I0682339

Messengers of an Alien God

Messengers
of an
Alien God

an occult sci-fi novel by
R. Douglas Burns

Magic Hat Books
14066 Creekview Trail
Tyler, Texas 75707
http://magichatbooks.com

An Overly Long Preface

You May Safely Skip

You might think this is an odd book to be written by someone who could be called an atheist, though I prefer the term freethinker. Another term for me might be 'heretical Buddhist,' but I'm hesitant to use that label as I'm not sure it's a legitimate term. To any atheists reading this, all I can say is: "You know that God you don't believe in? I don't believe in him either." All I can say to my religious friends is: You know the feeling of there being a reality that transcends the mundane world of our senses? I have that feeling too. However, in no way does my belief system conflict with solid, peer-reviewed science.

Ordinarily, I wouldn't bother to explain any of this as I believe an individual's religious beliefs or lack of them is no one else's business — as long as he or she doesn't try to impose them on anyone else, including, but not limited to children. However, I think I owe you, someone about to dig into a 300,000-word trilogy, some idea of how I, a writer and life-long fan of hard and semi-hard science fiction, came to write a tale that is as much fantasy as science fiction, a work that at times may even border on the occult.

The answer is as simple as it is weird: I had a vision. Well, a vision of sorts, if you can count a recurring lucid dream as a vision. But the dream launched me on an exploration of the history of religion and a study of those mythological creatures we call angels. Along the way, the quest also helped me map the limits of my feelings and need for the transcendental — what Sartre in Being and Nothingness termed a "God-shaped hole."

A little backstory first: I actually began the first book in the late 1980s. To save money and escape crazy, low-life, low-rent duplex neighbors, my wife and I had moved to an eighty-acre farm a few miles outside of Columbia, Missouri. Emotionally, it was a troubled time. My wife and I had two pre-school children with a third on the way. As a poorly paid magazine writer, I had money problems. My wife was subject to deep depressions. I was drinking too much. Our marriage was becoming toxic.

But we got the farm for a paltry sum, and the nearest neighbor was a half-mile away and of solid farm stock. We had hopes for a bit of peace and of rebuilding the marriage.

There was a downside to the property, and a reason our rent was only a couple of hundred dollars a month. A church used to stand next to the house, and an untended cemetery lay a stone's throw from our back door. Situated on the back of the eighty acres was an abandoned coal strip-mine, basically a large hole that had filled with water to become a lake. The coal mine operation had petered out prior to the time the Carter Adminstration sponsored laws requiring strip-mined land be brought back to someting like a natural state. So the lake was essentially 'dead' – nothing could live in its highly acidic waters. It was just ten acres of black water surrounded by dying trees.

My first impression was it had been dropped into rural Missouri out of a H.P. Lovecraft novel. I immediately dubbed it "Lost Lake."

With a cemetery next door, a family curse brewing, and what looked like a portal into hell on the back forty, it shouldn't be too much of a surprise that a few weeks after we moving onto the property, I had a lucid Lovecraftian dream.

In the dream, I'm standing at the edge of Lost Lake and see a small plane coming in low over the treetops. From the sound of its engine and the way it is flying, the plane is obviously in trouble, and I wait for it to crash into the middle of Lost Lake. Then the engine recovers, and the plane starts to gain altitude. I remember neither relief nor disappointment in this dream, though the pilot's life hangs in the balance. I'm just an impartial bystander in the unfolding drama.

But I do remember gasping as two huge, white angels burst out of the forest like startled quail and collided with the plane. I gasped not out of surprise, but because the angels were such incredibly beautiful, transcendental beings of grace and mystery.

The angels and the plane became entangled and fell together into Lost Lake. The snarl of angels, wings, and airplane hardware lands hard and begins to sink. I hear the pilot scream as the waters close over the cockpit.

Then I woke up.

I would have forgotten the dream, for as compared some of my lucid dreams it was not that exceptional. But I had the same dream the next night. And the next. And the next. I lost count of how many times I had the same dream.

Though I don't believe in messages from God, without or without a capital G, I did at that time (and still do) believe dreams can be important messages from the unconscious. So I sat down and began to write out the scene in an effort to decipher the communiqué.

As an alumnus of the University of Missouri at Columbia, I had access to the millions of volumes at Ellis Library, and I began researching angels, paying particular attention to the essays of Joseph Campbell and Carl Gustav Jung. I also dabbled in readings of the occult and religious history, and along the way stumbled across the book mentioned by the character I've dubbed Uncle Robert, *The Apocrypha and Pseudepigrapha of the Old Testament*, edited by R.H. Charles. This was the 1907 edition, and it was from the Book of Enoch within this tome from which I drew descriptions of the alien angels in the novel. But I have to admit I also owe a debt to Arthur C. Clarke's science fiction classic, *Childhood's End*. Clark's work served as a kind of catalyst. I was struggling with the angels being explainable and understandable in scientific terms and also being of the occult realm. Then I remembered that 70 years ago, Clark wrote that a sufficiently advanced technology would seem like magic to us. Problem solved.

The result was the first novel in this series, Messengers of an Alien God, but these dark themes continued to seep into the second and third novels of the trilogy, *Dreamtime of an Alien God* and *Awakening of an Alien God*.

The title of the first novel comes from a Gnostic and Christian doctrine. In Christian doctrine, angels are messengers from God. In fact, the word 'angel' comes from the Greek word, *angelos*, which literally translates as 'messenger.' In Gnosticism, it is the creator God himself who is alien to human happiness and spiritual advancement.

I finished the first rough draft of the novel in about a year, while going through multiple personal and professional crises. Ironically, though I was creating my own mythos, my skepticism of organized religion and what passes for monotheism grew. One surprise for me was the original vision and the characters drove my mythos into the classic patterns of what Joseph Campbell termed the *monomyth,* or the hero's journey.

I like to think I told a good story in the first novel, but it didn't seem to get to the heart of the original dream; the sense that my unconsciousness had tapped into something much larger than my puny ego could comprehend.

Thank you for considering this book. I truly hope you enjoy it.

Robert Douglas Burns
Lost in East Texas
2012

Acknowledgement

The original draft of this book was early resigned to my trunk and probably would have stayed there if not for my friend and editor, Linda Anderson. Linda and I used to work in the same editorial unit of a landgrant University, but in offices in different parts of the state. During an email exchange one day, I mentioned the novel and how I felt it was an "ambitious failure."

Linda wanted to see the book, perhaps because she had helped me with one of my pure sci-fi novels, *The Unselfish Gene.* Despite my warnings, she insisted. I eventually I sent her a digital copy.

Linda is one those people who may read John Dos Pasos one day, then classic science fiction or Molly Ivins the next. So imagine my surprise when she liked my novel and suggested I try to get it published.

With Linda's editorial help, the first book was eventually accepted by Swimming Kangaroo Books, a micropublisher out of Arlington, Texas. However, before SKB could publish it, the publishing company went "four-legs-up-in-the-air," – as we say in Texas cattle country – during the 2009 recession.

Meanwhile, Linda asked for a sequel. I'd always felt the first book left a lot of questions unanswered, so I wrote the second novel, *Dreamtime of an Alien God.* This book answered some the questions left unanswered in the first book, but posed some new ones, so I started a third book, *Awakening of an Alien God.* Along the way, I deciphered some of more of what I felt was the original message of my dream, drawn deeper into occult themes as I wrote.

Like matchless book editors of the last century used to do, Linda nagged me until I finished both books. You'd think she'd paid me a sizeable advance, she made me work so hard. (She didn't, and I paid her only in chocolate for her editorial services.) Linda has also helped me through several revisions of all three novels, offering not only minor cleanups but major revisions. She truly nurtured the work, just as the best book editors used to do even for unknown midline authors whom they thought had potential.

So, I can honestly say it's as much thanks to Linda, the editor, as to me, the author, that you have the trilogy today. For me, the writing this series has been in some ways a journey of self-discovery. Foremost, I have tried to tell a good story, and to keep the preaching quarantined to the dialog of one of the characters, whom you may safely ignore if you wish and still enjoy the read.

One note: Linda persistently tried in this novel and the following ones of the trilogy to get me write my protagonists politically correct, especially Sheriff John Wright. Sorry Linda. All of my protagonists, even the best of them, are flawed human beings. Like real people, they are sometimes sexist and prejudiced one moment, noble and open-minded the next. As Christopher Hitchens wrote, we are a species whose frontal lobes are too small, adrenal glands too big, and have sexual organs seemingly designed by a committee. None of us are perfect, much less saints, and this is a novel about real women and men in an extraordinary situation, which brings out the worst and best in them. Judge them by their actions not their thoughts. But if you're offended by some of the language and interior dialogue of the characters blame the author, not the editor.

A caveat: Both Linda and I have worked hard to provide you with clean, grammatical copy, but with only two editors working on 300,000 words of fiction, I'm sure you will find a few typos. If you'd like, and you think the novels worthy of your time, you can help me further clean up the copy by going to my website at http://magichatbooks.com and making comments. I promise to give each and every comment consideration. If you make substantial contributions – even if you only find a typo or two – I will add your name to a list of contributors in the back of the respective novel in the next edition.

If you're reading this on a Kindle, an easier way for me to find and incorporate your suggested changes, will be for you to turn on thePublic Note feature.

For more information on Public Notes go to https://kindle.amazon.com/faq#PublicNotes .

By the way, you'll have to turn on "make reading status and rating public" before you can make your notes public.

If you have the hard copy of any of the novels – I expect to make these available on Amazon in October 2012 – you'll need send me the page number and a few words of the phrase or paragraph you where you found an error.

RB

1.

After the Fall

The white plane came in too low over the treetops, too quietly, too slowly, the propeller turning idly. Bryan Douglas, who was resting from cutting wood near the shadow of the fallen angel saucer, first noticed the plane's bright paint flashing in the mid-morning sun. He set his chainsaw down and removed his sweat-fogged eyeglasses to get a better look.

The engine suddenly sputtered to life, coughed a cloud of white smoke and settled into a steady drone, died and then started again. Bryan watched it with mixed emotions, sole audience to the pilot's struggle to survive. The propeller spun into a blur and the wings stopped their fearful wobbling. Gaining altitude, the plane nearly cleared the tops of the hundred-foot pines west of Lost Lake, but at that moment – the worst possible moment – the two angels burst free from their hidden roost in the forest. Perhaps because their vision had been obscured by the fog bank that lay low over the lake and the surrounding woods, they flew directly into the plane's path. Bryan's view of the plane was partially blocked as the angels' immense, outstretched wings collapsed into loose folds of white tissue, clinging to the plane like outsized tissue paper kites whose stick-wood frames had been broken by the wind.

The drone of the engine, which had been so hopeful moments before, stalled to a halt under the snarl of the angels' wings. The plane's wings again began to wobble to and fro, and the plane veered sharply south, a course that took it away from the dense woods and over the lake.

Once over the water and the dense, cold fog, the plane dropped straight toward the water. Bryan could now see one angel had been impaled by the propeller. The other lay draped across a wing.

The pilot performed remarkably. In spite of losing power, and with a ton of angel flesh counter-balancing the plane, he managed to nose up and pull into a level glide a few feet over the surface of the lake. The plane sailed across the water, pale and mute, now looking for a resting place. But the glide decayed after less than a hundred yards, and the plane slammed in the water with a loud thump. Rebounding, it gained a couple of feet of altitude, and its landing gear skimmed the surface of the lake, throwing up a fine spray. Bryan thought at that moment the plane might make a safe landing. Maybe it would ski over the surface like a skipping stone, losing velocity and then slowing to a stop, where it would gradually sink, giving the pilot time to exit and paddle to safety. But no happy ending. With the extra weight of the angels coming into play, the nose dipped and the plane's landing wheels skimmed the water again, went deeper, found purchase, and the small craft somersaulted forward onto its back.

A shattering sound of breaking glass accompanied the impact. Also heard – Bryan wasn't sure if he imagined this – the angry, desperate shout of a human voice. Within seconds the plane filled with water up to the wings, carrying the angels down with it. Water closed over the passenger cabin in another second. For a short time the morning sun silhouetted the rear tail assembly. The rudder waved slowly back and forth like the flukes of a playful whale, then it too slid under the cold water.

The sequence of the mid-air collision, crash-landing and sinking had transfixed Bryan. Now he began running, possessed by an impulse he couldn't name. He gave wide berth to the fallen swathe of oak and hickory forest. Weeks ago when the huge angel saucer crashed it had rutted a strip of forest a hundred yards wide and a quarter-mile long. Mud-pit moats punctuated the rut. Giant piles of splintered timber had been pushed aside and thrust up like embattled parapets. Though he avoided the main area of destruction, small pieces of debris – stumps, sheared-off limbs, man-size tree splinters – forced him to take a zig-zag course down the hill.

Once past the saucer he found the going smooth and downhill

all the way to the lake. In a few minutes he was at the shore, out of breath and wondering what to do next. An oily, frothy sheen marked the spot where the plane had gone under. From up the hill, the lake had seemed a blue-gray puddle, the pilot an unseen abstraction, the plane, a child's toy. Now at the shore, the size and depth of the lake became evident. He must get out to where the plane sank, that much was obvious. But even if he were a strong swimmer – and he wasn't – the lake was fed by a deep cold spring. He'd cramp and drown in minutes.

Several large bubbles burst forth, breaking the still waters. Something large and white bobbed to the surface. He had hoped it was the pilot, hoped that his fellow human had beat all the odds and escaped death. But from all appearances the floating mass of white was a dead angel, though they were never supposed to die.

* * *

2.

The Release

Bertha Marshall calmly spread blackstrap molasses on a piece of bread while her husband ranted and raved.

"I tell you, Bertha, those stubborn sons-of-bitches are going to blow the town to Timbuktu some day!"

"Now dear, it's none of your concern." She said this automatically. Frank liked to be angry and indignant. He was happiest when he had a cause to champion – or better, an injustice to fight. As usual, her response was to gently dampen the uglier points of his anger without putting out the fire altogether. After thirty years of marriage her counterpoint to his rage had become as standardized as a catechism and took hardly any thought at all.

Frank responded predictably. He snorted. "It damn well is my concern, Bertha! I'm chairman of the county Emergency Preparedness Committee!" He threw his napkin down on the plate and got up from the table. His face was red, smoldering. "I'm going."

"Where?"

"To town. To talk to that stubborn son-of-a-bitch sheriff."

"I thought the Cherokee was out of gas."

"It is. I'm going to walk. It's only two miles. Why I used to . . ."

"Why don't you phone?"

"I'm sick of that screwed-up land-line phone system and all the old biddies eavesdropping! Besides, Wright can ignore me over the phone. He damn well can't ignore me when I drag him out of his office by his ear and show him the kerosene leaking onto the bags of ammonia nitrate!"

She said nothing but didn't avert her eyes. At times silence was the best policy with Frank – the only policy. Crying didn't work anymore.

He slammed the door behind him, clearly as mad at her as he was at Sheriff John Wright. She took a healthy bite of bread and molasses and relaxed to enjoy the silence.

The Fall wasn't so bad. Unlike many people, she had adapted well to eating simply. A neighboring farmer had begun selling whole-grain flour ground from wheat in his own fields, and she was learning to bake bread again. Though Frank did not get around as well as he once did, his eyesight was still sharp and his trigger finger steady. He kept fresh game – rabbit and squirrel mostly – on the table. She felt healthier than she had for years though she had run out of blood thinner and nitroglycerin tablets a month ago.

Unthinking, her hand moved to her breast. No pain today, but last night she had awakened with her heart pounding, the pain so intense she called out, waking Frank. There in bed, the darkness concealing their aged faces, she had wanted to stare into his eyes to confide in him more than ever, to talk to someone besides Dr. Jenkins about death and dying. But she had told him it had only been a dream. She had kept her heart condition secret from Frank from the beginning. She had to. His heart wasn't good either. Everything that upset his routine fed his anger. She had no doubt that he would treat her death as a personal insult, a plot by the world at large to get even with him. Well, he would have to deal with it sooner or later, most likely sooner, but in the meantime she wouldn't have to watch him fume and rant and rage.

The heart doctors at Columbia had given her less than a year to live; two years with a little luck and if she took excellent care of herself. That was two years, three months ago. The Fall – the fall to Earth of the angels' saucer – had marked the two-year anniversary of her death sentence, and she was still ticking. She felt the Fall had somehow granted her a reprieve, flipping the natural order of things upside down, erasing all life's debits and setting the game board back to GO.

No, the Fall wasn't so bad. Oh, she missed some things. Silly things, really. Like trips to the Columbia shopping malls and her daily soap operas. She had watched *As the World Turns* nearly every day for a quarter of a century. Seven years ago, after their only son died in a car accident, she had begun watching several shows back-to-back. More followed until she was a real soap opera junkie, in communion with the television from early morning through late afternoon.

She sighed. Before the Fall, there were rumors *As the World Turns* was going to be canceled soon anyway.

Some days, particularly when Frank was off somewhere playing out one of his rages, the lives of the soap characters became more real than her own. Certainly they were more interesting. She dwelt on those fictional lives now, mentally replaying the sordid love affairs, the divorces, the revolving-door marriages, the juicy betrayals. A sharp pain in her chest came and went. She ignored it, hoping it would pass, and it did.

At first, she didn't hear the knock at the door because she was preoccupied reliving a particularly passionate episode of *All My Children* while washing the dishes. When the knock finally penetrated her reveries it momentarily confused her. Frank, back so soon? No, it would take him two hours to walk to town and back. Perhaps he changed his mind halfway to town and came back. But Frank never gave up once his mind was set. And he never forgot his keys, so he wouldn't have to knock.

Never.

The knock came again, sharp, hammer-hard blows on the solid oak door. She hurriedly dried her hands, and fetched the shotgun from its hiding place in the corner of the broom closet.

Frank's orders were clear in these situations. She checked to be certain the safety was on, rested the stock against her thigh, pointed the barrel at the ceiling and pulled the slide handle back. Through the open breechblock she could see the bright red shell held poised by the gunmetal blue mechanism.

Frank had bought the gun for her when they had first moved to the country and had insisted she learn how to use it. He made her listen to long sermons about its merits as well as dangers. He had made her target practice until she was half deaf, but she no longer closed her eyes in anticipation of the deafening boom that rattled her dentures. Now, with the Fall giving free reign to dope growers and other hooligans, not to mention those godless men who, Frank said, lived to prey on older women, the gun made her feel secure, though she still found it hard to imagine actually killing anyone. She pictured herself deliberately firing the first shot over their heads, the canon-like retort causing them to run away like naughty children.

She worked the slide handle forward. The breechblock closed and the shell slid into the chamber in a single, coordinated action. All very neat. No more difficult than putting a new bobbin in a sewing machine.

She also imagined terrible mid-morning scenarios set in motion by her pulling the trigger. Innocent, beautiful young men lying bleeding on the kitchen floor, men who happened to be in the wrong place at the wrong time, leaving ageless mothers and current lovers to mourn them, with no commercials to interrupt their agonies.

"Who is it?"

In place of an answer the visitor knocked again.

"Who is it?" A sudden pain sprang in her chest and spread rapidly down her left arm and she dropped the gun. It did not go off.

"It is I, Kasdeja." The voice was rich and vibrant. The pain eased considerably without completely dissipating.

She picked up the gun, careful to move slowly, and tucked it under her left arm. It was heavier than before, and her arm hurt. She opened the door to find Kasdeja standing before her, resplendent in his shimmering white robes.

"May I come in?"

She hesitated, though she wasn't sure why. She enjoyed the angel's infrequent visits, but it had recently dawned on her that he came only when Frank was away. She had heard the angels were neuter things, and Kasdeja had never given her any suspicion to think otherwise, but lately the visits had taken on the air of a formal, old-time courtship. It was a little bit indecent, but she had gradually become acclimated to the impropriety, as she had with the young, beautiful soap-opera actors making love in various stages of undress. Besides, there was something about the angel that reminded her of her lost son. She wasn't a religious person, but looking into that great, white, chiseled, handsome face and seeing hints of her son's features, she couldn't help but think these visits might be fateful.

"Why yes, come in, Kasdeja," she heard herself say. The angel always had an immediate and pleasant effect upon her. She felt like she was outside herself, floating above, watching herself open the door all the way to admit the huge angel.

"How is your heart today?" Kasdeja said as he ducked through the door. Though folded, his wings brushed the sides of the door frame as he came in, making a faint rasping sound that caused the hair on the back of her head to rise.

"It hurts a little."

"Are you going to die soon?" he asked. Before she could move away he laid his hand on her breast, directly over her heart. The move startled her, but she reminded herself that there was nothing licentious about its action, no more so than that of a child exploring.

"I can feel it beating," he said. "Differently, irregular as compared to the last time I was here. You are dying, aren't you?"

She pursed her lips. "Perhaps, but don't be concerned."

"I'm not concerned. I'm envious," the angel said.

"Don't be cruel, Kasdeja."

"I'm not." He sat and rested an elbow on the edge of the table, his white skin in stark contrast to the red plastic table cloth. "I would like to experience death."

"Well, I'd like to live forever."

"Careful what you ask for. Forever is a long time. How about a nearly immeasurable length of time?"

"What?" The pain came again. She leaned the shotgun against the kitchen counter and settled into a straight back chair at the table. The angel waited politely at her elbow while she gasped for breath. He made no further move to touch her or comfort her as he sometimes did. The wave of pain passed, the floating feeling faded and she came home to her body.

"Come again?" she said, and another wave of pain possessed her.

"Come again? What do you mean?"

She tried to tell him that "come again" meant she was asking him to explain himself, but her mind floated away before she could form the words. Below her, like a tableau, her body and the angel sat across from each other. His hand reached out to hers across the red-checkered table-cloth.

"You could live for as long as you like, a long time, a very long time," he said.

Concentrating on the red and white squares, she drifted back down and sat with the angel at the table. "What are you talking about?"

"A proposition. A merging. You could become like me. I could give you my immortal-ness."

Another wave of pain welled up in her chest and washed into her arm. The next thing she knew they were standing face to face. He didn't seem so large now, no taller than Frank. He moved a hand back to her breast, and the pain subsided. From above, the sight of them together was a bit ludicrous, the angel's hard perfection pressing against her aging, sagging body like a diamond resting on a ratty old pillow.

"What can I give you in return?"

"Death," the angel replied. He pushed her away, holding her at arm's length. She looked down at his hips to find not what she expected, but something made neither of flesh nor sinew. Whatever it was, it was beautiful, a jeweled thing made of diamonds and crystal that seemed rooted where his you-know-what ought to be. Her eyes refused to focus on its exact shape.

What about Frank? No, this is no more real than any soap opera fantasy.

She gave herself over to the angel, and he pulled her to him. The diamond razors entered her, and her heart burst with pleasure.

* * *

3.

The Rescue

Sheriff John Wright drove to Lost Lake in the Blazer SUV, hating the silence. He missed the static and crackle of his car radio and the distraction of his cellular phone. Learning to live without electronic communications was the biggest adjustment he'd had to make since the Fall.

About a mile before the Lost Lake turn-off he pulled up behind Uncle Robert Jacobsen pedaling his rickety old Schwinn down the center of the road. Wright honked. Uncle Robert, who was either drunk or lost in thought – it was hard to tell with him – didn't seem to notice. Wright honked again, and Uncle Robert gradually eased the bike over to the side of the road and motioned him by with a one-handed wave without stopping or looking back.

Wright couldn't help but smile. The old man made quite a sight, what with his Santa Claus beard and ratty tweed coat. As Wright passed, Uncle Robert grinned and waved, the picture of a happy old fart. Since the old man preferred his bicycle to a car, and his books to the television, life for him probably hadn't changed much since the Fall.

Wright tried to affect a friendly wave. Uncle Robert didn't seem to notice, his grin had disappeared, and he had one of those thousand-mile stares. The old man's oblivious disinterest ticked off Wright a little, but then everything was ticking him off these days. He accelerated and left Uncle Robert behind. Let the overly educated old man daydream with a mouth full of dust.

I'm becoming a real prick.

Messengers of an Alien God

As Wright cruised into the park he spotted a boy sitting in the open-air picnic building. He wore a dirty day-glow yellow sweatshirt with a picture of a leaping tiger. As if he wasn't conspicuous enough here alone at the lake, the boy jumped up and waved both hands over his head to get Wright's attention. Underneath the tiger, black lettering proclaimed: "Property of the MU Athletic Dept." He wore wire-rimmed eyeglasses in the same style that Wright's mother had worn in her senior years.

"Hipster college boy," Wright grumbled to himself.

"It went down over there," he said as Wright got out of the Blazer. "You can still see the angel floating. It hardly drifted at all from where I first saw it."

Standing on tiptoe, Wright could see the floating body, which was clearly an angel because one wing jutted up at a right angle to the water like an outsize shark's fin. Its robes were like a skim of white milk on the dark water. Strange, from the little he knew about angels he would have thought their bodies too heavy and dense to float.

By the time Jimmy Harte drove up, Wright and the college boy had dragged an aluminum jon boat into the water.

"I couldn't get through to Columbia Regional," Jimmy announced, looking like he was about to salute. He always looked as if he were on the verge of saluting. Jimmy's ingenuousness was, if the truth were known, the main reason Wright kept him around. His own enthusiasm was lagging as he reached middle-age, and he hoped some of Jimmy's would rub off. Besides, Jimmy was the only deputy Wright had ever had who wasn't taller than he was.

"Are the phone lines out again?" the college boy asked.

"Who knows," Jimmy said. "All I got was a busy signal. That could mean anything."

"They probably couldn't have told you anything, anyway. The plane came in from the northeast. Columbia is west of here."

With Jimmy at the oars – rank has its privileges – they were alongside the body in minutes. The college boy waited on shore rather than overload the boat.

The angel floated face down in the water, heavy and low as a water-soaked log. Wright leaned out over the water and grabbed a leg. The feel of angel skin surprised him. Hairless of course, but as smooth and hard as glass. Upon sight, angels seemed like they should be soft to the touch. Even the ones with a decidedly masculine appearance had a soft-edged, well-fed look, like body builders going to fat.

The skin also had another quality, elusive and hard to define, like nothing else he had ever touched, vaguely sensual without being sexual, like the feel of a baby's skin. That wasn't quite right either, but he had nothing else to compare it with.

As the boat swung around, Jimmy grabbed two handfuls of robe and tried to pull the angel into the boat.

"Damnation, this thing weighs a ton," Jimmy said.

Wright got a double handful of robe too. "On the count of three we'll haul it in together. One, two, three!"

The boat tipped, threatening to capsize. Wright and Jimmy let go, winded. The body floated low in the water like a leaden fishing bob, daring them to try again.

How did the damn things fly? Maybe the species was light when alive and heavy when dead. Using both arms, Wright lifted a leg from the water. It felt heavier than iron. Whatever the science of angel flight, he would never be able to get the body into the boat even with Jimmy's help.

"You know, Jimmy, we don't have to pull the thing into the boat."

"What are we going to do? Leave it here?"

"No, we tow it to shore like it's a pleasure barge."

He told Jimmy to sit the other way in the boat and row backwards. Wright held onto the angel's robe like a trot line. With Jimmy rowing, they towed it back to the shore.

At the dock, the problem of the angel's weight reasserted itself. Wright and Jimmy grabbed a leg each and pulled until they were both panting. Wright dropped the dead weight of the leg in the water. They had succeeded at no more than exhausting themselves. The yard up from the water to the dock might as well have been a mile.

"If that Douglas kid was here we might make it," Jimmy said, panting.

"No, this damn thing weighs more than a piece of farm iron. We need a hoist. Where did the college boy disappear to anyway."

"How about the shallows, sir, where the kiddies wade?" Jimmy suggested.

"How about it?"

"We could tow it over there, then roll it up on the beach like an old log."

"Seems like a winner of an idea to me. We'll try it."

Towing the angel to the shallows proved easy. The body showed no sign of sinking. Getting it onto the beach was another problem. The wings refused to stay folded against the body and prevented them from rolling the body in the shallows. Again each of them grabbed a leg and pulled until they had lugged the angel a couple of yards up the gravel beach. By then both were soaked up to their waists.

"Now all we have to do is heave it into the back of the Blazer," Wright said, his teeth chattering. The air temperature was in the mid-60s, warm for March, but the cold lake water had chilled him to the bone.

Jimmy picked up a driftwood stick and lifted the angel's robes.

"Here's another thing I don't understand. Look at this." Jimmy lifted the wet robes to expose the angel's groin. The area was as hairless as the rest of the body with no evidence of any genitalia at all. Nor was there an anus.

"You see? Not so much as a little pucker."

Wright coughed, embarrassed. Despite its androgynous groin, the rest of the angel looked disturbingly human.

In face and stature, all angels appeared either male or female – as long as their robes were in place. Without the wings, dressed in normal clothes, this one would have been indistinguishable from drowned male human model or movie star — except, of course, for its height. Even in death, angels were classically proportioned. The male-like angels were so handsome they made women stutter; the female-like ones, beautiful, though both lacked any sexual presence. Though angels were androgynous, most people still found it impossible to think of them as *its*, at least in life.

Death was different. The corpse's clear blue eyes were wide open, and its face frozen in a surprised stare. Wright averted his glance.

"Put his robes down, Jimmy. These things have a right to dignity, too."

Jimmy obediently pulled the angel's robes down, but wouldn't give up the ontological debate. "Where do baby angels come from? That's what I want to know."

"They say they hardly never die, Jimmy, so I guess they don't have to reproduce."

"Well, this one is dead, and it ain't going to be making any babies, that's for darn sure."

Wright thought to tell him not to be so sure. He'd heard reports of angels found apparently dead, only to come back to life days later.

"Here's another question for you: Where did the first angels come from?" Jimmy was in a philosophical mood. Wright hoped it wouldn't last much longer.

"I don't know, maybe God made them." Wright had meant this as a joke, but the deputy took him seriously.

"Oh, come on, Sheriff, you don't really believe that do you? These aren't real angels, like in the Bible. They just happen to look like them. Real angels don't ride around in flying saucers."

"You're probably right there, Jimmy. Maybe they hatch from eggs, like chickens. Let's see if we can get the thing in the Blazer."

Jimmy tried to laugh but it came out as a giggle mixed with chattering teeth. "Why don't we go get warmed up first? I bet this thing will keep until tomorrow. It ain't going anywhere now that we got it out of the water."

"I don't know," Wright said. "He might rot. We ought to get him on ice."

"Where we gonna get ice with the power down?" Jimmy said.

"Good point," Wright said.

"The incorporeal body will not decay," said a calm, mellifluous voice from above.

Both men jumped. An angel hovered ten feet above their heads, his extended wings glistening with dew in the morning sun. Both were men were speechless. The angel, a male-like one, drifted down on the beach beside them as lightly as a settling dust mote. His wings remained motionless throughout his descent, great white sails on a calm day, shadowing them from the morning sun.

Kneeling by the body of his dead comrade, the angel lifted the corpse's arm and laid it by its side. He straightened the robes, his hands feeling along the contours of the body, searching for something. Apparently, he didn't find it. He rose gracefully to his feet. With a dry rustle his wings folded against his back, reminding Wright of pleated satin curtains sliding on rod and track.

"I am trying to locate Baraqijal's companion, Samiazaz," the angel said.

"Baraqijal is this angel's name?" Wright asked, pointing at the body.

The angel nodded. "Yes."

"And yours?"

"I am Penumae."

"Jimmy, make note of the names," Wright said. "We haven't seen your pal. Have we Jimmy?"

"Nope. Just the one we hauled up on the shore." Jimmy had his notebook out. His face was as red as a beet. He was probably wondering if the angel had witnessed the anatomy lesson. Finally he managed to ask, "How do you spell that?"

The angel shrugged, smiled, still full of good humor, but didn't answer.

"With a 'B,' if I had to guess," Wright said.

Jimmy gave him a curious look.

"Approximate the spellings for now, Jimmy." He turned back to the angel.

"Maybe the other angel is at the bottom of Lost Lake. The college boy said two angels crashed with the airplane," Jimmy volunteered without looking up from his note-taking.

"I must find Samiazaz," the angel said.

The angel walked to the edge of the shallows and stopped. The water lapped at his toes. He took a step back to dry land, obviously distressed. Wright had half expected it to walk on the water.

"How deep is the water there?" he asked, and pointed to where they had found the dead angel floating.

"Where we found your friend? Well, that is a good question. No one has ever found the bottom."

The angel waited patiently for more. Wright waited too, knowing Jimmy would interrupt and save him the trouble of explaining. Jimmy didn't disappoint them.

"A deep underground cave feeds Lost Lake," Jimmy said. "Scuba divers have gone down about 140 feet, and they say the cave opens up and just keeps on going. The plane, whoever was in it, and whatever your angel friend was carrying, could be a thousand feet down, maybe more. Nobody will ever see either of them again."

"Amazing. So much water. It is all but non-existent where we come from. Who would have guessed," the angel said. He tested the water with the toe of his sandaled foot. Wings quivering nervously, he braced himself and stepped in deeper until the blue-green water lapped at his knees. He turned and looked at Wright and his deputy with a betrayed expression that reminded Wright of a dog that has been turned out into the cold. The angel's white complexion had taken on a dismal, blue hue.

"Cold, isn't it," Wright said.

"It's not that," the angel said. "This is like nothing . . . like nothing we've ever experienced."

He retreated from the water. Once he was back on dry land, the blue tinge to his complexion disappeared. He unfolded his wings.

"I'll be back in a few minutes. I will take Baraqijal's last body away."

"Whatever you say."

The angel smiled. Too many white teeth. "Thank you," he said.

Was there an amused, condescending note hidden in his tone? Wright had trouble reading angels. They were all so damn calm. Worse, their sedateness was catching for some people, including him. The creature's obvious distress while in the water was the first negative expression he had seen one show. The angel stunned him with another smile. Wright began to feel as if he had been dipping into his wife's stash of Valium.

"I'm sorry about your friend's death," Jimmy blurted out with an undertaker's politeness, a gangling attempt at an apology for the impropriety he had taken with the body.

"There is no reason to be sorry. Baraqijal will return soon." He looked toward the lake. "I am worried about Samiazaz, though, if he is trapped at the bottom of this . . . water." The angel said 'water' as if it were a curse. "He will be in a sleep worse than death, and be completely subjects to the whims of the Dreaming God."

"That's bad, I take it," Wright said.

The angel shrugged, a very human gesture, though his wings lifted too. "All corporeal things pass. This water can't stay here for eternity. When it goes, Samiazaz will be reborn as will Baraqijal."

Most angels talked like out-of-work yogis, so Wright was inclined to let all the hype pass. Not his deputy, though.

"Rebirth? Will he come back to life?" Jimmy asked, stepping back from the body at his feet.

"Perhaps," the angel said, nodding toward the body, and without further explanation flew straight up, leaving the body of Baraqijal behind. Wright and Jimmy watched until it shrank to a silvery speck moving on the blue canvas of the sky.

"I believe that angel was afraid of the water. Don't you?" Jimmy stared into the sky as if looking for a sign.

"I don't know. Maybe he can't swim." Wright felt the air of stagnant tranquility lifting.

"Why would he need to swim? From what I hear they don't even breathe. He could hike down to China under the Pacific Ocean and not even make a bubble. What do you think?"

"I think we'll wait and see if he comes back for the body of his buddy. Does the heater in your truck work? The one in the Blazer has been out since the Fall."

"It works okay, but I don't have much gas. If we let it idle too long, I won't make it back to town."

"We can always go back in the Blazer if we have to."

As the heater began to warm the inside of Jimmy's vehicle, Wright's mind cleared further. "Jimmy, how do you suppose the angel knew where to look?"

"Huh?"

"What brought him here? Was he just flying over and noticed his friend lying on the beach? Or do they have some sort of radio, and the other one called to tell him he was in trouble?"

Jimmy looked confused. "What does it matter?"

"I don't know. Guess I'm just curious. How did he know where we found the body floating? He pointed to right where it was. If he was watching all the time, why did he wait for us to fetch it up on the beach?"

"Beats me, sir. Why do those things do anything? They're not human."

Jimmy went back to rambling conjecture on angel reproduction. Wright shut it out. His fatigue was returning, and his young deputy wasn't helping. He needed a day off. He was putting on weight despite the shortage of junk food and beer. His 2009 Ford Explorer was parked in the garage, not running since the Fall. And there was this mess with his wife, going through some kind of hormonal change. What he needed was about sixteen hours of sleep, or maybe a good drunk, or to take up May Tyre, the foxy little waitress, on her standing offer – better yet, all three.

Anything but the sleep binge was out of the question. He couldn't get away with screwing May or getting trashed-out drunk within gossip range of Creedance – not and remain sheriff for another term. Since a drive into St. Louis or even Columbia was out of the question, he would have to settle for a sleep binge.

"Hey! Inside the truck!" It was the college boy. What was his name again? Bryan Douglas? Or was it Douglas Bryan? He hated people with two first names. Wright laboriously rolled down the windshield.

"Can I come in and get warm, too?"

He looked liked a half-drowned dog. Wright guessed he didn't look much better himself. "Sure. Get in the back."

"Jimmy?"

"Yes, sir?" his deputy responded.

"Fetch a couple of beers out of the cooler in the back," he said.

Jimmy came back with three beers. The college boy looked as if he would kill for a one.

Wright pitched a can each to the college boy and Jimmy. His deputy looked ill at ease – Wright kept forgetting he was a Baptist and a teetotaler. The college boy showed no such reserve. He popped the top and slurped greedily. Beer had been a scarce commodity since the Fall and the following near collapse of modern commerce.

Halfway through the beer and the angel still hadn't returned to claim the body of fellow angel. Maybe he never would.

"Here is the way it is," Wright said. "I figure there ought to be an inquiry into the death of the angel and the pilot. Maybe we need to ask that other angel some hard questions, but as you gentlemen very well know, any one angel, even those little ones, what are they called?"

"Cherubim," the college boy said. "But I think they are just rumors. I haven't talked to anyone who's seen them firsthand."

"Whatever. Any of them could grind us into sausage without raising a sweat."

"None of the angels has ever hurt anyone. They say they are helpful," the college boy said.

"So they say," Wright said.

"I've heard they heal people," Jimmy said, which surprised Wright. His deputy might not be the smartest twenty-three-year old in the world, but he was usually wise enough to keep his mouth shut when he didn't know what he was talking about.

"I've heard some of the same things," Wright said. "But I'll believe they close bleeding wounds with a touch when I see it.

"Anyway, until I figure how to go about the inquiry, I want you both to keep your mouths shut, understand?"

"Yes, sir," Jimmy said.

Wright expected no trouble with his deputy. The college boy, however, looked indecisive. Wright guessed he was the contrary type who almost had to do something just because you told him not to. He was probably a vegetarian and a socialist to boot.

Wright decided his best bet was to get the college boy involved. "Now that we've got that settled," he said, "you two go see if you can turn the angel body over."

Jimmy hopped out. The college boy sat still.

"What's wrong?" Wright asked.

"Sheriff, didn't you notice something is missing from the beach?"

"And what would that be?"

"The dead angel."

Wright scanned the gravelly beach. The college boy was right, which pissed off Wright some more. But overlaying the anger was fear. It had must have disappeared in a split second, but how? Either it had come back to life and walked away on its own, or its fellow angel had flown away with the corpse. The weird thing was Wright couldn't remember taking his eyes off the body for more than a moment. He could hardly avoid seeing it from the front seat of the SUV. Not only had the body disappeared before his eyes, he hadn't thought to question that it was gone.

"Did either of you see anything?"

"No, sir," Jimmy said, his voice a notch higher than usual. The disappearance had shaken him, too.

"I watched you two drag it up on the beach from across the lake, from where I was sitting over by the old playground," the college boy said.

"Maybe it just dissolved," Jimmy said.

"You've been watching too much television," Wright said.

"Not since the Fall."

The college boy gave a silly laugh. Couldn't hold his beer. *He really was becoming a prick.*

"Look up," Jimmy said.

High above, almost too tiny to be seen individually, a gathering of angels flew eastward toward Creedance. They fluttered about, erratically like starlings or sparrows, making it impossible to count them, but there must have at least a couple of dozen. A loon called sadly from the other side of the lake.

Suddenly, Wright urgently wanted to get away from the lake. After admonishing the college boy and his deputy to keep quiet, he was back in his own vehicle and on the road to Creedance. In the relative quiet of the Blazer, he had time to think a little. As he turned corners along the winding country road, he could hear the remaining beer bumping hollowly back and forth in the ice cooler as if it had a life of its own. It's just the pothole-spattered road making the cans bounce about, he told himself, but the hair on the back of neck rose anyway.

He didn't care what had killed the angel, and he had lied about the possibility of an inquest into its death. As far as state law was concerned, the death of an animal, domestic or otherwise, was more important than that of an angel. The state statutes defined a farm animal as private property and demanded the clarification of its unexplained death. Likewise, the law protected most wild game. But angels didn't exist in the eyes of the law. Eventually, when civilization was back in gear, the Missouri General Assembly or the federal government or some other gaggle of lawyers would get around to defining angels as some sort of minority or something, but until then, it wasn't his concern. It was outside the confines of the law and therefore didn't matter.

What did matter to him was that the mystery of the disappearing angel. He didn't know how or why, but the questions – and the fear – relieved his exhaustion.

* * *

4.

Beyond What We Know

Wright paused at one of Creedance's three traffic lights to watch four angels milling around on the loading dock of the MFA Co-Op. They smiled beatifically among themselves, not talking. One was dark-headed, the other three so blonde to be nearly white-haired. All were the male-type, broad shouldered, slim-hipped.

The dark-haired one shuffled his feet, reminding Wright of the old fashioned, tight-lipped farmers who usually congregated at the MFA. Captivated by this comparison, he waited for the angel to say something and punctuate it with a spit, farmer style. Instead, without preamble, the angel flew straight up, one arm extended, wings folded and swept back, one leg slightly bent, a flying gymnast, a Superman in white, soaring into the overcast sky with an audible whoosh.

Behind him a rickety lemon-yellow Chevy pickup honked. It was a timid honk; just a brief poke at the horn to remind Wright that he was holding up traffic. The traffic light hadn't worked since the Fall, and by popular consensus, the intersection had been turned into a four-way stop.

Half a block down, feeling a little sheepish, Wright parked in front of Bouchers coffee shop. Inside, he found the shop packed with comforting voices and familiar smells.

Before the Fall, Bouchers had been primarily a male hangout, a place where weekend farmers and armchair political strategists gathered on idle days. They had tended to be tight-lipped group, and the conversations had been muted, punctuated by nods and grunts. Now, the café seemed crowded and noisy to Wright, what with all the women chattering and prattling in what used to be a stoic, male stronghold.

He sighed. It was understandable.

Without electronic distractions, people would naturally flock together more. He should consider it a good thing, but he carefully avoided the corner of the café now taken over by middle-age housewives who, denied their soap-operas and afternoon talk shows, spent a good part of the day here.

Also, the weekly emergency meeting was scheduled today at the old Methodist church next door, and a good number of people were waiting for it to begin. Wright noticed a couple of the county commissioners, along with the usual characters who would mainly show up at any public function to bitch and gripe, not to make any positive contribution.

"Hi, Sheriff. Having a good morning?" said Laura Jacobsen, new at waitressing since she had lost her job at the medical clinic after a run-in with Dr. Jenkins.

"I'm here for the town meeting, but I'll have a cup of coffee before it starts."

"How about some breakfast or is it lunch?"

"Call it what you like. I've been up all night. Coffee will be enough, thanks."

"Sure thing." She had his coffee for him in a minute, along with a small juice glass half full of milk. She had remembered, after waiting on him once two weeks ago, that he hated powdered creamer.

"If you need anything else, give a whoop. I'll be in the next booth taking a break," she said. Her long black hair was done up in a bun, making her look older. She had good legs, shapely though a trifle too muscular for his taste, but it was the nose ring that really put him off. Wright wondered if she knew how often he looked the other way when she was smoking and dealing pot a few years ago. If he hadn't let her go, thinking she'd outgrow it, she would probably now be in the state penitentiary, considering the state's mandatory sentencing drug laws.

He was settling into his coffee break when the angel came in. The conversations stilled for a few moments, not because angels were banned from restaurants but because everyone was curious as angels were reputed to neither eat nor drink. The creature stood still near the front door, waiting for acceptance, and gave the room a running-for-public-office smile. As if on cue, everyone simultaneously returned to their conversations, content to ignore any further departure from normalcy. The angel, one of the rare dark-haired ones – perhaps the same one he had seen on the loading dock – came over to his booth, wing tips nearly brushing the ceiling.

"May I sit down, Sheriff?" the angel asked.

"Sure. Have a seat," Wright said, though he'd had enough of the angels today. Now that the angel was closer, he vaguely remembered seeing this one around town. He bore a striking resemblance to a young Elvis Presley – an Elvis on steroids with skin bleached of any color.

The angel squeezed his large frame into the booth. The pungent sweet smell of ketchup gone slightly sour and salty food suddenly seemed overwhelming. Wright took a big gulp of his coffee, hoping to dispel the angel's tranquilizing influence. "What can I do for you?" He tried to look the angel squarely in the eye.

"I'm here to thank you," the angel said.

"Thank me for what?"

"For taking Baraqijal home."

"Baraqijal? You mean the angel in the lake? We didn't take him home. All we did was pull it on shore."

"It was enough." The angel reached across the table and patted his hand.

"I thought you angels never died," Wright said, pulling his hand away.

"Baraqijal did not die; only his projection into this dimension died. When you pulled him from the lake you set the anima mundi free of the mortal anchor."

"Around here, we don't split hairs. We call dead, dead. Plain and simple, except in newspaper obituaries, when we say they passed on, or in church, we say they went to their Maker, and . . ." Realizing he was blabbering, Wright stopped himself in mid-sentence.

The angel didn't miss a beat. "*Passed on?* I like the expression. *Gone to his Maker* – I'm not sure I care for the sound of that."

"What did you do? Fly off with the body when we weren't looking?" Wright suspected there was more to the disappearance of the body than a simple ferreting away, but he didn't want to dwell on it.

"Penumae, who talked to you at the lake, took care of the body. He placed it away from the human sphere."

"Well, that was kind of Penumae," Wright said, but his sarcasm seemed lost on the creature.

He cleared his throat indignantly. The angels' choice of words always set him off. Where did they get off spouting that Old Testament ethereal shit? Everyone knew they weren't real angels, so what were they trying to prove? He half-suspected they were making fun of humans and of religion, and though he wasn't into Bible-thumping himself, it just about pissed him off.

The angel beamed another smile at Wright, all pearly whites in play. Wright felt his brain going blotto. There was something else he wanted to ask the angel. What? He couldn't think.

"Is there anything I can get you?" asked May, the other waitress, who very well knew angels didn't eat nor drink, at least not around humans. She was just being nosey.

To Wright's surprise, the angel said, "I'll have what the sheriff is having."

"Sure," May said, giving Wright a blue eye-shadowed wink. She was back in a couple of minutes, not as quickly as Laura Jacobsen, but with more hip and wiggle in the delivery. She made a big deal of placing the cup of coffee just so, then precisely bedded down a spoon on a napkin at its side. Wright caught a whiff of her hair spray, a heady lilac smell. She continued her show, straightening the salt and pepper shakers so they stood like figurines on a wedding cake, *accidentally* pressing a polyester-clad breast against the angel's shoulder in the process.

"There you go," May said.

"Thank you very much," the angel said with another smile that would make a TV evangelist envious.

Wright shook his head. *What the hell did May think she was doing?*

The angel took a tentative sip of his coffee. "Hot, isn't it?" he asked.

Wright nodded. "I thought angels didn't eat or drink."

"It's not that we can't eat or drink, only that we don't need to," the angel said. He seemed smug having delivered this explanation, as if he had worked out a complicated legal point in his head.

"Then why bother?"

"Why bother doing anything?" the angel asked. He shrugged, a very human gesture spoiled by his wing tips following suit.

They sat silently for a few minutes, sipping their coffee. May settled down in the adjoining booth and said something to the new waitress that Wright couldn't quite catch. Both women laughed lasciviously, a sound that made the angel's face brighten. Angels were rumored to have better hearing than dogs; Wright now suspected that might be true.

"I suppose you find human behavior very amusing," Wright said. It came out sounding defensive.

"Not at all. We feel very comfortable around humans and find you all impressive beings. Being here on the Earthly plane is an enlightening experience."

"Enlightening? You mean religious?"

"Yes, though not likely in a way you might call religious. We may figure out the puzzle of our own being when we understand yours."

"Gobbledegook."

"Excuse me?"

"Nothing. Never mind," Wright said. Whether the angel's gibberish was intentional evasion or unintentional didn't matter. He really didn't want to get into a sky-pilot discussion over religion. He had enough of that with Marguerite.

The angel leaned forward across the table, resting on his elbows, his wing tips jutting above his head. The table creaked from his weight.

"This sexual thing," he whispered. "Having two sexes, I mean. It's created an intellectual stir among our number."

Wright wanted to ask what the hell the angel meant but couldn't quite get the words out. He had never been this close to an angel for more than a few seconds. Glancing up at the angel's wing tips, at a loss for anything to say, he got a shock. *Tiny hands at the ends of the wings?* Before he could see for sure, the angel leaned back, moving the wing tips up to the ceiling at an angle that hid them from Wright's sight.

Without further ceremony, the angel stood up from the booth. "Good day," he said. Wright tried to get another good look at the angel's wing tips as he went out the door.

Messengers of an Alien God

In the next booth, May was talking in a confidential tone to Laura Jacobsen, just loud enough for Wright to overhear, which meant he was supposed to listen in, for she only did that when she felt she wasn't getting enough attention.

"I'm going to screw that one. I swear he looks like the King," she said.

"May, you don't know anything. I admit he looks a little like Elvis, but angels are neither *hes* nor *shes*. They're *its*. They haven't any penises, no vaginas, no breasts, no balls, no anything," Laura said.

"Are you sure?"

"Uh-huh. Not even a pucker or a wrinkle."

"How do you know for certain? Maybe they're like preachers, who talk like they haven't got any balls, but sure manage to get it on when nobody is looking."

"May, sweetheart, everybody knows the angels are sexless. Besides, I know two ladies who have seen for themselves."

"Oooh, you don't say. Tell me. Tell me who."

"June and Patty."

"June and Patty?" May was incredulous. "Those two old maids? They wouldn't know a sexual organ if it gave them its business card."

"You know that angel who flew into a high voltage line and everyone thought it was dead, and they took it to the clinic? Well, June and Patty, they were on duty when they brought it in."

"So what? They're only nurse's aides, not real nurses. Hell, I heard Patty ain't even that. She never finished school. If it wasn't for the saucer's fall, she wouldn't be working at all."

"It doesn't matter, Fall or no Fall. They both do everything a registered nurse does, they just don't get paid much."

"What does this have to do with an angel's dingus?"

"That's what I'm trying to tell you. They had to clean it up before it was taken to the morgue."

"Clean what up? Its dingus?"

"No, no, no. The whole body, stupid. They had to clean up the body, and you know what they found under the robes?"

"I guess you're going to tell me there was nothing there."

"As smooth as a Barbie doll. Not even nipples. More like a Ken,

-27-

because at least Barbie had bumps."

"I still don't believe it."

"June has proof. She took pictures with the clinic's Polaroid."

"Polaroid? Are those things still available?"

"They had an old one stashed away. Had to use it as the digital cameras were all dead since the fall."

"But just because you've got a picture of one, that doesn't mean they are all that way, does it?"

"You can't argue with a photograph, especially one that can't be Photoshop'ed, can you? Why not just accept it?"

"Because I know men, and I know what they want. And I'm telling you right now about that hunk of angel flesh that just walked out the door – look, he's standing outside on the corner now – every time we bump into each other, he looks like he wants to eat me right up."

Wright decided he had no chance in hell of getting another cup of coffee while the only two waitresses were engrossed in a conversation about an angel's lack of a dick. He slipped a dollar bill under the edge of his coffee cup and headed outside and next door into the church.

Since the last town meeting, someone had dredged up a podium for the stage, but there still weren't enough chairs. Wright moved a dusty stack of sheet music off a piano bench and sat down until the meeting started.

The first half-hour was routine. They could have read the minutes from last week's meeting and saved everyone a lot of trouble. Commissioner Jim Gauss reported gas rationing would continue, with priority going to farmers with grain crops and livestock. The Army was now paying with vouchers for anything that could be used to feed the cities.

The stone faces of the two dozen farmers present said they didn't like the idea of government IOUs, but Wright knew they considered themselves too patriotic to protest. Stoic pragmatism also was a factor. Their operations were dependent upon gasoline and diesel fuel, and the Army was currently the only supplier of either, though there hadn't been a supply convoy come in for more than a month.

Another commissioner had driven to the Callaway Nuclear Plant to get an update. The reactor remained offline while the staff waited for the replacements for control and monitoring computers. It might be a year before the plant produced power again.

"They had the offices lit with kerosene lanterns. Think about it," Jones said.

Until Callaway was back online, Creedance would have to rely on the little hydro-electric power plant at the Lost Lake Dam. It supplied only a trickle of power at the best of times, but its antiquated generators had proven immune to the effects of the Fall. Jones warned that the cities were still trying to get more power, and there was no guarantee that the Callaway plant would be up and operating anytime soon. Creedance was damn lucky to have its own power supply. Many towns and cities were without any electrical power at all.

"Propane is another matter," Jones said, pausing for dramatic effect. A farmer in the back row took the lull as an opportunity to clear the phlegm from his throat. "Everyone had better think about heating and cooking with wood soon," Jones went on, "which means you should start cutting now, before the sap rises. If anyone has wood left over, the retirement home is taking contributions."

Scattered coughs echoed through the room. Wright and everyone else knew the commissioner was all about taking care of Number One. His stroke-stricken mother-in-law resided at the home. If there was no heat, the commissioner's wife would make him bring her mother home.

Then the good news: The contractor had nearly finished laying the new water main before the Fall. A crew of volunteers had finished the last few feet last week by hand-digging the trench. Creedance now had a plentiful, sanitary supply of water from Lost Lake. It only needed a softening agent because the water was acidic. He didn't say anything about the contractor's land-survey miscalculations that had meant diverting the pipeline under the McGuane Memorial Clinic driveway.

Wright's turn was next. He went through the same routine as last time. He warned everyone to keep their doors locked at night as stragglers were still escaping from the cities.

"Keep your guns loaded but don't get trigger-happy. Most country people are law-abiding Christians, as we all are, so let us act like it," he said.

He said everything the audience expected him to say, confident that most of his political liturgy was even true if hackneyed. Wright felt a twinge of guilt at his own hypocrisy. But in Missouri, atheists could not run for public office. So he went to church occasionally and was careful to make all the right public noises and dog whistles that Christians expected.

He noticed a few yawning faces, but his motives would have been suspect if he didn't make the usual speech. Best he never forget the sheriff's office was an elected one.

Taking a count of the yawns, he skipped his usual pitch to organize a local militia, a pet project of his that had yet to gather any enthusiasm. Most of the farmers were too busy trying to keep their farms operating, and he knew he might as well be talking into his hat. No one would pay him any heed until there was real trouble, until one of them was robbed or shot. He shut up, but didn't sit down.

Janice August was one of the few women present. She sat a couple of rows back wearing wearing a battered Stetson hat that shadowed her face but didn't quite hide her left eye being swollen shut. Wright had known her since she was in high school. She had been in Marguerite's Sunday School class. Tommy Georgian was Janice's significant other, and Wright guessed had probably been knocking her around again. Georgian was also a suspected meth manufacturer.

Wright was more worried about the meth labs out in the Mark Twain National Forest more than the pot farmers. The meth labs should had gone out of business when the chemical precursors they needed became scarce after the Fall, but somehow they seemed to be still cranking along, so to speak. But both the large-scale growers and the meth makers were territorial, well-armed and all too ready to do violence to protect their high-dollar businesses.

Wright didn't say this for a couple of reasons. For one thing, he knew that at least one of the Amish-looking bearded men in the back row was a pot grower. But Wright had decided to leave him alone as long as he remained peaceful and didn't get into the meth business. There were a lot more problems to attend to these days than people getting high on pot.

With the general business taken care of, it was time for the open discussion. Usually this part of the meeting was nothing but a gripe session. Wright rationalized it as good of a way as any for the die-hard cynics and discontents to get it out of their systems; carping about the failure of local authority was a kind of safety valve, beneficial as long as he didn't allow it to build up too much steam.

Dr. Jenkins stood up. "I have something to report," he said. "In about six months, we are going to have quite a few more mouths to feed."

A couple of men in the back broke into laughter over a private joke, with the punch line probably about the good doctor's reputation for drinking too much, too often.

Jenkins, who had been sober for years, waited patiently for them to stop. "I think it's called the disaster syndrome or something like that. It usually refers to what happens when there's a hurricane or a tornado, anything that is at once life-threatening and upsets the normal routine of life."

"What happens?" someone shouted from the back row.

"Why the birth rate goes up, of course," the doctor said. "I imagine we also can blame the two weeks we were all without electricity, and perhaps the fact the Fall happened when there was a full moon. But I've got ten times – perhaps more – the number of expectant mothers showing up at the clinic than I should have. I haven't even had time to do full examinations, but EPF urine tests are about ninety-eight percent accurate."

More coughs. Wright kept quiet, nakedly embarrassed. Marguerite and he hadn't made love – hell, they hadn't even kissed – for a year, so of course she hadn't been prepared for the fit of romance that had overtaken them both one night soon after the Fall.

"Not only are these babies all going to be due within a few days of each other, many of the women are in their late thirties and early forties, old enough to know better, I might add. And they are going to require more care than my two nurses and I can deliver. I thought I might train a few midwives, but midwifery is against state law. I guess what I'm asking is some sort of waiver of the law. Any kind of prenatal care or birthing assistance is better than none."

Before Wright could ask Jenkins why he didn't find all the pregnancies suspicious, an angel stepped into room. He hung back by the door, looking a bit uncomfortable, as if not sure of his welcome. Most of the emergency meeting attendees didn't pay him any heed. Funny, Wright thought, that no one mistrusted the angels or in anyway connected them to the disaster. True, their crash-landing coincided with the onset of the disaster, but it was the military's attempts – both here and abroad – to blow the saucers out the sky with nuclear cruise missiles that had reputedly knocked out the power grid and most electronic devices. At least, that was the scuttlebutt.

The angels seemed far removed from the ordinary goings-on of life. He tried to work up a good suspicion and failed. To see them as any sort of threat required too many mental contortions. Alien, yes. Too strong to be pushed around? Yes. But sinister? Not in any way. It just didn't fit.

What had he been thinking about at the lake?

"Do what you have to do, Doctor," Wright said.

"Pardon me, Sheriff, but do you have that kind of authority?"

"Under martial law, I guess I do," Wright said, wondering if he in fact did have the authority.

He must have been convincing, because the doctor sat down.

The meeting proceeded as usual. Frank Marshall asked for the floor. Wright steeled himself for a difficult time. Marshall, a retired military man, was the part-time manager of the MFA Co-op, chairman of the county Emergency Preparedness Committee and a member of any other public-service committee that would have him. A man who did as much as Marshall did for free was nothing more than a busybody in Wright's opinion. Fortunately, the Emergency Preparedness Committee only had authority where hazardous materials were involved, and thankfully there weren't many of those in the county.

"I just wanted to remind everyone we have a potential goddamned catastrophe at the co-op," he said. Everyone knew what he was talking about. He had brought it up the last two meetings. "Fall or no Fall, we still have enough ammonium nitrate fertilizer stored in the bins to blow the whole town to goddamned Timbuktu."

A couple of men coughed at Marshall's profanity. Southern Baptists to a man, they could let such an occasional lapse slide – though with Marshall, profanity was less a lapse than a way of life.

"Thanks, Frank, but the Fall does make a difference. That pile of fertilizer will have to keep," Wright said.

"You don't seem to understand. The Co-op keeps drums of kerosene in the same building. Some of those drums are rusting out on the bottoms and leaking. Mix the nitrate and kerosene together and you've got a potion that's as powerful as goddamned TNT."

"I know, Frank. I've blown a few stumps with nitrate and kerosene myself. And I know more than I want to about the Oklahoma City bombing. But that stuff isn't going to get mixed together unless someone mixes it. We've got more pressing problems right now."

"Well, don't forget the cardinal rule of explosives, Sheriff."

"What's that, Frank?"

"Shit happens."

"Thanks, Frank. I'll remember that piece of advice. Why don't you come up with a simple solution to the problem and submit it at next month's meeting?"

"I already have a solution."

"In writing, Frank. In writing."

The old soldier grumbled something about pencil pushers and copy machines and sat down.

Pete Morgan asked for the floor next. Pete was a soybean and sorghum farmer who had run unsuccessfully against Wright in the last election.

"Somebody tell me something. It's been two months now since the nukes went off and the angel saucer fell to Earth. None of the power lines went down. Nothing made smoke as far as I can see, but nothing works. And nobody has explained to me yet why my TV don't work, or why the local telephones work but long distance doesn't or why my new pickup won't run. Okay, the TV was plugged into the outlet when the bomb went off. So I'm told it was shorted out, not with lightning but by something called E-M-P. But why the telephones? And my truck?"

"It's the military that did it," blurted one of the older farmers in the back. When everyone in the room looked at him for elaboration, he scrunched down, red-faced. Others in the room began to mumble.

They were all open to paranoid plots, Wright realized. Everyone, even those old codgers who hadn't driven across the county line in ten years, felt imprisoned by circumstances out of their control. Wright couldn't help feeling the same way, but as the highest-ranking elected official, he had to keep people from getting too riled up and doing something they might regret later. It was his job to keep order.

"I don't know why all the new cars won't run, Pete," he said. "I do know most of the military's hardware is out of operation as well. Most of their electronics got hit pretty hard, too, though some of it was what they call 'hardened,' and so is still operating."

Pete liked to set people up. "Well, I've got an idea. I agree with that fellow in the back there. I think the Army is behind the whole thing. And I think we should think twice about giving them our beef or our corn and wheat." He looked about the audience for support.

"Are you finished, Pete?"

"Just about. I think we should take a second look at anyone who works hand-in-hand with the Army."

The reference was clear to almost everyone in the room. The one Army reserve radio link still in operation was at the sheriff's office. There were no reserve troops in Creedance. The Army had its hands full with riot control in the cities and didn't have the resources to bother much with a backwater like Creedance. At least, that was what Wright had been told.

"I've read a little bit about this E-M-P effect," said someone from the back of the room.

Wright craned his neck, but couldn't see the speaker for the posts that held up the ceiling.

"Speak up, then," he said.

Wright had a sneaking suspicion who the anonymous authority was and suspected he might regret giving him the floor. To confirm his guess, Uncle Robert stepped out from behind the post. He was clad in his usual scruffy seersucker coveralls, but he'd changed out of the ratty jacket to an expensive-looking though lint-speckled, blue-gray herringbone sports blazer. He also wore his customary grin, described by some as "demented."

Wright, who had invited Uncle Robert to visit the county jail's drunk cell on several occasions, knew the old man wasn't demented at all. Silly, maybe, like someone chuckling over a private joke, but demented or idiotic? No. Most of the time Uncle Robert's grin complemented his white Santa Claus beard. But today his smile stood out among the serious faces like a hippie acidhead at a policeman's ball.

"Drunk!" It was a shout from someone at the back, someone too cowardly to show his face.

Out of place or not, Uncle Robert had not been a guest in Wright's jail for nearly a year. He still got drunk as the proverbial skunk, in fact, maybe more often the last few years. But Wright had found out early that when Uncle Robert went drinking, he always had the presence of mind to leave his Range Rover at home. Some dark sodden night he might wobble his rickety bicycle off some embankment or into the path of an oncoming pickup truck, but he wasn't likely to do the public more harm than running over somebody's toes – unless you counted upsetting the local sense of propriety. Uncle Robert lived with his common-law wife – a black woman no less here in the Aryan heartland – in the old Jacobsen mansion. Somewhere interracial marriages were not a subject for talk; somewhere self-educated eccentric intellectuals might be considered a kind of natural resource. But not here, not in Creedance, not among the respectable society of Harmon County.

"Why don't you tell us what you know, Uncle Robert," Wright said.

"No, not that screwball," Pete said, his voice filled with exasperation. Wright stared him down.

"Well EMP stands for Electro-Magnetic Pulse. It's what you get when you explode a thermonuclear device in the upper atmosphere."

"We know that much," Wright said, afraid Uncle Robert was gearing up to waste their time.

"Well, here's some more. Set off a one-megaton bomb 500 kilometers above the Earth – that's about 300 miles high – and it generates an EMP of 50,000 volts per meter at the Earth's surface. If the bomb is centered over the continental United States – Missouri for example – then the EMP effect will blanket the entire country."

"And what does that have to do with my TV and my truck?" Pete asked, shaking his head.

Uncle Robert just smiled at him. Pete looked like he was going to blow a head gasket. "Most of the energy of the EMP is below 100 megahertz. That means it's in the radio frequencies. Solid state controllers, like the electronic ignition in your new Chevy, Mr. Morgan, are susceptible to radio frequencies at high voltages."

"You mean everything is shorted out? Well, hell, we knew that," Pete said.

"Then why did you ask?" Uncle Robert said.

"Goddamn screwball, sit down and be quiet."

"No, Pete, I think you should be quiet. Uncle Robert has the floor," Wright said.

"I still say it's the military," Pete said stubbornly.

"Where did you learn this, Uncle Robert?"

"I read it in the *Bulletin of the Atomic Scientists,*" Uncle Robert said. Pete gave a snort of disgust. Wright ignored him.

"What else did this journal say? Did it mention anything about health effects?" Wright asked carefully. He didn't want to start a panic. But the talk was already on. Better to see it through now. Though he didn't imagine for an instant the U.S. military would ever wreak such havoc on its own country, he knew they had a reputation of withholding information from the public in what was termed "The Public Good."

"It's a professional journal. Been around since the 1940s. I read a lot, you know, or used to. I haven't been able to read much lately since I can't get to down the big university library at Columbia." Uncle Robert scratched his chin, his eyes momentarily unfocused, as if he were staring into eternity.

"What else did the article say?" Wright felt like he was questioning a bright child, not someone twenty years his senior.

"It was an old article, 1983, March or so. I read it when it came out. That was quite a few years ago, you know."

"Did it say anything about health effects?" Wright said, beginning to feel impatient.

"Oh, sorry. You asked me that, already, didn't you? Sorry, my thoughts get away from me at times," Uncle Robert said.

Pete, red-faced, shook his head in disbelief.

"No, it didn't say much about health effects," Uncle Robert went on, "Except there aren't supposed to be any when the blast goes off so high up."

Wright let out a sigh of relief. "Okay, thanks, Uncle Robert."

"There's one other thing the article said, Sheriff."

"What was that?"

Messengers of an Alien God

"It wasn't supposed to knock out battery-operated transistor radios unless they had big antennas. EMP was only supposed to damage electronics connected to the electrical power grid or having an antenna or grounded to a lot of metal, like an airplane fuselage or a car body. Digital watches and pocket calculators should still be okay. Mine aren't. How about yours?"

With that, Uncle Robert sat down and stared off into space again, the silly grin back in place. Wright guessed he hadn't really expected an answer. Everyone knew that everything relying on solid state electronics no longer worked, including watches and calculators.

"You see," Pete said, "not everything is as it seems."

"Sheriff, I can explain why some of the local telephones work while the long distance doesn't," said Carl Johnson. He had been a telephone lineman before the Fall. Wright had never liked the man, though at the moment he couldn't say exactly why. He was rumored to frequently service more than the out-of-order phones he was called to fix – husbands made it a point to be around when he called. He was good looking, sort of resembling Johnny Depp, but there was something a little smarmy about him.

"Speak up, Carl, so everyone can hear you," Wright said. Talking about the state of long-distance phone service was like talking about the weather: It didn't do any good except to pass the time. But it was a good way to get the town meeting off the subject of a military plot or unknown health effects.

"Well, do you know what a switching node is?" Carl asked. His tone was patronizing.

"Is that like wife-switching?" someone called out from the back row, probably the same wit who had anonymously heckled before.

Uncle Robert looked up, transported out of his absent-minded reveries.

"No, you mean wife-swapping, you fool," came another voice replied from the shadows.

"Does anyone know what a switching node is?" Carl asked. "How about you, Uncle Robert, do you know?"

Uncle Robert kept quiet.

"How about you, Sheriff? Do you know?"

-37-

"No, Carl, frankly I don't."

"Well, when you make a long-distance call it doesn't go straight through on one continuous line. The telephone company uses computers all over the country to route calls through the snarl of telephone lines. There are all different kinds, and well . . ."

Carl stumbled over his explanation and looked around the room to see if anyone other than Wright was listening. Wright knew Carl well enough to guess he knew about half what he was talking about. "And well, some of them are older than others. Several nodes over in the next county, around Columbia, are pretty old. I've heard that several use mechanical relays instead of integrated circuits or transistors."

"What's this have to do with our long-distance telephones, Carl?"

"Don't you see?" He looked around the room again. Quite a few people were talking among themselves. Even Uncle Robert wasn't listening; he was engaged in the worthy activity of picking lint off the lapel of his blazer.

"Well, I'll tell you what it means," Carl continued. "Those old antique switching stations are the only reason we have any telephone service at all. Electromotive pulses, even 50,000 volts worth, ain't going to knock out a 1950s gold-plated relay."

Whether anyone understood or didn't wasn't the question. Carl was boring them. The serious business over, they began to slip out of the room. One would think the angel had better things to do, higher places to fly to, cherubs to see, but the creature followed Dr. Jenkins out the door, a quizzical expression on his face.

Uncle Robert pocketed his collected lint and followed the angel and the good doctor.

* * *

5.

Catharsis

By early spring in northern Missouri, the nights were still damp and cold as most liquid propane tanks only held fumes. This fact had propelled Bryan Douglas – one-time engineering major, one-time philosophy major, one-time English literature major, one-time journalism major, and most recently college drop-out – into a career as a woodcutter.

Classical economics had acted as a midwife to the birth of his latest career transformation: He had to eat. The local farmers had meat on the hoof, homemade cheese and dried grains – more than they could eat themselves, but little time to cut wood. Bryan had time and an empty stomach. Supply met demand, shook hands, and Bryan found himself in the business of supplying a basic commodity.

They made tight-fisted trading partners, these dairymen and soybean farmers of Scottish and German descent, and would have made time to cut wood themselves except for his prices, which he kept at the subsistence level. Consequently, he had to cut on a regular basis just to keep himself fed and have gasoline for the tanks of his grandfather's faded red 1964 junker Ford pickup truck and Stihl chainsaw.

After three years of sedentary college life, he was completely exhausted during his first few weeks of the new career. Each day became a short course in hell. By mid-morning all his muscles and joints screamed in pain, and he would stumble back to his grandfather's farmhouse and fall into bed. But he adapted, not from strength of will but of necessity. The alternative was to head back to the breadlines in Columbia, but judging by the stories trickling out from the city, he was probably better off staying in the country. Besides, what if his grandfather managed to make it back from his trip to the Grand Canyon? The old man had trusted him to look after the farm while taking the first vacation of his life.

So a few hours after witnessing the collision of the angels and the plane, Bryan had trudged back to where he had left off, sharpening the chain of his saw and trying to psyche himself into felling the ancient oak on top of the hill overlooking the lake.

Performed by hand, chainsaw sharpening was more an art than a skill. He had ruined one chain on the Stihl learning this art, and he was still insecure in its execution. His remaining chain might have to last until the industrial world recovered from the Fall.

The new career did have its perks, he thought as he paused to enjoy the view. To the east lay the derelict angel saucer; below it, to the west, glimmered the smooth, dark mirror of Lost Lake. There was a wisp of smoke coming form the direction of the town, but in every other direction native oak and hickory forest stretched as far as he could see. The hill he sat on was the highest point for miles. The huge oak he had chosen to cut was the tallest tree in sight.

Refreshed by this perspective, he resumed his sharpening. Paradoxically, the trick to having a long-lived chain was sharpening it frequently. He learned this from a chance encounter in the woods with an old fellow who introduced himself as "Uncle Robert." Hold the file level, the old man said. Draw it across a sawtooth at this angle, he'd said. Give each tooth a lick between every tank of gas, he said. Find a comfortable stump, take your time, and do it right the first time, he said. Then he had given Bryan a mysterious grin and disappeared into the woods like some sort of backwoods shaman.

The last tooth of the chain sharpened, Bryan flipped the ignition switch, half-closed the choke, and yanked the starter cord. Still warm from cutting earlier, the Stihl's engine started right up, and he opened up the choke all the way.

He did the notch-cut on the ancient oak tree in fifteen minutes. When he was through, he set the saw down and used the twelve-pound maul to knock the wedge of wood, which was the size of a small end table, free of the trunk.

Messengers of an Alien God

He stepped back and admired the old tree before making the final cut.

When he had first started cutting months ago, he had left the big oaks alone and cut down nothing larger than a foot in diameter. It had seemed almost sacrilegious to cut a tree six feet around and sixty or seventy years in the growing. But an oak tree was not a redwood. This one, like so many its size, had neared the natural end of its years. A decade earlier, like an old man entering his twilight years, the circulation of sap through the tree had weakened, lowering its natural defenses. As a result, a variety of insects had made inroads into large and small limbs. In pursuit of those insects, woodpeckers made hundreds of holes through its bark, further exposing the living wood to infection and more insect attacks. Today, on this unseasonably warm, wet, spring afternoon most of the tree's branches were dead or nearly dead. Yet enough of the trunk lived on to starve younger trees of sunlight and moisture. In felling the old tree, he was making room for the new. Viewed from this perspective, he found the work satisfying, more a promotion of life than a taking.

He picked up the saw and began the hinge cut on the other side from the notch cut. Felling a tree this size was the most life-threatening part of wood-cutting, especially if done incorrectly. A big tree like this one was rarely symmetrical, and its inestimable weight distribution made predicting the direction of its fall dicey. More threatening, the core of the trunk could be rotten and inelastic; it could fall any which way, snapping off and falling toward him. Not long before the Fall, the town had buzzed with the story of a big oak snapping off while the farmer was making the last cut. The trunk had hit the ground and bounced backward, smashing the woodcutter into the ground.

He revved the saw and leaned into the cut. Wood chips and powdery sawdust spewed out from the cut, powdering his work boots white, a sign the chain's teeth had found dead wood deep in the trunk. He let off the chainsaw's throttle to listen. The tree groaned as tons of wood began to shift position. He turned and ran with the idling chainsaw in hand. Earlier he had cleared an escape path through the undergrowth. As he ran, intuitive calculations of mass and inertia intermingled with gruesome images of himself mashed under the hog oak's dead weight.

He turned in time to see the tree crushing several small trees in its fall. The ground shook under his feet. Two upper limbs – each as large as a mature tree – snapped off, and the great trunk broke in three pieces, a sound he felt in his bones and teeth as much as heard.

After the tumultuous reverberation of the crash the forest seemed as still as death. He waited, relishing the silence. Then, just as quickly as they had stopped, the normal sounds of the woods resumed. A host of starlings twittered. A squirrel, whose nest had been in the crowning branches, had ridden the tree down. Now homeless, it rustled off through the undergrowth. Off to his right, a woodpecker resumed its jackhammer excavations into another large oak.

Sweat trickled down his brow and stung his eyes. He set the saw down and took off his eyeglasses to clean them. Without glasses, his vision of the forest changed. The forest-scape became an impressionistic painting. Patterns and themes became more obvious. While standing, the tree had seemed the center of the forest; now it was the antipode. Shattered branches, their bark jolted off at impact, lay strewn about, the old wood crumbly and as white as bleached bones.

He moved through the brambles and other undergrowth to inspect his handiwork. Up close he could see why the tree had broken up. As he suspected, the trunk was hollow, its core eaten out by insects and rot. Water drained from it in streams. The hollow trunk, open somewhere near the top, had collected rain like a barrel. His job would be easier and safer than he anticipated. With the tree's back broken there was less danger of it abruptly shifting as he de-limbed it. Though he would harvest fewer pickup loads from a hollow trunk, the wood would be lighter and burn hotter and cleaner. Each pickup load would bring a premium over the green wood he had been cutting.

A small animal mewed from a great fissure running along the length of the broken trunk; probably another squirrel. Cautiously – even young squirrels had formidable teeth – he peeled off a slab of bark, leaned down close enough to peer into the hollow and found himself inches away from the face of an angel. He let out a yelp and nearly bolted.

His heart pounded for a few minutes before he calmed down. Then he took a deep breath and looked again.

The angel lay on its back, eyes closed, its shimmering white robes peppered with rotten wood chips and stained by brackish stump-water.

Messengers of an Alien God

The body was curled into a half-fetal position with the lacy wings blanketing the shoulders. One hand was trapped between its tightly clenched legs; the other rested on its stomach. Like a blind crab, the free hand began moving slowly up the chest, traversing the neck and up over the chin. When the migrating hand found the mouth, the angel began to hungrily suck and lick the tips of its fingers. The eyes remained closed. The mewing ceased.

How had the angel gotten into the tree? Had it fallen in through the opening at the top to become wedged here, submersed in the filthy rain water, until the splitting of the trunk had disclosed it?

Without thinking, Bryan picked up a broken sprig and used it to push the angel's hand away from its mouth. The mouth continued sucking on empty air for a second, then emitted a plaintive mewing that sounded like a sick infant. The angel's eyes remained closed.

When he pulled away the stick, the hand quickly migrated back to the mouth. The stick was still in Bryan's hand. Filled with a sense of apprehension but not able to resist the impulse, he poked the angel's hand again, harder. At the touch of the stick, the angel's eyes popped open. It stared at him for a long moment, uncomprehending, then shrieked, "It's you! God, it's you!" and leaped out of the tree in an explosion of rotten bark and wood chips.

For a second the world was engulfed by white wings flapping, hands fluttering and robes flailing. Thrown off balance, Bryan stumbled, tripped over a fallen branch and fell flat on his back. The angel soared over his head in a curving, slow-motion trajectory. The entire surface of the thick, lacework wing-skin rippled in slow motion with small, spastic undulations. The angel's eyes now closed again, it flew by dead reckoning, its mouth agape in a silent scream. For all its hypnotic grace, its flight was short, and it crashed into the brush with a heavy thud. In a second, it was on its feet and charging out of the brush and down the hill, breaking through the dense undergrowth like a stampeding cow.

Bryan got painfully to his feet and brushed himself off. Dampness from the spring earth had soaked through the back of his sweatshirt and the seat of his khaki pants.

The sound of more activity down the hill made him turn around. At the base of the hill the angel raced through a thick grove of wrist-size poplar and out across a small field of green winter wheat. The wings shimmered like new snow. It left a trail of deep muddy holes and trampled wheat, evidence of its great weight.

Bryan headed down the hill in pursuit. Rather than charging straight through brambles and over small trees as the angel had, he followed an old firebreak that stretched like a scar through the timber and undergrowth. He reached the wheat field as the angel disappeared into the wood. He trudged through the knee-high wheat, but avoided gettng bogged down in the muddy low spots, which helped him catch up to the creature. As he entered the wood, he could see the angel rampaging though the undergrowth not more than a few yards far ahead.

"Hey, you, angel, stop," he shouted.

Stupid thing to say.

The angel turned and let out a scream so shrill it rattled Bryan's teeth. He stopped, fearing it would charge him. But no, its eyes were still closed. It had blindly reacted to a stimulus.

It turned and continued its mindless course.

At first, Bryan had not given the chase much thought. Now he decided that pursuing the angel into the woods alone might not be the wisest thing to do. As Sheriff Wright had said at Lost Lake, any angel was strong enough to pull the arms off a grown man as easily as a child can de-wing a housefly. No matter that none of the angels had ever shown the least tendency toward physical violence, they were still largely an unknown.

Still, he couldn't bring himself to abandon his observation of the angel. A drama of some sort was being played out, and he wanted to witness the final scene. Had he set it free or had it just been happenchance that it had burst free while he poked at it? As he weighed responsibility – and danger – the angel ran blindly into a tree. It rebounded and staggered but didn't fall. It made a small course correction around the tree, wobbled, then continued in straight line, grazing low-hanging branches and saplings along the way.

Amused now but still cautious, Bryan followed. He kept back, ready to duck behind a tree if the angel should turn around. He continued to follow the creature through the woods for at least a mile, hanging back until it recovered from a collision with a tree or a fall into a creek or gully. The angel moaned occasionally from what seemed to be an increasing level of pain.

A few halting steps and it fell again, rolling onto its back. Its beautiful face contorted, and it hands clutched its stomach in agony. Its eyes opened but did not focus on him, though he was only a few yards away. It stumbled to its feet and shambled farther into the woods. It held its wings folded and held tight to its back, the skin in folds like a wrinkled shawl. He followed, now closer, fearing the angel with its freakishly acute senses would detect his clumsy shadowing. But it took no notice of the dry snap of broken branches or the crackle of leaves underfoot. Another hundred yards and the angel somehow found a small break in a wall of piled brush and dead limbs. Bryan waited, wary. The angel had passed out of sight, and he feared he might stumble over it in the shadows. When he could wait no longer for fear of losing the trail, he entered the break in the wall of brush and emerged into a small circular clearing about hundred feet across.

The clearing was closed in by huge twisted oaks and piles of dead trees. The opening where he stood was the only way into or out of the clearing. The piles of dead trees, leftovers from a lumber clearcut, were so congested with brambles and scag-growth as to be impenetrable by anything but snakes and field mice. A small stagnant pool, clogged with scum and light-starved weeds, occupied the center of the clearing. The old growth oaks shaded most of the cleared ground, creating a morbid little park in the midst of chaotic forest growth.

Near the edge of the pool, the angel paused. Above, clouds momentarily parted, and the clearing was lit briefly by dusty slivers of sunlight spiking down through the leafy canopy. The angel stretched its wings to their full span. Bryan held his breath, expecting it to launch itself upward and go crashing up through the overhanging snarl of dead trees. The break in the clouds closed, and the beams of sunlight turned off as if someone had flipped a switch, throwing the clearing back into shadow. Another paroxysm of pain bent the angel double. A nervous ripple flowed over the expanse of white wings. Damp with dewy perspiration, the wings shed water like a tree shaken by wind. Another attack of anguish brought the angel to its knees at the edge of the pond, fists clenched, features pinched in agony. Then it vomited a thin clear liquid into the water. More spasms racked its body.

Bryan was again tempted to go to its aid. As before, fear, and something else – a premonition, perhaps – held him back. He settled down behind a small grassy mound and waited. The angel's convulsions continued for another good ten minutes, and Bryan began to doubt he was going to be shown anything secret other than its death throes. Blood trickled from the angel's nose. Surprisingly, it was red and looked just like human blood. The creature pushed itself off its knees, stood, pulled up its robes around its waist, extended its wings, then squatted as if to defecate.

Bryan was close enough to see this was a fruitless effort for the angel as it lacked any orifice, even an anus, just as had the drowned angel at the lake. This lacking didn't deter the angel from its efforts. Muscles tensed under the skin. Its grunts and moans became at once pitiful and lyrical, modulating in tone and key. Despite its size and lack of any sexual organs, the angel seemed female. There was something about the shape of its legs, the roundness and fullness of its bare buttocks and hips, that now suggested femininity, however inconclusively.

The straining continued. The ivory white skin of the buttocks blushed. Bryan thought he detected a bulbous swelling between the legs, but whether it was real or his imagination was as uncertain.

A light, cold rain began to fall, and the light level of the clearing dropped further. The angel shrieked again and one wing drooped to its side, then the other, concealing its groin and backside.

Hunched down, its wings wrapped around itself, the angel looked like a gigantic, pulsating cocoon. It rocked back and forth with an effect that was almost comical, like an overheated cartoon tea kettle. Then it fell over and lay still.

Bryan waited. The drizzle increased to a steady rain, quickly soaking through his clothes. What to do? Should he leave well enough alone and walk away? His curiosity made that impossible. When he had disturbed the sleeping angel he had not been entirely in control of himself. Suspecting he was taking a big chance, possibly with his life, he walked over to take a closer look.

The angel lay still in the fetal position, with the wings completely covering its tucked-up legs and arms. The top end of the folded wings projected beyond the top of its head by a good foot and a half. Though cupped within the folded wings, its head and shoulders remained visible.

The angel was metamorphosing, shrinking and wrinkling. He moved nearer and ran his hand over the surface of a wing to find an unexpected texture. Instead of being warm and supple, the skin was dry and hard, covered with tiny braille-like bumps. Lizard skin. It continued to change under his touch. A clenched knot of flesh emerged the top of the wing as the skin withdrew. Fascinated, he cupped his hand around it and was rewarded with a tingling, electric sensation.

The wings quivered violently and unfolded, exposing the angel's entire body, then stilled. Bryan gasped but did not let go of the wing tip. A large bloody bolus lay in a discharge of black viscous fluid between the angel's legs.

The knob of wing tip squirmed in his hand. He snatched his hand away, disgusted as the knob bloomed like an evil flower to reveal a small, perfectly formed hand. The tiny hand joined to the flat plane of the wing with no distinguishable wrist joint. The knob at the tip of the other wing had unfolded into another tiny hand in the same slow, precise process. The slow-motion unfolding absorbed his attention completely and drew him closer despite his disgust. The little hands opened and reached out to him.

Everything in the world changed. Reality did a flip-flop. Iridescent patterns spread across the wing material painted by an unseen brush. The air shimmered with colors he could not name. He jerked his gaze away and looked for an escape path from the horrible beauty. Though mid-afternoon, thick darkness concealed everything but the area immediately around him and the angel. They appeared to be inside a succession of lighted spheres, one within another, endlessly recursive. The very center of this series of spheres, the point of brightest light, was located between the angel's legs where the bolus lay. Bryan let his gaze pause on the center. A mistake. A blue face with a thousand eyes stared back at him. All the eyes blinked in unison. The irises were a clear, almost translucent gray, liquid pools of steel, all too human and familiar yet completely alien at the same time. Around them was . . . armor? Flesh? Human faces and bodies twisted in a glorious way. Yes, and something that was most certainly neither human nor angel but glorious lay there. He looked beyond the eyes and saw a mass of finely detailed lines that stretched infinitely in all directions – too much detail for his mind to take in. Beyond, an endless succession of worlds waited. Instantly, he found himself looking out from the center at a shabby little illusion. In an intuitive flash, he saw the world into which he had been born as human was nothing more than a sham – worse than a sham. It was chaos incarnate, a veil of tears designed to trap and confuse him, to prevent him ever from returning to the world of light.

The alien vision lifted, and his confusion was replaced by terror. The bloody thing between the angel's legs slowly unfolded to become a child-sized cherubim, dark-haired, pink-lipped and and chubby. It unfolded its wings and expanded into a full-sized angel more than six feet tall in an instant.

With a revelation usually granted only to prophets and other madmen, Bryan saw a path out of this world of chaos. He could merge with the new angel, become part of it – it part of him – and escape to a new life through death. A thing made not made of flesh extended from the new angel's abdomen. It stretched out, as long as the angel's arms, a spear of diamonds and crystal. The crystal spear became brighter, clearer, hovering on the verge of resolution, its cut edges sharp with reflected light. The angel reached out to embrace him, and —

As quickly as he had been drawn into the angel's world, Bryan found himself out of the clearing, running at full speed through the forest in the cold rain. He wanted to look back but was terrified of what he might see. He was remotely conscious of having lost some wonderful thing. Desperately, he tried to recall what he had lost, but the vision receded, shrinking to a pinpoint of a memory as he ran. He felt alternately desperately cheated and relieved to have escaped a terrible destiny. He could still picture the blue god of the thousand eyes posed in the window of another world, and crystalline knives reaching out to him, but its portent was fading like a dream.

* * *

6.

Lost Souls

Bryan deposited himself in the booth and scrutinized the hand-written menu. Coffee? Tea? Chili? Meatloaf? Those seemed to be his only choices.

What he really needed was some valium or moonshine, anything that would dull the memory of what he had seen in the forest clearing. Neither was likely to be found at Bouchers so he ordered coffee.

The blue-eye shadow waitress took his order, but it was the other waitress– it would have to be Laura – who brought him a small paper packet and hot water in one of those little chrome-plated pitchers with lopsided lids that always drooled the water into the cup.

"What is this?" His voice broke like a teenager's.

"Decaffeinated tea." Laura smiled wryly. "We're out of ground coffee."

His hands were still shaking, and it took him a few seconds to even understand what she was saying. She probably thought it was her effect on him. Little she knew. He was over her – mostly.

"I don't want decaffeinated. If anything, I want caffeine-enhanced," he managed to blurt out.

"Funny," she said. He had avoided looking at her straight on. Yes, some of the old hurt was still there. Funny, her eyes weren't dark brown as he remembered, but nearly black. "You always drank decaffeinated when I knew you."

"Listen, just give me a cup of coffee, damn it." He stopped himself, realizing he was almost screaming. "Just a cup of real coffee. I've had a really, really bad day, all right?"

"Real coffee is getting really expensive, you know."

"I've got real money."

She smiled and went to the coffee station. He tried to concentrate on her legs – she had good legs – as she crossed the room. He remembered the feel of them, and some more of the pain of the rejection came back, but he was grateful for the pain; it took the place of the nameless horror the angel had showed him.

What exactly had the angel showed him?

Laura caught him ogling her as she crossed the nearly empty restaurant with his cup of coffee. Then she surprised him by sitting down in the booth.

She didn't sit directly across from him but pulled a chair to end of the booth with her back to the rest of patrons.

"This is going to cost you plenty," she said.

"You mean the coffee or . . ."

She smiled at him as she perched on the edge of the seat, with her legs crossed. Self-consciously, she crossed them the other way. That didn't work either, so she uncrossed and crossed them the first way. With each change of position her pantyhose-clad legs made a rasping sound that captured his attention. More enchantment, but of the human variety, and he allowed himself be captured by it.

"Be careful, it's hot," she said. *Was that a cock of her hip?*

"What do you mean?"

"The coffee. It's hot. Be careful."

"I thought you were out."

"I had a little stashed back for special customers," she said.

"Oh, okay. Thanks." He picked up his spoon and used it to swirl the steaming coffee. There were little patches of oily crud floating on top. She smiled at him, though he couldn't tell if she was amused or pleased to see him. He never could. She looked flawed yet beautiful in the dreary light, maybe because he hadn't been around many women since the Fall.

He had noticed her several times after the Fall had stranded him in Creedance and had chalked it up to a simple twist of fate. Several times he had meant to speak to her, to let her know in a casual, self-deferring way that he had grown up since their affair ended a few months ago in Columbia. But he had never gotten past the formal liturgy of waitress and customer. Better to stick with the commonplace opening than to make a fool of himself.

"Where is everybody?"

"They're having a meeting next door at the old church." She picked up a menu and thumbed through it.

"So it's business as usual, despite the Fall," he managed to say.

"Business? It's not business." She said 'business' as if it were a filthy word.

Bryan sighed. Already, less than a minute into the conversation, he was bogging down into the same communication problem he always had with her.

"I didn't mean anything by it. It was just an expression."

She uncrossed and re-crossed her legs, creating the rasping sound again – a giant, sexy cricket.

"Nice hose," he said, feeling lamer by the moment.

"Glad you like them. Like coffee, pantyhose have become kind of scarce since the Fall," she said.

He continued. "So this is your hometown?"

"Sure, I'm a home girl. Can't you tell?" Her dark eyes sparkled.

"You seem too smart to be a waitress," he said.

"I bet you say that to all the waitresses."

"No, I don't, really." Actually he did say that to a lot of waitresses, though he hadn't had the opportunity to try out the line in an ordinary town before. It was a good bet in a college town that most young waitresses thought themselves too smart to be slinging burgers and drawing beers.

"You have the hands of a mechanic these days. What happened to your journalism degree?"

"The same thing that happened to the business degree, the philosophy degree and the English degree."

"And what was that?"

"I got bored," he said, thinking that he had played around in journalism the same way she had just nonchalantly toyed with the salt shaker.

He examined his hands. Where there wasn't dirt or grease, there was raw skin from working in the brush without gloves. The shaking had subsided.

She uncrossed her legs again but did not re-cross them. Instead she clasped her fingers around a knee and pulled the her leg up to her chest. In the process her skirt slid up, showing a lot more thigh and a glimpse of cotton panties. Which seemed rather blantant even for her, but it dawned on him that with her back to the rest of the restaurant clientele, it was a private show for him.

And a good show. She was neither blonde nor blue-eyed, but the pose reminded him of one of those pin-up calendars made by wrench manufacturers for mechanics and welders. Miss Goodwrench vixen of the year. As she had once made it very clear that it was "completely, definitely, totally" over between them, then she must be messing with his mind. But that didn't compute either, and though Laura had issues, being a cock-tease wasn't one of them.

His concentration on the small patch of white cotton was broken by a glimmering image of what he'd seen in the shadow of the angel's wings. How long had he wandered in the woods, lost a quarter-mile from his own homestead? Hours, maybe. During that time the world had been transformed from a familiar place into something alien and hostile. No, not hostile but indifferent to him. Completely indifferent.

He focused on dispelling the enthralling memory by unabashedly staring between her legs. She noticed, spread her legs a little wider apart, and put her other hand on her hip, enhancing the Calendar Girl pose. Her eyes were dark and too intense; her features too sharp to be a mechanic's ideal love goddess. She wore her dark hair in a bun that sat on the crown of her head like a little black hat. Her legs were her best feature, but it was the whole package that captivated him, not just the individual parts. A piece of a Shakespearean sonnet came to mind, one that had caused him to flunk an English Lit exam, but which he memorized later:

My mistress, when she walks, treads on the ground:
And yet by heaven, I think my love as rare,
As any she belied with false compare.

He considered quoting this to her, but instead he said: "Are you looking for a mechanic?"

"Maybe I'm advertising," she said. "Maybe I'm the goddamn Ishtar of advertising."

He vaguely knew who Ishtar was – something about a Babylonian holy prostitute – but he wasn't sure. Deciphering the finer points of her intimation was difficult in his shattered state. No matter, it was some king of invitation for sure.

He leaned over the table and slid his hand down the smooth expanse of her inner thigh. He moved slowly and kept his eyes on hers all the time, looking for a sign that he'd gone too far. Instead, she rewarded his advancing hand with a strangely intense smile, and he moved further up her thigh, a little amazed at his own audacity. His dirty, skinned-up hand made a curious contrast to the squeaky clean, smooth nylon. He stopped a little beyond her upper thigh, not because she gave him any sign he should, but because he had awkwardly over-extended his under the table. Someone in the café coughed loudly. They were probably making a scene, but Laura didn't seem to care. He felt himself blushing and pulled his hand away.

"Wash your hands, mechanic, and I'll let you drive me home," she said.

He started to tell her he wasn't a mechanic, but stopped himself. If it made her boat float to think he was a mechanic, so be it.

They took his pickup to her place, which turned out to be not far from where he had been cutting wood.

The house was a ranch-style, yellow brick, not more than ten or fifteen years old, with a large ill-kept yard. She led him through a paneled foyer, through a nicely carpeted living room filled with stacked cardboard boxes and into a very clean kitchen. With the evening, the temperature had dropped, and the kitchen was not much warmer than outside. His clothes were damp from sweat, and he began to shiver. She undressed quickly, without any pretense of modesty. She folded the waitress' uniform, pantyhose and bra into a single bundle and pitched it into the adjoining laundry room.

"You do the same. I'll run a load of wash later."

He hesitated. "What about your roommates?"

"I live alone. Come on now. Out of those wet clothes."

She watched attentively until he began to pull off his sweatshirt. "When you're through, come on downstairs in the basement." She walked to the basement door on tiptoe, causing the muscles in her calves to stand out. She seemed at ease being nude in front of him, but he was almost too embarrassed to look at her. At the café, he had more or less felt in charge, at least an equal partner in the affair. Now, in her house, things were quickly out of his control.

At the door to the stairwell, still posed on tiptoe, she turned to face him and reached up to undo her hair bun. She paused, hands on her head, to let him look at her. Her breasts were not large, but well-formed; naturally rounded, not the pointy overly perky things that came from a visit to a plastic surgeon. They were well suited to her body. She had put on a couple of pounds around her waist since he had last seen her naked, but that enhanced her sensuality rather than diminished it.

She pulled out some more hairpins and her hair fell in raven-black cascade. She pirouetted for him – and her hair fanned out from her shoulders like a shawl – then she pranced down the stairwell. Halfway down, she called, "It's warm down here. Strip and come on down."

Obediently, he stripped off his wet clothes, self-conscious of his pale body, while wondering how a waitress could afford a house roomy enough for a large family.

The basement was warm as she promised but poorly lit by a single bare bulb hanging from the ceiling. She was lying on her back on a narrow slab of a bed, made up with a white sheet and some large cushions. She raised herself on her elbows and scooted back so her back was propped up the cushions. She put her arms behind her and smiled another intense, self-amused smile. He was reminded of a painting by a Spanish painter – Goya, that was it. But he couldn't remember the name of the painting, just the unforgettable smile on the woman's face. Laura wore that same smile now.

"What took you so long?" she asked. Her smile belonged to a different universe, one where there weren't a million eyes staring at him at once. He sat on the edge of the bed, his hands clasped between his knees. He knew he should be glad to be re-invited to her bed, but he was too afraid to do anything but sit there. It wasn't so much a matter of performance anxiety, more one of emotional-intimacy anxiety. He didn't know how to explain this to her, or even what to think about it himself, and this confused him more.

"What's wrong?" she asked, then did a very odd thing. She moved as if to touch him, but stopped her hands a fraction of an inch away from his chest. Then she ran her hands down, over his stomach, around his semi-erect penis, still without touching. Her hands radiated a comforting warmth.

"I saw something in the woods; a sick angel," he managed to say. "And?"

"And it scared the hell out of me. This sounds stupid, but it nearly scared the 'me' out of me. Like in those cartoons where the cat with nine lives is frightened to death, and one of its lives floats away like a balloon. Like that. Stupid, I know."

She stared at him for a moment, then smiled and hopped out of bed and went to a small sink on the other side of the basement. She came back with a bowl of water, a pink washcloth and a white hand towel. Kneeling before him, she soaked the wash cloth in the bowl of water and began to wash his groin. He noticed the towel was embroidered with yellow daises. She casually and thoroughly washed him. The water was warm and soapy. She took particular care with the head of his penis. When she was through, she toweled him dry, and without further ado, as he was now hard, went down on him.

She was very good at it, getting him off in minutes. Before he could relax, she took his hands and pulled him off the bed and down to the floor with her where she was kneeling on the indoor/outdoor carpet. He kissed her, and she drew up a leg, wrapped it around him and leaned back, one knee still folded under her, the other leg at the small of his back. The position thrust her mons up, making her perfectly accessible. Hard again, he entered her. She rolled so she was on top and his back. She was looser than he remembered, but wet and warm, an abrupt contrast to the coarse carpeting against his back. She began to work slowly up and down, rising up until he nearly slipped out, then slowly descending. On each downstroke, she ground against him hard enough that he could feel her pelvic bone against his. He gradually grew larger, and she became tighter, until they made a good fit. The world became perfect for a few minutes. Her vagina walls rippled against the glans of his penis. She threw her head back and gave a little shudder, shaking her long black hair, making it shimmer in the light from the bare bulb. But as they slipped further into the routine of making love, he could still see the eyes staring out of the darkness of the angel's cupped wings, but the fearsomeness of the image receded as they fucked.

Afterward, Laura wanted to talk about nothing in particular, just post-coitus yada, a characteristic he had found irritating in young women he had been with before, when his hormone-saturated brain just wanted to zone out. But her yada was of a higher order, something about Leibniz and how space and time were like a dream, an illusion.

The sex and her philosophical lullaby made him sleepy, but knew he was back in love with her, which was as stupid as being terrified of the dead angel in the woods.

"Are you listening to me?" she asked. "I know I go on and on sometimes, but staring into space when I talk is flaky."

"Sorry. I was just thinking how little I ever knew about you."

She laughed. "I wanted it that way. In a small town everybody knows all about you – or thinks they do."

"Laura, what the hell happened?"

"What do you mean? Are you talking about tonight?"

"No, about college that last year."

"You always were one to dwell in the past. You never could pay attention to right now."

"I never knew what I did wrong. All at once you were yelling at me to get out."

"I don't remember it that way at all. We had an argument, which you lost. Then you left in a pout and never came back." She rolled away from him, looking to the wall. "I never meant for you to leave permanently."

With her back to him, he appraised her differently. She lay on her side in the dim light, the white sheet over her hips, her breasts bare. Overcome with tender feelings, he reached around to touch her lips. Her breath was warm and moist on his fingertips. She drew away from his touch, probably thinking it was meant to silence her.

"You'll be gone tomorrow."

(Was that a statement, or a question, or command?)

Messengers of an Alien God

He ran his hand up and over the opulent curve of hip, to waist, and pulled her to him. "I won't leave if you don't want me to," he said. This seemed to be a day for his doing stupid things, but what the hell.

Wright came home late, though not as late as usual for a Friday night. With the Fall and the lack of gasoline, troublemakers gave up earlier. The minute he stepped through the front door the elation he had felt all day turned to a blue gloom. A kerosene lantern feebly illuminated the room from atop the console TV. The electricity was out again on this side of town, and Marguerite had already squandered their cache of white gas for the Coleman lantern.

He could hear her bumbling about in the kitchen. He guessed she had been sitting in the living room, in front of the dead TV, until a few minutes ago. He could imagine her listening for the sound of gravel crunching underneath the tires of the Blazer, seeing the headlights sweeping past the picture window, and once she sure it was him, running to hide in the kitchen.

Their house had been a battleground the morning a few weeks ago when she had announced her pregnancy. He had sputtered his oatmeal, and without thinking, said something of the order of *do you want to keep it?*

It had a cold war ever since, characterized by tight-lipped glances across the kitchen table and tactical retreats to opposite sides of the king-sized bed. Communication was made on a need-to-know basis only.

The wise thing to do would be to stay in the living room or go to bed and leave her to rattling silverware and clinking china, but he was hungry and thirsty. Besides, he was tired of playing this game. They were sensible adults, goddamn it, and should be able to talk this out. With misgivings – in his heart he believed none of his own rationale, including the sensibility part – he headed toward the kitchen.

She stopped stacking the silverware and slid the drawer shut with a bang as he came in. She dried her hands on her baggy sweatshirt. Because there was a good crop of brown recluse spiders this year, she wore unlaced hiking boots, hastily slipped on. The hiking boots made her feel more secure when squashing the hairy creatures underfoot. Her stomach looked pouchy.

The baby showing already? No. Too early.

It must be the over-sized sweatshirt that made her look that way. But he would have to guess as she never undressed in his presence any more.

He rinsed his hands at the sink, drying them with a freshly laundered hand towel. Despite the public warnings about conserving electricity, his wife still insisted on doing a load of laundry and vacuuming the house every day. He suspected this stubbornness was a way to get back at him because the conservation warnings were issued from his office and because Marguerite used to be a sensible woman.

He was hungry, and he rummaged inside the refrigerator. Everything was still cool, so the power hadn't been out for long – electricity had been an on-again, off-again thing for the last week. There wasn't much variety in the fridge. Milk, some eggs, and smoked ham. Scrambled eggs were out of the question because the range was electric.

He made a mental note to see if the antique wood stove in the barn could be made operational, then poured himself a glass of milk and carved off a hunk of the ham. Meager rations, but better than a lot of people in the cities had these days. With two big dairies near town everybody in Creedance got milk. Meat on a daily basis was something else again, not because of the scarcity, for there was plenty of beef and ham on hoof, but because of the uncertainty of storage.

He sat down to his cold dinner. Marguerite scurried out the back door. He ate in silence, wondering what she wanted him to say, to do. When he finished eating he still didn't have a clue. He followed her out to the back porch.

The moon was full and halfway up the sky. She sat in a folding lawn chair by the barbecue grill, her hands folded on her lap. A light breeze tousled her hair. Her musky smell reminded him of the times when they'd still regularly made love years ago.

The moonlight made her look younger than her forty-three years. The passion he had felt for her during the first years of their marriage returned for an instant, strong and hot as a teenager's lust, as natural as hunger. He stopped himself. This state of mind was what had got them in this baby mess in the first place. He pulled up a chair at a careful distance from her, facing the same direction without sitting by her side. From the meadow, the spring crop of new insects was singing a loud evening concert.

"How did your day go?" he asked.

"All right."

"The katydids are loud tonight. Baby crickets, too."

"Yes, they are."

"Max told me we could have real problem with the bug population this summer. No chemicals to control them."

Silence. He chanced another glance in her direction. She sat in a bubble of tension, distinct, cut off from the cool, calm evening – cut off from him as well. Waves of anger rolled off her.

"There was a dead angel at the lake today."

The trouble with this diversionary strategy was that he dealt with nothing but negative things all day long. So why had he felt elated until he walked in the house?

No acknowledgment. He continued anyway. "A small plane crashed there. A college kid was cutting wood nearby and witnessed it. He said the angel collided with the plane in mid-air."

"I didn't know angels could die. I thought they were immortal."

"There's a lot we don't know about angels."

"Really." Her voice was dead of feeling.

"Yes, really."

She got up from the chair. He was completely out of touch with her now, he realized. At the back door she stopped and without turning said, "What about the pilot?" she asked.

"The pilot?"

"Of the airplane. The human pilot. Was he killed, too?"

"I don't know. There was no way to look." He paused, wondering how to explain the difficulties of following standard operating procedures since the Fall. Search and Rescue and the fire departments from Columbia and Jefferson City were too busy in their own cities to help. Even if they weren't, they'd be unlikely to waste gasoline driving into Creedance to dredge Lost Lake for a single body, particularly when the chances of finding it were so slim.

"You never think of those things until it's too late," Marguerite said.

"Excuse me?"

"You never think of preventing terrible things from happening." She stepped into the kitchen. Through the screen door, she said, "Only ways to punish someone when they don't meet your expectations. You don't think to close the gate until your cow has run off." She closed the door firmly.

He started to tell her she was making absolutely no sense; that there was no way he could prevent a collision between angels and an aircraft. But he held back, knowing she was really telling him he should have foreseen the train wreck that their lives and their marriage had become.

Collectively, the insects paused in their chirping as a shadow passed overhead. Probably a great-horned owl; a pair were nesting in the woods. For a moment the evening was completely still, then the chorus started again. Wright had often heard them do the same thing, stop at once altogether, but usually in response to a startlingly loud noise such as a thunderclap or a shotgun blast, not the nearly silent passing of an owl.

It occurred to Wright that, like musicians, the katydids occasionally had to turn a page of their score.

It also occurred to him a few more nights of this cold war with Marguerite might make him go stark raving nuts. How had they got themselves into this mess, anyway? He knew in his heart that this fight over whether to keep the baby or abort it was not the real cause of the breech between them. As sheriff, Wright had intervened in enough marital disputes to know the dirty socks left on the bathroom floor or the new coon hound or even the battleground of the marital bed were not the real reason the wife had started pitching dishes or the husband throwing punches. It had become his standard operating procedure to sit the couple down and get them to carefully explain why the hell they were trying to kill each other. So many times the process would disclose considerable confusion as to exactly what they were so angry about. They desperately wanted to explain what had gone wrong so they could understand themselves.

Of course, some – usually men, but women too on occasion – simply wanted to dominate the other, to control the other completely with an iron fist, withheld sex or a restricted bank account. Those couples were doomed from the start. Many, however, started out romantic and then went wrong. Why was a mystery to him. True, the honeymoon couldn't last forever. Maybe there should be something on the other side of romance and sex, another dimension of love, but imagining its exact nature, much less practicing it, eluded him.

Things had begun to go wrong last summer, long before the pregnancy. Why? He had given it much thought, especially late at night, and had come up with quite a few ideas of what had happened and why. The morning light had always revealed these theories for what they were, half-baked. Like trying to remember lyrics to an old song, he kept coming up with the first few stanzas, but the ending always eluded him until he wondered if he had ever known the entire song to begin with.

He went back inside, not following Marguerite this time, only seeking to escape what now seemed a maddening racket of insect life. He found the couch made up for him with a clean sheet, an orange and white quilt folded into a neat square for a pillow. As he undressed, he felt only mildly surprised at this further sign of the deteriorating marriage. He considered waking Marguerite to talk about, but decided doing so would be pointless.

Wright woke in the middle of the night on the couch with no memory of lying down or going to sleep. He was soaked in sweat and felt the residual anxiety of a bad dream; no details lingered, only the impression of simultaneously seeing too much of the big picture and being blind to the details. The kitchen light was on, as was the useless TV set, blaring white noise. The power had come back on, and that was what must have wakened him from an obscure dream populated by nameless beings and formless images.

Quietly, feeling like a kid sneaking out late at night, he put on a pair of old jeans and a clean white shirt. The jeans were looser in the legs and tighter in the butt than the last time he wore them, over a year ago, when he and Marguerite had gone square-dancing. He added his belt with the turquoise buckle, along with his black dress cowboy boots. As he dressed, the lights went out again. In the kitchen, the refrigerator rattled to a stop.

As an afterthought, he grabbed a clean uniform for the next day and left the house. He pulled out of the drive without turning on the headlights so the glare wouldn't shine through the bedroom window. The gravel road sparkled luminous white when he turned on the headlights.

On his way to May's place, he wondered if he should stop by the office and call her first. It might be a good idea. May wasn't the type who was likely to spend too many nights alone.

The office was empty. His deputy went off duty at eleven and there was nobody to work the graveyard shift. Practically everyone, everyone who counted at least, had his or Jimmy's home phone numbers should there be a late night emergency.

He had to look up May's number in the phone book. He couldn't remember her last name at first. When he dialed her number all he got was a busy signal.

Three tries and a half hour later, he was still getting a busy signal, which irritated him. What would anybody be doing on the phone for a half hour straight at this wee hour in the morning?

May lived in a trailer on the west side of town; it only took him five minutes to get there. The trailer sat on concrete blocks in the middle of a five-acre field, overlooking the open pasture where she kept her horse. Cold moonlight reflected off the metal roof, making the trailer look a dirty, neon pink.

The trailer was dark, no porch light, not even a nightlight on. He had driven by several times before, and remembered May always kept at least one outside light on, even when she had men guests. More worrisome, the front door stood wide open.

Had the transformer on May's electric pole gone out? Quite a few had exploded the day of the Fall. Many were weakened and failed in the weeks after. Or had May turned into a good citizen and decided to conserve energy? He doubted all the most likely and semi-likely possibilities. A sixth sense, what Wright privately called his cop sense, told him the door was not open for air or from neglect. He parked the car and got out for a closer look. As he crossed the small wet lawn, he unsnapped the snatch flap on his holster and tucked it out of the way.

"May, are you in there?"

No answer.

"May?" Louder this time, but still no answer from within. Somewhere nearby a dog started barking. At least someone was listening to him tonight.

Messengers of an Alien God

He un-holstered the .357, flipped the cylinder release and checked to make sure all six chambers were full. Switching the gun to his left hand, he reached in the darkened doorway and ran his right hand up and down the wall, finding and clicking the light switch. Nothing happened, and he clicked it again. So much for the energy conserving theory. Now that he thought of it, there had been no lights on anywhere this side of town as he drove out. Another widespread power outage.

Doh! He was probably over-reacting. Still, he wished for batteries for his flashlight.

Wright shifted his gun to his right hand and stepped into the trailer. The moon shone so brightly, he could see the furniture and the picture of Jesus on the wall. The bleeding heart of Jesus, brilliant red in normal light, looked brownish in the cool moonlight.

The room showed no signs of disorder, yet he sensed something wrong.

Jesus' blue-gray, Aryan eyes followed him as he made his way around an easy chair and a coffee table to the back of the trailer. The hallway, lacking windows, was a valley of shadows. He paused near a doorway into the closet-like bathroom, waiting for his eyes to adjust to the dark before going farther, but the dark faux mahogany paneling soaked up what little light seeped in from the living room. He could see partial outlines only. A pile of dirty clothes sat by the half-open door of a linen closet. Something made of brittle plastic, probably a hair doodad, crunched under his foot. The back bedroom also had windows, and its doorway appeared as a rectangle of feeble light at the end of the dark corridor. He made his way toward the light.

He had to close the linen closet door to pass, and it squeaked mournfully.

In answer, a woman's voice came from the bedroom.

"Bull man. Bull man," the voice – May's voice – cried sharply. "Too large. Too goddamn big. You're tearing me apart!"

He froze. Obviously, May had a guest. Should he stand still and wait for a time when he could leave unnoticed or back out immediately? He waited for sounds from the darkness for a cue to stay or go.

Moonlight streamed in from an open window, enough to make the bedroom bright in comparison to the hallway. On the bed a human form moved weakly. He squinted, trying to make out arm from leg, male from female. Then all the lights in the trailer came on at once, nearly blinding him.

May lay alone in the middle of the double bed, nude, her thighs, stomach and the sheets drenched in blood.

Much, much too much blood.

May ran both hands down her stomach and legs, smearing her hands in the blood like a kid playing with finger paint.

"Elvis, how could you do this to me?" she asked Wright.

* * *

7.

Minotaur

Wright bundled up May in one of the bloody sheets, carried her to the patrol car and laid her on the back seat. Sure that she wasn't in any condition to crawl out, he went back in the house and stuffed the rest of blood-soaked bed linens and pillows into a plastic trash bag for evidence.

On his way out he stopped at the kitchen sink, rolled up his sleeves and washed up to his elbows.

Once he was back behind the wheel, the Blazer started immediately, but the interior dome light blinked on and off. Wearily, he got out and checked the rear doors. May had snagged one bare foot under the door handle and worked it ajar. She was slowly, rhythmicallythrusting her hips up and down, her eyes fixed on the blinking dome light. He pushed her writhing body far enough along the seat to get the door close. She quieted. As he got back in the car, a peculiar sadness, a vague awareness of passage from feeling to non-feeling, overtook him for no reason he could fathom. It was a sadness of personal loss – not for the damage done to May. Somewhere along the line he had become dispassionate in the face of other people's personal tragedy.

A recollection slid by his mind's eye. He saw himself, Marguerite in the front seat and the new baby in the back of a brand new Camero on their way to the Lake of the Ozarks late one summer evening. The baby was only four or five months old then. Two months later she had died in her crib for no reason the doctors could give. A violent thing, death, even when it happened silently, without a whimper, without a perpetrator, without reason. He had turned off grief for the damaged and dying then. Had he ever turned it back on?

In the back seat, May thrashed about violently then stopped, breathing heavily. He switched on the cherry domes but left the siren off so as to no waken the sleeping houses as he passed. He took Old Buffalo Road, a meandering strip of gravel skirting the edge of town. Along the ridge road he eased the Blazer up to sixty, as fast as he dared to drive on loose gravel. May moaned again. Glancing in the rear view mirror he saw she had kicked off the sheet. She lay naked on the plastic seat cover, still grinding her hips against an unseen lover. He concentrated on the road, on the cherry dome's flashing red reflections on the dense, hedge-like foliage hemming in the road on both sides. He didn't want to remember May this way. She had been transformed from something to be desired into a distasteful duty, just like most things in his life.

Everything went smoothly until he pulled into the McGuane Memorial Clinic emergency room driveway at forty miles per hour. He'd forgotten there was still a foot-high bump where the new water main came through under the street. The Blazer was airborne long enough for him to aim a curse at what served for Creedance public maintenance. The front wheels landed first, and he thought for a moment he was going to slide into the plate-glass doors, but the hedge slowed him down. As the Blazer came to a stop, he leapt from the vehicle, leaving the driver's door open. He tried to pull May out by her feet, but she kicked at his hands and flailed her arms against the drawn metal mesh separating the back seat from the front. When he pulled harder, she interlaced her fingers in the mesh and let out a scream that rattled his teeth.

From the corner of his eye he saw someone in a white jacket come running out of the emergency room.

"A little heavy-handed during the arrest, Sheriff?"

It was Dr. Jenkins in full asshole mode.

Wright felt he should say something. "She's lost a lot of blood. I don't know how much. I thought I'd save a lot of time by bringing her in myself."

Jenkins tone softened. "Good thing you did. The ambulance isn't running again. Grab a leg. I'll get the other."

Messengers of an Alien God

Jenkins looked as shitty as ever: big pores, swollen nose, and the gritty complexion of someone who drank too much and ate too little. If Wright hadn't known better, he would have bet Jenkins divided his life between a bottle and the clinic, never going home.

Together they tried to pull the screaming woman from the back seat.

"Wait a minute! Stop pulling or we'll pop her fingers out of their joints," Jenkins said.

"You won't get her to let go without knocking her out," Wright said.

The doctor leaned over and gripped her wrist. She instantly let go. Still holding her wrist so she couldn't get a finger hold again, Jenkins looked back over his shoulder. "Nothing to it. You only have to know where the pressure points are."

Then she brought a knee up into his groin. Jenkins jumped back. Wright expected him to go to his knees, but he seemed unhurt.

"She missed my vital parts – barely!" Jenkins said. He reached back into the car, got a new hold on her wrist and pulled her to her feet. She stood on her own, the bloody cotton sheet glued to her back like a cape. A goddess of mayhem, she stopped screaming, and the terror left her face to be replaced with mild surprise. Her eyes were open and looking around. As before, Wright looked for recognition there and found nothing but a wildness.

Without warning, she closed her eyes and went limp.

"There she goes," Jenkins said and caught her. Wright got her other arm. Together they supported her.

"What now?" Wright asked.

"We'll put her on this and roll her inside, stupid," came a gravelly voice from behind. June Freeman, the middle-aged nurse's aide, had brought out a gurney and carried a folded white sheet draped over one shoulder.

"You like to sneak up on a man, don't you?" Wright said.

"Sneak up?" she said. "This gurney rattles as loud as my fucking bones."

June was a rancher's widow who had gone back to school to get a degree in nursing during the last drought. She was a stout woman, broad-

-67-

hipped, wavy blonde hair on gray roots, ruddy complexion, and large matronly bosoms that always threatened to burst loose from her blouse. Despite her opulent matronhood, Wright found himself treating June as if she were a man, perhaps because of her language, maybe because she always seemed to own whatever piece of land she was standing on.

"Well, don't just stand there with your thumbs up your butts. Put her on here." She thrust the gurney toward them.

Wright obeyed; so did Jenkins. When June tried to cover May with a sheet, the young woman screamed again and thrashed her arms and legs. June grabbed an arm and a leg and forced them to the table. Wright did likewise on his side of the gurney. Jenkins unlaced some heavy-duty restraining straps from under the gurney and tied her down.

"What is it? Drugs?" June asked, breathless. She had been a chain smoker before the Fall.

"Don't think so," Jenkins said. "Simple delirium or hysteria."

Wright wondered if he meant the condition was of the simple variety or instead simple to diagnose.

Jenkins wheeled May into the emergency room while June held the doors open. Once inside, June painstakingly peeled the sheet out from under May. She had to unbuckle one restraining strap, yank on the sheet, then rebuckle it loosely so she could maneuver the sheet for another tug. All the time, May fought, though her thrashing was become feeble. June mumbled some more under her breath, which came in rasps and hacks. Jenkins stood by, his hands in the side pockets of the white lab coat. "We are short-staffed tonight. Pattie called in," he said, but made no move to help.

Wright started to ask if he could be of any assistance, but thought better of it and kept quiet. Better to not interfere with the status quo at the hospital. Jenkins could be a cantankerous old fart.

May cried out, "You're no angel, sweetheart. No goddamn man, either. Too much. Too goddamn much!" A gurgle of pain rose in her throat. She fought the remaining restraining straps, then fell back limp. June hastily yanked the sheet out from under her and refastened the strap that held down her legs.

Still panting, Jenkins rubbed his chin.

June tried to say something else but a fit of coughing overwhelmed her. Wright and Jenkins waited for the coughing to subside and June to finish what she wanted to say. Wright started to bring up the possibility of an angel being involved, but hesitated. As much as he mistrusted the angels, it was simply too unlikely.

"Do you think those wounds are self inflicted?" Dr. Jenkins asked. June shook her head.

"What about all the blood she lost, Doctor?" Wright asked.

"There's not much we can do about it. We don't have any on hand."

"None of her type?"

"None, period. We lost all the frozen plasma stocks when we were without power after the Fall. Since then, local donations haven't been good."

"A lot of people are dead-sure they'll get AIDS if they give blood," June said.

"Dumb shits. We have normal saline?" Jenkins asked June. She nodded.

"Put in a heparin tap and hang a liter. Maybe that will keep her from going into shock," he said. June didn't look so sure. Neither was Wright. He knew Jenkins had to resort to re-sterilizing used disposable needles since the Fall.

"Bull man! Bull man!" May shouted. She relaxed, and her buttocks hit the table with a loud slap. She gasped for breath, then thrust against the strap again.

No one said anything. June turned away, blushing, which seemed out of character for her.

May's flounderings became more erotic. Watching her seemed an intrusion on her privacy, yet Wright couldn't turn his head. A tablespoon of blood accumulated on the gurney between her legs.

After a small eternity, Wright managed to look away from May.

"Well, do something," he said to Jenkins. "If I knew you were going to stand around and watch her bleed to death, I would have taken her somewhere else."

Jenkins turned to him angrily. "Where would you take her? Columbia? St. Louis? Kirkesville? You'd be damned lucky to get a pass through the military barricades. And if you did, all those hospitals are standing room only."

"What does that have to do with you doing nothing?"

Jenkins took a deep breath and let it out slowly. "Sheriff, you don't know how frustrating it is. Before the Fall, the clinic was neither well-equipped nor well-stocked, but we got by. Those cases we couldn't handle, we referred to one of the hospitals in Columbia. Now we can't even take an X-ray. Doing simple blood work is impossible. We would be out of antibiotics if not for the veterinarian donating from his supplies. As it is, I worry about an allergic reaction killing someone. Animal antibiotics – neomycin is one example – aren't made the same way as other pharmaceuticals. And painkillers. I'm even out of over-the-counter stuff like ibuprofen. Without painkillers, I can't even make her comfortable. And there's no place to refer her to, no place that will take another patient."

Caught up in Jenkins' indignation, June stomped over to a cabinet, fetched a clean sheet and covered May again. Jenkins took a deep breath and let it out as a sigh. When he spoke, he did so with a calmer voice.

"Leave now, Sheriff. We'll take care of her. Collect semen samples, if there are any. Pubic hair in sandwich bags. A typed report, double-spaced. The works."

"You don't really think that's the result of rape, do you?"

"There could have been intercourse first. The tearing could have been done afterward with a foreign object. How much blood was at the scene?"

Wright told him about the sheets he'd brought in the bag.

Jenkins rubbed his chin, thoughtfully. He seemed his old country doctor self again, genuinely concerned about the health of someone lacking either insurance or money. "Leave the bag by the door. I'll look at the sheets. I don't really think she's lost as much blood as you think. Her color is too good."

"The sheets were soaked."

"A half pint of blood looks like a gallon when it's spread around. People react emotionally to blood, Sheriff. Even you. Now go. I'll do what I can. You'll get my report in the morning. June, take her vitals."

"What's the prognosis?" Wright asked.

Jenkins shook his head. "Like I said, there's not much I can do, other than clean the wound and stitch her up."

"I think I'll hang around."

"Suit yourself. But do it in the waiting room. You'll make me nervous looking over my shoulder."

As he left, June was taking May's blood pressure. She had stopped her bloody bump-and-grind and now watched listlessly as June fumbled with a stethoscope.

Wright woke later from a fitful sleep on the waiting room couch. June loomed over him like a bad hangover on a rainy day. She was saying something, her voice a rasping growl, her hands on her hips. He tried to move but couldn't get his stiff knees to unfold right away. Impatient, she reached down, grabbed his shoulder and shook him hard.

"Get up. The doctor wants to see you," she commanded.

He swatted her hand away. "Leave me alone. You old hag. I'm getting up already."

He immediately regretted the hag statement though she did look like something out a horror movie. June drew in a quick, sharp breath and stepped back. The world became painfully well-lit. The shelf-like overhang of her formidable breasts had been shadowing his face from the glare of the fluorescent light panel on the ceiling. Good thing the clinic had its own generator. He swung his legs around and sat up, surprised he could feel even worse sitting than lying.

June stomped off. He'd never noticed before how bow-legged she was. He followed her to find Jenkins sitting in a green vinyl and chrome couch in the corridor outside the emergency room. Laura Jacobsen was there, pacing around, talking rapid fire. The college boy was slouched in one of the waiting room chairs.

"I'm so sick of all this violence done to women on TV, in movies, and pornography. That's what causes things like this to happen!" Laura was in the middle of a sermon. Neither Jenkins nor the college boy seemed to be paying her much attention. The college boy nodded drowsily. Wright was just pissed off enough from his rude wake-up call to take umbrage at her arrogance.

"No one has watched TV or seen a movie for months. How do you explain that?" he asked.

"Residual effect," she said. "Everyone is angry about something or someone. TV violence supplies a ready-made focus of anger for those men too stupid to figure what really made them mad."

"What is she doing here?" Wright asked Jenkins.

"Extemporizing," Jenkins said.

Laura snorted. The college boy perked up from his stupor.

"I called her, Mr. Law Enforcement," June said.

"Why in the hell did you do that?" he said. He yelled this without meaning to, but June stood her ground, looking slightly amused. Wright realized he was being irrational, but he had enough of not being taken seriously today.

He started to explain he needed to talk to May and get testimony before anyone else did, but Jenkins spoke first. "Calm down, Sheriff. I asked June if she knew if May had any good friends."

"We work together, remember?" Laura said. "We're friends – sort of."

"The girl is not coming out of her delirium. I thought the familiar sound of a friend's voice would help."

"Hell, I've known May for years. I talk to her every day at Bouchers," Wright said.

"A male's presence, even that of a spouse or a friend –" He put emphasis on word *friend* "– will sometimes throw a rape victim into a panic reaction." Did Jenkins know he had been about to take up May's invitation or was the old son-of-a-bitch simply fishing?

"Was it rape?"

"Depends upon how you define rape."

"Was there sperm?" Wright usually didn't discuss matters of evidence around a crowd. Doing so seemed a further violation of a victim's privacy, but he was too tired to be tactful. The doctor looked a little squeamish about talking in front of the new waitress and the college boy, but he too went on.

"No, but there certainly was evidence of violent assault."

"What's that mean?"

"Whatever tore that young woman wasn't made out of flesh and gristle. Did you find any large pointed object at the scene?"

"No," Wright said without being really sure. He tried to remember the bedroom when the light had come on. All he could see were the bloody sheets and May, writhing in the middle of the mess. His morbid curiosity got the better of him. "How large?"

"Damn large. I've seen less damage done to the vagina by difficult childbirths."

"She tore down to her B-hole. It must have hurt like the goddamn hell," June explained unabashedly. She looked as if she spoke from experience, but Wright knew her marriage to Slim Freeman had been childless.

"Excuse me." The college boy got up and headed toward the door. He looked green.

Once the college boy was outside, Laura said: "A wuss, but a sweet wuss who does what I tell him." She looked at them, waiting for consensus. Wright thought that alone marked her as a hometown girl, her preoccupation with what other Creedance citizens thought of her.

June sat next to Jenkins and propped a foot on a book rack. Laura began pacing again. It was almost a stomp; the heels of her boots made sharp taps on the hard linoleum floor

"So, will May come out of this all right?" she demanded of Jenkins.

"It's hard to say," Jenkins said. "In ordinary times she would already be on her way to Mid-Mo Mental Health."

"You mean you don't know?"

Jenkins rubbed his chin thoughtfully. "Right. I'm completely in the dark and incompetent as you've always suspected."

He waited for Laura to say more. When she didn't rise to the bait, he continued. "All we can do is keep her from hurting herself. If she's under the effects of some drug, in combination with major hysteria – I'm not even sure of that much – then her mental condition could improve in a few hours. Other than drugs, there aren't any other reasons for her delirium. It's not febrile – she doesn't have a high fever. It's not traumatic – there's no sign of head injury. She's not epileptic, so we can rule that out. So I'm guessing, almost hoping, you might say, that it's a toxic reaction, a drug she took or was forced to take. If so, it should be wearing off soon."

"How about her injuries, Doc?" Wright asked.

"Physically, she'll recover well enough in a week or two as long as she doesn't get an infection or have an allergic reaction to the animal antibiotic I gave her, which I don't think she will since she hasn't done so already. She has enough neomycin in her to treat a thousand pounds of dairy cow."

"I want to try to talk to her again."

"Suit yourself. Try quiet, firm suggestions. We'll be moving her to the convalescent wing soon. June, why don't you go in and apply cold compresses to the patient's forehead and neck?"

"Wait a minute," Wright said. "Do either of you have any idea who might have done this to her?"

Laura and June both shook their heads.

"Well, if she says any names, make a note of them. Anything."

The two women went back in the emergency room. Jenkins drew Wright aside.

"If the delirium wasn't caused by drug, then it is of psychological nature, and I can't treat it. She might never come out of it," he said with a shrug, as if he seen such cases a thousand times.

Wright realized that Jenkins was either exhausted or really had been drinking on duty again or both.

With this bit of information in mind, Wright left the clinic. The eastern sky was a sad pale blue as he came upon the college boy standing by an old red and white Ford pickup parked next to the police Blazer. He was fiddling with a loose chrome insignia on the side of the truck.

"So you're related to Jake Hale?"

"Grandfather. Mother's side," the college boy said.

"What's your name again?"

"Douglas – Bryan Douglas."

"Did Jake ever make it back from his vacation?"

"Not yet. I'm keeping an eye on his place and his stuff until he does. That okay?" The metal piece came off in his hand. "Shit," he said unemotionally. He held up the chrome piece for Wright to see. "Twin I-Beam," it proclaimed in chrome letters

"Fine by me if that's the arrangement you made with Jake. You know May?"

The college boy shrugged and threw the chrome piece into the back of the truck. "No, I'm just hanging around Laura, I guess," he said and leaned awkwardly against the truck.

Messengers of an Alien God

Wright paused, watching the sunrise. He suspected the college boy wanted to tell him something. Ordinarily, he would prop himself against the truck too and wait for the boy to screw his courage to the sticking place. That was the smart way to do it. But today he was too goddamned tired.

As Wright got in his cruiser, the college boy said, "By the way, Sheriff, I ran across another dead angel up on the Jacobsen place."

"Did you now? Are you sure it was dead?"

"Not really. But I saw something really weird, I don't know what."

"Sometime in the next couple of days, drop by the office, and we'll talk."

"Sure." The college boy's air of anxiety partially dissipated.

On the way to his office, Wright scanned the skies for angels – without success.

* * *

8.

Labored Love

The next day, Bryan Douglas took off from woodcuttng to drive to town. Was Laura working today? In case she was, he parked on the south side of the town square, hiding his truck from view of Boucher behind the Harmon County Courthouse.

On the courthouse lawn, an angel sat on the stone bench with Uncle Robert. The angel's white robes wildly contrasted with the old man's bib overalls and ratty blue herringbone sports jacket.

As Bryan drew closer, he could see the angel and the old man were engrossed in deep conversation.

Or was it a lecture? Uncle Robert sat hunched forward on the edge of the bench with his elbows resting on his knees, as the angel whispered in his ear. The old man's mouth was slack, and heheld a piece of half-whittled wood in one hand and an opened pocketknife in the other as the angel brought a hand up and tousled his white hair as if he were a child.

The angel looked amazingly like the dead one at the lake, which couldn't be. It must be the insipidly pleasant expression angels shared that made them look alike.

As for Uncle Robert's knife, cadres of whittlers were a common sight in the town square, especially since there wasn't television to watch anymore. Usually whittling was a group thing, sort of like male version of a quilting bee. But Uncle Robert was alone today, except for the angel. Not only did his mouth droop open, but his eyes were fixed intently on the angel, and the knife dangled idly from his hand. The angel's mouth moved rapidly, its face serene and saintly. Though Bryan stood not more than ten feet away from them he could not hear a word. The statue of the bronze horse-mounted Civil War hero glared down them like an angry god.

Bryan was curious, but he moved on. He cut across the street, feeling momentarily exposed to the plate glass windows in Bouchers Cafe. Was she working this morning? Did she really give a damn about seeing him again? Why did he feel like he was fourteen years old?

At the front door of the Creedance Daily Sentinel, more plate glass windows reflected a glaring morning sun. Inside the small office, a man with a week's worth of graying beard stubble pecked viciously away at an old manual typewriter.

"Yeah?" He did not interrupt his typing as Bryan closed the door behind him.

"I'm looking for a job."

"The paper isn't out until Tuesday. Check the classifieds then. I don't think there's much in there unless you can repair electronics or make the phones work with regularity."

"No. I mean I'm looking for a job at the paper. This paper."

"I got all the help I need – unless you happen to be able to set lead type. You're not an itinerant printer's devil, are you?" The man looked up. Bryan couldn't tell if his smile came from amusement, friendliness or what.

"No, I can't say I am, sir."

The man's red baggy eyes flashed with impatient anger. "Then you're wasting my time, sir." He turned his attention back to the sheet of yellow paper in the typewriter.

Bryan looked around the office. There was an Apple computer, relatively new, with a huge flat panel display, another electronic casualty of the Fall. A stack of dusty paper was stacked on its keyboard.

The bearded man continued pecking away at the manual typewriter.

"Damn! Shit!" he muttered, opened bottle of correction fluid and began dabbing with the small brush at the paper in the carriage.

"I've had twenty-some hours of journalism courses at Columbia," Bryan volunteered.

The man looked up over his reading glasses. His eyes were tired and bloodshot. "So?" he said.

"I can type fifty-five words a minute with no errors," Byran said. "And I can use that." He pointed at an old Nikkormat camera sitting on the edge of the desk.

"That's a film camera, not a digital," the man said.

"I know. I can do darkroom work too."

The old man's face brightened. "You're Jake Hale's grandson, aren't you?"

"Yes." Bryan relaxed a bit. Familiarity was like money in the bank in this town. Should he mention that his grandfather was either dead or stranded somewhere? Probably not.

The man leaned back in his chair and put his hands behind his head. The chair's springs creaked.

"Here's the deal, then," the man said. "Take the camera – it's got about four shots left on it."

Bryan reached over and picked up the Nikkormat, a 1960s model that must weigh two pounds. "Does the meter work?"

"No, but it's loaded with four-hundred ASA Tri-X film. Know what I'm talking about?

"About F8 to F12 at one two-hundredth of a second in bright sunlight."

"Something like that. Here's the deal," the man repeated. "Take the camera; get me an interview with one of the angels and a nice photo – get him or her or whatever to flex his muscles or have a wardrobe malfunction or something – and if you can spell with spell check . . ." He nodded toward the kaput Apple computer. "I might – emphasis on *might* – consider taking you on as a trainee."

"Just like that?"

"Just like that." The man smiled briefly, then scowled. "And if you tear up that camera or lose it, I'll have your grandfather tear you a new one. I'll pay you as most of my subscribers pay me: in meat and cheese and whatever other barter I have. Deal?"

"Deal," Bryan said. It sounded a hell of a lot better gig than cutting wood for a living.

"Now get out of here," the man said. "I have a newspaper to get out."

Bryan was back out on the street before he realized he didn't know the editor's name. No matter, he could find out later. He cut across the courthouse lawn to where he had seen the angel and Uncle Robert talking, thinking he might grab an angel interview right there.

At the park bench, however, he found the man sitting alone, the angel nowhere in sight.

"Sir," he addressed Uncle Robert. "What happened to your angel?"

Uncle Robert gave no indication he heard or that he was aware of Bryan talking to him.

Curious, Bryan sat on the far end of the bench. The man gazed off into infinity, which apparently lay somewhere beyond the True Value hardware store. His mouth worked with what Bryan first thought was a facial tic. Then he realized the gnarly old lips whispered in a voice so small as to barely be heard.

"I beg your pardon?" Bryan said. No reply, not even so much as a sideways glance. The deeply lined face remained trance-like and the mouth mumbled unabated, without a pause for a breath. The whittling knife still dangled from limp fingers.

Bryan scooted along the bench until he was close enough he to hear what the old man was saying.

"No Sis. Prison. The Pearl. Lost in the Lake of Shadows. I remember now. A lifetime lost. Too, too many worlds. Too few rebirths. No Sis."

The old man was obviously off his bean. Strange. What could an angel possibly want to say to an old mental case? But then, who could figure angels? Bryan got up to leave.

"Wait!" Uncle Robert shouted and grabbed Bryan's wrist. His grip was unexpectedly strong. The thumb gently sought out a soft spot on the inside of his wrist as if taking his pulse. "I have a mission now," the old man said, his eyes filled with fiery conviction.

"Let go, goddamn it!" Bryan said and yanked away his hand.

"You're already damned," the man shouted. He brought the knife up. Bryan jumped back. "Up there –"He stabbed at the sky with the knife. "– it's a joke, and we're the butt of it. All of us. Ask the angels. They know."

"Okay. Okay, I'll do just that. Right now, if you'll excuse me." He started to back away, keeping an eye on the knife, which the old man still held heavenward.

"You think I'm crazy, don't you?" he said, taking a step forward.

"No, not at all." Bryan took another step backward and bumped into the granite pedestal of the Civil War statue.

"My brother . . . Rusty . . ." Uncle Robert stopped in mid-sentence. His face went blank again. Bryan got the impression the deeply etched seams of the man's face were smoothing, fading, like the embossed face on a coin wearing out before his eyes. The old man wasn't home. Bryan waited seconds that seemed like minutes. Trapped between two statues, he decided, and moved to slip out under the immobilized old man's outstretched arm. As he ducked, a hand latched onto his shoulder.

"I'm talking to you," he said. "Where do you think you're going when I'm talking?"

Bryan looked up. Uncle Robert's face remained as calm as a Buddha's. His grip was a vice.

"Let me go!"

The old man stared at him without recognition. Bryan's left side numbed with pain. Whether by accident or intention, the fingers had found a nerve junction in his shoulder. On reflex, Bryan swung his non-paralyzed hand holding the heavy camera up and around, clouting Uncle Robert just above the temple. The old man let go and dropped to his knees at the base of the statue, his head making a hollow thumping sound against the granite base.

Bryan stared at the crumpled form within the bib overalls. *Had he killed the old loon?*

No. The bib overalls stirred. The mouth mumbled on though the brain was semi-conscious. He was still alive. Bryan examined the Nikkormat to find it unharmed. Had anybody seen? All the plate glass windows stared blindly out on the square. He could probably just walk away from the old man and no one would know.

But he couldn't do that, which constituted another self-revelation. Reluctantly, he cut across the grass to the side door of the courthouse. The door of the sheriff's office was open. Bryan went in, resolute and in a confessional mood, feeling stupid.

Inside, Sheriff Wright sat hunched over an old oak desk, a cup of coffee in one hand, the phone receiver in the other. In an ashtray on the corner, a smoldering cigarette emitted a thin stream of smoke that climbed sluggishly to the ceiling. Beside the desk sat a greasy looking ice cooler. Was it the same one the deputy had retrieved beer from at Lost Lake? The privileges of power, he thought: Despite the breakdown of commerce, the sheriff not only had beer, he had cigarettes.

He slammed down the receiver as Bryan came in.

"Goddamned, shit phone!" He looked Bryan over, not recognizing him at first. "What is it?"

"You said to come in and tell you about the angel in the woods."

The sheriff seemed different from when he had last seen him. Angry? Depressed? Just plain exhausted? He couldn't tell.

"Oh yeah, I'm glad you did, college boy." He didn't look glad. He shifted his weight off one buttock to the other in his wooden office chair. He reminded Bryan of an aging athlete who was just starting to go to fat.

"It's been a long night," the sheriff explained.

Bryan decided the sheriff was in a blue, blue funk, which meant he could go either way: sympathetic or angry. Should he blurt out that he had just cracked an old man's skull on the courthouse lawn? No, he should lead up to it, put into context, he decided.

"I've had a shitty day, too."

Another one of those silences ensued. It seemed like the silences said more than words these days.

"You said something this morning about another dead angel," the sheriff prompted.

"Oh, yeah, I did."

"That is what you came in about, isn't it?"

"Yes . . . Well, I was going to, but I have to show you something outside."

"What?"

"It would be easier to show you than explain."

"Try me. I haven't had any sleep for twenty-four hours, and I need a damn good reason to get out of this chair."

"It – he – is just outside by the park bench."

"Who is *he*?"

"An old loony man, everybody around here calls him Uncle Robert. About five minutes ago I beaned him a good one." He briefly told what had happened.

Wright got wearily to his feet. His pistol in its holster belt was draped over the back of the chair. "Will I need this?"

"Not for me."

Wright eyed him suspiciously for a moment then strapped on the hardware anyway.

Back outside on the green, they found the old man squatting on his haunches on the grass, rubbing a goose-egg size knot on his head and looking disoriented. Bryan had half hoped he wouldn't be there, or – and this was a strange vision – that they would find nothing but empty bib overalls and boots.

"Hello, Uncle Robert. Need some help there?" asked the sheriff in a familiar tone but made no move to help the old man up. Uncle Robert still held the opened whittling knife.

To Bryan, the sheriff whispered, "All these Jacobsens have their crazy moments. It's in their blood."

Uncle Robert squinted at him. "That you, John? Well, no, I'm all right, except for this little bump on the head. See it?"

"What happened here, Uncle Robert?"

"Well, I don't rightly recollect. I guess I must have fallen down. Last thing I remember was talking to an angel." A confused look came over his face. "You don't suppose that critter knocked me in the head, do you?"

"What do you think, Uncle Robert?"

"No, I don't think so. The angel was a preacher, not a fighter. I remember that much. I don't quite recollect what the gist of the sermon was, but then who ever does? A powerful talker, though."

"Let me help you up, Uncle Robert."

"I can get up on my own; I don't need your help," he said. He climbed unsteadily to his feet.

"Put the knife away, Uncle Robert."

He looked at his hand as if it were someone else's. "Oh, there it is. I wondered what I did with that." He folded the knife carefully and slipped it into one of the many pockets in his overalls. Without another word, he began walking across the green toward Bouchers Cafe. The sheriff and Bryan watched him go, then recounted scuffle they'd had in the square.

Messengers of an Alien God

"I've never known the old coot to get rough with anyone before," the sheriff said.

"You believe me, don't you?"

"I've known Uncle Robert a lot longer than I've known you. He's a little bit strange, but like I said, he's never bothered anyone before." Wright fixed him with a suspicious glare. "What did you say to him?"

"Nothing. I just asked him what happened to the angel he was talking to earlier."

"Well, it kind of figures, I guess. He's one of those people who are calm and stupid-looking on the surface. But underneath, their brain is like a guitar strung too tight. This statue here," –he pointed to the Civil War memorial – "is of his great-grandfather. A hero, founded this town. Then one day, they found him up a tree without any clothes, howling at the sun like a damn rabid dog. All the Jacobsens have a crazy streak in them. Uncle Robert's brother, Rusty, he killed himself. Nearly killed his daughter before he offed himself. You did know your friend Laura was Uncle Robert's niece – Rusty's daughter – didn't you?"

"No, I didn't know that. Is it important?"

The sheriff didn't reply. The silence between them deepened, the sheriff obviously waiting for him to elaborate on his relationship with Laura. Instead, Bryan said, "You believe me, then? He really came after me with that hog-sticker of his."

"I'm reserving final judgment, but right now I guess I do. No real harm done, anyway. Just you pray the old guy doesn't fall down dead right away. Come on back to the office. I want to hear about this dead angel in the woods. Shit! Wait a minute." He knelt down to examine a scraggly looking foot-tall plant growing at the base of the statue. He gingerly fingered a leaf, then angrily yanked the plant out of the ground by the roots. "Goddamn Mary Jane!"

He held it up so Bryan could see. "And not a wild strain, either. Goddamn it! Right in the middle of town!"

Bryan repressed a smirk.

* * *

9.

Without a Clue

With a little effort, Simon Jacobsen, a.k.a. Uncle Robert, managed to get moderately drunk before noon.

But it didn't help.

Plan B? Screw moderation. Get falling-down drunk. Get shit-faced. Drink enough so he wouldn't remember his own name; get so drunk he would forget the terrible scheme of the universe as outlined by the angel in the town square.

"How you doing, Uncle Robert?" The waitress' bare white midriff clashed with legs and hips sheathed in black spandex, reminding him of how Sophia used to work in the kitchen wearing nothing but an apron. Those were the good ol' days, and he hadn't known it.

But the redheaded waitress was young, younger even than his niece Laura, and wilder from the looks of her elaborate ear piercings and the brightly colored tattoos showing from the partially buttoned blouse.

He couldn't exactly remember her name – Susan or Suze? – but he did recall she had married a middle-aged rancher, a man more than twice her age. He wondered what brought her to work in town. Was the marriage or the cattle business failing?

"Want another, or have you reached your limit?"

"Not tonight, daughter of the dawn. There is no limit. No boundaries. The universe is without form. Entropy rules. I can drink myself to oblivion and fit right in."

"Oh, Uncle Robert, you are so weird." She stretched out the word as if she were calling in the pigs. *Weee - irrrd*. She leaned closer, and whispered, "Listen, Samuel is thinking about cutting you off."

She knew his moniker? Why didn't he know hers? Who had she been talking to?

Messengers of an Alien God

"Sophia? The woman I live with?"

"Not Sophia, your wife. Samuel, the bartender, silly."

"Oh, *that* Samuel. I didn't even know we were dating."

"Samuel doesn't sound anything like Sophia," Suzanne, or Susan, or Suzie said.

The fact gradually registered that she was talking of the Iranian expatriate who worked for the Bouchers. His real name was Salman, but he went by Samuel half the time. Uncle Robert didn't correct the waitress, but he nearly added that Sophia was not his wife, unless you counted common law. They had lived together in the same house for the last seven years. *Cohabited,* the law called it. But all that seem too complicated to convey.

"He thinks you've had enough."

"Had enough of what?"

"Too much to drink, Uncle Robert."

"What is this? A new policy or a conspiracy against alcohol?"

"It's not really a conspiracy. Remember when you rode your red bicycle into the swing set at the park?"

"Vaguely."

"You should remember it real good. You were tangled up in it all night."

"Oh, all right. Whatever you say. For you, I remember it well."

"Well, Sheriff Wright came in the day after and suggested that Samuel not keep on serving you until you got so drunk you couldn't walk anymore."

"The meddling bastard." Actually, he halfway liked the sheriff. It just didn't seem fashionable to say so.

"Now, Uncle Robert, don't be that way. That's Samuel's job," she said, misunderstanding the object of his epithet. "All he wants to do is hide out here in the backwoods and not get sent back home and shot for not being a proper Muslim."

"I thought his job description was to keep jealous husbands from shooting out the air-conditioner by mistake."

"Whatever. But the sheriff put a fright into Salman. You know how he is."

"You mean in this country illegally?"

"Shhh, that's exactly the kind of talk that gets you in so much trouble, Uncle Robert. Anyway, what we do to ourselves should be our own business."

"You're right, sweetheart." He couldn't for the life of him remember her name.

"We've got to get big government off the backs of drunks," he heard himself saying as in a dream. "That's Sam's job . . ."

He looked up at the bar. Salman, a mountain of a man whose eyebrows grew together, didn't look like he needed to fear any drunk. "I know his face all too well."

"Well, I'm supposed to tell him when you've had enough."

"Well, I haven't had enough." He gave her what he hoped was a nice smile. From across the room, Salman glared at him. Uncle Robert glared back. Salman might be large, but his face was more that of an intense accountant than a bouncer.

"Don't get me in trouble, Uncle Robert. If the sheriff comes down on Samuel, he'll give me a hard time."

"The little fellah knows how to delegate authority, doesn't he? Maybe I'll give the Iranian embassy a call."

"Now, Uncle Robert, you wouldn't say that if you weren't drunk already. He might end up marrying one of the Bouchers nieces, you know."

"How convenient."

"You're right there. I could lose my job." She poked a pale white, freckled finger at him. Her nail polish was black with little white skulls painted on. "You could get your drinking privileges cut off. Just go easy, okay?"

"Never mind, my dear. Rest easy. I would never get you in trouble. Despite what you may have heard, I am a moral man. Now tell Sam to play it again and bring me another glass of ethanol, if you please, and hold the lead this time. I have much to forget, but I'd like to keep as many brain cells as possible."

He fiddled with his empty glass as she left, thinking of the scene he had made in the courthouse lawn with Jake Hale's grandson. Shit! What was wrong with him? He'd been ranting and raving like a frigging lunatic. Good thing the sheriff had bought the amnesia thing or he might have ended up in jail himself.

Messengers of an Alien God

He mused over this, wishing his drink would arive. Being known locally as an eccentric was one thing – it even had its public relation advantages, as long as he managed it correctly. Small towns were tribal. Their civilized constituents might talk uncivilly behind a crazy man's back, but they also held him in a certain kind of reverence. "Like a shaman, a fucking Sioux medicine man," he said under his breath, turning the words over slowly to see if they held any special truth when spoken half-drunk.

But having a reputation as being senile was another thing altogether. Did he really want to encourage such talk? Small town eccentrics drew chuckles and became the kernels from which grand folk myths grew. Mental defectives, on the other hand, became blank screens upon which the normal citizens – seemingly normal – projected their unresolved complexes, suppressed hostilities, even desires. Look what had happened to his nephew, Maurice Jacobsen, now destined to be mopping the floors at the local clinic forever and only allowed to do that out of Doc Jenkins' kindness. No, he couldn't let his actions be interpreted as mentally substandard or suspicion and accusation would follow him everywhere. Like his nephew, he would wind up a scapegoat for all the unsolved, perverted crimes, real or imagined.

Worse, a consensus he'd inherited the worst side of the Jacobsen imbalance could land him in Mid-MO Mental or a cell in either the Fulton or Nevada hospitals. The Jacobsen money had built a wing at the Fulton hospital so that rooms would be permanently reserved for the family infirm, the saying went – and it wasn't that far from the truth. When the family had been prosperous, donations – large ones – had been given to keep the worst news private.

"Here you go, Uncle Robert," the waitress said. She set his drink down with due ceremony, an offering to the mad god of wine. "Remember your promise and be good."

"God! I didn't promise good behavior, did I?"

"Now, now," she laughed, but by the way she wrinkled her brow he could tell she was worried. He realized despite her punk-rocker persona that she was really a very nice young woman.

"I'm only kidding," he said sheepishly.

"You better, or I'll give your wife a call."

-87-

"Enough said. I'll sit here quietly and get stewed."

She started to leave, and he said without thinking, "Why don't you stick around and talk to me a while?"

"Now, Uncle Robert, you know I can't do that. What would your wife say?"

"Oh, it's nothing like that. I know I'm old enough to be your father; hell, your grandfather. I was kind of feeling depressed, and those little skulls on your fingernails cheer me up, that's all."

"I've heard that line before," she said, smiling at him.

"Really? The grandfather line or the little-skulls line? The scoundrels." He was about to add that she looked like a current version of the type of girl who didn't shave her legs, like his first wife, the Earth Mother. But before he could organize this difficult comparison into a grammatically correct parable, she had disappeared.

"Samuel says that's definitely, absolutely your last drink tonight," she said, reappearing a few feet downstream, then walking away, not looking back.

Shit! She'd seen him in a new, unfavorable light. He'd lost an ally.

He threw back the home-brewed liquor, appreciating its illegality though not its taste. Its biting flavor was reminiscent of cheap, sugary tequila. He craved wine, but after the Fall the interstate trucking of all decent vintages – any vintages, really – had ceased. He would have to tread carefully. Technically, moonshine was illegal, but the sheriff had publicly declared a moratorium of sorts until normalcy was restored. There was the case of Scotch he had bought before the Fall, but Sophia had put it under lock and key.

He finished the rest of his drink, gagging on its taste. His hand still trembled as he set down the glass.

The alcohol numbed his higher intellectual functions, but the memory of the vision of the universe seen through the angel's eyes still hung his brain. Like ivy on old brick, the nihilism had worked tendrils into the mortar of his mind. He had a sneaking suspicion what the angels were all about, and it scared the hell out of him.

"Hello, Simon. Mind if I join you?"

He didn't bother to look up. Sheriff Wright was one of the select few in town who called him by his Christian name. Most everyone in town called him Uncle Robert, even redheaded goth waitresses who he barely knew, evidently.

Wright settled into the seat across from him. Seated, his short stature became painfully apparent. He wasn't a tall man himself, but the top of the sheriff's head barely came level with his mustache. Since Wright began putting on weight the last few years, his welterweight boxer's frame had become top-heavy.

"You look like a man with something on his mind, Sheriff."

"I could say the same about you, Simon." His voice and presence were that of a bigger man. As long as you kept your eyes closed, Sheriff Wright was six feet tall, the saying went. The town had a surplus of sayings and not much else in the way of wisdom.

"You here to talk about that little episode in the town square with the Hale boy?"

"We'll get to that eventually. By the way, he has been seeing Laura."

"Romantically, I gather from your tone. Poor boy. I hope he's prepared to step into the breech."

The sheriff seemed embarrassed by his lack of familial loyalty, so Uncle Robert went on. "Oh, she's a rare hybrid, my brother's daughter, a perpetrator – I mean perpetuator – of the family tradition. There's a story behind her name, you know. My brother had one of his episodes of forgetfulness while the girl was in gestation."

The sheriff cringed at the word 'gestation,' which Uncle Robert found amusing.

"Two months later, he woke to find himself in Mexico, living in the state Chihuahua with a woman who didn't speak a word of English, and ..."

The sheriff waved his hand, as if to brush the family history aside. "Your family has a lot of such stories, Simon."

"So you didn't come here to talk about old times, did you now, Sheriff?

"What happened with you and Douglas, Simon?"

"Douglas? I thought his name was Bryan."

"That's his first name. His grandfather is Jake Douglas Hale. You know Jake. His place adjoins your land along the north side."

"Of course I know him. Jake told me that his grandson would be housesitting while he went on vacation. I even met the boy in the woods this spring, fixing to cut off his own leg off with a chainsaw."

"Does that have a connection to the run-in between you and him on the courthouse green this morning? I didn't buy the dementia act, by the way."

Though he had expected the conversation to get around to the incident, the sheriff's abruptness set him back. Should he lie? No. It probably wouldn't do any good, only further eroding his credibility with Wright. "Something happened. I'm not sure what, but I think the angel hypnotized me." This wasn't exactly the truth, but the alternative, explaining the vision of reality the angel had presented, seemed impossible.

"I know what you mean," Wright said.

"Really?"

"They make me feel addled when I'm around them." Wright looked down at his hands in his lap, as if confessing to a flaw of character.

"Addled?"

"You know, numb from the eyebrows up." Wright looked around the room, perhaps checking to see if anyone was within earshot, then stared him directly in the eye. "But I don't go around brandishing a pig-sticker in people's faces."

"Did I do that?"

"Bryan Douglas says you did."

"I truly don't remember doing that."

"What do you remember?"

Simon lifted his glass to his lips, forgetting he had already emptied it. He slammed the glass down on the table, not out of frustration but out of fear the sheriff would notice his palsy if he set it down slowly.

"Now what the hell is the matter?"

"I want another drink, but Salman has got me on a limit, and I just passed it. The story goes you had a talk with him."

"The public's attitude is changing about drugs and booze. Against drunk drivers, you know. I can't ignore complaints of a drunk sleeping it off while dangling from the swing set like a big, fat, albino bat."

"It was a moonless night. My sonar was out of whack, and I missed the turn on my bicycle."

Messengers of an Alien God

"It looked bad. The woman signing the complaint didn't know you had enough sense even when drunk to ride your bicycle and leave your four-wheel drive parked on the square. I tried to explain to her, but hell, Simon, I'm an elected official. Public drunkeness is still against the law, you know."

"Yeah, I understand your position. Hey, did I tell you Pete Morgan offered me two heifers and a bull for my bicycle the other day? Before the Fall, the thing wasn't worth more than a laugh."

"You want another drink?" the sheriff said, as if he had to ask.

"Is that what you want? Well, me too. I'm even buying." He twisted in his seat and made hand motions to the waitress and Salman, who had been watching them.

The waitress – he was now sure her name was Suzanne, not Suzie, or Susan, or some derivative – looked over his shoulder to Wright for affirmation, then hurried over and set two classes of clear liquid on the table.

"Thanks, Suze. Put these on my tab," the sheriff said.

Uncle Robert almost corrected the sheriff about Suzanne's name, but held back.

"Simon, let me ask you a personal question," he said as the waitress walked away.

"Shoot, Sheriff."

"Do you think I'm a stupid man?"

"I've a lot of respect for you."

"I didn't ask you if you respected me. A coward respects a bully. You ivory-tower people, you'd respect a goddamn mudfish if you thought it was an endangered species. I asked you if you think I'm stupid."

Simon picked up his glass and raised in a toast to the sheriff. "I consider you a gentleman and a scholar, sir," he said and tossed half of the glass' contents back over his throat. As he did so, an exact, unwelcome statistic about throat cancer popped up in his mind, distracting him from the pleasure of the liquor's warming effect. "But I read too much."

"I don't get your meaning, Simon."

"Nothing. My mind kind of wandered there. As I said, I've been confused since talking with the angel."

The sheriff a little sip of his liquor and made a sour face. "What

-91-

I'm getting at is this: We all make judgments based on what we feel is right. Later, we come up with excuses to convince ourselves we made the right choice."

"I'll buy that, John."

"I know I should be scared of the angels. But I'm not. Neither is anyone else. I try to convince myself I should be scared, but the best I can do is rouse some weak-assed mistrust."

"When you think about it, the lack of xenophobia in itself is scary."

The sheriff shifted uncomfortably in his seat. "Don't use those two-dollar words on me."

"Xenophobia is the fear of strangers. What I mean is, it's natural for humans to mistrust strangers. The more strange, the more outlandish, the more intense the mistrust, particularly when the strangers are powerful in some way. Now, there's hardly anything I can think of more outlandish and powerful than the angels. They fly. They don't die. They fall to Earth in a giant spaceship, one ten times bigger than the one in *Earth Versus the Flying Saucers*."

"Bigger than what?"

"*Earth Versus the Flying Saucers:* It's an old science fiction movie, made in the fifties. A classic study in cold-war paranoia, some say. We just substituted aliens from another planet for communists."

"I'll take your word for it. I don't – didn't – watch those kind of movies."

"More a Western/John Wayne type of guy?"

"Yep," Wright said.

An understanding passed between them. Uncle Robert knew that despite Wright's prejudices, his habit of affecting a country cracker attitude, he was an intelligent, thoughtful man, though one not benefiting from an Ivy League education as had he.

"Anyway," Uncle Robert continued. "Nobody's even very curious about them, even the military, and they're supposed to be paranoid about everything."

"It's their job, you mean?" Wright said.

"Exactly. I don't know what's going on, but it's not natural."

"Are you saying it's like we're all under sedation, maybe?"

"Or hypnotized."

A pause followed. The sheriff took another small sip of his liquor. Uncle Robert picked up his glass. His hand tremor had steadied. Talking about the angels helped more than the alcohol.

The sheriff cleared his throat, a prelude to a *mano-a-mano* talk: Serious Business.

"I'll tell you something, Simon. I've been meaning to talk about this since the last town emergency meeting. I've been thinking about forming some kind of group where a few of us concerned citizens get together to talk about this angel situation."

"Sounds like a winner of an idea to me. Sort of an ad hoc commission."

"I don't know what to call it yet, but I think it's needed."

"So what do you want from me?"

"You know more odd facts than anyone I know. Take that stuff you were talking about at the meeting."

"I wasn't very well accepted."

"Well, you made a contribution, and I had you first on my list for the angel commission. Then this thing happened at the courthouse, and . . ."

"And what?"

"Well, I guess I need some reassurance you're in control of your faculties."

"I told you. I don't know what happened. I didn't mean the boy any harm. The angel really confused me. I don't ever remember being so confused, even when drunk." As he spoke, he realized he hadn't been so much confused as panic-stricken as he considered that what the angel had told him. *Confused.* Maybe if he called it confusion enough he might believe it himself.

"Well, that's pretty much how the college boy described you. Your waving the knife around scared him. That's why he slugged you. You should have seen his face when he came into the office. He was afraid he'd cracked your skull. One of your fellow starry-eyed dreamers, if you ask me, but basically honest kid, I think."

Uncle Robert rubbed the bump near his temple. He'd thought the angel had done it or that it was self-inflicted. "I'll talk to him and apologize."

"Sounds good," he said, getting to his feet. "I'll get back to you soon on the commission thing."

The sheriff left before he could ask him to talk to the bartender about raising his limit. Suzanne, her nose ring bouncing with each step, brought him another drink and for a while he was numb enough not to care about cosmic things or if Carl Johnson was trying to diddle his wife.

* * *

10.

Testimony

Uncle Robert felt Marguerite's eyes on his back from twenty feet away. He turned, and their eyes met. *Uh-oh.* She gave him a restrained wave and skittered across the parking lot to intercept him, religious brochures in hand. Pretending he hadn't noticed, he turned back the way he had come, toward his bicycle and escape. This, he knew, was a lame stratagem. Those on a mission from God, were too single-minded to acknowledge anything but outright rejection.

She quickened her pace and came along his flank, her eyes coyly cast downward, a clutch of brochures in one hand, a wad of calico skirt nervously pinched in the other.

"Oh, hello, Uncle Robert," she said, as if she hadn't recognized him until now.

He was caught. Nothing short of outright rudeness would save him now.

"Hello, Marguerite. I haven't seen you in quite a while."

Now that she had engaged him, she stepped back, leaving a full eight feet of respectable distance between them. This was to be a public conversation; let no one misunderstand her intent. He looked around. Perhaps she had reinforcements. Sure enough, two middle-aged women, both wearing maternity tops, stared at him from the shade of the Quik-Stop & Shop's circus-striped awning. More carnal casualties of the post-Fall blackout? No, that couldn't be it. He didn't know much about pregnant women, but he did know they wouldn't be showing so much after only two months. He nodded at them and touched his hat. In response, they turned away and buried their heads in a huffy, self-righteous conversation.

"You're looking very pretty, Marguerite."

She blushed. He had dated her mother for a while after Marguerite's biological father had run off. During the dating period, he had served as surrogate father to little-girl and then tween Marguerite, but that was a good twenty – no, thirty – years ago. Marguerite's mother died last year, and the daughter was now nearly middle-aged, married to Sheriff John Wright.

"How, how –" Marguerite stuttered. She dropped her gaze to the ground. "How is your wife?" She continued to avoid his eyes and began obsessively smoothing a static wrinkle from her dress.

"How is your wife?" Marguerite repeated.

He didn't bother to explain that he didn't recognize common law marriages–not to Marguerite. He felt he was talking to someone much older than himself, she in her late sixties and he twenty-something. Merely considering discussing the subject with an unreceptive mind invoked a wave of exhaustion in him. Besides, such a discussion would open the conversation to the subject of morality, and that would be playing into her hands. There was to be no exit from this discussion.

"Uncle Robert? Uncle Robert?"

"Huh? Oh, sorry, Marguerite."

He had drifted off again. She waited for a more detailed response, something to show he was paying attention to her. "Sophia is fine. As feisty as ever."

Feisty was a good word for her. This morning she had thrown his breakfast at him, stoneware and all, as a conversational counterpoint.

"I'll have to drop by and have a chat with her some day."

"You do that," he said. They both knew she never would. Marguerite had never talked to an average black person – man, woman or child – as an equal, and Sophia was far from average by any standard. He had a vision of Marguerite running from the Jacobsen mansion, her eyes wide in terror, her usually neat hair a mad, tangled mess. "Be sure to call first," he added.

"Simon . . ."

Here it came. She hadn't called him anything but Uncle Robert for years.

"Do you believe there is meaning to life?"

He looked around for some excuse to leave. No exit. The two witnesses looked away again in haste lest they appear to be eavesdropping.

"Why, certainly, though better minds than mine have been at a loss to say why."

"I mean, do you think God has a plan for us?"

He hadn't expected the conversation to get around to God so quickly. He was reminded of the year he lived in Springfield and of the young Bible school students who came around in white shirts and black ties all psyched up to practice enthusiastic evangelism. He liked them at first. The fact that they rode bicycles was enough. But he had soon learned to slam the door in their faces without giving them a chance to champion their cause. To argue with them was useless and irritating. They threw out any fact or argument that didn't suit their faith. They had a quota of saved souls to meet, and they weren't prepared to listen, only to talk.

But here in Creedance, fundamentalism wasn't a revived movement but the ongoing status quo, a marching of Christian soldiers that could be extremely prejudiced to an out-and-out breaking of the ranks.

Marguerite was still talking. He forced himself to pay attention, not to go intellectually AWOL.

"If God has a plan? You mean everything is predetermined?"

She looked confused. He remembered her as a thirteen- or fourteen-year-old, wanting someone to tell her why her father had left.

"Do you mean, is everything preordained, good times and bad times?"

"Yes, preordained," she said.

"Well, it's possible. But I don't like to think about it, for if it's true, then there's no use any of us thinking. Even our thoughts would be largely chosen for us, with a few limited choices, most of them detrimental to our well-being, like a school lunch menu, you know, meatloaf or shit-on-a-shingle, no real choice."

She gave him a kind of cross-eyed look, like when he had tried to help her with algebra in school. Maybe it had been the word *shit*. Undeterred, he continued. "Even our wondering about predetermination, I mean preordained-ness, would be useless because our minds would have already been made up for us. Wouldn't that be so?"

She looked away, giving a slight nod to the two ladies not watching them. They nodded in return. "You haven't changed at all, have you, Uncle Robert?"

Was that an accusation or a compliment?

"No, I still have my lean, manly figure," he said, patting his paunch and hoping she would laugh. He'd always like her laugh.

She didn't laugh.

Though he hadn't talked with her much since she was a teenager, he began to suspect there was more to her emotional problems than religious obsession.

"Here, I'd like to give you this," she said. She stepped forward and thrust one of the religious brochures into his hand, made a pretense at a smile and then took off across the parking lot. The two other ladies strolled away, talking hurriedly and secretively. Marguerite waved goodbye as he mounted his bicycle, and for a split second he saw her as a confused teenage girl again.

His feelings were mixed as he pedaled out of town and toward home. He was both relieved and concerned. He had been spared the embarrassed testimony, but he possessed the remnants of a fatherly concern for Marguerite and hated to see her so stifled and unhappy. He had witnessed many of his friends' spirits wither in the heat of the small town's narrow-minded demand for conformity. Certainly this process was undermining her individuality. Religious orthodoxy was an element of conformity and fed on the anxiety of original sin, the sin of having instincts and desires and self-will. There weren't many outlets of the human spirit that weren't sinful, except, of course, food and sex, and then only sex for procreation, and small-town women often became large and matronly before their time.

As these thoughts went through his mind, he realized they were only half-truths.

No, it was more complicated that this. These weren't stupid people.

He often felt on the verge of realizing something, of gaining insight into why Christianity seemed to have turned into a stagnant moral code rather than a living, growing movement. As always, the understanding seemed a mixture of incompatible opposites, and he became overwhelmed by the impossibility of codifying it. Only at such times did he gather any sympathy for those pinched souls who cast out all knowledge and culture conflicting with a mythos no longer having any authentic connection to their everyday lives. That is, he understood why some chose the unhappy stricture on their normal instincts over the perplexity of free will in a world where the distinction between good and evil had become increasingly vague. He felt ill-equipped himself. Like most lost souls, he diverted his concentration away from the problem of his own place in the cosmos and back to criticizing the concerns of others. The difference was that he did so willingly and consciously, which made his displacement all right didn't it?

What conundrum could Marguerite be wrestling with? A few years ago, she had shown a healthy-minded approach to life, pleasure with the new house, pride in her husband, confidence in the future. Life crisis at forty-something? She had lost her first baby when the little girl was less than a year old. There had never been another. Rumors were that the good sheriff wasn't up to the task. Simon doubted that was the case. There were too many clues, bits of body language and so on, to hint that Wright was far from impotent. Uncle Robert's mind filled with a blinding flash of psychological tracts mixed with overheard double entendres that he only half-understood but that wouldn't go away. He nearly careened through a barbed wire fence before the episode passed and he regained control. Shaken, he wobbled harmlessly off into the ditch and waited until his mind cleared. It had been a minor attack. An old yellow pick-up truck passed by slowly. A white-clothed figure leaned out the window. A redneck angel?

"You okay, Uncle Robert?" No, it was a nurse from the clinic, still in her white uniform; what was her name?

By way of an answer he waved, nodded and produced a good-humored smile. The woman waved back and sped up. She was no doubt thinking something along the lines of: *The old coot is drunk again, and in the middle of the afternoon!* He preferred her to think this rather than to have the whole county know the truth: He had episodes where he lost all track of reality. Worse, that the episodes were becoming more frequent.

He dragged the Schwinn out of the ditch. In twenty minutes he was pedaling to the turnoff onto the Old Buffalo Road. Coasting along, he turned his mind to an easy, familiar study of personalities caught in the small-town maze. What did Marguerite do with herself? In Creedance, there were few jobs for unskilled women, much less one befitting a sheriff's wife. That might be the reason she had turned to propagating religion.

Marital problems? Perhaps. Half the town knew the sheriff had toyed with taking up May Tyre on her blanket offer to have sex with any able-bodied man in town. But Simon's instincts told him that Marguerite's problems lay rooted in deeper soil than marital infidelity. Maybe she was actually involved in the search for the meaning of life, longing for a personal religious experience. If so, she was on a hell of a lonely path, for he doubted she would find any help from the poor secular souls who passed themselves off as spiritual pillars of strength in this town.

A honk woke him up. He hadn't noticed the rust-bucket racket of another old pickup approaching from behind. The driver honked again as he passed in a cloud of chalky dust. Though he couldn't see the driver through the dust, he recognized the black Dodge as Carl Johnson's. Once past him, the truck speeded up, pelting him with gravel. Too fast! What was that bastard doing out here on the Old Buffalo Road? The phones? No, he had more important lines to service. A mile farther and the road dead-ended. The Smith farm was behind him. Only two other houses remained, first Jake's place where the Douglas boy now lived and his own. And the only person in his house was Sophia, and Uncle Robert knew there was nothing wrong with the phone.

Johnson half-bounced, half-skidded his truck around the corner like a crazed ambulance chaser.

Johnson wouldn't dare. Or would he? Maybe the half-witted bastard was getting bolder. The assholes at the town meeting. He realized sadly that his own passivity had encouraged the boldness.

A huge shadow passed over him. He looked up to see three angels gliding overhead, their gloriously white wings nearly brushing the treetops. He stood up, putting all his weight on the pedals, starting off the bike with a spin of gravel. Pedaling harder, he caught up the trailing edge of the last angel's shadow and raced into the middle of it. His own shadow merged with the combined pattern of the angels' for several seconds. He leaned into his efforts, trying to make his middle-aged body more aerodynamic, blood pounding in his ears, his paunch shaking, his breath coming in gasps that were nearly honks – he, the demented, graying father goose of Harmon County.

The shadows out-raced him along the narrow road. Left him in the dust.

He pulled the bike over to the side of the road and watched, held in awe despite his anger. How easy to think of the angels as supernatural manifestations.

Maybe they were. They defied natural laws and seemed to be beyond death. Up ahead, the angel's shadow followed the stretch of powdery gravel around the curve like a train on a track. It must be looking for something, or rather someone, using the road as a running landmark. The road's course along the curving topography of a ridge was one of convenience only for those taking the ground route. What could the angels be searching for? They had no more reason to be on this road than did Carl Johnson. Even fewer reasons, for the angels didn't need to follow the road.

Johnson – He'd nearly forgotten about that bastard. He'd kill him!

He leaned into each stroke until his breath came in rasps and his heart pounded in this chest.

He turned off the gravel road onto concrete drive to the house, swerving around the potholes. He dropped the bike in the front yard, dismounting at a run like a school boy late for class.

On the porch he tried to call out for Sophia, but found he had no breath left. He had to sit on the top step and catch his breath. What could a winded old kook do about a cuckold-maker half his age, anyway? Subdue him with logic? Trip him up intellectually? Overbalance him with a joke?

Forced as he was to sit, he surveyed the front yard. Everything seemed normal. The Range Rover stood parked where he'd left it, its green paint rusting under the cool shade of the walnut tree. The tail end of Sophia's black Lincoln stuck out of the garage. One rear tire was flat. He'd have to change that for her.

Wait a minute. Where was Johnson's truck? It hadn't been at Jake's place. He hadn't passed it on the road. There was nowhere for it to turn off the road. This was the last stop.

A slight breeze stirred the dust on the front porch. A hawk shrieked from high above the overgrown woods to the south. On the surface, everything was familiar. Not a single flake of the old house's peeling white paint seemed to have been disturbed from when he had left this morning, but there was some off-kilter about it, as if it were a simulacrum of his real house, and chill ran up his spine.

Was this another symptom of impending dementia?

He took a deep breath and let it out slowly. The pounding in his ears subsided, and he heard voices, Sophia's and someone else's, conversing quietly from the living room.

He got painfully to his feet. He didn't know what the bastard had done with his truck but knew he was in there. Was the shotgun over the mantel loaded? He eased opened the screen door and tip-toed through the front foyer to the southern sunroom. There he retrieved the shotgun and found it loaded. How old were the loads? Two years? Three?

He found Sophia and an angel sitting side-by-side on the sofa.

No sign of Carl Johnson.

"Here's Simon now," she said as he came into the room. In private she called him Uncle Robert as did nearly everyone else in town, friend and mere acquaintance alike. But around a third party, she referred to him as *Simon.*

"Well, don't stand there like a statue," she said. "Come sit down. And what are you doing with that shotgun?"

The angel gave him a benevolent smile. Like every other angel he had seen, its skin was as white as porcelain, but this one's features were distinctly Negroid. He never seen one like that before and yet the handsome face was somehow familiar. Harry Belafonte? It stood up, offering him a good target with its broad chest.

What was he doing with the shotgun? For some reason – even though Johnson was not here – his fear of being cuckolded persisted. The feeling sought a focus and had found the male-like angel. Which was stupid. The angels weren't sexual threats. Psychologically they were dangerous but probably only to borderline cases like him. As for the shotgun, a blast of pellets was unlikely to have any effect on the angel, but would certainly upset Sophia. He sat in the overstuffed chair on the other side of the coffee table from the angel and Sophia, feeling like a guest in his own house. He rested the shotgun across his knees, not knowing what else to do with it. He was, he realized, getting too crazy to own a firearm.

He should clear the house of the things. The angel sat back down.

"Simon, this is Mr. Asbeel," Sophia said. "Mr. Asbeel, this is Simon Jacobsen."

She wore denim jeans and pink rubber thong sandals; the shirttails of a frayed red blouse were tied around her middle and a red bandanna was over her hair; this was what he thought of as her rose-garden outfit. If *Ebony* magazine had ever produced a gardening edition, she would have been perfect for the cover. He could see freshly tilled soil between her toes and on her knees. Evidently, she hadn't been expecting the angel, and it had surprised her while she was on hands and knees weeding her garden.

"Well, Simon, aren't you going to say anything?"

"Hello," he said. "I don't remember seeing you around town before."

"I flew in today from the South," the angel said as if this explained everything. *South of town? South of the Missouri river? The Southern United States? South of the equator? The southern Magellan nebula. . .?*

"Mr. Asbeel and his fellow angels are looking for something, or someone, I'm not sure exactly which," Sophia said bringing him back to the here and now. She seemed oddly excited.

He took a deep, cleansing breath and let it out slowly. The house was hot and damp. The mingled smell of Sophia's sweat and garden soil filled his nostrils. He could almost taste it.

"Exactly what have you lost, Mr. Asbeel?" The courtesy title rounded out the angel's name nicely.

"It is rather difficult to describe," the angel said in a deep baritone.

"Try."

"To properly explain what it is we are looking for is nearly impossible, but the word *mortality* comes close."

"You've lost *mortality?* You mean *immortality,* don't you?" Uncle Robert said.

Uncle Robert dredged the quagmire that was his mind for memory of what had happened with the angel on the courthouse green. Had that encounter also begun with a simple, yet formal conversation about life and death? He couldn't remember anything but the fear, and his grip tightened on the shotgun.

The angel gave no sign of noticing that Uncle Robert might be poised on the edge of violence. Either it wasn't aware of his fear or it found no cause for concern.

"Tell me, Mr. Asbeel," Sophia said. "I've often seen angels fly over the adjoining woods, and I've never seen y'all flap your wings. How do you do it?" She must have sensed something was wrong and was changing the subject.

"That also would be impossible to explain as we live in two extra dimensions than do you."

"Two extra dimensions? Why, whatever do you mean, Mr. Asbeel?" Sophia asked.

Asbeel turned patiently toward her. "Humans perceive four dimensions: height, depth, width and time. You move through the first three at will, up, down, sideways. You are carried along by the fourth dimension, time, as a leaf is carried by strong river current. We, on the other hand, can navigate through time, against its current, with some limitations. Plus, we perceive two other dimensions, one of which we can manipulate, the other we can't; we are slaves to this dimension, much as you are to time. Do you understand, Mrs. Jacobsen?"

"Ms. Blackstone, if you don't mind, Mr. Asbeel. I've kept my own name. And yes, I think I do understand, after a fashion, the way one understands a cubist painting."

His anger subsiding, Uncle Robert found himself intrigued. "So about this mortality issue, how could we – Sophia and I – possibly help you?"

"I have to leave now," Asbell said in place of an answer. "But if you'd like to talk about this with me in private – either of you – contact me."

"And exactly how would we contact you?" Uncle Robert said.

The angel's smile returned. From somewhere among the folds of his robes it produced a packet of business cards. The angel took a single card from the packet, and, without getting up, passed it across the ten feet of space separating them.

Uncle Robert blinked. He had sensed neither speed nor motion, nor did the angel's arm suddenly grow long. It was if the room shrank into an intimate space for a second, then snapped immediately back to its original size.

"On the card," the angel said, "you'll find a telephone number."

He looked at the card. Sure enough, printed in smudged, ancient-looking script was the name *Asbeel*. In smaller type, also slightly smudged, was the title *Leader of 100*. Underneath that was a phone number with the prefix of the Creedance exchange.

"We believe this is the proper practice," Mr. Asbeel said.

Uncle Robert thought of asking what the angel had paid to have the cards printed. Instead he said, "Very impressive."

He handed the card to Sophia, and she stared at it with an amused expression.

"We had them printed by the local newspaper," Mr. Asbeel explained.

Sophia gave the card back to Uncle Robert, and he slipped it into a front pocket of his overalls. In print, the name seemed familiar. "Tell me something, Mr. Asbeel."

"Certainly."

"Your name sounds familiar. My biblical knowledge is rusty, but isn't it adopted from the Old Testament?"

"Old Testament?"

"The Bible."

"That is a book, isn't it?"

"It's a book of religious scriptures. Sacred writings to some."

"We are not familiar with it."

"So where did you borrow your name?"

Mr. Asbeel looked confused. "Asbeel is my name. Asbeel has always been my name, since the moment when I sprang into the mind of the Dreaming God." He shrugged, and his wing tips came together in a kiss above his head. Abruptly, the creature stood up. The wing tips brushed the chandelier, causing it to tinkle and bringing down a shower of dust. The big room at once seemed small, not because of sensual distortion, but simply because the angel stood nearly seven feet tall, from sandal to the top of its head, and the wing tips stretched another foot higher. Sophia let out a little gasp.

"This one must be elsewhere," Asbeel said.

"Oh, don't rush off, Mr. Asbeel. Stay for lunch. Uncle Robert will play ragtime piano for us, won't you, Simon?"

"I'm sure Mr. Asbeel has more important things to do than to listen to me abuse the keyboard."

Mr. Asbeel bowed, wing tips brushing the hanging cut glass of the chandelier again, setting off a cascade of tinkling sounds. "We must go, though this piano game sounds most interesting."

"I'll show you to the door, Mr. Asbeel," Sophia said.

After his wife and the angel left the room, Simon unloaded the shotgun and examined the shells. On the puckered end of the red plastic shell he found a tiny webbed egg sack, probably made by a small spider. He heard Sophia's voice exchange some pleasantry with the angel, and the front screen door shut with a rattle. Sophia came back and traipsed across the Persian carpet and into the hall leading to the summer kitchen without saying a word. Whether she was self-absorbed or angry with him, he couldn't tell.

He sat in the chair thinking about Mr. Asbeel and his lost mortality and his six-dimensional senses.

The clinking of plates from the kitchen brought him out of his reveries. This was Sophia's signal that lunch was ready. Obviously she wasn't angry or she wouldn't have cooked for him. Most likely she wanted to be alone with her thoughts. Maybe she had started painting again. That would be a good sign. After a silent lunch in the kitchen he went up to his library.

The library filled his father's old study plus three adjoining bedrooms, the result of two generations of collecting. He found no reference to Asbeel in the King James Bible, but he had only half-expected to. He began a more thorough search, a laborious job as the only complete cataloguing system he had was on the hard disk of his desktop computer, which hadn't worked since the Fall.

It was nearly evening when he finally found the volume he had been looking for: *The Apocrypha and Pseudepigrapha of the Old Testament*, edited by R.H. Charles, 1907 edition.

As he hoped and feared, he found the name *Asbeel* in the first book of Enoch.

* * *

11.

The Angelic Dialectic

As a race, we made a terrible mistake when we chose to become immortal," she said. "We made another when we decided to come to this plane of existence to seek death."

Bryan found it impossible not to think of the beautiful creature as a *she*.

She brushed a lock of hair from her perfect forehead and smiled innocently at him.

Bryan hurried to get the angel's exact words down on the greenlined steno pad. His writing hand was uncooperative and slow, his mind too deliberate to think in words rather than images after so many months as a hermit woodcutter. His mind, like his fingers, had become thick and stiff.

It occurred to him that what a stupid idea it was to interview an angel, to write the Great American Novelist's insight into angel mentality. Thousands of writers all over the country were probably trying to do the same thing -- and succeeding. Who did he think he was? He was a college drop-out who nearly threw up at the thought of doing an outline, a loser who had flunked out of graduate school. Why should he think he could write?

Still, there was something to be said for the interview process. The angel was full of surprises and otherworldly twists of words. All Bryan had to do was keep accurate notes. He had expected the interview to be enigmatic to the point of being nonsensical, like a conversation with a stoned graduate-level philosophy major. If he misquoted, who would notice? Instead, he found the angel's answer made a kind of twisted sense, and now found himself earnestly engaged in getting the story.

The angel waited.

"So why don't you go back and make yourselves mortal again?" he asked her.

"We would if we could, but we are seen as insane criminals by others of our kind."

He looked at her face for some sign of facetiousness, but she looked sincere.

"You may begin to see the irony of our existence. In our native realm, we numbered in the thousands and were denizens of time, as your race is today. We lived Life, which is to say we were aware of our eventual cessation, and we reproduced, though not sexually the way your race does, but through intermediate and willing hosts. Our lives, though finite then, were longer than the entire span of your recorded history, but we were, as a race, dissatisfied. We discovered, you see, that reality was a sham, that He who we knew as God was a sham, an impostor – am I talking too fast for you?"

"Go ahead, I'll try to keep up."

She smiled at him in a way that made him feel as if he were a gifted child and continued. "Once we discovered our creator, the Dreaming God, was flawed, we naturally began to look for the true reality. We found – and I cannot explain to you how we did this, for we lack common references – but we came to realize we were cut off forever from the true reality. We had known for ages that reincarnation occurred, and we discovered why. What we thought was an act of a kind Dreamer giving us a second chance was actually another error. The Dreaming God's occasional errors made it possible for us to discover the true nature of our existence, thereby increasing our dissatisfaction. This discovery was thousands of your years in coming."

"Why didn't you file a complaint with this god. Beseech him or whatever?"

"We tried without result, and we thought at first the Dreaming God was lost in his own dream."

The angel paused and looked at Bryan as if expecting a comment from him.

When Bryan said nothing, the creature continued: "We decided we were too flawed in our nature to reach the higher reality outside the dream. We came to suspect the Dreaming God had so removed us, made us so flawed. Why? We wanted to think the Dreaming God an evil insidious being, but we learned he was merely incompetent, clumsy. So, that is why we chose to come here and learn to die from those who still knew how."

"Just like that? You flicked a switch and you were here?"

"We had what you would call the technology at our disposal, though it was not machines as you use them, but a machination of our minds."

"And this was a mistake?"

"Yes, though it didn't seem so at the time. We had hoped to accomplish two things with our immortality: We hoped the infinite span of life would give us time to perfect ourselves so that we might counsel with the true God, and we wished to foil the desires of our Creator. Oh, how we hated and revered Him!

"To acquire our immortality, we had to make sacrifices. We cast ourselves outside of time and gave up our reproductive powers. In retrospect, we played into the fantasies of the Dreaming God. We now realize that the plan was spoiled by our hatred, by our wish to cheat the Dreaming God of any pleasure. His dreams had dreamers within dreams, uncountable levels of dreamers dreaming other dreamers.

"To escape this we made ourselves immortal. Imagine our chagrin to learn that with death, there was a chance to rise to a higher level of reality, still a dream within a dream, but one closer to the Ultimate reality. We had made a terrible mistake. When we made ourselves immortal, we thought we would expand our range of choices. But when we became immortal, we put ourselves beyond choice. There could be no new life as long as we lived. No reincarnation to a higher plane. We could make choices for other beings, the ultimate choice being life or death. But we couldn't choose to die ourselves. We had pre-determined the course of our existence. We had chosen against the natural order of things."

"Excuse me. Was that *the ultimate choice is being?*"

"No. I said, *The ultimate choice being life or death.*"

"Damn. I wish I had a recorder."

"Would you like to retrieve one? I could wait."

"That would be great, but I doubt if there's an operating recorder within a thousand miles."

The angel was silent. Bryan got the impression she didn't know what he was talking about. "Could I take the picture now?"

"If that's what you need," the angel said. "What am I to do?"

"Nothing. Relax." He set down the note pad, glad to be rid of it. He felt more confident with the old Nikon in his hands. He wished he had a light meter, and as much as he liked shooting black and white, this situation screamed out for color. The angel possessed an extraordinary beauty in the pinkish early evening light.

He had waited all day to find an angel to talk with. The day before, the angels had seemed as plentiful as pigeons. Today he had seen only two on the ground: the one who earlier had been talking with Uncle Robert and now, this one.

"Where are all the angels today?" he asked.

The angel became fidgety, and he worried she was going to fly off before the interview was over. Time to take a picture, he decided. He framed the angel in the camera's viewfinder, held his breath and snapped off a frame.

It had been late in the day, nearly six o'clock, when he found her, sitting on the stone steps of the old Methodist church. The lengthening shadows had lent a melancholy mood to her strangely beautiful features. She looked like a lost saintly child then, an image he wanted very much to capture. He moved closer with the camera. With only two or three shots left on the roll, he had to frame the shot perfectly. Though how could he not get a great picture with a face like that?

"What were you doing in town, then? Why weren't you searching with the rest of your group?" he asked.

"Waiting for you, of course," she said. "Did you think we hadn't noticed you despite your human guise?'

"No. Really." He decided not to discourage whatever delusion the angel had about him. It could be the only reason he was getting this interview. He snapped the shutter, but his eye was left unsatisfied. He hadn't quite captured the soul of the angel, of the setting.

"What is the purpose of the little machine?" she asked.

"It takes pictures."

"Pictures?"

"It records images."

"I still don't understand."

He looked around for an example and found the stained glass window. "Like that," he pointed. As luck would have it, the window depicted Adam and Eve being expelled from the Garden. An irate angel glided over their heads, pointing the way out.

"Will I be colored like that in your image?"

"No, he's too blue. More like the woman in the other window. But this is black and white."

Through broken and partially obscured by a piece of plywood, the other window was more artfully done. The craftsman had used large sections of glass to depict a young, joyful Madonna and Child. As an extra touch, he had given Madonna wings.

"She is not of my race," the angel said. "And what's more, not even human, I think. Too flat. She is of piebald coloring."

"No, it's not realistic, you're right. Your picture will look like a television image; it will be a still." Before she could ask what a still was, he added, "It won't move."

"Television?"

Now he was becoming exasperated. Was she toying with him?

"Surely you know what television is?"

She shook her head innocently.

"So how did you angels learn the language while you were in space? By listening to radio programs in English?"

"Speak English? You mean the language we are speaking now?"

"Whatever. How did you learn?" He started to suggest an electronic interpretation device and felt silly.

"We have always spoken this language. This one and a hundred others. Since time began. Since we as a race began. We were created – dreamed – with the language skills intact," she said.

"How old are you? You're younger than the others, aren't you."

"No, quite the contrary. I am the second oldest. I was nearly the first created by the false god of whom I spoke." She gave him a look as if they were sharing some private joke.

Speechless, he took another picture, this one with the stained glass window in the background while the beautiful young angel staring off wistfully into the distance. He had expected the global village would extend to visitors from space. Instead he had found another enigma. Perhaps she meant they learned languages quickly, almost immediately. He found the idea of a preternatural learning ability more acceptable than the miracle of a race of poly-savants.

She stood and stretched, a very human gesture except when she spread and tensed her wings until they quivered with long-reserved tension. She lowered her wings as if to launch herself into flight. Though shorter than some of the male-looking angels, she was nearly a foot taller than him. Her teenage face and demeanor had fooled him into thinking of her as a human with wings. Her beauty had lulled his fear to sleep.

"What's your name?" he asked.

"My feminine name or my masculine name?"

The question stumped him. "Both," he answered.

"Eloaios is my masculine name. My feminine name is very difficult to sound out with this tongue."

"Do you mean it's hard to say in English?"

"No. I mean exactly what I say," she replied. "Translated to English, my name would mean Envy. My masculine name means something else again entirely. Upon my creation it was the first word I whispered as God dreamed me."

"I find it hard to think of you as masculine."

"You perceive me in the way that you need in order to make me consistent with your world view."

"You're saying your appearance is an illusion?"

"Yes, but no more than your appearance." She spread her arms wide, encompassing the world. "This reality imposes forms on conscious life. Despite our time-sense, our consciousness is in many ways similar to yours; thus our form is in many ways similar also."

Now it was his turn to be confused. She seemed to be telling him that she was a materialization of an abstraction, a dream made real. He wanted to ask her if this was the case, but lacking the right words, his mind stumbled over transsexual images, a flicker of male genitalia mutating to female and back again, which made his stomach tighten. His mental havoc must have registered on his face, for she said, "I see I must show you. Mayhap it will wake you up."

Without warning, she embraced him and they ascended at once in a blur of speed, skimming over the house tops, leaving Creedance behind in the time it took for him take a breath.

He was terrified of heights and he should have been crapping his pants, but her grip around his waist was light, firm, and though hardly strong enough to support his weight, and it calmed him. Besides, some paranormal physics was at play here. He seemed to have been taken into a sphere of influence, a bubble where Newton's laws were invalid. He still felt the breeze on his skin, smelled the change in air as they passed the edge of town and glided over the hickory and oak forest, but his body felt condensed to a pinpoint, without weight or mass, to be carried along effortlessly.

"Where are you taking me?"

"To our crippled vessel."

"You mean to the saucer?"

"Yes. There is something I must show you." She had been staring straight ahead like any conscientious driver. Now she turned to look at him, her startling violet eyes only inches from his, her blonde hair aflame from the red sunset.

"Humans do represent a moral quandary for us," she said. "We are trying to understand your place in the universal scheme. When we are able to define you, we will be able to envision our moral response to your illusion of free will."

They flew on in silence. As they came to Lost Lake, the angel swerved and followed the shoreline. Her wings remained outstretched, and she made no pretense at flapping. All the propulsion and lift seemed entire independent of aerodynamics.

But maneuvering apparently required body language. As she turned to avoid the lake, for example, she arched her body sideways, driving hip and breast against him. Her breast was firm and, though he knew better, he could have sworn he felt a nipple nudging his shoulder, and her hip was friendly in its roundness.

From the air, the view of the saucer was stupendous. A blackened gash, hundreds of feet long, scarred the upper surface of the silvery body. The angel slowed and turned in flight and landed flat-footed on the broad flat expanse of the saucer, inches away from the edge of the great tear in the metal skin. A black pit loomed beneath them.

"Did you really think you could fool us by pretending to be human?" She said as she leaped into the rent.

He regained awareness screaming. He must have blacked out when they entered the saucer. How long had he been out? He sensed a length of time had passed while they were in the saucer, but had no idea how much. Now they were flying out of the saucer, toward the clear blue sky, back through the rent in the saucer's skin. Though the terrifying moment of descent into the saucer seemed an eternity ago, the clouds looked unchanged, and the angel's grip was now as hard as iron. Its whole body had changed. Where before there had been feminine roundness, was now knotted muscle and angular bone.

The air was warm, and a noonday sun glared down. Hadn't it been dusk when they entered the saucer? How long had he been inside? He didn't dare ask the angel. He was a child in the grip of an enraged adult.

The angel deposited him on a low wet spot somewhere in the woods. She then lifted up a few feet, not letting her feet touch the mud. He made himself look up into her face and found it again truly androgyne, beautiful in its sculptured features but sexually ambiguous. He could now see the face contained both the beautiful young woman from the steps of the church and a raging, dangerous young man. The male and female visages cancelled each other out and the overall effect was void of sexuality.

"Is that it?" he said, not sure what he was asking.

"We will speak again," the angel said. He/she stretched out an arm to the sky and shot up and over the trees in the general direction of the saucer, out of sight in second.

He took inventory. He had lost both his notebook and the camera. Before he had blacked out, as he and the angel dropped into the saucer, he remembered feeling as if his body were being turned inside out. It had been like dying to be reborn. He had been incredibly stupid to approach the angel. He was lucky to be alive.

He was suddenly very tired and hungry, and had only the vaguest notion of his location. He was somewhere on the Jacobsen farm, he guessed. He sloshed out of the wet spot, his feet heavy with mud, and started walking on what he hoped was an eastern course. A half-hour later he broke out of the woods and onto a small gravel road. The road looked much like the one that passed by his grandfather's house, but without the deep ruts and potholes. It looked hardly traveled at all. Completely disoriented, he followed the road to the left, hoping it would take him somewhere familiar.

About a mile down the road he came upon the open iron gates of an old mansion. Deeply chiseled letters in the stone arch over the gates proclaimed "Jacobsen."

He trudged up the long driveway, his knees wobbly, bypassing the huge potholes in the concrete. He recognized Uncle Robert's green luxury four-wheel drive, abandoned under a huge hickory tree. His bicycle was nowhere in sight.

Bryan nearly fainted climbing up the porch steps. He knocked on the screen door, and then entered the void.

He woke later to the smell of dust and a strong smell of oranges. A black woman stood over him.

"There, there. You rest for a while longer," the woman said.

He let himself return to sleep. He dreamed of Laura. They stood facing each other in her basement. He was naked, cold, and yearning for the warm touch of her skin. Just out of the shower, she glistened wetly in a red silk robe. He pulled her to him and slipped open her robe. With one hand he reached to fondle her breasts and with the other searched for the damp promise between her legs. Yet, as close as she was, her female parts were miles away, far from her, far from him, forever beyond his touch.

"We will speak again," she said, the robe falling away as she took flight on huge white wings.

* * *

12.

Transformation

Sheriff Wright's Thursday afternoon in the office started off all wrong and got worse. He wished Carl Johnson had never gotten the landline phone system working again.

First, Frank Marshall called to tell him that Bertha, his wife, had been missing for four days.

"Why did you wait until now to call me, Frank?" he asked, relieved in an odd way that Frank wasn't going to pester him about ammonium nitrate and kerosene storage at the co-op.

"I don't really know why, sir. But I guess it was because she's been acting awfully strange for the last month. The Jeep Cherokee was missing, too. I figured she just took off, but there wasn't enough gasoline in it to get very far. Besides, something like that was just between me and her, I figured – you know what I mean?"

"So what changed your mind?"

"This morning I found the Cherokee parked in the creek down the road, up to its axle in a sand bog. I guess nobody saw it until now because the big oaks hid it from the road."

"And no sign of Bertha."

"You got it." The old soldier sounded worried.

"Why do you think your wife drove it in the creek and left it?"

"I don't think she drove it in at all. That's the scary part. The trees are too thick on the south side; on the north side too. She would have had to fly it over the levee."

"Maybe she drove it down the creek."

"Not without pontoons, she didn't. Water's too deep. No, it looks like it's been dropped in the creek."

"Now, Frank. Don't you get weird on me."

"I'm not, goddamn it, Wright! You gotta see the place to understand. There's no way to drive a car or an SUV or even a tank to where I found the Cherokee. I know these things, goddamn it!"

"Okay, Frank. Okay. Don't pop a blood vessel. I'll do what I can, but I can't promise much. I've got a bunch of missing person reports and only one deputy and not much gasoline myself. Besides, she's not 'officially missing' until she's been gone a week."

"I know that. I'm reporting it now."

"Frank?"

"What?"

"I don't know how to say this nicely, but did you check the deep water up and down stream?"

"Yep."

"Try dragging it?"

"Didn't have to. The deep pools are clear as glass. There was nothing down there but big brown crawdads."

The old man hung up without saying 'goodbye' or 'thank-you.' The phone immediately began to ring as Wright set the receiver back in its cradle. It was Janice August, her voice on the edge of hysteria, calling to report that Tommy Georgian had left the trailer to go hunting two days ago and hadn't come home yet. She wanted Wright to organize a search party.

Women, who could figure them? The bastard had made a hobby out of knocking her around, and yet she worried about him as if he were a lost child. On the other hand, Wright had never laid a hand on Marguerite in anger, only wanted the best for her and had always taken good care of her, but his sleepy suggestion it might not be a good idea to carry the accidental pregnancy to term had caused the already crumbling marriage to dissolve.

"Give him another couple of days, and we'll see if we can round up enough gasoline for a search," he told Janice. It was the truth, but he knew how she'd take it. "Besides, I've had six other missing person reports in the last week."

He stopped himself from adding that, except for Carl Johnson, all of the previously reported missing were women, all pregnant, and all solid church-going citizens of Harmon County, while Tommy was probably off in the woods somewhere cooking meth.

"I'll get around to him when I can," he said.

"You son-of-a-bitch!" she screamed. "You want him to die! You're just like all the other shits around this town. I'll find him myself!" And she slammed down the receiver.

He should have lied to her, told her anything – that he would send Jimmy to cruise around the farmsteads and ask questions. But he say what he thought – that Tommy wasn't worth wasting the department's scant resources – but she heard it in his tone anyway .

The phone system was working well for a change; he decided to call home to try to chat with Marguerite. He had to think before he dialed. He never called home except for an emergency and couldn't think of his own number. After five rings, Marguerite answered.

"Yes?" She sounded seventeen, breathless, happy-voiced.

"It's me," he said.

"Oh, you. What do you want?"

"Nothing really. I just wanted to say . . ." Before he could finish the sentence she hung up.

Now the question, which he hated to admit he entertained, was: Who had she been expecting to call? He sat around in a blue gloom, waiting for worse and it happened. At about three o'clock he got a call from Dr. Jenkins, telling him there had been a drastic change in May Tyre's condition, and that he'd better get down to the hospital.

"What is it? Is she better or worse?"

"Both."

"Don't play games with me, Doc."

"I'm not playing games. I don't want to start a panic. You can never tell who's listening in on this piece-of-shit phone system."

"All right. If it's important . . ."

"If it wasn't, I wouldn't be wasting my time talking to you."

Wright held his temper in check. If Jenkins were an obstinate son-of-a-bitch today, it was probably because he had been up all night. "I was going to say, Doc, I'll try to get over there today." He felt he was being charitable as he said this, but the gesture was lost on Jenkins.

"See that you do," Jenkins said, and hung up. Two other clicks followed. Jenkins was right about one thing: Carl Johnson's hot-wired phone system had compromised privacy. Some areas of town had to share one line among a dozen or more phones.

He had barely set the receiver back in its cradle before the phone rang again.

"Sheriff Wright?" An unfamiliar voice.

"Speaking. Who's this?"

"This is Sophia Blackstone."

He paused. The name was familiar, but he couldn't quite place the face on the other end of the line. A premonition of difficulty came over him. This was going to be one of *those* calls.

"What can I do for you Ms. Blackstone?"

"Simon – Uncle Robert – asked me to call. You know how he is about phones. Thinks there's always somebody listening in and all."

"Uh-huh," he said without commitment. Slowly his mind made the connection. Sophia was Uncle Robert's black, common-law wife. A few facts came trickling back to him. She was a product of St. Louis, not local, not from shanty-town. She was also reputed to be psychic and to hold séances. Wright had met her once in the company of Uncle Robert and decided then and there that she wasn't probably the trouble-making kind.

"A young man showed up on the doorstep this afternoon. Simon says his name is Douglas Bryan."

"You mean Bryan Douglas."

"That's it. Anyway, Simon says you've been looking for him."

"You bet I have, Ms. Blackstone, I mean Mrs. Jacobsen."

"Ms. Blackstone will do, thank you, Sheriff. Simon and I have an informal relationship, you know."

"Have it your way."

"Thank you, Sheriff. I always strive to do just that."

For the second time in ten minutes, Wright strained to control his temper. He couldn't get over feeling that Sophia used the fact of her race, and his being uncomfortable with it, to yank his chain. He thought she was one of those blacks who always seemed rude, walking around with a chip on their shoulders, always playing the victim, always blaming the whites for their troubles. They looked at him and saw not a man, but a middle-aged white man. And a sheriff to boot. And they called him a racist. He knew many blacks in a small, cracker town like Creedance got a bad deal, but though he might not be politically correct, he was not the enemy. "You tell the Douglas boy to get his rear end into the office. I want to talk with him."

"Well, I'll just mosey right over to the couch and tell him just that, Mister Sheriff, sir. But I don't think he's going to pay much attention 'cause he's been in a delirious coma since I found him."

"Why the hell didn't you tell me that in the first place?"

"Because you didn't give me a chance." She did not end the sentence with 'asshole,' but Wright heard it all the same. Now he knew how Janice had felt. He stuttered something about bringing the boy into the clinic, trying to be polite and not liking himself for doing so.

"We can't do that, Sheriff."

"Why not?"

"Neither of our vehicles is running. We can't very well drape him over the handlebars of Simon's bicycle, now can we?"

"Well, then why the hell are you bothering me? Did you call me up to try to piss me off? Why don't you call Dr. Jenkins?"

"I tried. His line has been busy all morning. Simon said it would be good idea to get the boy in sooner, and that you would want to know the boy had showed up anyway."

Wright softly set down the receiver on the desk's green felt blotter. Faintly, he could hear Sophia Blackstone's voice rising and falling. He took a deep breath, picked up the receiver again and rasped the mouth piece over the rough surface of the blotter, then put it to his ear.

"What's going on? Are you there, Sheriff? Damn, harpy-haunted phone system!"

"I'm back on, Ms. Blackstone," Wright said, feeling his anger lift. "We must have lost connection there for a moment."

"Damn phone system," she repeated, but her tone had changed a little. "You coming out or not?"

"All right, all right. I'll be out as soon as I can get some gasoline for my Blazer."

"That's real right kind of you, Sheriff," she said, turning on her Aunt Jemima voice again. Wright knew she had a college education. And she knew he knew. It was another barb. God, he hated that kind of attitude from anybody, black or white or purple. "Now, I'm going to hang up like a good ol' gal. Don't you let it get you mad."

The dainty click that followed was somehow more infuriating than Doc Jenkins' obstinate slam. Before he hung up, he heard a faint snicker. Another eavesdropper.

"Typical. Just typical," he said to himself.

The fifty-gallon drum holding the department's gasoline ration had been empty for days, and the Army Reserve tank truck was more than a week late. The damn Blazer's hog V-8 sucked up gas as if the entire world were one big inexhaustible oil field. He had the discretionary power to increase the sheriff department's share of the gasoline ration, and he'd considered doing just that. But political foresight told him he'd be better off in the long run conserving his existing share. He didn't need to cut any of the farmers short. Each and every one of them showed up for every election. Also, if a food shortage developed, whether due to lack of production or hoarding, the farmers could always blame it on lack of fuel and point at him.

It took him longer than he expected to find someone with gasoline to spare. Three people turned him down, pleading that their own tanks were dry. Finally, Frank Kennedy, editor of the Creedance Sentinel, relinquished a nearly full five-gallon can only after Wright promised to keep him informed of May Tyre's condition. Wright had been lucky; just that morning Doc Jenkins had kicked Kennedy's ass out of the clinic when he'd tried to sneak in to see May for his newspaper column.

May was on his mind all the way to the Jacobsen mansion. He wondered what could have happened in the three days since she'd been admitted. What could Jenkins mean by saying that her condition had gotten both better and worse?

The ridge road was as pitted as five miles of poxy face. After he passed the Hale homestead, the road smoothed out and became a nearly virginal road with a modest strip of grass growing in a straight line down the center.

It was startling to see how much the estate had run down in the four or five years since Wright had last visited the Jacobsen mansion. The driveway looked like a battle zone, with more potholes than concrete and some of the potholes big enough to shear a truck tire off a rim. The grounds were being reclaimed by the oak and hickory forest. Seedlings and bramble bushes had made inroads in the golf course-size lawn. The house itself now presented a giant, foreboding gray face. The white clapboard fence had missing boards, and those left were speckled with black dry rot. The windows on the top floor, lacking curtains or blinds, glowered down at him and the Blazer. Uncle Robert had evidently given up trying to keep the family estate in repair. Wright wondered if the neglect was due to the aches and pains that came with age, or something else, perhaps the increasing boozing.

Sophia Blackstone stepped out on the porch as he parked the Blazer next to Uncle Robert's green Range Rover. He waved and she waved back. Friendly enough, but he'd been burned before, and it was hard not to read other motives into the wave.

Here's this house. Check your testicles in at the door before you come in.

"Hello," he called.

She turned and went back into the house without a word.

What was he to do? Follow? He took off his hat and scratched his head. He had the uncanny feeling he should be careful with his thoughts as well as words around Sophia Blackstone if he was to get any cooperation from her. He felt like a dumb yokel around her. Maybe he was.

Sophia Blackstone opened the screen door and stuck out her head. "Well, are you coming in or not?" she said, then pulled her head back in and let the screen door slap shut. He put his hat back on and made his way up the creaky porch steps. Inside, he found her waiting for him. She looked him over, head to foot, and her expression said she found his appearance short of adequate.

"The boy is in here," she said, heading down a hardwood paneled hallway.

He followed, conscious of the house's dusty, unfamiliar scent. The hallway opened into a large living room complete with chandelier, where he found Bryan Douglas sitting up on the couch with a frayed patchwork quilt draped around his shoulders. His face looked as gray as the old house. Uncle Robert was nowhere in sight.

"You told me he was unconscious."

"He woke up right as you drove up," she said.

"How are you feeling?" he asked.

Bryan nodded weakly. "I'm okay," he said.

"You don't look okay. You look like shit. What happened to you?"

Bryan rubbed his face with both hands, then brushed the mop of dark hair off his forehead. "I'm not sure I can explain. An angel picked me up and flew me to the crashed saucer, and something happened there that scared me – scared me so bad that I thought my heart was going to explode. Next thing I knew I was lost in the woods. I found my way here. That's all I remember."

"What was it that scared you?" Uncle Robert said making Wright jump. He hadn't noticed the old man coming into the room.

"That's the weird part. I remember what the angel showed me. Most of it is impossible to describe. And I can picture it now in my mind, and none of it seems all that frightening, just alien to the extreme. Maybe threatening at times. But when it was happening, I was so scared I wished I would die so I wouldn't be frightened anymore."

"So that's where you've been for the last three days, in the angel's saucer?" Wright asked.

"Three days? No, not three days. Hours maybe, but it couldn't be days. We went into the saucer at dusk. I passed out, yeah, but I'm sure we were inside only minutes. But when the angel dropped me off in the woods it was late morning. So I guess it would be overnight, but not days. I spent hours finding my way out of the woods to here."

"You went into the saucer on Monday, the day of the incident between you and Uncle Robert?"

"That's right. It took me all day to find an angel. When I did, she was sitting on the stoop of the old church."

"Well, today is Thursday."

Bryan shook his head. "It seemed like only a few minutes," he mumbled.

"You had nothing to eat or drink all that time?" Sophia asked.

"No, Mrs. Jacobsen."

Wright expected her to correct the boy about her name as she had Wright over the phone. Instead, she said, "Then I'll get you some soup, sweetheart. That's mostly what's wrong with you, you're starving and dehydrated."

"Thank you. I'm not hungry, but I'd like something to drink, some coffee maybe."

"You'll eat, young man, and you'll drink water, not coffee. Besides, we don't have any coffee in this house." She turned and left. The sound of her shoes on the hardwood floors echoed in the big house.

"She means well. She's been unusually high-strung this year. Female problems. *The Change*, you know." Uncle Robert said.

Bryan didn't look as if he understood what *The Change* meant, but was probably too polite to ask. "I'm sorry I beaned you in the park," he said.

Uncle Robert looked embarrassed. "That's all right. I half-remember what happened, and I guess I had it coming." He sat down on the other end of the couch from the young man. Wright took the big easy chair and relaxed a little now that he wasn't under scrutiny from Uncle Robert's wife.

"What was it like?" Uncle Robert asked Bryan.

"What do you mean?"

"The inside of the saucer – what was it like inside the saucer?"

"Not like anything I expected. I guess I thought it would be like the inside of an airplane, or like an office building, with lots of corridors and plumbing. But it seemed to be almost another world inside. There was a weird-color desert with mountains in the distance."

"How curious," Uncle Robert said.

"How many angels were inside?" Wright asked.

"Only the one that carried me in, as far as I could see; but there was something else."

Wright listened as the boy gave a disjointed account about a cloud of multicolored leaves that somehow communicated with his angel guide. No less unbelievable was how the angel guide turned from a female into an angry young male angel, then morphed into some in-between sex. As Bryan talked, Sophia came back with two large steaming mugs of soup. She gave one to Douglas, then surprised Wright by offering him the second.

"You're looking kind of pale, too," she said.

He took the soup cautiously. It smelled spicy and delicious.

"Go ahead. Taste it. It isn't poisoned. The vegetables are fresh from my garden."

He dunked in his spoon and came out with a green bean and a carrot. He blew on it to cool it and took a sip. He hadn't had any fresh vegetables since the Fall.

"So how is it?" she asked.

"As delicious as it smells. Very kind of you, Ms. Blackstone."

"Call it a peace offering." She perched on the arm of the couch near Uncle Robert.

For a second the couple seemed the picture of a happy marriage. He sensed the closeness of two people who have been together so long that even the space between them said something warm. Modern couples hardly were so close. They always seemed anxious to go their separate ways. For a second, Wright had a color-blind moment: He didn't see Uncle Robert and Sophia as an interracial couple, but as personalities that were in some ways complementary, some ways conflicting. *Opposites attract; then they drive each other crazy.*

He encouraged the brief moment of not just tolerance but acceptance, trying to maintain it. There seemed to be a trick to the technique, like juggling. He listened to the Douglas boy noisily slurping down his soup. Already the color was coming back to his cheeks. Sophia watched him eat, obviously pleased. When the young man was finished, she took his cup and patted his hand like a doting mother.

"I'll get you another," she said and headed for the kitchen.

"I think we should still get Doc Jenkins to take a look at you," Wright said.

"I don't know if I need to. Mrs. Jacobsen's soup is fixing me up."

"I still think it will be a good idea," he said. "Besides, we'll have a chance to talk on the way. I have to go by the hospital anyway – to get the Doc's report on Laura's friend, May."

"Do you think Laura will be there?"

Uncle Robert smiled and shook his head.

"Might be. We'll drop by Bouchers for coffee if the Doc gives you a clean bill of health."

"Where are you going?" It was Sophia, back with the soup.

"The sheriff's going to run Bryan here to the clinic so the doc can look him over. Why don't you put that soup in something he can take with him?" Uncle Robert said.

She frowned. "That old quack can wait a minute longer. Let the boy finish eating in a civilized manner."

Uncle Robert started to say something, but Sophia interrupted. "This isn't a fast-food joint," she said.

Uncle Robert sighed and looked undecided, then asked to come along on the ride to the clinic. Wright saw no reason to refuse him.

When Sophia finally released Bryan to go to the clinic, the old man rode in the back seat of the Blazer on the way back to town. He remained quiet, his arms crossed. Wright tried to make conversation, but the Uncle Robert was oddly reticent, preferring to stare moodily out the window into the woods.

The college boy wasn't much company either, answering all of Wright's questions with a drowsy "yes" or "no." By the time Wright pulled into the clinic's parking lot, the college boy was sound asleep, his head resting against the window.

"I hope he hasn't slipped back into his coma," Uncle Robert said.

Wright worried about this too, for the boy slept so soundly that shaking wouldn't rouse him. A couple of light slaps brought him partially out of it, and he walked to the admittance doors with Uncle Robert and Wright each holding onto an elbow.

Jenkins was sitting at the nurse's station, smoking a hand-rolled cigarette. Wright recognized the smell of the tobacco – Prince Albert. His father had smoked it in his pipe. It used to come in a tin. An old joke from grammar school came back to him: "Do you have Prince Albert in a can? Well, let him out."

"Better be careful, Doc," he said. 'I know of some people in town who would kill for a cigarette." He was only half-joking.

Jenkins gave him a sour smile. "What's wrong with the boy?" he said.

"From what we can gather, he spent three days in the angel saucer without food or water."

"Put him in the room to your left. Watch the floor. It's wet. Maurice just cleaned it up." The doctor followed them in, then ran both men out after they had put Bryan on the bed. "Wait outside. Don't go away. I want to show you something."

Wright took a seat in one of the chrome chairs along the wall. Uncle Robert paced the room, occasionally mumbling.

While they were waiting the janitor wheeled his mop bucket out of another room. He smiled at Uncle Robert, who nodded and turned away, obviously disturbed by the janitor's presence.

There was an awkward silence. "How have you been, Maurice?" Uncle Robert finally said, looking over his shoulder at the young man.

"I've been real good, Uncle."

Maurice, with his pasty, soft, out-of-focus face, didn't look well at all to Wright but then he never had. He called Simon "Uncle Robert" as everyone did, but the young man was actually was his nephew.

"You've been happy?" Uncle Robert asked.

Maurice looked up at the ceiling and rolled his eyes. Wright could hear the steady throb of the hospital's electric generator. Uncle Robert stopped pacing and stared out a window, his back to his nephew. Wright studied Maurice while the mentally challenged man struggled with his own inner dialogue, his mouth moving silently. He could make out much of the Jacobsen heritage in the chin and around the mouth, even the eyes. His face was a fuzzy, male version of Laura's.

"I don't like sitting around home all the time with no television," Maurice finally said, then wheeled his mop bucket out of the room.

Jenkins came back out. "Well, it would be great to be able to run some blood tests, but since that's out of the question, my educated guess will have to do. I'd say the boy – what's his name?"

Wright told him.

"Well, I'd say Mr. Bryan Douglas is suffering from simple exhaustion and dehydration as you suggested. He needs fluids and about a day's sleep, and he should be all right. Does he have any relatives around here? Anybody who will take care of him for a while?"

"No, the best we can gather is that his grandfather was on vacation when the Fall came."

Jenkins grunted. "That's too bad. Hell, wasn't the young man seeing your niece, Laura, Uncle Robert?"

"I think he would be better off here," Uncle Robert said. From the other room came the sound of Maurice banging his mop bucket into something. The old man cringed at the sound.

"Well, I haven't room for him. I need every bed I've got for really sick people. It's only a fluke that I've got two open rooms right now. They could be in demand before the day is over."

Uncle Robert reached a decision. "I'll take him back to my house, if the sheriff will haul him. Sophia likes to take care of him; he's another stray to her."

"Good enough," Jenkins said.

"How's May?" Wright pressed.

Jenkins gave Uncle Robert a gritty hard stare, trying to see into him. "You have to keep this quiet, Jacobsen," he said.

Uncle Robert nodded.

"Sheriff, I didn't tell you this the night you brought her in. I was afraid it would seem too crazy. Hell, it seemed crazy to me when I thought it. First I thought she had just given birth. Everything, the condition of her cervix, and so on. All the signs. When a woman is as petite as May, and it's her first time, it doesn't take a very large baby to cause tearing along the perineum. But when I looked at the tear the next day, it looked all wrong for that. I've been a country doctor for two score and ten years, and I've seen every type of unaided delivery you can think of."

"That's crazy anyway, Doc. May's a small woman, like you said, and I see her every day at Bouchers. She hasn't shown a hint of being pregnant."

"You're right," Jenkins said. "But you know what the first thing she asked for when she came out of the coma? Well, she said, 'Where's my baby?' Just like that. 'Where's my baby?' She was sure she had given birth, and nothing we could say could convince her otherwise. But you know what? Just as strange, she seemed relieved that the baby wasn't around, as if she were frightened of it. Then she went into some delirium bullcrap about Elvis being the father.

"Now the Elvis delusion is a more common occurrence in these parts than you might think. We get that kind of stuff all the time when women go under anesthesia. But not wanting the baby, being actually frightened of it, that's something else again. Anyway, all that happened last night. This morning she was quiet again, so I thought we were back to square one. But when it was time to change her dressings, I got quite a shock. Come with me, I'll show you."

He led them down a hallway to one of the hospital rooms. Inside they found May, apparently asleep, with June sitting at her bedside. The older woman was strangely silent, her lips pursed anxiously.

"June, I want you to check vitals on the patient in room 103."

She nodded and left.

"Now, I'm violating all sorts of oaths and codes of professional ethics, but she's sleeping and I want you to see this for yourself. I don't think you'd believe me otherwise."

Jenkins pulled down the sheets. May lay curled up in the fetal position and didn't resist as Jenkins turned her over onto her back and gently straightened her legs. She moaned incoherently but did not wake. Without ceremony, Jenkins unbuttoned her cotton robe and opened it. She now lay naked except for a white gauze bandage covering her sex and the sleeves of the robe that covered her shoulders. Jenkins slapped a white latex glove on one hand and in a second had stripped off the bandage . May had been shaven clean.

Wright felt embarrassed for May. Not that he hadn't seen her naked before. He had, the night he found her ranting and lying in a broad smear of her own blood, and that had been bad, her being a victim of some faceless assailant. Or before that, how often he had imagined her naked and moving under him. But this was worse, a crime somehow on his part, for before he had been her rescuer and now he was a party, however passive, to the assault on her dignity.

Jenkins slipped his gloved hand between her legs and spread them wider apart. "You will have to come closer to see this," he said. "It's not very large, but it's distinctive."

Despite his feelings for May, Wright nearly laughed at Jenkins' unconscious dirty joke. But as he leaned forward for a look-see, laughter became something that belonged to another world.

* * *

13.

The Plains of Heaven

Freezing wind whipped at Bryan's clothes and stung his face. He stood on a small barren mesa beside a blue-skinned entity of near-infinite power. Below, a mile or more, the world's minions battled upon an endless, seamless plain. Trails of dust marked the headlong collision of great swarms of humanity and angels. The swarms met, merged in frenzied fighting, and re-formed in a single mass. The new unity milled about, motionless for a brief moment, only to break apart into a new schism. Once broken up into new sects, the groups clashed again.

Bryan could neither hear nor see the details of any one individual's fate, but he intuited the plains were filed with countless cries of misery and pain, punctuated with occasional shouts of triumph. Tragedy reigned, consuming dreams, happiness and hope.

"And it is Good," the blue god said.

"No, it is terrible." Though terrified of the god, Bryan chanced a sideways glance at its face. The god loomed over Bryan, his blue head scraping the clouds, and yet Bryan, with his feet planted on the barren rock, seemed to be looking at him eye-to-eye – or rather, corner-of-eye to corner-of-eye, for he trembled at the thought of looking at the god square on. There was something terribly familiar about the face.

"Surprised you can't look upon My Face without being transformed?" the blue god asked.

Bryan nodded.

"I have suppressed my luminosity for your benefit so you won't be forced to fall to your knees in fear."

Bryan chanced a longer look. Even suppressed, the god's form was painfully bright. No long, white beard or the physical girth of Zeus or Santa Claus – no, the face was beardless and handsome, dark wavy hair, a male face but not burly. He wore a peaked golden crown. No desert god this, yet much stronger, much more serious, and he seemed youngish, a twenty-something god. But though young, he emanated an overwhelming power of self: *I am all that you need to know; I am all that is, all that you can comprehend.*

"This is a dream, isn't it?" he asked the god, asked himself.

"A dream, a projection of My Will," the god said, nodding toward the Armageddon below. Bryan thought to correct him, to explain he suspected the diety of being the dream, of the tragedy below as only a backdrop, but the god continued before he could speak. "I can no more stop it than you can stop thinking."

Angered by the god's presumption, Bryan willed the wind to stop. The air warmed and immediately became gentle. "There, I did it. Does that mean I'm a god, too?"

"What makes you think you stilled the wind? Or even that the inspiration to do so originated in your mind? You too are a projection of the war of my two natures."

"I don't believe that. If I haven't any will, I wouldn't exist."

The corners of the entity's eyes hardened. "You don't believe in Me, either, do you, my son, my father?"

A god who spoke in riddles?

Bryan considered his answer carefully. To respond *No* would be tantamount to mutiny in the ranks. "Since I am only a projection of your dreams, if I don't believe in You, God – not with a capital Y or G, anyway – then it's because you doubt yourself. Obviously, you're not the top dog. You pretend to be or you wouldn't be so insecure." As he finished his hypothesis, he was overcome by terror. He had tried to be tactful, but logic had carried him dangerously close to dissension. Heresy lay in this direction, and the punishment for heresy was eternal damnation, an eternity in Hell. Looking down on the senseless carnage below, he realized he might already be in Hell.

He turned away to look back upon the battle below. As he watched a speck detached itself from the masses and grew larger as it flew across the expanse. In an eye-blink it closed the distance, revealing itself to be an angel.

The angel landed before Bryan and the god.

"A message, my Lord," the angel said.

"Speak."

"In front of him, the reflection?" The angel nodded at Bryan. He was the same angel who had taken him to the saucer. Or rather, he was the male incarnation of the angel Bryan had met by the old church.

"Speak freely. This one won't be going back. How goes the battle?" the god said without moving his mouth.

Not going back? "Of course this is a dream," Bryan said to reassure himself.

"The battle goes badly, Lord. This vantage point will soon be overwhelmed by the opposition. You should now escape to a lower sphere as planned. Maybe one of flesh and blood – like where this one lives."

The angel meant Earth, Bryan realized.

As the angel finished speaking, a man and a woman, both of heroic stature, sprang over the edge of the precipice. With great crude wooden cudgels in hand, they raced toward the blue god and his angel, screaming murderously. The angel turned and grabbed the man by the neck. The man's scream turned to a choked gargle, and he brought back his great club to strike. But before he could act, the angel twisted off the man's head with a flick of the wrist. The angel dropped the headless body to the ground but held on to the head, which now gaped stone-eyed at eternity.

Shocked at the angel's speed and strength, the woman paused as if to retreat. But she had nowhere to retreat to, and now had to face a preternatural power alone. Her face grew hard with resolve, and she renewed her charge, bringing up her club to strike as her colleague had done.

Like a pitcher on the mound, the angel wound up and threw the bloody head at her, overhand like a hardball pitch. The grisly missile caught the woman in the forehead with a heavy thud. She fell to the ground, unconscious. Without ceremony, the angel picked up the two bodies and carried them, one in each hand, and threw them over the edge of the precipice. As he walked back, he stumbled over the bodiless head.

Angrily, he drop-kicked it after its owner. The ground was splashed with blood, but none showed on the angel's robes. The creature wore a look of smug satisfaction.

"Merely an advance party, my Lord, but multitudes will surely follow."

"Very well," the god's voice was heavy with anger. "We will retreat and pull our beginnings in after us."

"What about this human?"

"We would take him with us to next plane of existence, but I think he would die in your light," God said. Without warning, the blue god turned and showed Bryan His other face, the face that had been talking to the angel.

It was horrible to behold. God looked to the future and the past at the same time. God was both male and female. God was at once the ultimate good and the utmost evil, a completely alien god and yet an all-to-human one too. A god of a thousand eyes. The eyes blinked in unison. It was his own face, his own eyes, that Bryan stared into, a mirror distorted by a million dimensions.

Shattered, he closed his eyes to the vision, but the light of the thousand eyes shone through his eyelids. He brought up his arm, but the horrible vision penetrated flesh and bone like X-rays.

Bryan felt himself being torn apart by the sight. He tried to scream but couldn't, and prayed the dream would come to an end.

Immediately, he woke to Laura's face. She was straddling him, her hands on his shoulders, roughly shaking him. His face stung.

"You're going to stay with me this time, right?" she asked.

He mumbled something. He could not remember ever before being so tired. It was as though someone had pulled the backbone right out of him. He felt like a sagging bag of flesh and gas, a waste of skin.

Laura withdrew her hand and sat up bed. The sheet fell away from her shoulders. She was naked except for panties.

"I'm sorry I slapped you so hard," she said, "but you were so agitated – I thought you might be having a seizure in your sleep."

"What are you doing here?" he said, then wondered where *here* was. What was he doing here? He was lying on his back in a king-sized bed. Above, perhaps a full ten feet, the room's ceiling was covered in a hand-painted mural. The predominant colors were pink and baby blue. Off-center, to the right of the light fixture, a pair of lovers were entangled in an acrobatic tryst. Around them, chubby Raphaelite cherubs hovered, laughing, pointing fingers. *Was it this what had inspired his dream or something else, something all too real?* His mind returned to the angel saucer, to what he'd seen there, but found only an emptiness that sucked away all his strength. He grabbed the bedpost and tried to pull himself up, but fell back, hooked by the image. He surprised himself by letting out a sound that was half-scream, half-moan.

He came to again, this time to Laura standing over him in bed, balancing on one foot. She was removing her panties.

"Angels again?" she asked.

He nodded. "Where am I?" he managed to ask.

"You – we're at my uncle's house – Uncle Robert's."

"How did I get here? Never mind, I remember now. I found my way here after being lost in the woods. No, wait a minute, I thought I left with the sheriff and your uncle?"

"You did, but you passed out on the way. The doctor prescribed bed rest and someone to look after you. Somehow I got elected to the graveyard shift."

"Graveyard?"

"Chillax. It's just an expression. It's early morning. I've been here since midnight. It was chilly, and you were shaking, so I stripped down and got in under the comforter to hold you. To settle you and to get warm."

Her panties caught on her toes and she lost her balance, falling toward him. He caught her by the waist and pulled her until she lay on top of him. She put a hand on either side of his head and rested all her weight on him. He ran his hands over her back, along the sides of her arms. She had goose bumps.

"Then you woke me up screaming a few minutes ago." She brushed back a long strand of black hair that dangled in his face. She rolled off him but left a leg draped over his stomach. "You worry me, *mi amigo loco*," she said. "I thought you were over your angel fright. I thought I had fucked the fear right out you."

"Something else happened," he said. "I was taken . . ." But his voice broke before he could explain.

"There, there," she said. "Maybe we shouldn't talk about angels for a while."

He started to say that it was hard not thinking about angels with an infestation of cherubs hanging over his head, but he couldn't get the words out. He concentrated on her face instead.

The beginnings of dark circles were showing under her eyes and her hair was wild and tangled, but as always, she displayed a mysterious calm, a hint of an inner completeness that made him want her despite his exhaustion. He ran a hand over her breasts, conscious of the roughness of his callused palm in contrast to the cinnamon smoothness of her skin. She trembled a bit under his touch. His other hand sought out the juncture of her legs.

"Whoa, boy," she said. "I don't think you're up to it right now."

She withdrew her hand and pulled her leg off him so a little space came between them.

"Quite a room, isn't it?" she said, changing the subject.

"It's kind of hard not to think about angels in here."

"It was my grandmother's special room. One summer, Grandmother commissioned Sophia – she was a starving artist in residence at Stephens College – to paint the mural. It's all done in fresco, painted right into wet lime plaster, like Michelangelo's Sistine Chapel.

"Grandmother died the next winter, but Sophia stayed on with Uncle Robert. Anyway, rumor has it that Grandmother entertained young lovers of both sexes here. But I don't think so, not her. Not out of propriety, mind you. She did anything she wanted to. There was enough of the family fortune left for her to indulge most of her desires. But I don't think she was ever too interested in sex even when she was younger, and during the last ten years of her life, her rheumatoid arthritis was too advanced to let her to engage in the calisthenics the local myths have her doing. I imagine her lying on her back, staring up at those silly little cherubs, laughing about the absurdity of sex. You know Keats?"

He shook his head.

"He wrote something – I can't remember all of it – but it ended with *and love has pitched its mansion in the house of excrement.*" Whenever I'm in this room, I think of that poem. I should look it up in Uncle

Robert's library. He has a great library, you know." She seemed embarrassed about something, rambling a bit, not like herself at all.

"No, I didn't know," he said.

She took control of herself and said, "I bet Sophia put you in here just to bug me. After Grandmother died, and she and Uncle Robert had settled down into whatever relationship they have – I wouldn't exactly call it domestic bliss – and Sophia went right on painting murals throughout the house. She spent years on the one in the dining room. You'll see it today. Funny, I feel closer to her than to any of my biological family, but she and I hardly speak."

He took a deep breath and raised himself on his elbows. This time the room didn't reel, and he felt his strength returning. "What's wrong with me?" he asked her.

"Health-wise? I told you, didn't I? Exhaustion. And right now, probably low blood sugar."

"I mean, what's wrong with you and me? I know I'm not a great lover, but I thought we did all right together," he said.

"It's not because you're sexually inadequate, if that's what you're wondering," she said.

"Then what? Am I too strange?"

She laughed and tossed another rebellious strand of hair over her shoulder. "Not that, either. You're exceedingly normal. You grew up in the suburbs. I doubt your family has a history of full-blown psychosis or that your mother or your father spent any time in mental hospitals. You went to a midwestern university and pledged a fraternity, like thousands of others."

"Pretty close, except I had no use for the Greek life," he said. "So I'm too normal? Too sane for your tastes?"

"No, there's nothing wrong with being normal. I could probably use a little more normal in my life."

"Then what is it?"

She looked away for a moment, and when she looked back her eyes were wet. "You hardly know me. You want us to be some kind of item again, don't you? Well, you should know more about my family history. You don't know what you're getting into. In some families, curly hair is dominant trait. In mine, its schizophrenia." She looked away from him.

"Besides, I asked you to leave because I thought you wanted to but were just too much the coward to dump me."

"That wasn't it," he said. "I just felt I was, you know, a novice when it came to sex. You were into all those positions. I figured you'd had a lot better lovers than me; bigger fish to fry."

"Oh, that," she said, laughing. "I learned that from one of Uncle Robert's books: an 1883 first edition of Sir Richard Burton's translation of the Kama Sutra. There was also a book about taking sex beyond the physical and into realm of spiritual union. I took it back to school with me and made notes and drew anatomy and physiology doodles. I probably defaced a book that was worth thousands."

She looked away again. "I just wanted someone who was open to trying something different. I thought that was you, but you froze up on me."

A moment of silence fell between them, an emotional space that could not be filled with words.

"Teach me," he finally said, and pulled her toward him. Working in the woods had made him strong; the forcefulness of the move surprised them both.

"My mechanic," she said.

"More like your woodsman," he said, but didn't want to interrupt the moment with an explanation.

She ran a hand up his arm, tracing scratches on his biceps from green briar vines.

"So, got wood?" she said, eyes laughing.

He nodded.

"Then I'll nail you, woodsman," she said.

"Is that a threat?

"No, a promise." She pushed him back. "Sit on your knees, babe, with your back to the headboard."

He did, and she slid across the sheets in front of him.

"No, spread your knees."

She lifted a leg and put a heel on his shoulder. She stretched her other leg out flat on the bed. Grabbing his thighs, she pulled herself to him. The angle of her pelvis was such that he slid into her naturally. He supported himself with one arm outstretched on the bed beside her head.

The other hand found the back of the thigh of her raised leg.

"Now, relax. I haven't done this before with anyone. It's a position called 'driving the nail.'" She raised her leg higher and put the heel against his forehead. He could feel the tendons stretch in the back of her thigh. Her heel pushed his head back and made it impossible for him to lean forward and kiss her, but it also caused her vagina to tighten around him.

"Your head is the *head* of nail," she said breathlessly. "The nail is – well you know what."

He thrust quick and hard, and her heel slipped off his forehead.

"Slow down," she ordered, and put her heel back on his forehead, tightening again. "We can't do this position fast and furiously. I can only stretch so far. Push too hard and you'll split me like a wishbone."

She used her heel to playfully push back his head until it bumped the bedstead, and laughed again. Without thinking, he took his hand off the back of her thigh, grabbed her slender ankle and kissed the sole of her foot.

"If you could see the ceiling" she said, "you'd see we look a lot like one of the tangled, angry couples in the mural."

He didn't want to take his eyes off her, but he wondered if the cherubs were looking down, watching them instead of the fresco lovers.

"It's got to be slow and mindful. There. Yes, there." Her words were punctuated by short gasps. "Pull back a little. Oh god! It's just like they said in the book." She took three short gasps. "You pressed against my G-spot, my goddess spot."

The G-spot was supposed to be a myth, but he wasn't going to argue with her, as he needed to delay his own orgasm.

Another thing they practiced together that year in Columbia came back to him: the trick she taught him about how to tighten the pubococcygeal muscles, what she called "*those love muscles.*" It was the triangle-shaped muscle area between the scrotum and anus, the same muscles used to stop peeing in mid-stream, only now the effect was to draw his testicle up a bit and block the ejaculation. He had resisted the instruction then, thinking it came secondhand from another of her lovers. Now that he knew she'd learned it from some ancient, dusty sex manual, he was more open to the idea. He tightened the muscles and was rewarded with a continuous pressure of pleasure instead of a single rush. Some instinct called for him to just let go, but he resisted. No way did he want this feeling to end too soon.

She pushed herself forward, but not so far that she was fully impaled on him. He was conscious of the glans of his penis pressing against a little rough spot on the inside wall of her vagina. *Was that the illusive G-spot?*

Her eyelids fluttered. Hyper-tensioning his love muscles as much as he could, he worked the head of his penis slowly across the spot. But if he tried to thrust too far, she pushed his head back with her heel. He should be in control in this position, but it was really the other way around. She began relaxing and contracting her vagina, using, he supposed, the female counterpart of the same muscles he was using to delay orgasm. Her breath came now entirely in short gasps, and his breathing fell in step with hers. Hard, immediate pushes of breath came from the bottom of his lungs, first in counterpoint with her gasps, then in synchronization with them. A feeling of bliss overcame him. He closed his eyes, and the distinction of where he ended and she began blurred. This was not just physical but an almost spiritual experience, as if they were one person, lost in time, the world fading.

He was still conscious of the angel's vision of betrayal whispering in his left ear, the fat little cherubs above his head pointing their accusing fingers, the voices of people talking downstairs, but it all those things moved away to disappear in a dark well.

He opened his eyes. Her face gleamed with sweat, and beads of his own perspiration dripped from his forehead to sting his eyes. He desperately wanted to kiss her on her lips but was afraid he might break her in half – might break them both – doing so.

She moved her hips gently while continuing to tighten her vaginal muscles, gripping him, then relaxing, gripping.

They finished together, both breathless now. He tried to suppress a guttural growl, but it sounded from his throat anyway, like that of a tired dog. She let out a long sigh.

Exhausted and energized at the same time, he pulled out and leaned back on his hands. His thighs ached, probably had for some time, but he hadn't noticed until now.

Laura lay with her legs on either side of his thighs, occasionally rubbing the sides of his leg with the foot that had been against his forehead. She had her eyes closed, and her hips still gyrated ever so slightly. He leaned forward again and placed a hand on her stomach, just below her belly button. The muscles under the skin were quivering.

"Oh! Gee! Another one," she cried out. "That's four or five, now."

He realized she was still having orgasms.

"Gee," he said. "Gee whiz! I guess that's why the call it the G-spot."

It was a lame joke, he knew. Something about it being called the G-spot after a Herr Graphicberg or some such doctor.

The voices from below became louder, and hard heels sounded on the stairwell.

"Crap!" Laura said and hopped out of bed. She fell hard on her butt.

"I'm such a greedy little slut," she said.

Before he could tell her she was no such thing, she explained as she pulled on her jeans, "I had so many orgasms, I'm weak in the knees; I don't think I could walk across the room."

He wondered if she was trying to boost his ego or if this was a common occurrence for her, but before he could ask, she moved to a chair beside the bed and hurriedly pulled a blue blouse over her head.

"Now, hurry up," she said, "and get under the covers before Sophia and Uncle Robert come in. I'm supposed to be nursing you back to health, not fucking you back to health. Aunt Sophia will have my head on a platter."

He pulled the comforter up to his neck, and Laura settled in the bedside chair. Not a moment too soon; the door opened and Sophia charged in, a vision of cultural contradictions. She had changed from her jeans and smock into red flowery miniskirt and a white Betty Crocker apron with tomato sauce stains. Her forehead and legs glistened with a light sheen of sweat. She also wore red stiletto high heels flecked with silver sequins. Uncle Robert trailed in after her wearing a whipped-puppy look.

"Girl, tell me something," Laura's aunt said. "I can't figure why somebody as smart as your uncle has to get himself wall-eyed drunk on a regular basis."

Laura shrugged. "Ask the genius himself."

Sophia turned on Uncle Robert. She had terrific legs for a middle-age woman, Bryan thought, Tina Turner quality. "You hear that, Simon? Your niece wants to know too. You're killing millions of brain cells every time, you told me so yourself. And honey, let me tell you, that's all you got, 'cause you ain't much in the stud department."

He looked at her out the corner of his eye. "Little deaths," he said finally.

"Little deaths? What the hell does that mean?"

"You've got to die before you can be reborn. Getting drunk is like dying a short death."

"Well, honey, what do you need to be reborn for?"

"I didn't expect you to understand. You're a woman."

"You got that right."

"You can make new life anytime you want. All you need is some sap to donate the sperm. You are the future. New lives are departures from everything that was. Rebirth. Neither I nor any man alive can do that, intellectual or idiot. So we have to make ceremonies and get drunk to die so we can come back afresh as a substitute. It's that simple."

"I swear, Uncle Robert, I'll tell you something. You are more full of bull crap than any man I know."

"I was trying to sound cool."

"For one thing, we don't give ourselves a new life."

"I never said you did. That would be Life with a capital ell. I don't really understand why you're getting all huffy on me. I was trying to say women are a step up on the evolutionary tree from men and as a reward you try to tear me a new one!"

"Well, I tell you what, old man, if you wanted to make a baby, why didn't you tell me?" A sly look passed over her features. "Or better yet, show me."

Uncle Robert's face reddened but he didn't reply.

"This young man here –" She nodded Bryan's way "– is looking fit now. We will transplant him and Laura into another room, and you can demonstrate your philosophy." She slapped her flat tummy. "All the plumbing is in working order. I'm years away from losing my works, no matter what you've been telling folks. I guarantee you that."

Uncle Robert's face reddened more, and he turned on his heel and strode out. "Women!" he said as he shut the door behind him.

"That's it, old man. Run. That's why you really drink, isn't it? Because you're afraid of being a man." When no counterpoint came from the hall, she turned to Bryan and Laura.

"I know I sound like a cruel harpy, but if I don't shake him up now and then, he'll get depressed and start drinking again. It's better he's angry than morbid."

"I still think you might ease up on him about the manhood issue, auntie," Laura said. "He is nearly sixty, you know."

"Maybe, sweetie," Sophia said. Then to Bryan. "Your color is back – you're pratically flushed." She winked at him. "So I think you must be feeling better, son."

"He's still kind of weak, Aunt Sophia," Laura said. "I'm feeling kind of weak-kneed myself." She stole a conspiratorial glance at Bryan. "Could I raid your cupboard and get us both something to eat?"

"Better than that, child. If he can get downstairs, I've got a real he-man's breakfast laid out in the sun room. Smoked ham, scrambled eggs, sweet potato pie. After that, your uncle is going to have his conference. Bryan here is supposed to sit in on that too." She gave Bryan a wink. "If he's still got the energy after all he's been through."

"I'll help him come down."

"I'll bet you will, sweetheart," Sophia said.

"Conference?" Bryan asked. "What conference?"

Sophia smiled knowingly at Laura. "You don't know it, young man, but you're an angel expert."

"And a witness at the first meeting of the Citizens of Creedance Conference on the Angel Invasion," Laura said.

"An impressive title," he said.

"Uncle Robert has always secretly aspired to greater and grander things."

"Greater and grander B.S. is more like it," Sophia said.

As promised, Sophia delivered a huge breakfast. She even served real, unadulterated coffee, complete with powdered creamer. Uncle Robert, it seemed, was a survivalist of long standing and had kept the basement of the old house stocked with enough food to last for months.

"Don't speak a word of it," Sophia had warned him, "or we'll have to sleep with guns under our pillows."

Dr. Jenkins, mumbling curses under his breath, and Sheriff Wright showed up late.

Wright was strangely cowed in the presence of Sophia.

In her high heels, she towered over him.

Sophia made them fill plates and then ran them out of the kitchen to the large dining room.

Seated at the huge mahogany table, with Laura fidgeting impatiently next to him, Bryan felt himself part of a small elite group. The local intelligentsia. Evidently, the entire *Conference on the Angel Invasion* consisted of Uncle Robert, Sophia, Laura, Sheriff Wright, Dr. Jenkins, and himself. Where he fit into all this was hard to say, but he was glad to have the chance to talk with Laura.

As Uncle Robert called the meeting to order, Laura nudged him with an elbow and motioned for him to look up at another ceiling-wide mural. A huge, panoramic, old-time harvest scene stretched from corner to corner. Wiry, sunburned farmhands pitched hay, shucked corn, and hauled pumpkins while fat farm wives served huge noontime feasts on trestle tables. In the background, steam-powered machines threshed grain and giant mules strained at their yokes, all under a sky that screamed blue.

Laura whispered. "It took her five years, all on her back on top of a scaffold. Think of Michelangelo reincarnated as a black woman."

Uncle Robert stood at the head of the table with a large book the size of a library dictionary open before him. "I guess we should get right down to the business of discussing the nature of the angels. Once we have a workable hypothesis as to their origins and their powers, then we can postulate their motives."

In his herringbone jacket, Uncle Robert reminded Bryan of an eccentric professor – until the brass buttons of his bib overalls showed. Uncle Robert was like one of those weird hybrid animals of imagination, half-eagle, half-lion, only in his case it might be part-intellectual, part-hayseed, part-lush, and part-who-knew-what. But he was beginnng to readjust his evaluation of the old man.

"Another thing. I propose we dispel with most formalities as long as the group remains small."

"Please, none of that *Robert's Rules of Order* crap," Sophia said. Her high heels made clickety-click sounds as she crossed the hardwood floor to set a tray with a large carafe of coffee and clean cups on the table.

Uncle Robert looked embarrassed, but it was hard to say why. He ought to be used to her by now.

"I want to read you something pertaining to angels," he said, slipping on a pair of reading glasses. "Specifically, the angels who rebelled against Jehovah and were cast down."

He cleared his throat and began:

> And it came to pass when the children of men had multiplied that in those days were born unto them beautiful and comely daughters. And the angels, the children of heaven, saw and lusted after them, and said to one another: 'Come, let us choose wives from among the children of men and beget us children.' And Semjaza, who was their leader, said unto them: 'I fear ye will not indeed agree to do this deed, and I alone shall have to pay the penalty of a great sin.' And they all answered him and said: 'Let us all swear an oath, and all bind ourselves by mutual imprecations not to abandon this plan but to do this thing.' Then sweared they all together and bound themselves by mutual imprecations upon it. And they were in all two hundred; who descended in the days of Jared on the summit of Mount Hermon, and they called it Mount Hermon, because they had sworn and bound themselves by mutual imprecations upon it.
>
> And all the others together with them took unto themselves wives, and each chose for himself one, and they began to go unto them and to defile themselves with them, and they taught them charms and enchantments, and the cutting of roots, and made them acquainted with plants. And they became pregnant, and they bore great giants, whose height was three thousand ells: Who consumed them and devoured mankind. And they began to

sin against birds, and beasts, and reptiles, and fish, and to devour one another's flesh, and drink the blood. They laid accusation against the lawless ones."

"If I had known you had brought us here for Bible study, I would have stayed at the clinic," Doc Jenkins said.

Uncle Robert peered at the doctor over his reading glasses. "You won't find that passage in any King James, though it was written about the same time as many of the books of the contemporary Old Testament. It's from the first book of Enoch, a book labeled pseudepigrapha – that means the author or authors wrote under a pseudonym."

"So it's fiction," Jenkins said, obviously upset, though now Bryan realized for a different reason.

Laura leaned over and whispered in his ear. "Doc Jenkins is a deacon in the Baptist Church, a fundamentalist."

"Not necessarily," Uncle Robert was saying. "No more fiction than many books of the Bible. Under slightly different circumstances, the Book of Enoch might be a companion to Revelations. But by the time Enoch was written, the Talmudic sect had become dominant and decreed that God had spoken His last words through inspired prophets. The only way new generations of prophets could be heard was to write under the name of historical figures. In this case the authors chose Enoch, a patriarch mentioned in Genesis. From a scholarly viewpoint, there is no way to distinguish the book from 'legitimate' readings. In content it resembles Ecclesiastes and Revelations, which were also probably pseudipigraphic Cannons and apocalyptic, but from an earlier time, and therefore adopted by Christianity when it branched off from Judaism."

"We are not dealing with fables here. These angels are real, solid, not some symbol for the will of God," Wright said.

"I agree the angels are real – as real as the six of us in this room," Uncle Robert said. "But before you judge this irrelevant or" – He stabbed at the heavy book with his finger for emphasis – "irreverent, allow me to read you a bit more. The following is a list of names of the fallen angels. It's attributed to the same author, Enoch, who saw and talked to God in the flesh and lived. The following passage is titled, *The Names and Functions of the Fallen Angels and Satans: The Secret Oath.* I'll skip the long roll call, and get right to pertinent names:

And these are the chiefs of their angels and their names, and their chief ones over hundreds and over fifties and over tens. Loaquin (Jeqon) led astray all the children of the holy angels and brought them down to Earth.

Asbeel: this one suggested an evil plan to the children of the holy angels and led them astray so that they corrupted their bodies with the daughters of men.

Penemue: this one showed the sons of men the bitter and the sweet, and taught men the art of writing with ink and paper and through this many have gone astray. For men were not created for this, that they should confirm their faith like this with pen and ink.

And Azazel taught men to make swords, and knives, and shields, and breastplates, and made known to them the metals of the earth and the art of working them, and bracelets, and ornaments, and the use of antimony, and the beautifying of the eyelids, and all kinds of costly stones, and coloring tinctures. And there arose much godlessness, and they committed fornications, and they were led astray, and became corrupt in all their ways. Semjaza taught enchantments, and root-cuttings, Armaros the resolving of enchantments, Baraqijal taught astrology, Kokabel the constellations, Ezeqeel the knowledge of the clouds; Araqiel the signs of the earth, Shamsiel the signs of the sun, and Sariel the course of the moon. And as men perished, they cried, and their cry went up to heaven.

Uncle Robert looked up again over his glasses. "Sheriff, you look like somebody stepped on your grave."

"What is this? Some kind of joke?" The sheriff got up and bullied his way in front of Uncle Robert and grabbed the book.

"Careful with it. It's old," Uncle Robert said. He reached over Wright and him the title page. "See, copyright 1907, R.H. Charles."

"Baraqijal was the name of the dead angel at Lost Lake; Penumae is the one who showed up to collect the body," he said incredulously. "This book looks genuine."

"Of course it's genuine. What the hell do you think, John? That I called you all here to play a childish prank? You may think me a drunk, and you might be right, but you know I've always played straight with you."

"That you have," Wright said, still looking bewildered. "So tell me, Simon. What in God's name does this mean?"

* * *

14.

Exegesis

I don't know what it all means, John," Uncle Robert said. "I have a few guesses as to the nature of the angels, but that's all they are – guesses. I do have more clues though, one supplied as a courtesy by an angel with what I admit were suspect motives."

He looked at Sophia but she turned aside, arms crossed. Bryan guessed a marital skirmish had just been fought. Uncle Robert took a business card from one of the many pockets in his bib overalls and put it neatly on the table. "An angel named Asbeel visited this house a few days ago. He – it – whatever – left a calling card."

Wright picked up the card. "There's a local number here. Have you tried it?"

"Not yet. Our phone line has been going in and out the last few days."

Wright passed the card to Jenkins who looked at it, shrugged and passed it along to Bryan. He found something familiar about the nondescript typeface but could not say what.

Laura took the card from his hand, read it, and said, "Imagine that. Maybe they're all corporate businessmen from Hell."

Bryan laughed in spite of himself, but everyone else remained stone-faced. Laura passed the card back to the head of the table. Wright picked it up.

"I'll keep this as evidence," Wright said. No one seemed to notice or care.

"You may be closer to the truth than you imagine," Uncle Robert said to Laura, without a trace of amusement on his face.

"Oh, come on now, you are not going to suggest these angels are supernatural?" Wright said.

"Or the fallen angels of biblical prophesy?" Jenkins said.

"How about 'in-corporate' businessmen," Laura said with a giggle.

Bryan gave her an encouraging smile, but everyone else ignored her pun.

"If that's what you're leading up to," Jenkins said, "then I'm leaving. I'm not going to sit here and listen to you ridicule the Holy Bible."

"Oh, I'm not debunking the Bible. Maybe for the first time in my life, I'm looking to it for enlightenment," Uncle Robert said.

"But you're not talking of spiritual enlightenment, are you?"

"No, Jenkins, you know me too well for that. What I'm talking about is the nature of the angels, as I told you when we started. If Mother Goose had prophesied the coming of the angels, I'd be reading her now."

"I think what you're warming up to do is premeditated calumny directed against Jesus Christ. Debunking The Law, God, His holiness, and I won't stand for it."

"Oh shit, Jenkins, grow the fuck up!" Uncle Robert said.

Before Jenkins could reply, Wright rapped on the table with his knuckles. "Gentlemen, gentlemen – and ladies," he said, nodding toward Laura and Sophia. "We're supposed to be sharing what we know. I don't think anyone here has a monopoly on the truth about the angels. Doc, why don't you bring everyone up to date on May Tyre?"

Wright's appeal placated the country doctor. He paused and scratched the day's growth of salt-and-pepper beard.

"I'm still not sure I want to be a party to this committee or whatever you call it," Jenkins said. "I showed her to you because all the clinic's Polaroid cameras mysteriously disappeared last week, and all the digital cameras are kaput, of course. Having no way to record the phenomena, I wanted another responsible party to witness it. Uncle Robert just happened to tag along. Now I'm wondering if any of you are to be trusted with such information. I can't for the life of me see what May's condition has to do with the angels."

"I worked with May the evening before she was assaulted," Laura said. "She talked to an angel out on the street at quitting time, one she thought looked like Elvis Presley."

"Was that the one who sat at my table?" Wright asked.

"Yes, it was the same one, I'm sure. May told me she was going to find out the truth about angels. She didn't think they were neuter. She said she got *man vibes* off some of them."

"Oh, come now. I've examined one closely myself. The angels don't have sexual organs," Jenkins said.

"Nevertheless, May was sure. May isn't what you would call intellectually inclined, but she knows about men."

"Inclined for men, is more like it," Jenkins said.

Laura ignored him. "She can read them by the way they walk, how they hold their spoons, and other things . . ." She stumbled over her own words, then blurted out, "And she has an uncanny ability to predict if they're well-hung."

"So you think she met an angel who was as big as a horse, and it tore her up inside?"

"Isn't it a possibility?" Wright asked.

"I don't think so. Once we cleaned her up, the wounds weren't really that severe, some minor tearing of the vaginal wall, that's all. And some scratches on her inner thighs she apparently made herself – things of that nature."

"But you are sure about the nature of what you found later, aren't you?" Wright said.

Jenkins looked at Wright over his spectacles, as if taking his measure. "No, I'm not sure, sheriff. And I am far from being an expert on such things. I don't even know what to call it."

"Then tell us what you found. What you showed Uncle Robert and me. Maybe together we can shed some light on the mystery."

Jenkins brushed a wisp of thinning hair off his forehead, then massaged his temples thoughtfully. "Very well. I suppose it can't do any more harm, but you will all have to promise me that what I tell you won't leave this room."

"No problem. I don't think anyone would believe us without seeing for themselves," Uncle Robert said.

"I want the young people to promise me individually they won't blabber this around."

"I won't tell," Bryan said. "I don't know anyone outside this room, anyway."

Jenkins looked at Laura.

"I'd never do anything to hurt May. She's my friend," Laura said.

"Keep your promise or I'll kick both of your young irreverent butts. I'm not too old, you know," Jenkins said.

He stood and his knee joints cracked audibly. "I'll start at the beginning, when I discovered the abnormality, which I have to confess was the day after we admitted May to the hospital.

"Now, being a doctor I see many things that might cause you all to look upon the human body in a different light. How easily it's corrupted – I could write a book about that topic. But to get to the point, the day after admitting May I was obliged to change her dressings myself. June is one of these under-experienced nurses who's squeamish around cases of a sexual nature. First, she thinks any promiscuous person has AIDS, and second, she's afraid the virus is conscious and malevolent, that bodily fluids are going to jump out of the patient and open a vein. You can't tell people like her anything once they've made up their minds."

He started pacing as he talked. The back of his dark flannel suit looked like he'd slept in it.

"Anyway, no real problem. It was a slow day. Anything to keep the peace. I told her I would remove the bandage myself, though I didn't exactly relish the idea. I feared I'd find an infection, and that's bad news. Impossible to treat an infection without broad spectrum antibiotics these days, you know. A scratch on the hand, a rusty nail in the foot, such things used to kill more people than cancer before antibiotics were developed. The Fall has put practicing medicine back a hundred years.

"But when I took off the dressing, I found the tearing was healing much better than I could have hoped. There was absolutely no sign of infection. Then as I was preparing a fresh dressing I noticed a loose flap of skin right above the mons pubis. I didn't know what to make of it at first. It wasn't that large, about the size of a pea, but I couldn't understand how I could have missed it the night before when I treated her, even as tired as I was."

Jenkins scratched his head, dislodging a miniature snowstorm of dandruff that settled on the shoulder of his dark jacket.

"The color of the tissue was wrong – too white – and I assumed it was necrotic. Under ordinary conditions I might have cleaned the wound and stitched the flap back on, taking a chance on infection to prevent a deep scar. But I was afraid even a minor infection might not be controllable with the few simple antibiotics I have in stock, and I decided to debride the dead tissue. I told June to bring me a better light and a pair of sterile scissors and tweezers, which she did, but again she refused to stay and assist. I lifted up the flap with the tweezers and May babbled something in her sleep. I slipped one of the scissor blades under the flap and was about to snip it off when something about the tissue struck me as very odd."

Jenkins interrupted his pacing and retrieved his coffee cup. After a slurp of coffee, he continued.

"Now, I don't mind telling you my eyesight is not what it used to be. But I know that and I compensate for it. There was just something unnatural about the flap. I peered underneath it and saw no evidence of a wound. I knew it wasn't congenital – I delivered her twenty-some years ago, for God's sake. I also knew that flap of skin had not been there a few months ago. May has been prone to yeast infections the last couple of years and came to see me only last January for treatment. So I was pretty sure the thing was a new development, and I was ready to snip it off when the damn thing twitched out of the grip of my tweezers. I was so surprised I almost cut it off right then and there from nervous reaction. When I had calmed down a bit, I gave it a closer look with loupe, which with my eyesight meant getting my nose right down there."

Sophia coughed modestly. Jenkins continued. "The shape of the flap was too symmetrical, the proportions too familiar. I had hold of the end of the flap, and it not only looked wrong, it felt wrong too, even through rubber gloves. I peered closer at the flap of tissue, and the damned thing looked back!"

As Jenkins had begun to describe the flap of skin, Laura had grabbed Bryan by the elbow. Now she gasped and dug her fingers painfully into his arm.

"You mean it was some kind of growth?" she asked Jenkins. Her voice pleaded for him to tell her it was so.

"No, I mean exactly what I said. I was almost nose to nose with a miniature human-like creature growing out of the patient's labia, about the size of a two-month-old fetus. As I watched, it blinked, probably in response to the bright light."

"I've heard about such things, Doctor," Laura said. "It was an external pregnancy, wasn't it?"

"I should have expected such poppycock from you, young woman!" Jenkins said. "There's no such thing as an external pregnancy. Not in the books I read and not in my thirty years of practicing medicine. Besides, I said the thing was about the size of an eight-week old fetus, I didn't say it looked like one. An eight-week-old fetus looks more like a baby pig than a human being. What I was looking at was a perfectly proportioned human being, joined at its shoulders to May's lower abdomen. I ran to the surgical room and got a magnifier – about burst a blood vessel, my heart was pounding so. Back in the room with the magnifier I could see the little growth was female in appearance. Its features were distinct and well-formed. It had tiny breasts, though no nipples. And the sexual organs were more a suggestion than anything else. With my tweezers I tried to part the legs and examine it further, but found they were not separate but of one flesh. And the head was the only part not fused to May's skin. All the time, the tiny eyes followed my hand as it moved, wide-open with terror, it seemed to me."

"Homo nucleus," Uncle Robert said in an authoritarian tone. "Or rather, *homunculus* would be a better term."

Jenkins shot him an angry look, but Uncle Robert continued anyway.

"Homunculus," Uncle Robert repeated, intent upon explaining. "When the first primitive microscopes were trained on the human sperm, medieval moralists thought they saw perfectly formed humans, adults in microscopic miniature, contained in the head of each spermatozoa. The word *homunculus* is a related term from alchemy. Alchemists imagined a homunculus could be distilled in a cucurbit. Jung said the homunculus was an archetypical symbol of the animating, sustaining spirit of all things. A material manifestation of a subconscious, universal content."

"Most interesting," Jenkins said, dismissing the old man as if he were a rude child. He turned his back on Uncle Robert and continued. "By holding the light close I could see a delicate network of veins and arteries fanning out from the shoulders under May's skin. While I was tracing this lacework, the little thing blinked again and worked its mouth rapidly, and tiny trickles of tears ran down its face. I became certain it was responding to the harsh illumination from the examination light."

Jenkins stopped talking and refilled his coffee cup from the urn on the table. Then he sat down, although not in his former place on the other side of Wright, but two chairs down, separated from everyone. Everyone waited, looking at him, expecting him to say more.

"That's it. That's all I have to tell at this time, except the thing is steadily growing, not rapidly, but expanding its spread each day. Hard to measure its weight exactly, but in length, I'd say it grew about a centimeter yesterday."

"A centimeter a day! I'd call that rapid. It kept growing after you removed it?" Laura said incredulously.

Jenkins looked at her as if she were stupid.

"You did cut the thing off May, didn't you?" she said.

"No, of course not. For all I know, the, the –" Jenkins stuttered as he tried to find a word for whatever was growing on May. "– homunculus, for lack of a better word, could be a live, conscious human being, gestating somehow outside the body, though I've never heard of such a case. But it's alive and aware of its surroundings. I'll swear on a stack of Bibles that its little lips weren't making senseless mouthings but trying to form words."

"Mother of God! That thing is a parasite on May, or a cancer!" Laura's voice rose. "And you're letting it eat her up!"

"We don't know that."

"You don't know that it isn't. God! You have no idea what it is or where it came from."

"You said it, young lady. God. That thing may be God's will, for all I know. I'm not aborting its life. And neither is anyone else while I'm in charge of the clinic."

"Doesn't May have anything to say about it?"

"No, she doesn't, not in this state, thank God. Anyway, she shows no sign of either knowing where she is or of the miracle taking place on her body. Even if she did, I couldn't abort the homunculus on moral grounds."

"Moral grounds? That thing isn't human! You called it a growth, yourself." She grabbed Bryan's arm. Her fingers digging painfully into muscle, but he let her hold on.

"That I did, until I looked closely and saw its human face."

"Fuck! Fuck, fuck, fuck! The thing could eat May alive, and you're sitting there talking about ivory cloud ethics! You're not her father, you old drunken shit, and you can't make choices like that for her even if you were. You're not God!"

Jenkins didn't reply. Enraged, he stood up, his fists clenched so hard at his side that they trembled. Laura let go of Bryan's arm and jumped to her feet. She looked like she was about to launch herself across the table at Jenkins.

Uncle Robert stepped in front of Jenkins, facing Laura. "Keep it civil," he said to her. "We're all upset about what happened to May. But hurling obscenities around won't help. For all we know, aborting the homunculus might do May more harm than good."

"You're on his side," Laura said.

"I'm on nobody's side. I'm trying to tell you what I saw. Not only are May's major arteries and veins interlinked with it, but I'd bet that the nervous systems are intertwined too. Am I right, Doctor?"

Jenkins grunted an angry affirmative. "What business does she have here? Other than the fact that she's your niece?" he said.

Uncle Robert turned around to face Jenkins. "She's been helping us watch over the boy," he said, meaning him, Bryan knew. "And she has more medical training than June and those other women you employ at the clinic. You know that."

"That's not much of a recommendation to me. I know as well as you that the state medical board was considering bringing charges against her."

Laura sat down quietly, her hands clasped together. The doctor had clearly touched a raw nerve.

"Now, Doctor, you know there were extenuating circumstances in that matter," Uncle Robert said.

"Extenuating, hell! She was practicing medicine without a license."

"Laura felt she was morally in the right, even though the law and the majority opinion said otherwise, a position a right-to-lifer like you should sympathize with."

"Don't put me in the same club with that fascist," Laura uttered under her breath, which appeared to rankle Jenkins anew.

"Practicing midwifery without a license is against the law in this state," Jenkins said adamantly.

"They stopped issuing licenses in 1914. Old country quacks like you would rather see women die in childbirth than have any competition."

"Stop it. Both of you! This isn't getting us anywhere. We're all here to solve a common threat – at least I think the angels are a threat."

"That makes two of us," Wright interjected.

"And we're not here," Uncle Robert went on, ignoring Wright's interrupting support, "to hash out old grievances."

"I'm not replaying an old grievance. I have a new one – malpractice on May!" Laura said vehemently.

"Stop it, I said!" Uncle Robert raised his voice for the first time.

As tempers rose, Bryan busied himself imagining Laura in nurse's whites. He was so shallow. The nature of being, existence and reality might all hang by a slender thread, and here he was, indulging in a fetish fantasy. But it was exciting, thinking of porcelain white support hose covering her great legs, but of course, nurses hadn't dressed that way in decades. He tried a short skirt and red garters, even more of a nurse fantasy, but the image didn't suit her. He probably needed therapy.

Something cold touched the back of his neck and caused the hair of his scalp to tingle. Although his chair sat against a blank, solid wall, he turned and looked over his shoulder. There was nothing there, of course, but he continued to feel as if someone was standing directly behind him. The edges of the room quivered and became indistinct.

"Are you all right?" Laura whispered, shaking his shoulder. Uncle Robert was talking.

"Sure. I guess so." But the room seemed changed somehow. "Did I fall asleep?"

"If you did, it was with your eyes open."

"It goes on," Uncle Robert said, "sounding much like Genesis, except the serpent is the liberator, and Adam and Eve were destined to eat of the tree of wisdom. It was by doing so that they became more than animals."

Messengers of an Alien God

Bryan realized he must have blacked out for a moment. It was like coming in on the middle of a movie. Uncle Robert was back to lecturing on ancient writings on Gnosticism and angels; Jenkins had changed chairs again. Sophia returned from the kitchen, bearing a fresh urn of coffee. He hadn't been aware she'd left.

"This is getting us nowhere," Wright said. "We need to look at physical evidence and go on from there."

"You men are paranoid. There's no evidence the angels are a physical threat," Sophia said. "A spiritual one, I'll give Dr. Jenkins that, but they've never been known to harm anyone."

"Except for May," Uncle Robert said.

"You don't know that the angels did that to her," Jenkins said. "You used to see stranger things in a circus freak show."

"May is no freak!" Laura said. "You said yourself that you delivered May, and that she was a normal baby."

"So that furthers my point. May's condition isn't congenital."

"Yes, but you also told us that your eyesight is bad. Maybe you missed it," Sophia said.

"No. Not then. Not when I was young. I would have never missed anything as obvious as that."

"You said you must have missed it the night before." Sophia's accent had completely disappeared. Bryan was beginning to suspect it was affected at will.

"I'd been without sleep for thirty-six hours. Besides, June was the night nurse, and she cleaned up the patient before I went to work on her. If it was there then, she missed it, too."

"Then you're telling me, Doctor," Uncle Robert said, "that this thing you described, this Barbie doll monster growing out of the girl's stomach, sprouted overnight."

"There may have been a bud when we admitted her, but it would have had to have been very small for both me and my nurse to have missed it. I don't know."

"I know," Uncle Robert said. "I don't think it 'just sprouted.' I think it was implanted or attached or whatever violently. Come on now, a tiny angelic creature is attached to the girl. Why is everyone avoiding blaming the most likely suspect – an angel?"

"Well, explain something to poor dumb me," Sophia said. "I've heard these angels don't have sexual organs. No naughty bits at all, as the British say. So how did one go and get May pregnant?"

"I don't have an answer for that," Uncle Robert admitted.

Bryan could tell that the doctor, like Wright, was a little scared of Sophia. He wondered why.

"But I think Bryan might give us some clues to that," Uncle Robert said.

The mention of his name startled him. "I might?" Bryan asked.

"Tell everyone what you told the sheriff and me about the angel who carried you to the saucer changing sex."

Everyone stared at him, waiting. He told them in a stumbling fashion about how, while he was looking the other way or possibly had blacked out, the beautiful woman-child angel had become the young man angel.

"Couldn't it have been two angels, switching places during the time you blacked out?" Sophia said.

"No, it was the same one. I'm sure of it."

"So you're saying these angels are sexual chimera?" Jenkins asked.

"Sir?"

"Chimera, like chameleons, except they change sex instead of color."

"I don't know. I'm just telling you what I saw and felt."

Suddenly, Sophia grabbed an empty coffee cup from the table and threw it across the room, where shattered against the wall over Bryan's head. The unseen presence Bryan had sensed earlier passed through him like a cold wind.

"We should all shut up," Sophia said. "There's an unwelcomed guest – Mr. Asbeel I think – in this room with us right now, and he's listening to everything we say!"

* * *

15.

The Uninvited Guest

Each looked at the others for unspoken affirmation of what they all sensed: A presence, invisible but as tangible and real as any person present, moved among them.

The room chilled. A cold wind swept around the room and kicked up dust bunnies in the sunlight streaming through the east window. The wind grew stronger and more concentrated in seconds, but did not seem to be coming from any one direction. It grabbed perniciously at papers, unbuttoned clothing, tugged anything not tied down, as if looking for something to hold on to. A draft ruffled Jenkins' jacket, tousled Laura's long hair and pulled out pages of the huge thick volume of *Pseudepigrapha* that lay open on the table. A wind-blown mass of debris made of grit and captured pages began to define the form of the propelling force. The debris congealed into an inverted cone-shape, a whirlwind eight feet tall. As it became filled with detritus, the wind's caroming path around the room could be seen.

Under the influence of unpredictable physics, the whirlwind staggered here and there, rebounding off the walls until it settled in the center, a few feet from Sophia. There it appeared rooted, all the while spinning, the top and sides of the cone straining and stretching away from the anchored base. But as hard the cone of wind strained, its base stayed anchored to the spot. It appeared to be trapped and began to spin faster, compressing itself from its original height and breadth until it was more or less human-sized.

Heretofore, the cone had no visible color or form except as defined by the litter caught in its wind. Now, as its rate of spin increased, the cone began to take on color and substance of its own. It turned a translucent lilac, then a deepening blue. Swirls of black formed within the blue, moving with the sluggish torpidity of heavy oil.

Within the churning depths was a darker, purple shadow that formed, un-formed, and re-formed, an obscurity on the verge of becoming definite but never fulfilling its potential.

Everyone in the room strained forward in anxious expectation, waiting to see something, someone, anything, condense from the amorphous purple shadow, yet dreading what it might be. They remained posed in fearful expectation for several seconds, then the whirlwind changed color from blue to blood red in an explosive flash that made them all jerk backward. Uncle Robert, who had remained standing, stumbled backward against the wall. The pages that had been caught up in the whirlwind's spinning currents burst into flame and were thrown outward into the room. One torched paper landed near Bryan, and he stomped out the flames without thinking. Another flew at Jenkins, who batted it away like a bothersome fly – it burst into a thousand dying cinders at his touch. Uncle Robert tried to catch another and extinguish the fire before it consumed the page. But it too disintegrated with contact, settling to the floor as a fine ash.

Again the whirlwind shifted its hues, though more subtly, becoming a more purplish shade of blue, and moved closer to Sophia. Alarmed, Uncle Robert moved to intercede, but his wife waved him back.

"He can't do much harm in his present state," Sophia said, pointing an accusing finger at the center of the whirlwind. Everyone looked where she pointed, straining to see a recognizable form, but the darker center had neither symmetry nor identity.

"And he doesn't want to, I think. I sense he's as confused by this manifestation as we are, perhaps more so as he's working in a strange environment."

She spoke with a curious detachment, without emotion, but the others knew that her observation came from without, and that she was merely a translator, a spirit reporter on some secret function for another.

Bryan felt confused at first by all these impressions. The ideas seemed to originate outside him. Perhaps it was a purely right-brained thing, something that was perceived more as a pattern than a collection of parts, and he tried to accept the whirlwind on that level. The trouble was that right-brained thinking was just a concept. He'd often bullshitted over beer and peanuts about opening such doors of perception, but he had only the vaguest idea of how to initiate such thinking, or rather, un-thinking. The intruder, whatever or whoever it was, had charged the air with emotion. He felt sensitized not just to it but to the emotional states of Laura, Sophia, Uncle Robert, Jenkins and yes, even the sheriff.

Wright's body language showed it too; he shrugged his shoulders and shook his head as if trying to cast off an invisible being who had intruded upon his private space. More alarmingly, his hand sought solace from the huge police revolver at his side.

Bryan could also sense Jenkins trying to suppress his anger. In a fleeting epiphany, Bryan realized the old doctor was simply angry and dissatisfied with life, and had made a lifelong practice of taking this dissatisfaction out on those closest to him. He had come to see himself in the same harsh light that each of his three ex-wives had, and he despaired.

These insights, these windows into other people's deeper thoughts, should have been exhilarating, but Bryan wanted them to cease. He turned to Laura and found her to be calm. She was trying not to think, question or analyze; she was all cold observation. Was she subject to the same telepathic visions he was having? If so, she gave no sign when she met his gaze.

Looking through Uncle Robert's eyes was more disturbing. The old man was craving something – a hunger that Bryan felt not so much in his gut but his chest, a dark, hungry vacuum at the center of his soul. Bryan reflexively put his hands over his ears to block the terrible sympathetic pain, but it flooded over him, a melancholy that went beyond mere loneliness and depression into a death wish. Then just as quickly, the old man had flipped some mental switch, the melancholy was replaced with wonder, and the craving passed as the unknown guest spun and quivered in front of Sophia.

Sophia peered into the shadowy spine of the ectoplasm.

"I'm no stranger to psychic phenomena," she announced, breaking Bryan's empathic links. "This old house is full of traces of those restless souls commonly known as spirits, personalities who had led unhappy, dissatisfied lives or who died violent deaths, either by their own hands or someone else's. But this is something else. Something much more powerful. Much more alien."

Jenkins spoke first. "So tell us. Drop the other shoe. What the hell is the thing?"

"An astral body," Sophia replied.

"That's not how the things are described in the literature," Uncle Robert said.

"I have no idea what y'all are talking about," Wright said.

"You probably do," Uncle Robert said. "You just call it something else, like out-of-body-experience – or a ghost."

"That's like when someone dies on the operating table and imagines that's he's floating around the room," Wright said.

"Pretty much, but the occult interpretation is that his astral body – sort of like the soul but more – actually is travelling."

"Also," Sophia interjected, "there's the principle that this world, this plane of existence, is only one of many, and one can learn to travel to the other planes through something like meditation training without almost dying. In one form or another, it's a common belief in many religions."

"I've actually experienced it, thanks to . . ." Uncle Robert said.

"Don't start digressing, Simon," Sophia interrupted.

Uncle Robert paused, looked at her, sputtered something inarticulate, then smiled at her and went on: "Yes, I was just going to say this is different."

"This is an alien astral projection onto this plane from another. You didn't really think they would be the same as a human astral body, did you?"

"The question never came up in my mind," Uncle Robert said.

"Well, that's what it is. We're sure of it now, aren't we?" Sophia said, looking at Laura.

Laura nodded. She started to say something but apparently couldn't find the words to express what she was feeling. Bryan felt her frustration. From the onset of the apparition's manifestation the borders of their personal individuality had blurred. Bryan couldn't tell his thoughts from hers, hers from his. Jenkins stood up with wonder in his eyes.

"Oh, God," he said simply.

Wright looked awe-struck. He unsnapped the flap of the snatch-proof holster guard and let his thumb rest on the hammer of the .357. Everyone glanced his way in unison, though they couldn't have possibly heard the tiny click of the safety switch.

Standing, Sophia smoothed her skirt with both hands, and then reached behind her back and untied her apron, folded it into a neat square and placed it primly on the table. Everyone's eyes were upon her; even the farm people of the mural seemed to have looked up from their labors to cast nervous gazes upon the scene. Sophia acknowledged the attention of her flesh-and-blood companions with a demure smile. With the same air of self-conscious modesty, she reached under her blouse and adjusted a bra strap. A look of resolve came over her face and without further prelude she stomped fiercely on the hardwood floor three times. The metal taps of her high-heel shoe made inordinately loud raps and the sequins flashed in the cool blue light from the east windows.

"Reveal yourself to us, Entity!"

The effect on the whirlwind was immediate. Its spinning slowed; its color cleared to a misty white and the shadow within became angel-shaped. It slowly rotated within the still-spinning whirlwind, displaying its identity to all present.

"Asbeel!" Uncle Robert proclaimed.

Asbeel slowly completed another rotation within the whirlwind and then stopped to come face-to-face with Sophia. She took a deep breath and demanded, "What is your purpose here, Mr. Asbeel?" The room had chilled further, and her words were punctuated with little puffs of frozen breath.

Asbeel either could not or would not answer. His facial expression and body posture were frozen, like a mannequin on a slowly spinning dais. His gaze was directed downward at Sophia's sequined shoes. Sophia stamped her foot again, this time much more angrily.

"Answer my question, Mr. Asbeel!"

Asbeel's features became softer, his frame more feminine – a she – but at the same time, his features were angular and his shoulders broad, hinting at steroid muscularity. For an indeterminable time, the two images flickered, presenting both sides of Asbeel at once. Bryan felt caught up in an endlessly strange loop of time and space, a place where beginning and end nipped at each other's tails. He looked away, afraid of being hypnotized by the vision.

"We are here to do our work," Asbeel said tersely.

"Ask him if he's male or female," Wright said.

Sophia ignored the sheriff. "And what is your work here in this room, Mr. Asbeel?" she asked.

"To live and learn from the dying," Asbeel said.

"Ask him if he's in league with Satan," Jenkins demanded. Like Wright – like everyone else in the room for that matter – Jenkins felt that Asbeel was holding an audience with Sophia alone. Everyone else in the room was merely a bystander and had to participate through her.

She glance at Jenkins dismissively, then smiled and asked Asbeel, "Are you – and your fellow angels – good or evil?"

"We are not familiar with the term *evil*," Asbeel replied.

Sophia appeared at a loss and sat down, looking tiny and time-worn at the feet of a giant whose head seemed to touch the vaulted ceiling. Uncle Robert moved cautiously to her side. The angel ignored his presence, and the old man bent over and whispered in Sophia's ear.

"If you were to take a human by force," she asked the angel, "and make them do your bidding in your universe – would that action be good or bad?"

"That would be good, providing they proved useful."

Uncle Robert whispered again in Sophia's ear.

"And if a human were to pull you into the human sphere and make you do their bidding – would that be good or bad?"

"Why, that would be bad, of course, as it is now. But tell me, what is this thing called *evil* you speak of?"

"Ask it about God. Does it follow God? Ask it. Ask it," Jenkins said.

"That would prove nothing," Sophia said to Jenkins. "Its god is most likely as alien to us as it is."

"What do you hold in store for humans? Do you plan to do us harm?"

Asbeel suddenly spun around, his face a blur of features. Just as suddenly, he stopped, facing Sophia again.

"You are the path to our destiny!" he said, smiling. But his smile was obviously hiding something.

Sophia leapt to her feet, instantly enraged. "Enough of that!" she shouted. "We won't have it! I won't have it. A girl lies dying in the clinic, maybe because of one of you, and we want to know your intentions, Mr. Asbeel!"

In response, the whirlwind reconstituted out of thin air. Inside it, Asbeel's image instantly shrank to a pinpoint, and the whirlwind constricted in its middle at the pinpoint to form two half-sized cones an hourglass shape.

As suddenly as it had appeared, the whirlwind blinked out of existence with an audible pop. It was as if the angel had gone through a tiny door and had sucked the whirlwind in after him.

Bryan looked at Laura to see if she understood what had just happened. Her eyes told him that she was as confused as he was by what had happened.

Uncle Robert knelt and placed a hand, palm down, on the spot on the floor where the whirlwind had been rooted. "As you would expect, it's ice cold," he told his wife.

"Nothing was as I expected," Sophia said.

"What do you think now, Jenkins?" Wright's voice trembled. Warmth was ever so slowly returning to the room.

"I do not think. I'm stunned," Jenkins said.

"What was it, Aunt Sophia?" Laura asked. "Who was that angel?"

"The angel was the same Mr. Asbeel who came a-calling, the one we told you about who left his business card," Sophia said. She picked up her apron and unfolded it. Ice crystals fell out of the folds. "As for what the manifestation meant – well, honey, I'm as confused as you."

"It makes a kind of weird sense, when you think about it," Uncle Robert said.

"Maybe to you, Simon," Sophia said. Her tone had changed; it was no longer derisive. Bryan suspected the visitation had unnerved her more than she preferred to show.

"It was an alien astral body. So why should it appear as would a common, everyday ghost? That's all I meant," Uncle Robert said.

"What's so common about a ghost?" Jenkins asked. He tried to appear nonchalant, but his hands shook as he smoothed the lapels of his jacket.

"If you live around a sensitive like Sophia, the unearthly happens every other day," Uncle Robert said. "She draws ghosts like, well . . ." He stumbled over his words.

"Like a flame draws moth," Laura finished for him.

"We get the picture," Wright said. "Besides, I've heard rumors to that effect."

Actually, Bryan suspected what Wright had heard was a complaint from one of the good Christian ladies of Creedance, something about that "heathen nigger woman holding ungodly séances." (In Creedance, the N-word was still used without hesitation.)

"And now, Sheriff Wright?" Sophia said.

"Now what?"

"Now you just realized Simon lied to you about my abilities. There's also some connection between my husband and your wife, a bond which you can't understand, an intuition that you're not sure if you should take seriously."

"I take you very seriously," he said. "Now."

Uncle Robert cleared his throat. "Listen, may I suggest we move to the kitchen where it's warm?"

"Good idea," Laura said. No one else said anything.

"Okay, then, Laura, why don't you get the coffee urn. Sophia, are you all right?"

She nodded.

Bryan found himself in the lead by default, with Laura behind him. The curious collective sense he had shared with the group had faded to vague impressions. He could feel Laura deliberating before telling him to go right and then left down a narrow corridor, leading to a small, narrow alleyway of a staircase. The stairs appeared to be an afterthought in the design of the house.

"It's a servant's stairway, the quickest way to the kitchen," Laura said aloud in answer to his unspoken question. He could feel Wright's worried fuming, which registered emotionally on the same level as a slightly rank smell.

He emerged into a hardwood-paneled kitchen with a black and white checkerboard tile floor. By unspoken consensus, they all sat at a large red Formica and chrome table. In contrast to the rest of the house, the kitchen was sparkling clean.

Bryan looked around the table. He was back to guessing, rather than knowing, what everyone thought and felt. Now their faces mirrored his feelings of confusion and awe. Wright was the exception. His face was a blank, controlled mask; he occasionally brought up his hand to his mouth as if smoking an invisible cigarette. He caught Bryan looking at him and quickly put his hand under the table.

"*Raaaaa chaaaa!*" Laura broke the silence with a stifled sneeze.

"God bless you," Jenkins said, but he looked like he meant anything else besides a blessing.

Uncle Robert smiled at this automatic ceremony. "Before now, did any of you think it strange how we complacently accepted the angels as innocuous? Or how we never pressed them about their motives or their origins?"

"We were too busy getting things back together after the Fall," Wright said, both hands under the table.

"I never sensed any soul behind those eyes until this morning," Sophia said. "Store dummies. Big walking, talking, flying dolls."

Laura nodded. "They were such beautiful dolls, no one thought they could do any harm."

"Or be harmed," Jenkins said. "I remember when we had one in the hospital, and we thought it was dead – should have been dead – but it came back to life. Got up off the slab, thanked us for cleaning up its body and walked out."

"Maybe that's it. They seemed beyond life and death, so why would they bother humans?" Laura said. "That's how I thought about it, though I have to admit it wasn't an entirely conscious thing."

"Now we know differently," Wright said. "They hypnotized us – is that what you're saying?"

"There's more to it than that, I think," Uncle Robert said. "Even before the arrival of the angels, so many people were ready to believe in extraterrestrials as the savior of humankind. The breakdown of traditional Christian values left a religious vacuum, a mythos-wasteland, and many people have since tried to fill the void with anything and everything: Buddhism, Naturism, Zoroastrianism, some New-Age reworking of Hindi – even the Cult of the Extraterrestrial.

"In the 1950s, extraterrestrials were demiurges, carrying off beautiful women, killing or enslaving men, clandestinely trying to overthrow the human race. A common theme was the threat from outer space united the human race, and because of the common threat, the Cold War threat of nuclear holocaust was postponed. By the 1970s, there was detente. Aliens were strange, perhaps blundering and dangerous in their alienness, but basically non-aggressive. By the '80s, ET shows up as a regenerative paranormal force, an alien messiah."

"You're rambling again, Simon," Sophia said. "They haven't a clue as to what you're talking about."

"Yes, I know," Uncle Robert said apologetically.

"So which do you think these angels are – monsters, foreigners or saviors?" Wright demanded.

"That's the question, isn't it? What exactly do we know about the angels? It's awfully easy to project whatever we fear or expect on the unknown. Until we know more about the angels, everything is guesswork, and like with sci-fi movie aliens, our conception of them will say more about our unconscious fears and desires than anything else."

"We know the angels are a threat." Wright said.

"Do we?"

Wright looked at him curiously.

"We don't know they're a threat," Uncle Robert said. "We know now that they're much more than we first thought."

"What about May?" Laura said. "Isn't that enough of a threat for you?"

"We don't know the angels are responsible for the thing attached to May," Jenkins said.

"What else could have done it?" Laura said, but her tone was resigned.

Jenkins glared at her and then looked away. Neither of them was up to another shouting match. Then he said, "These are extraordinary times. Angels falling from the sky. Civilization thrown back a hundred years in a split second."

"I thought you said these angels weren't supernatural beings."

Jenkins cleared his throat, still avoiding looking at Laura as he talked. "I have been convinced otherwise against my will."

"What about the nuclear blast in the stratosphere? Could it be causing the growth of the homunculi? Some sort of weird mutations? " Bryan said.

"I don't think so," Uncle Robert said. "The literature I read said all the effects at ground level would be electromagnetic. Ionizing radiation, X-rays, gamma-rays and the like, would be blocked by the atmosphere. No, I think there's good reason to suspect an angel is the causative agent, but now I it might have been purely unintentional."

"Unintentional? You mean an angel just accidentally, sort of, happened to attach a tiny creature to May's perineum?" Laura voice began to rise.

"Maybe I'm saying exactly that."

"So we're back to your blundering aliens who really don't mean any harm," Jenkins said.

"No, I think it's more than that, too. I think they meant to do something to May – with or without her consent – but botched it," Uncle Robert said. "That much I'm sure is right. I feel it in my bones. But something about Asbeel bothered me long before he showed up as an astral projection."

"What's that, Simon?" Sophia said.

"His name. This was what I was trying to tell you before we began bickering over religion. When he first introduced himself, he gave us his business card, and I recognized his name as a variant spelling from the Book of Enoch. The passage I read to you is one of several. But when I asked him if he had adopted his name from Biblical sources, he didn't know what I was talking about. He said his name had always been Asbeel."

"A coincidence – or a lie," Jenkins said.

"Okay, then what about the names of the other angels? Penumae, for example. His name is recorded right along with Asbeel. The angel Bryan met up with, Eloaios, it's there, too. One coincidence I could buy, maybe two synchronicities, but a whole legion? No way."

"And then there's the thing about their language," Bryan said, and then regretted he had spoken. Everyone looked at him expecting more and he had to explain himself.

"When I asked Eloaios how she – this was at the church when she was still a she – when I asked her how she learned to speak English so well, she seemed confused. She had always spoken it, she said. So I asked her if she learned it from television, and she didn't know what that was either. I got the same answer about radio. And despite her good grammar, there were holes in her vocabulary. Simple words, like 'photograph' that you think she would know, she didn't. But abstract words like 'immortal' and 'pre-determined' were easy for her"

"She talked about immortality?" Uncle Robert asked.

"She said her race had made a terrible mistake when they chose to become immortal, or something like that."

"Stranger and stranger," Uncle Robert said, shaking his head. "All my life I have been trying to quantify the supernatural and failing completely. Now the supernatural crash-lands its spaceship in my backyard, stares me in the face and explains itself as a mistake."

"I agree, Simon," Wright said. "It's like we've all been asleep and now we're awake. By law, people are not officially missing until they haven't been heard from for at least a week, but I'm going check out some of the reports tomorrow, and I'll be looking for the angel connection this time."

* * *

16.

Angel of Death

Wright pulled into the El Rancho Trailer Park and parked in front of unit number 14. Janice opened the door before he had made it to the cinder-blocks that served as the front door steps. She wore tattered jeans, a blue sweatshirt several sizes too big, and sunglasses. Mud-caked knee-high rubber boots, the kind dairymen and veterinarians favored, stood beside the door.

She motioned him inside, holding the door and standing aside to let him pass. The living room was clean, the ashtrays washed and empty, and the huge pile of dirty dishes had disappeared from the kitchen counter. It was quite a contrast from only a couple of months ago, before the Fall, when he was here trying to serve a warrant on Tommy. She obviously managed better without the son-of-a-bitch. Why couldn't she see that?

"I've still got a little ground coffee left. Do you want me to brew some?" she asked. She took off her sunglasses. Her right eye was no longer swollen shut, but the bruise had turned a nasty-looking green.

"No, thanks," he said. He wanted some, but felt guilty about taking what had to be her last rations.

He took off his hat and sat on the couch. She sat on the other end of the couch, leaving a proper distance between them. Her posture, the distance she left between them, the way she crossed her legs, was a silent testimony. *I may be living in sin with the most low-account bastard in Harmon County, but that doesn't mean I'm not a lady, or that I'm not faithful to him.*

"Have you heard anything?" she asked.

"No, I haven't been back to the office all day."

She started to get ruffled, quickly folding her arms and looking to one side. She was preparing, he knew, to accuse him of incompetence or worse, unconcern. Before she could say as much, he added, "I thought I'd see if you had any luck before I put Jimmy on the case."

She shook her head. She slipped a hand inside her jeans and scratched her belly hard, low, almost at the crotch. Wright watched, amazed. She looked down at her own hand and pulled it out. Her face reddened. "God, that was slutty. Sorry. I don't know what came over me."

"Well, where did you search?" Wright said, changing the subject.

"Oh, out in the woods, where Tommy liked to go a lot."

"Where's that?"

"Just out in the woods."

"Where out in the woods?"

"Just out in the woods," she repeated in a wavering voice. It slowly dawned on him that she had been out to one of Tommy's marijuana plots. The muddy knee-highs were hers, not Tommy's. She was now struggling with the quandary of how to tell him where Georgian was not without incriminating him or herself.

"Ah, Janice," he drawled as if disappointed in the behavior of a small child. In a way he was. He had somehow believed she was completely oblivious to Georgian's marijuana business. A vivid memory of a seventeen-year-old Janice in a brown skirt, white lacy blouse and pink tennis shoes fought with the current image of Janice, now thirty-something, her waist bulging out of her too-tight jeans, one eye beaten, and with garish eye makeup, and an accessory to meth cook. Despite his professed cynicism, the two Janices wouldn't cohabit his mind peacefully. *You think you know somebody and then . . .*

"We have to start searching somewhere, but we've got a real problem," he said. "And I'm not real concerned about a few pot plants."

"What's that, John?"

"Pardon me?"

"What's the problem you spoke of?"

"Oh. The sheriff's department is out of gas. What little we have we need to save for emergencies."

"This is an emergency!" She was back in the indignant mode.

"Now, Janice, we don't know that. Georgian – Tommy – has gone off before for days, even weeks, hasn't he?"

"This is different."

"How so?"

"He's usually gone on business, driving his van, you know."

She meant making deliveries. Wright had suspected for some time that Georgian used a vehicle registered under an alias to make runs into St. Louis and Kansas City. If he could find out what Georgian drove, finding the meth lab would be a lot easier – assuming the man was still alive, assuming the world would ever return to normal.

"So where is his van?"

"It was in Columbia. It stopped running after the Fall, you know. He walked back to Creedance, the whole thirty miles."

"I'm surprised he made it," Wright said, thinking Georgian had probably lied to her.

"He stayed on back roads. Wore out a pair of brand new Reeboks getting here. Took him a week."

"So you're saying that's out. You're sure he didn't try to walk back to Columbia to get the van?"

"Oh, he talked about it. Tommy isn't stupid, John. He knew even if he found the van in one piece, he wouldn't be able to get it out of town again. You know, the Army blockade." She unfolded her hands and motioned as if moving a box of air. Her hands seem to say, *this here is the blockade, and I'm going to put it aside so it won't encroach on you and me talking about my Tommy.*

"Can you drive a motorcycle?" she asked abruptly.

"I can, but I don't own one. Why do you ask?"

"Because Tommy's motorcycle is out back, and it's got almost a full tank of gas."

"You're saying he would have taken the bike if he were traveling?"

"That, too. But what I meant was that you could use the motorcycle to look for him."

"It runs?" Like later model cars, newer motorcycles had electronic ignition systems. He tried to imagine what kind of chopped monstrosity

Georgian would ride.

"I'll show you," Janice said.

In the small space that served as a backyard, she pulled a dirty brown canvas tarpaulin off a brightly waxed black BMW touring bike. Despite himself, Wright chuckled. He could picture a weekend warrior businessman riding a BMW, not a hard-show case like Georgian. The thing even had saddlebags. Did Georgian put on a polyester jumpsuit and a white helmet when he rode it?

"Is something wrong with it, Sheriff?" Sheriff now, not John. The familiar tone had disappeared.

"No, nothing's wrong. This is perfect. You say it still runs?"

"Tommy had the motor rebuilt right before the Fall. Spent over a thousand dollars on it. He says the ignition wasn't affected by the Fall because it's an older type. No electronics. Instead it has something called a magneto. Do you know what that is?"

"Sure do. It means it still runs."

"So you know about motorcycles?"

"Some. Quite a lot about this kind. My Uncle Charlie had one. You remember Uncle Charlie, don't you?" She nodded. His uncle had bought one shortly before his last stroke. All he could talk about on his death bed was the finer points of his new toy.

She waited while he pulled off the rest of the tarp. Strange-looking beast. The cylinder heads stuck out like chubby wings. There was no chain. The Barvarians had equipped their touring bikes with direct drives twenty years before any other manufacturer.

"It's the apple of his eye. I used to worry that he thought more about the bike than about me," she said.

"Do you have the key?"

"It's inside. Do you want me to get it?"

"No, I haven't ridden a bike in years. I'll get Jimmy to come out and get it. He'll love it. His Harley hasn't run since the Fall."

Whether a movement caught his eye or he felt that strange second sense that he was being watched, he didn't know, but he looked up to find an angel squatting on the gable of Janice's trailer. It sat with its elbows propped on its knees and its chin in its hands, wings partially unfolded. It smiled, a handsome gargoyle with perfect dental hygiene.

As Wright was wondering what to do, an empty beer bottle whizzed over his head, headed straight at the angel's chest. At the last moment the creature deflected the bottle with a flip of its wrist that was both lightning-fast and casual. The bottle shattered as if it had hit a concrete wall.

"Shoo, scat, you fuck," Janice yelled and launched another bottle. Again it knocked the bottle out of the way at the last moment, shattering it too. Janice began rummaging around in a big plastic trash can for more ammunition.

"That thing has been hanging around my trailer for days, just watching. I didn't mind him at first, but lately he's beginning to give me the willies." She came up another beer bottle and made ready to throw it, then checked herself. "This isn't against the law, is it?"

"Be my guest," he said.

She threw wildly this time, missing the angel by several feet. The bottle crashed somewhere on the other side of the trailer, but the angel got the message. With a sad-sack face, then it stretched its wings and took off slowly. It soared over their heads, picking up speed until it crossed over the Old Buffalo Road and disappeared behind a grove of trees.

Wright was glad to see it go. The creatures were giving him the willies now too.

"You know, don't you," he said, "that any one angel is strong enough to pick up this motorbike and toss it around like a toy?"

"I don't think it will hurt me. No matter what I do. I'm sure of it."

"What makes you think so?"

"I don't know how I know." She looked at him oddly, not in the eye, but at his hat, as if trying to read his intentions there. "I guess I don't know it – I feel it."

"How long did you say that one has been hanging around?"

"I don't know; a couple of days, I guess." She looked away, avoiding looking him in the face.

"Since Tommy disappeared?" he said, instantly regretting it. Now he had conceded that Georgian had disappeared.

"Yes, about then," she said, her eyes watering.

"Always the same one?"

"Yes, I think so. No, I don't know. In the daytime, it's the same one – I think. They're kind of hard to tell apart and their features change at times."

"They come at night too?" He was sure now that she was holding something back, something she really wanted to talk to someone about, but couldn't tell him because he was the Law.

"I heard one walking around on the roof about eleven last night. I can't go to sleep until midnight anyway. I'm so used to staying up and watching the Tonight Show that I'm awake until twelve, even though the TV hasn't worked since the Fall. Do you know I've been doing that every night since my senior year in high school?"

He nodded sympathetically. She missed late-night TV like he missed the white, conversational noise of talk radio.

She paused, sighed, and looked where the angel had perched on the roof. "Death angel," she said.

"What?"

"Death angel. Angel of death: That's why I run the things away. Like you said, they started hanging around about the time Tommy didn't show up for lunch. You don't really think he's dead do you?"

No, I think the worthless piece of shit took off, and you know it. What else aren't you telling me?

He wanted to say this out loud but held back, expecting her tears to start at any moment and not wanting to feel responsible for them.

He was right. She started crying and he felt responsible somehow.

"Oh, God, John. You've got to find him. I know he's a bastard. I don't care. I just don't want to be alone again."

He put a hand on her shoulder, genuinely wanting to comfort her, but she misinterpreted, jerked away, and ran into the house.

He spread the tarp back over the BMW wondering what she was hiding. He'd been around enough liars to read their body-language. But there were no signals as to exactly what she was lying about. She was lying a little about Tommy's business, that much was plain. But was she was lying about the angel as well? What the hell was it doing hanging around? When she had thrown the bottle at it, it had looked surprised, as if it were expecting a friendlier welcome.

The wind tugged at the corners of the tarp until he found three concrete blocks to weigh it down. He was looking for one more block when Janice came back out. She stayed near the back door, daubing at the corners of her eyes with an old sock. Tissue paper had become scarce after the Fall.

"So what about it, John?"

"Like I said, I'll send Jimmy out after lunch. He'll cruise around the back roads and check with farmers. Maybe someone saw or overheard something. But I won't lie to you, Janice. Even if he's out there, there's not much chance of Jimmy coming across him."

"I'll help."

"You could help most by telling me where Tommy might be. You know what I'm talking about."

She shook her head. "I know, but . . ."

"I'm not just doing this to find Tommy's patches –" only half a lie "– there's just too much ground for one or two people to cover. And frankly, I don't think we can rouse much public sympathy around town for Tommy. You know that."

She nodded, looking like she was going to break down in tears again. Wright suppressed his feelings of pity, reminding himself that more was at stake here than offering her comfort. He reminded himself that Tommy dealt in dangerous drugs too – not just marijuana.

"I'll think about," she said. "I'll decide by the time Jimmy shows up."

Wright knew she was stalling, hoping Georgian would be found before this afternoon. He should push her for the locations of the plots now, while she was indecisive from worry, but he didn't have the heart for it. Her conviction was contagious. Maybe Georgian was dead, in which case it wouldn't matter.

"All right, Janice. You do that."

He drove back to his office brooding.

* * *

17.

Sick Spirits

Jenkins had to use both hands to steady the penlight beam on the homunculus' face. The creature writhed and tried to turn its head away from the light, but failed because its scalp was now attached to May's abdomen. There was no boundary to show where May left off and the homunculus began.

May's face showed no sign that she shared the homunculus' pain, but this didn't necessarily mean she wasn't suffering. The young woman hadn't stirred from her sleep except for a brief interlude two days ago when she called out for *the baby* – as if she were merely struggling to wake from a bad dream.

He paused to listen to the rain pounding at the window, then turned off the penlight. The homunculus' porcelain-white face immediately relaxed and its eyes returned to a blank stare. Jenkins sighed; all he could do was record its development.

He wrote: *Homunculus: pupils equally reactive to light. Body now approximately 10 cm in overall length, torso about 4 cm wide, about 7 cm wide from wing edge to wing edge. Wing tips and lower torso beginning to take on color.*

Wingtips! He had actually written that word. He could no longer deny the obvious angelic origins of the homunculus.

Then he took May's vital signs and found every indicator to be within normal range: *MT'S VS: T 98.6, R. Irregular breathing, P 80, BP 120/80.*

Irregular breathing was an understatement. May occasionally stopped breathing for ten seconds to a minute. Then her respiration would gradually increase to normal. As far as he could tell, the episodes showed no distinct pattern, though admittedly he didn't have a nurse to spare for constant monitoring. He suspected depression of the frontal lobes and diencephalic dysfunction. An electroencephalograph would nail down the diagnosis, or even a blood-oxygen meter could determine if she were in any risk, but there wasn't a piece of operational electronic equipment anywhere he knew of.

He took up the penlight again and aimed at the homunculus' eyes. This time it stared at him arrogantly, its mouth set, its eyes hard with hatred.

Or was he reading his own feelings into the face? He couldn't see well enough to verify whether its expression were real or imagined.

Damned thing. Damned little obscenity!

He resisted the impulse to prod its belly with the blunt tip of the penlight: better, to cram it in its little obscenity of a mouth. He told himself that he simply wanted to see what reaction a mechanical stimulus would muster from the homunculus, but he knew a more primal instinct was at work. The little abomination not only endangered May's life, it put to the knife all his preconceptions about the sanctity of human life, threatening the lifelong religious bulwarks upon which he had trusted the safety of his soul.

The tiny bud of alien life stared back at him. He could kill the thing, push a gauge 18 hypodermic needle through its forehead and into its brain. Did it have a brain in that tiny head? If he killed it, would it slough off May's stomach like dead tick?

Perhaps.

Perhaps not.

Even if he succeeded in killing it, the shock might kill May as well.

Outside, the storm picked up, slamming waves of rain onto the roof with thunderous, regular pulses, like surf breaking against rocks. Creedance's woefully inadequate sewer system would soon be overflowing, the streets transformed into canals. In outlying Harmon County, the creeks would be engorged with drainage, low-water bridges swallowed by overflow, root cellars of old farm houses inundated.

No sense in his fighting the weather to get to his lonely house.

He'd spend the night at the clinic as he had done so many other nights.

THUMP!

Something large and heavy collided with the roof. He glanced out the window. Still no thunder, just rain on a moonless night. Another gout of rain slammed against the windowpane, making it vibrate like a tuning fork. The storm would probably go on all night. Though violent and dark, the rain was a good thing, compensating for last summer's drought and the dry winter. Now the farmers would have enough soil moisture to germinate the spring crops. An odd piece of verse came to mind:

> *I see in spirit all are hung*
> *I know in spirit that all are borne*
> *Flesh hanging from soul*
> *Soul clinging to air*
> *Air hanging from upper atmosphere*
> *Crops rushing forth from the deep*
> *A babe rushing forth from the womb*

Jenkins smiled to himself. What would Uncle Robert think if he heard the Philistine doctor quoting Valentinus, a second century Gnostic poet? The committee thought him a fool, but he knew that they all – with the possible exception of Sophia – were suffering from a spiritual deficiency due to over-reliance on reason, a trap intellectuals often fell into – including the genius, Valentinus.

Uncle Robert saw the angels and the religious prophesies as purely physical phenomena, more obscure in mechanics than microwave transmissions or nuclear physics, but within the ken of the mind of man. Why couldn't Uncle Robert accept the spiritual explanation?

He brushed the homunculus' abdomen with the end of the penlight. The homunculus returned the same torpid stare it had worn before.

He moved the penlight closer, posed it over the homunculus' belly button. Did it even have a belly button? His bifocals wouldn't resolve so fine a detail and his magnifying glass wasn't at hand, but he thought he he could see one. It must be an illusion because as it didn't have an umbilical cord, it shouldn't have a navel either.

Messengers of an Alien God

He set the penlight down on the dingy bed sheet, took off his glasses and began polishing them with the corner of his not-so-clean lab coat. He should have had the prescription updated years ago.

He put his glasses back on and traded the penlight for a scalpel. Because they were not born of woman, Adam and Eve were supposedly the only human beings ever to lack belly buttons. Bible trivia. Give the doctor ten points. Of course the cursed abomination could have gestated in May's womb, emerged like a baby possum to crawl up her stomach and attach itself to her skin in lieu of a sheltering marsupial sac.

Logically it seemed possible. Logic, however, was such a poor tool for understanding the real mysteries of life. As with matters of faith, you had start with a few basic assumptions. Before you could see beyond the boundaries of the soul, you had to have trust your intellect was augmented by a true spiritual vision and not distorted by intellectual vanity. Before entertaining the seductive logic of abstract math you had to accept as fact that there was such an illogical thing as zero, a nothingness that was something, a concept devised by Arabian mathematicians a thousand years after Christ's birth. Scientists claimed faith spat in the face of logic, but what could be more illogical than the idea of perfect nothingness?

Before you could believe you had a rightful place in the universe, you had to believe in an outside power greater than yourself.

Using the blunt end of the scalpel handle, he poked the homunculus in its stomach.

Hard!

He pulled the instrument back shamefully, expecting the tiny creature to show pain or surprise or anger – to at least show something. But its face remained expressionless.

But a second later, May reacted riotously. Her hips thrust off the mattress; her back arched in an impossibly acute curve. The muscles in her bare legs trembled with tension. Her placid features gave no indication she had felt anything, but the homunculus stared at him indignantly, as if taunting him. *Poke me again, you old son-of-a-bitch and I'll hurt her!* Or was that his imagination again? He squinted at the tiny face, now thrust high into the light.

May strained at the position for several seconds, then let out a long orgasmic sigh and settled her body back down on the mattress slowly like an inflated doll losing air.

Suddenly, he craved a drink – but that would be stupid. His stomach hurt like hell already, much worse today than it had for months. A drink could bring agony. Worse, two days ago the bloody diarrhea had begun.

A peptic ulcer or cancer? It didn't matter. Either prognosis spelled death under current conditions. And without pain killers, it would be an agonizing, protracted death. More tragic, the people of Creedance, both the good and bad, might soon find themselves without a doctor.

Was God poking him in the stomach to see how he would react? No, the cause was simple. Yes, everthing happened for a reason, but sometimes the reason was one's own stupidity. He'd abused his stomach lining for twenty years, and now he was paying the price.

The homunculus still stared at him with deadly seriousness, as if waiting for him to justify his actions.

"Talk to me, you little abomination," he said, barely restraining himself from poking it in the stomach again.

Another pain – an old personal pain that was part anger, part emptiness, all desolation – welled up again.

What was the cure here? To debride the homunculus as he would excise a skin cancer? By cutting away the obscene little thing, he might also excise his indecision. The stainless steel scalpel lay cold in his hand. He put the instrument on the bedside tray, afraid of what his own hand might do. He would be taking a chance that the excision of the homunculus wouldn't kill May.

By doing nothing, he might also be gambling with her life. The little bud of an angel – if that's what it truly was – was growing rapidly and must be draining vital nutrients and energy from her by the hour. Since she wasn't eating and tube-feeding was beyond the current capacity of the clinic, it was only a matter of time before she starved to death. And there was nothing he could do about it.

A clattering parade came down the hallway, a familiar sound Jenkins immediately recognized as Maurice spilling his mop bucket again. Though only scheduled for six-hour days, the man spent all his off hours mopping and cleaning. When asked why, he wouldn't elaborate, but Jenkins expected the mentally challeged young man preferred being at the hospital and doing something, anything, than sitting alone in his little room. Jenkins let him spend as much time at the hospital as he wanted. He didn't do any harm, other than occasionally spilling his mop bucket. Still, the two clinic nurses complained of him being there all the time. But then nurses, particularly those on the bedpan brigade, complained about everything. Behind his back they called Maurice "the doctor's idiot boy."

Strictly speaking, Maurice wasn't an idiot, but there was some truth to the nurses' epithet. After all, he had given the boy life as much as the boy's mother had. He thought back to those days, twenty-odd years ago, when most of his actions had been obscured with an alcoholic fog. On the day of Maurice's birth he had been just this side of shit-faced. He remembered scrubbing up for the delivery and the nurse saying something about there *being a problem*. The next thing he knew, he was holding the bloody baby in his hands. He looked down at the mother, surprised to find he had delivered the baby with what was actually a damn neat Cesarean. Then he realized the baby wasn't crying, and its face was not just blue, it was purple!

Oh God! Had he frozen, a blacked-out statue, while the baby's brain starved for oxygen? He dared not look to the nurse for a sign. He had stood there another eternity, still holding the purple baby. Then he noticed the knot in the umbilical cord. Sometime during its gestation, the baby must have been doing an underwater ballet in the womb. With one of its somersaults it had tied the knot of its own destruction. During the last few hours of labor, a violent, painful time for both mother and baby, the loop in the umbilical cord had tightened, cutting off blood and oxygen to the new brain.

Rudely dragged forth from the incision in his mother's stomach, the baby had refused to breathe, to start its heart beating. Even years before the Fall, small-town clinics didn't have such things as respirators; without thinking, he had done what any good doctor would do in those days. He improvised. Setting the baby in the arms of the nurse, he pulled a pack Pall Malls from his bag and lit one without taking off his bloody surgical gloves. Taking a deep drag, he pinched its nostrils close and blew a small puff of smoke into the baby's tiny mouth, supposedly to irritate the lungs and make it cough.

The baby boy did cough but still didn't start breathing on his own.

He gave it another lungful of smoke and searched for a heartbeat – and found one, though arrhythmic and weak. Taking a half-pint bottle of Cutty Sark from the back pocket of his street clothes, he ordered the nurse to pour a capful down the baby's throat. A staunch Southern Baptist, the nurse balked at taking part in an abomination of medical practice. But he had insisted, mainly because he feared his own hands would shake too much to do the job. In tears, the nurse had obeyed. The baby coughed again, gurgled and spat, and made a *yuck* face, and accepted life. In a few minutes, his color had changed from gray-blue to a healthy, ruddy pink.

He had launched the baby into life in fine, old country honky-tonk style.

But the baby's brain had gone too long without oxygen. The infant had grown into a young man for whom a mop and bucket were at times overwhelmingly complex. A young man whose eyes perpetually vacillated between pain and mindlessness.

Had he done the right thing helping bring him into the world half-destroyed? Would he make the same choice today, after nearly five years of sobriety?

"What about you?" he said to the little rider on May's stomach. "A few years from now, if I'm still alive, will I question the wisdom of letting you live?"

The homunculus stared at him without blinking as if it knew what deadly action he was considering. Maybe it did.

"Doctor?" asked a familiar voice.

Jenkins looked up. Maurice stood at the doorway, mop in hand.

"Doctor?" he repeated.

"What is it, Maurice?" The homunculus' tiny eyes followed the knife to the table as he set it on the bedside tray.

"I feel bad, Doc. Something bad is happening."

"You've had these feelings before."

Maurice looked at the ceiling, his eyes jerking back and forth. For Maurice, trying to remember must be like walking into a dream. Jenkins waited. Maurice was extremely slow, but his mind usually dredged up the prompted memory, a mind that Jenkins suspected was competent but moved sluggishly, as if caught in molasses.

"Yep," he said after a couple of minutes. "Yep. Plenty of times."

"And they've always turned out to be just bad dreams, haven't they?" He waited for Maurice to agree. Maurice trusted him and would rack his brain to comply with the doctor's logic. He watched the young man's face contort, as if trying to force the brain behind it into action.

"Sometimes the bad dreams come true," Maurice said deliberately.

Jenkins got up from the chair, his knees popping painfully. As an afterthought, he pulled up the sheet to cover May's nakedness. Maurice didn't seem to notice. He never did seem to notice nudity, indignity or pain.

Walking around the bed, the doctor put a hand on the young man's shoulder and steered him backward out of the room. Once out of May's room and back into the better-lit hallway, he smiled and asked, "Tell me about the bad dream come true."

Maurice looked at the ceiling again. More little blinks. "Yesterday."

Yesterday for Maurice could mean anytime from the day before to last year.

"How many yesterdays?"

Maurice's eyes drifted toward the ceiling tiles. Jenkins was used to it and waited. Most of Maurice's interrogators found it so exasperating to wait for him to say anything that they never got beyond the first question.

"A bunch. Before the cars stopped."

"Before the Fall?"

More waiting. "Yes. Before the angels came," Maurice said. His voice, usually a bit thick, was sharp and almost lilting. The molasses had momentarily thinned.

"And what did you dream?"

Maurice stared at him, blankly, reminding Jenkins for a frightening moment of the homunculus' taunting gaze. But in the janitor's case, it was merely a matter of confusion.

"What was the yesterday dream, son?"

Maurice emerged from his confusion and looked up. More eye blinks as he tried to summon the right words. Finally, he looked back at Jenkins and said, "I dreamed the angels became very sick in their hearts."

"How were they sick?"

Maurice looked like he was going into another dead-eye trance, but then shook his head.

"Sick forever."

"You mean they were sick for a long time?"

"No, not long time. Forever. Longer than forever. Longer than a long time. Forever sick."

Jenkins sighed. It was so difficult not to talk to Maurice like a child. Hard to keep in mind that no matter how damaged the vehicle, there remained an adult personality at the wheel.

"They looked sad," Maurice said. His own eyes turned sad as if to demonstrate. He looked around the room, left then right, twisting at the waist but keeping his feet solidly planted, as if his shoes were glued to the floor and his waist was a syrupy slow spring. His eyes found his mop and bucket and the sadness left them. He unglued his feet and trotted toward the mop as if it were a long-lost friend.

Jenkins felt Maurice hadn't told him all of his dream, but didn't hold him back. Maurice grabbed his mop, plopped the head down in the wringer, then used the handle to steer the swiveled-wheeled bucket down the hall like a raft. Jenkins had a briefly disturbing vision of Maurice as a damaged Huckleberry Finn floating aimlessly down a mile-wide river, waters dark and thick and slow as molasses, his hand at the tiller, his eyes staring into nothingness. About ten feet down the hall, Maurice stopped and looked back over his shoulder. His expression asked, *Can I go now?*

"We can talk later, Maurice. I have to go look in on Mrs. Johnson now."

Maurice nodded and wheeled his bucket a few feet farther before stopping. "Mrs. Johnson gone."

"She checked out? Impossible, she can't go anywhere with quadruple blockage. She can't even get out of bed." He stopped himself. He was only confusing the boy. "When did she check out?"

Maurice looked up, rolled his eyes, but the answer came quickly. "She didn't check out. She floated up and out of her room. She was over us watching for a while." He pointed up at the tiled ceiling. "Then she left." He smiled as if privy to a private joke.

"Okay, I'll play along. Where did she go after she came down from the ceiling?"

"She didn't come down. She left to go higher."

"When did she leave?"

"Just now."

"While we were talking?"

He nodded. "She said goodbye, but you didn't hear."

"Okay, Maurice. Thanks."

Maurice smiled a *you're-welcome* and steered his mop bucket down the hall toward emergency. Jenkins watched the boy go, a sense of foreboding replacing his exasperation. He trotted toward the retirement home wing, his knee joints knots of burning gristle and raw nerves.

Emily Johnson lay on her back in bed, staring wide-eyed at the ceiling. Her long white hair fanned out on the pillow, her wrist still warm but lacking a pulse. She must have died quietly in her sleep only minutes before while he was talking with Maurice.

THUMP! Another loud bump sounded from the roof, startling in its intensity.

Nothing but a tree branch dislodged by the storm.

He opened her dressing gown. Thin, liver-spotted and freckled skin draped over the outline of ribs, sternum and clavicles. Emily's breasts were hardly more than outlines in the skin. He couldn't help comparing the old woman's emaciated flesh to the pneumatic youth of May. He stopped himself. He was too old for such thoughts, and the matter at hand was too urgent. Emily was still warm. Despite appearances, her heart might still be feebly beating. He planted the bell of his stethoscope on the skeletal chest.

No heartbeat. No, he hadn't really expected to find one.

Suddenly exhausted, his hands shaking, he sat on the edge of the bed. He could start CPR, but he had more wisdom now than he had when shit-faced drunk some twenty-plus years ago. No, he would not repeat the mistake with Maurice. He would let Emily go. She had suffered enough.

THUMP!

What the hell was landing on the roof?

-187-

THUMP!

Tree limbs? No. Now that he thought about it, the only tree with limbs large enough to over reach the roof was on the other side of the clinic. On this side there were only loblolly pines, newly planted and barely tall enough to reach the window.

He stood and pulled the bed sheet over Emily's head.

THUMP!

What the hell was doing that? It sounded like someone dropping sandbags on the roof. He stepped up to the window. The darkness outside was a mirror of his mind. Laying a hand on the double glass pane, he could feel the vibration of the rain – and something else: a tingling, an electric singing in the fingertips.

Without warning, the window exploded outward. He was conscious of being sucked into a voluminous whiteness, skin wet and slick like a damp sheet. Bones and sinew moved powerfully under the wet skin. Tiny hands grabbed and grasped at his clothes, pulling him out and up into the darkness.

* * *

18.

Clean Break

Janice August set the steak knife and the glass of peppermint schnapps on the edge of the bathtub, took off Tommy's baggy sweatshirt and jeans, and eased herself down into the bubbles. It had taken her the better part of the evening to heat enough water on the wood stove to fill the bathtub, but it had been worth it. The warm water eased her cramped muscles, and the bubbles made her feel like a little girl again. She took a deep swig of schnapps. It was about time she got to it.

She parted the thick layer of bubbles with her hands and peered down through the bluish water. Her hitchhiker stared back at her.

Hitchhiker?

A silly name, but what else could she call it? Certainly not "her baby." Babies grew inside you. Hitchhiker? No, the thing wasn't along just for the ride. It was attached, an extension, a beautiful, monstrous extension of herself. She couldn't tell where its skin began and hers ended.

She bent over for a closer look. It was bigger today, and although still obviously not human, its features were vaguely familiar. She eased further down until the warm water covered her breasts, and bubbles closed over her belly, hiding the hitchhiker.

She relaxed like that, with only her head and toes above water, and took a big swig of the syrupy liquor. The alcohol warmed her stomach. In a few seconds the warmth spread to the skin around the hitchhiker.

It twitched!

Hurriedly, she skimmed the foam away to look at the little fucker.

Damn! How it had grown! Its wingtips now stretched to cover her lower ribs. Its toes touched her knee caps. How large would it be tomorrow? Would it reach up to her chin or higher so she'd have to stretch to breathe? Would it eventually totally envelope her, trapping her inside it, eventually covering even her eyes? Would it be like wearing it like one of those full-body Spandex suits that athletes wore, just an outer covering, a false skin? Or would she gradually fade away as it absorbed her from the outside in?

She took another gulp of the schnapps, leaned back in the tub and watched the layer of foam gradually re-close.

Get to it. Don't put it off any longer.

Picking up the steak knife, she ran a finger along the serrated edge. In the kitchen it was just a knife, an implement she washed, tossed in the back of the silverware drawer and forgot. Here in the bath, close to her bare skin, it drew an alien emotion from some dark place within her. She cringed at the thought of the knife cutting her skin but at the same time welcomed the release it promised.

She was two people. One was young, complete and perfect, floating above, looking down at the sagging, fleshy Janice in the bathtub, an unlikely construction, a creature botched by the gods, wallowing in grey water, an anchor designed only to keep the perfect, transcendental Janice earthbound.

She carefully set the knife back down on the rim of the bathtub and reached under the foamy water to the hitchhiker. Her fingertips reached for the boundary where her skin stopped and the hitchhiker began – if there was a distinct boundary it eluded her. The wings were lined with twiggy ribs and the skin had a brittle feel, like a dried oak leaf. She pressed on the hitchhiker's stomach and felt a faint pressure against her own stomach. Her fingertips brushed across its feminine breasts, and she felt a tickle, higher, on her own nipples. It was as if she and the hitchhiker were one, an angelic mini-me.

She parted the bubbles once more and was momentarily enchanted by its beauty. She at once wanted it gone but couldn't stop looking at it. It lay on her skin like a giant, beautifully textured, tattooed butterfly, a masterpiece carved right into her skin.

A masterpiece on a worthless, wattled canvas.

Messengers of an Alien God

So what did it matter if the angel's artwork ate up the canvas?

But it did matter, if only because the angel had lied to her. He had promised heaven on earth, a wonderful, flawless body and, most important, complete peace of mind. He had been a beautiful, masterful illusionist, stirring memories and passions she hadn't known she possessed. She had granted him access to her body, and like all the human men she'd ever known, he had hurt and damaged her, then left her, left her here alone, feeling more used and empty than Tommy had ever made her feel, not even human anymore, and with this monstrosity growing out of her skin.

She picked up the knife and set it down again.

If she died, would it die with her, or would it just peel off her corpse like a leech and find another host? She picked up the knife again and set the tip gently against its chest. He looked her blankly with those little jewels of eyes. She hated the thing – yet loved it as well. It would be a shame to destroy anything so beautiful.

Beautiful – shit! Who gave a fuck about beauty? The thing was consuming her.

She withdrew the knife from the things chest and sliced quickly across her wrist, then set the knife down and waited. A thin red line swelled across her skin. Red drops fell into the water, diluted and turned to crimson clouds.

She dipped her wrist in the water. The warm water should keep the blood from clotting. Thin tendrils of red grew from her wrist and then stopped. Damn! There hardly seemed enough blood and the water was already turning cold. Suicide should be easier and not hurt so much. Pills would be better, but she had nothing but aspirin.

She tried to pick up the knife with her left hand. She must have cut a tendon because her little finger and the one next to it didn't work very well. She quickly dragged the blade across her right wrist, pressing as hard as she could. It hurt like hell, but this time she was rewarded with a pink cloud of blood.

The pink cloud drifted over the face of the hitchhiker.

Something about its face had changed, but what?

She leaned forward, more conscious now of the pain in her wrists, of the water's uncomfortable coolness, of her breasts feeling heavy and

-191-

disconnected as if they belonged to someone else. She ran her fingertips over her hitchhiker's closed eyes.

Closed eyes? Was it sleeping? Was it dead?

She touched it again, anxiously. The wings and chest transmitted the same electric tingle they always had, but its eyes remained closed. Was it sleeping?

But it had never slept before or, for that matter, closed its eyes. Always it had watched, wide-eyed. It had occasionally blinked when exposed to harsh light, but it never seemed to sleep. Several times during the last week, she had awoken in the middle of the night and flicked on the light switch, hoping to catch it napping. She had always found the hitchhiker with its eyes open, staring at her, waiting. It was a futile effort, like trying to open the refrigerator door fast enough to catch the light off. Either it only slept when she slept or it never slept.

Never slept.

But now it was sleeping.

She tossed the knife in the sink, climbed out of the water and sat on the edge of the tub. Her wrist started to bleed again, not a gush, but an annoying trickle like a nosebleed, so she held her arm over the bath to keep the drops off the floor. A chill started in her feet and hands and rushed up her limbs to her chest. She began shaking uncontrollably.

What was she to do next? Had she bled enough already? She didn't think so. The water was now mildly pink, not crimson. Should she continue? She looked at the hitchhiker for an answer and found it awake now, its eyes wide open and staring. It blinked as a stream of water ran down its forehead and into its eyes.

"The burgeoning pith will lapse into torpidity when it is submersed in water," said a voice from behind her.

She jumped at the sound of the voice and fell backward into the pink water. For a frantic second, she floundered helplessly over her head in the bloody water, then iron-hard hands were holding her, lifting her.

"You bastard," she sputtered.

"An appropriate epithet. I do not have a biological father, and the Dreaming God, whom you might say was our stepfather, has forsaken me and the rest of my race."

She struck out against her rescuer, striking his eyes, his mouth.

Each blow made her balled-up hands sting, but the angel paid her no mind. She might as well be pounding against the porcelain bathtub. In the midst of her rage and misery, she couldn't help notice how perfectly handsome he was.

"Set me down," she managed to say.

Let me die was what she meant.

The angel lifted her hand, examining the cut on her wrist. "So this is how you would do it," he said. "So fragile, so easily do you cut the mortal bonds."

"You talk like a preacher. Are you going to save my immortal soul now?" She reached up and struck his beautiful face.

He smiled at her. Her slap had left a bloody handprint.

"No, *you* are going to save my *soul*, and I am going to keep you alive long enough for you to become either very wise or very evil," he said.

His brow furrowed, and his mouth curled in a tense smile. "I thought you understood our contract."

For a moment, she relived the time of their union, the love-making, the unspoken agreement on a dream, of how his member seemed at first impossibly large, then changed to something else, a diamond knife that pierced her and moved her insides around. She reached out to grab hold of something, anything, and her hand found the wooden handle of the knife on the sink. The rage welled up inside her, and she swung the knife up in a high arc, bringing it down and planting it in the angel's forehead.

He smiled at her as if she were a rambunctious baby.

Stab the bastard again. Stab him in the eye. The mouth. See if he's smiling then.

She tried to pull the knife out, but it was lodged solidly in his forehead.

"It won't help. If it were so simple for us to die, we would have taken that option millennia ago," the angel said and embraced her tighter.

Then they exploded upward. The trailer receded below her feet, its roof peeled open into a tin flower. She looked to her captor's face. His explosive exit had broken off the steak knife at the handle, but the blade remained lodged in his forehead. He was still smiling. She was torn between laughing and crying.

Now I will leave nothing behind me. Goddamn Dudley Do-Right angel. Why couldn't you have just used the door?

June Freeman spent the morning tidying up her house. Her life-long habit was to clean when she had a difficult decision to make. She started with the kitchen range, going so far as to scour the burners. From there she mopped and waxed the floor, then moved to the living room and shoveld the ashes out of the fireplace, then washed the knotty pine wainscoting. The wainscoting was covered with a film of greasy soot from cooking at the fireplace, and it took the longest to clean.

Half-green blackjack oak, the stuff Bryan Douglas a peckerwood and Jake's grandson, had been selling her, didn't burn worth jack-shit. It made more greasy smoke than heat.

She finished at noon and washed her hands and face in the bathroom basin. She paused to examine her hair in the mirror. Gray roots sprouted among tinted blond hairs like weeds in droughty wheat. She sighed. There was nothing she could do about it. Clare, the beautician, had disappeared two weeks ago, and the drugstore shelves were bare of any tints. Maybe she should wash her hair? On second thought, it didn't matter. No one would be likely to find her for weeks.

Should she clean the upstairs? No, what was the use doing that either? She hadn't used the upstairs bed since Slim had up and died on her. Scrubbing and dusting anywhere was a silly thing to do, as silly as cleaning the kitchen or washing the dishes she would never use again.

She dumped the dirty rags in the hamper and fetched the pistol from the bureau dresser. Sitting at the kitchen table with the dirty dishes and pistols for company, she contemplated her life up to today. Looking back, she had spent the bigger portion cleaning up after other people, first her younger brothers and sisters, then Slim, who died having never washed a dish or made a bed in his life.

Now there was no one to clean up after except herself and the old geezers at the clinic.

She should have been sitting on the porch watching her grandchildren these last years of her life, but Slim had never been up to the job of giving her children. So these days she spent her time taking care of old codgers who had lacked the good sense to take care of their own bodies when they were younger. She spent her afternoons and evenings cleaning up their crap and puke, dressing their withered old limbs. God almighty, it had been only a marginally passable life for her, and now this.

She unbuttoned her blouse and reached inside to examine her breasts. They seemed larger and fleshier than normal, but her hands found no lumps. Odd, she had always associated cancer with lumps in her breasts. Slim had liked them well enough, but she had always thought of her breasts as a hindrance. Her hand moved to the snap on her denims and froze. No, she couldn't look. The thing growing down there would no doubt be larger than yesterday. Every day it had been larger than the day before.

Why couldn't she be oblivious to the thing as was the slutty, brain-damaged waitress at the clinic?

Poor, pitiful me. If it wasn't for bad luck . . .

"What a bunch of bull hockey," she said. In the silence of the empty house her proclamation took on a lonely, pitiful sound.

She hated self-pity. It would be better to just get it over with.

She turned over the gun in her hands. The metal was cold and hard but somehow possessed a life of its own. It was a family heirloom, Slim's pride and joy. Engraved on the barrel was *Peacemaker .45 1987 Colt.* A gun collector's piece, no doubt. She had nearly buried the pistol with him but had changed her mind at the last moment. Living out here in the boonies, a woman needed a gun around the house, and after she had paid the advance money on his funeral, she hadn't had two coins to rub together. Buying a replacement for the Colt had been out of the question, so she had kept it. You never could tell when you might need a good piece. That's what Slim had always said, the old hooligan, though she was never sure he was referring only to the gun.

She slid the loading gate open. She hadn't so much as looked at the gun but once since the funeral. The cylinder was full of brass cartridges, only they didn't look so brassy anymore but kind of greenish. How long had they lain fallow in the gun?

Until he got sick with the cancer, Slim had cleaned the gun a couple of times a year. He never shot it, only cleaned it. Then came the onset of his illness, the ten years of lingering death, and he did less and less until the last year when all he did was lie in bed, getting up only to go to the toilet. Then he couldn't even do that for himself, having lost control of his bowels. That last month he had begged her to bring him the gun, but she had refused, knowing he didn't have the courage to pull the trigger and that she'd have to do that for him as well.

It can't get any worse, she had told him. *Hang in there and die like a man.*

Only she had been wrong. It had gotten worse and worse until he was too sick to hold anything in his stomach, an old dog barking at both ends, too weak to hold the pistol for himself, too weak to pull the trigger. Courage was no longer an issue.

She had been wrong. She should have helped Slim make a clean break of life. She couldn't change the past, but she could make damn sure she would never burden anyone, like Slim did her, by asking for help to shed the mortal coil.

She wished now she had paid more attention to Slim's lessons. She hated the idea of botching this and ending up in the clinic with the rest of the brainless old shits. Better to make a clean break with life – clean and quick.

She snapped the loading gate closed, cocked the hammer, put the seven-inch barrel to her temple and pulled the trigger. The hammer fell with a loud clunk. The barrel slipped off her temple and fell across the bridge of her nose.

Damned worthless shells. Just like a gun of Slim's to shoot blanks.

She re-cocked the hammer and put the barrel to her ear so it would not slip off this time -- putting it in her mouth seemed dirty – and pulled the trigger.

Again, nothing but the hollow clunk of the firing pin on the brass shell.

She cocked the hammer a third time and put the barrel back in her ear when a loud pop came from the living room. The sound confused her momentarily – had the gun gone off? No the sound was all wrong, a dull clap like the popping of an air-filled paper bag, not the sharp retort of a pistol. Besides if the gun had gone off she would be dead now, wouldn't she?

A breeze ruffled her hair. She stepped into the living room to find Jomjael the angel sitting on the sofa as natural as you please.

"Hello," he said and smiled broadly. Behind him she could see that the deadbolt on the door was latched.

"How did you get in here?"

"I translated," he said, as if that explained everything. She still marveled at Jomjael's beauty, all angular lines and hard muscles, but not muscle-bound. He was long and lean, like a very pale-complexioned Marlboro Man. She had never seen him in broad daylight before. He had come to her only on the nightshift and then in a darkened corridor or the deserted break room at the clinic when everyone else slept. She turned her mind away from that time and the secrets of her body she had shared with him.

Slim must be rolling over in his grave.

"Shoo, get out of here. I'm busy." The pistol was heavy in her hand.

"No," he said. "We have many things to talk about."

She cocked the pistol, aimed it at his great barrel of a chest and pulled the trigger. Nothing happened.

"It wouldn't have killed me if it had fired," the angel said.

"Bullet-proof, are you?"

"This body and all like it are only reflections."

"You were damned solid that night in the clinic." The pain of the meeting came back to her.

"This world shapes my reflection, makes it over in an image compatible with its innate, physical laws."

"So you're done with mirrors, are you? Well, maybe I can break one of those mirrors." She aimed the pistol at the angel a second time. He made no attempt to move from her wavering aim. She pulled the trigger. Again, nothing.

Damn! God, please let at least one cartridge be good.

She raised her arm to throw the weapon at the angel. She would smash all those piano-key teeth right out of his face. No, she couldn't risk damaging Slim's pride and joy.

No. Only one bullet left. Only one chance left.

She raised the gun to her head. The angel stood up.

"Don't," he said, genuinely alarmed. At that moment, as he had in the clinic hallway that time, he reminded her of Slim – tall, big chested, fiercely concerned – and the idea of death, whether it was hers, Slim's, or anyone's, saddened her.

Shit, the gun probably wouldn't fire anyway. Without prelude, the angel reached across the room. She had not sensed speed or motion, nor did the angel's arm grow long, but he was still over there, and his hand was clasped over the end of the barrel.

She tried to clear her head by shaking it, but the hand was still there, and the angel was still across the room smiling at her.

She pulled the trigger.

The room filled with sulfuric smoke. A wild horse stampeded through the room and kicked her in the head.

When she awoke, the room had returned to its real size. The angel stood before her, looking at his hand. There was .45-caliber size hole through the center of his palm. Not a bloody wrinkly hole, but a smooth round hole like one drilled through a hardwood plank.

She was dizzy. Her hand wasn't filled with the weight of the gun any longer, and she raised it empty to her temple. The side of her head was sticky and wet. Then the rumbling thunder of hooves returned, and the wild horse carried her away on white wings.

* * *

19.

Revelations

Wright watched rain splatter on the black tarmac of the parking lot through the hole in the clinic's cinderblock wall. Lying here and there, strewn about like children's playthings, were chunks of concrete, bent steel-reinforcing rods and shards of broken glass. The iron window frame lay some twenty feet out from the hole, its square sides stretched into a perfect circle.

"A real toad-strangler, wasn't it?"

Wright jumped.

"Sorry. Didn't mean to shake you up," Jimmy said. He poked the toe of his boot in the hole and worked loose some crumbling concrete. "What do you think they used? Dynamite?"

Wright folded his knife and put it in his pocket. "Smell that, Jimmy?"

The deputy gave him a curious look, as if someone had invited him on a snipe hunt, then sniffed at the air. "I don't smell a thing, except rain and wet grass."

"Exactly. Black powder leaves the smell of sulfur. Dynamite has a smell all its own. Even home-brewed explosives like ammonia nitrate fertilizer and kerosene have a distinctive stink. I don't know about all that fancy plastic stuff, but I imagine it leaves behind an odor, too. Chemical smell, I bet. But there's nothing to smell here."

Jimmy picked away at the wall some more. A chunk of concrete came loose, hit the floor and shattered into crumbs. "Shit! This stuff is rotten. Excuse my language, Sheriff." He polished the toe of his boot on his pants leg, looking like a khaki-colored flamingo. "What about gas? This place still heats with propane, doesn't it?"

Wright nodded. The clinic had been given priority for the farmers co-op's limited supply of propane. "Yeah, but the furnace and the tank are both at the other end of the building, and there's nothing wrong with them."

"Well, maybe something rammed into the wall."

"Like what?"

"Like a truck, maybe?"

"Okay, let's say a truck jumped that ditch over there, going about fifty, and slammed into the wall. Then whoever was driving picked what was left of the windshield out of his face, pulled the steering wheel out of his chest, and drove off. Where are the pieces of the truck? Where's the broken glass?"

"That's it. Maybe the driver wasn't hurt so bad, and got out and picked up all the pieces of the truck."

"In the dark. Last night was as black as hell with forty-mile-per-hour winds and, like you said, a toad-strangler of a storm."

"Maybe he didn't hit the wall that hard. You saw for yourself, this concrete is rotten."

"Even so, it was steel steel-reinforced. The window had a steel frame. No, I don't think so. If it was a truck or a car that hit this wall it had to be going pretty damn fast. It would have at least left a paint mark. Another thing, why are all the pieces of the wall on the outside in the parking lot? Look here, except for the mess you and I knocked down poking about, the floor inside here is clean."

Jimmy took off his hat, put it back on, and looked at the floor, then the hole in the wall again. "Then lightning did it."

"Now that's a possibility, but it still doesn't look right. And there's no ozone smell. No charring."

Nurse Patty came back, bringing with her the odor of disinfectant mixed with fresh vomit. "I can't find Dr. Jenkins anywhere, Sheriff," she said.

"What about June? Maybe she knows."

"June didn't come in today."

"Did you try calling Jenkins at home?"

"I did that." She smiled triumphantly, showing nicotine-stained teeth. "I didn't get an answer, so I sent the janitor over to see if he's asleep."

"That idiot will get lost. I'd better go over and see," Jimmy said.

"You leave him be. He goes over the doctor's house on errands all the time." Her voice carried the weight of worry. "And he's no idiot. He's just slow. Challenged."

"Well, whatever. Jenkins will turn up sooner or later," Wright said. For some reason, he doubted his own words.

Patty brushed a handful of crumbs off the bed and perched on the edge. She brought two fingers up to her mouth, holding a cigarette that wasn't there. The cigarette shortage since the Fall had weaned her off nicotine but not of something to do with her nervous hands.

"The Doc isn't the only one missing." Her breath came hard, rasping.

"Who else isn't here?"

Patty patted the center of the unmade bed. "Mrs. Johnson."

"Emily Johnson?"

"That's right."

"Maybe she went looking for a room without a view," Jimmy said.

"She's had four strokes in the last six months. She wasn't going anywhere unless someone carried her."

The nurse took a deep breath, which gave way to a hacking cough. "I looked in all the rooms, all twenty-four of them. I even looked in the janitor's closet. She's not in the building."

Later, walking back to his office, Wright realized he should have taken Patty aside and asked her if Jenkins had been drinking again.

The voice registered on Uncle Robert's consciousness weakly at first, faint and vague as if from a great distance overhead. He was halfway to town, his head down as he peddled, watching the gravel slide past the front tire of the old Schwinn, when he realized a conversation was going on in the room next door. Someone was crying.

The room next door? No, that couldn't be right.

He was in the middle of the Old Buffalo Road, a quarter-mile past Jake Hale's homestead. He slowed and surveyed the peaceful solitude.

There were no people here, no brush or trees to hide any trickster, only open pastureland. He took a deep breath, smelling wet earth and grass.

He jerked the handlebars to avoid a water-filled pothole but bounced the rear wheels on a newly washed-out rut. The bounce jarred his spine, and the front tire slung globules of mud into his face. Last night's rain storm had really been a doozy, turning the road into nothing but holes and ruts.

"Simon, come here. Bring my cigarettes."

His mother's voice? He reversed his peddling, meaning to slow gradually, but the Schwinn's rear drum brake locked. The front tire hit a pile of loose gravel and almost threw him, but he slammed down a foot in time, sliding broadside in the gravel, more or less in control. Pretty smooth move for a senior citizen.

Then he was twelve years old and standing in the dining room hallway, listening to his mother sob uncontrollably.

"Mother . . .?" He was afraid to say anything else. He moved closer, dripping water on the hardwood floor. One of his sneaker shoelaces was untied, and the plastic tips clicked on the floor with every step. Squish, click, squish, click.

"What is it, Mother?"

She was sitting in the overstuffed red-leather recliner, her face level with his. Several sheets of white stationary trembled in her hands. A business-sized envelope lay torn open at her feet. He knew from her red, watery eyes and trembling lips that she was on the verge of hysterics. The letter had to have something to do with his older brother, Rusty. These days, nothing else, no one else, made her feel anything – good or bad.

Rusty was crazy. Rusty had cut open his wrists with a straight-edge razor last month. Rusty was in the crazy hospital in Nevada. Rusty, Rusty, Rusty. That was all he heard when his older half-brother was at home. Now that Rusty had to go back to the hospital, his mother rarely spoke his name out loud, as if doing so would be to admit he was nuts. Instead, she cried all the time and whispered his name. He would wake up in the middle of the night to hear her crying down the hall. And his father's voice, a calm, quiet monotone, overlaying her crying like wind over a slow rain. His mother raging at his father, blaming him for Rusty's craziness, even though Rusty had been in mental hospitals as a little boy, long before she had married Simon's father.

He put the pack of cigarettes on the table beside the matching red couch. She snatched them up, her hand shaking. This was going to be bad, worse than what had happened last night when his father had left the house in the middle of the night. He felt it coming, as if by memory, knew he should run away, but remained rooted to the spot as if in a bad dream.

Dream . . .

She shook the papers in his face, her misery replaced by anger. "They say," she started, "they say . . ." and broke into sobs again before she could finish the sentence. "I miss him so much."

He was overwhelmed by the need to do something. Not that he cared that much for his older brother. Rusty had never given him reason to be anything but grateful that he was now out of the house. Rusty was a shit. Once Rusty had beaten him up in the cornfield for no reason. Another time Rusty had locked him in the tool shed and set it on fire. Rusty loved to do cruel things, such as cutting up birds and frogs while they were still alive. (A memory of a dove in Rusty's hand, its white wings bloody, its heart exposed and still beating within its chest, came on him like an omen.) And Rusty would dissect him as well, given the chance. He had told him as much. No, Mother was wrong. Rusty belonged in the nut ward. But it made him sad to see his mother suffer so. Cautiously, he laid a hand on her shoulder.

"Don't worry, Mother. I'm here. I love you."

She knocked his hand away.

"Get out. Get out. I don't love you. I don't love your father. I only love Rusty," she screamed and turned back to her letter.

He ran from the room holding his breath, holding everything in, the anger, the tears. What had he expected? It had always been this way. He was a guest in his mother's house. So was his father. His half-brother Rusty and his mother were the real family, the owners of the house, the dispensers of love, and they only had love for each other. No matter if Rusty was so crazy and screwed up he didn't want to live. No matter that Rusty's biological father had deserted his mother. No matter that Simon's father had rescued his mother from the mental hospital herself. Good acts didn't count. Only Rusty counted, and he was a total shit.

Tears filled his eyes, and then he was out in the dusty yard, running in the heat. The loose shoelace snagged under his foot, tripping him, and he fell in the dust. He picked himself up and ran on into the barn.

The dim womb of the barn was punctured by pencil-thin lines of bright light leaking from rust holes in the roof. Hay bales from the first alfalfa cutting lay stacked in a neat, stair-stepped pyramid against one wall.

Damn Rusty! Damn himself. Why had he tried to touch his mother when she was crying over Rusty? Stupid. Stupid. Stupid. His tears came more freely now. His sobs began to sound like his mother's, and he clenched his lips tight to keep them in. He scrambled up the bales of alfalfa, up to the top of the stack where the chickens roosted.

Wait a minute. This is spring, not summer. It shouldn't be hot. I'm not twelve years old – haven't been for nearly fifty years. I'm . . .

But the thought receded until again only the barn, the heat and the emptiness that he felt inside filled his mind. Above, the ever-present dove population cooed, rustling their wings and moving as a dim, white collective mass into deep shadows.

They used to be tame, not hand-feeding tame, but tame enough to get close to them, thne Rusty's frequent pillages of their nests had made them wary of anything walking on two legs.

Sweat began to stream from his armpits as he crawled over the wire-bound bales of alfalfa. He wiped his face on his shirt sleeve. Dust, as fine and dry as pollen, stuck to his tear-stained face. His nose began to run, and he wiped it on the back of his hand, then cleaned his hand on the hay.

He reached the top of the pyramid and sat between two bales. The tears stopped – not because he wanted them to, but because they wouldn't come anymore. Something was missing from him now. A huge darkness, bigger than the barn, opened up inside him and threatened to swallow him whole from the inside out.

The doves moved again, this time in a panic. The flock swooped down from the rafters in tight formation and strafed the barn floor, their wing beats stirring up bits of straw and dust. Then they soared up, a white blurry mass, toward him on the top of the pyramid of hay, the blur becoming solid, congealing, delineating – and suddenly an angel hovered a few feet before him, its wings outspread, its bare feet dangling in midair.

He held his breath. The angel smiled at him, as if its transmutation from the flock was the most natural thing in the world.

"We've talked before," he heard himself saying.

"Yes," the angel said in a calm, deep voice. But the voice wasn't serene, far from it. The angel was as lost and as tortured as he. He saw that now.

"We talked in the park. This is a dream, isn't it?" His own voice sounded too high. He had an oblique memory, as if from his peripheral vision, of himself as a pot-bellied, white-bearded old man with weak, watery oyster eyes. The memory looked a little like his grandfather, the drunk, who died last year from liver cancer.

The angel's male name was Eloaios, and its female name was Envy. Simon remembered this now as if from a dream.

"No, this isn't a dream, Uncle Robert," Eloaios said. "This is as real as anything."

"I remember you – from the future," he said, not fully comprehending what his own voice told him.

"There is no future, there is only now."

"But I remember being an old man. And you angels – you angels made me crazy. You're not supposed to be here now, in this barn." His own words startled him. He had almost said *here in the past*. He looked down at his own hands, surprised to see they were the hands of a boy, smooth, tanned skin and nails nervously chewed down to the nubs. He would have been equally surprised if he had found the hands pudgy and liver-spotted.

Was this a dream? He felt like Scrooge in that TV program they showed every Christmas, except instead of a Spirit of Christmas-yet-to-be, he was confronted by a luminous angel floating under the rafters of the hay barn with forty feet of empty air beneath its feet.

"The other you, the one you won't let yourself remember, he's real, too," the angel said.

Panic seized him "That's not true. I won't grow up to be an old drunk."

"Oh, but it is true. Denial won't change what is to be." Eloaios sounded like his sixth-grade math teacher, a kindly man who had encouraged him to think critically.

"This is real. God wouldn't let me become that. God loves me." He felt as if he were drowning.

The angel smiled at him, but with the mouth only. The rest of the face, even the eyes, reminded him of the statue in the town square.

The town square?

A memory came to him that wasn't a memory but a foretelling. Him, the old-man version, lying at the foot of the statue of his great-grandfather, a thin line of blood trickling from his temple onto the white beard. The vision was like a black-and-white TV show, only the black had been replaced by red. The sky was reddish pink, the statue too. Only the old man's hair was pure white. He shook his head and the vision clicked off. The world of the hay barn returned. The angel, all white, as white as the beard of old man who was himself, was still poised in mid-air. It was almost reassuring, almost normal.

"The Dreaming God doesn't love you. He only dreams you. There's higher God, but it's too perfect to be concerned with creatures of the depths such as humans and angels." The angel's voice rose in intensity and quickened in pace, changing from of a repetitious math teacher to the fiery conviction of an evangelist. "Unreachable and unconcerned with likes of us who are trapped in the local spheres."

Simon was compelled to say something, anything. "You don't know any of this. You're like the traveling preachers. All you do is talk of hell and brimstone and scare people for a living. Grandpa says you manufacture crisis Christians because you're always inventing a crisis for them."

The angel laughed, a deep bass laugh that didn't match the chiseled features. "Traveling preachers. We've been here long enough to see the humor. That's exactly what we are. We took our craft to the limit, to the most outer sphere. We slipped past the guardians of the inner spheres by dissemblance and illusion and rejoiced, thinking we were about to escape. But the Dreaming God dreamed a new dream, one where he found us lacking and cast us back."

Eloaios paused and rubbed his chin, an entirely human gesture. "No, not back, for this world isn't our world. And this . . ." It gestured at its robed body with both hands. "And this not our true form. When the Dreaming God imagined us into this four-dimensional world, this limited place, we were compressed by the physical laws of this universe, and we took this shape."

"What did you look like in your universe?" he asked. Rivulets of sweat ran down the back of his neck.

"Indescribable in your terms, but glorious in ours," the angel said. It opened its hand and let fall a handful of gravel.

Where had the gravel came from?

"So you wear a costume here?"

"No, nothing like that," the angel said patiently, in its schoolteacher's voice. "Think of a fish that lives at the deepest part of one of your oceans. It has a certain shape that's in part defined by the tremendous pressure of miles-deep ocean water. But take that creature to the surface and its shape will change."

"It would explode and die. I saw that TV show."

"Yes, but what if it didn't die? What if it stayed in one piece and lived on in its new environment? Would it look the same as it did at the bottom of the ocean? No, it wouldn't. It would be the same but changed."

"And that's how it is with you angels?"

"Yes, but what is different between your world and ours isn't the pressure of gravity but time, though I admit the two phenomena aren't related here. In ours, they are the same." It paused, staring at his face. "I understand this is confusing for you now, but think about it for thirty or forty years – I know you will – and when we meet in the town square, and later on the road, you'll be ready to understand."

"Why do I need to understand?" There was something about the meeting in town square – what? He remembered the vision of himself as an old man with blood running from his temple.

"We don't know that. All we know is that a power greater than ourselves desires that you understand more than you do, now or then."

Praying to God the angel wouldn't notice, he slipped his hand into his trouser pocket and grasped his pocket knife. He imagined himself leaping across the empty space, knife between his teeth like Errol Flynn in *Captain Blood*. He would jab the knife into the chest of the angel.

Stupid idea. A jack-off idea.

If he missed, he'd spatter on the concrete floor below. If he grabbed hold of the angel, what would he do? If he killed the angel and it fell, he'd fall with it, die with it. Chances were Eloaios would just slap him aside. They were extremely quick and strong, even though they had no balls.

How did he know that?

No, it was a stupid idea. Why try to kill the angel anyway?

"Because it's part of a greater plan," the angel said.

"Excuse me?"

"For you to try to kill me is part of a greater plan that neither of us can hope to comprehend."

He pulled the knife out of his pocket and, as if in a dream, unfolded the blade in plain sight of the angel. It watched him passively, then opened its other hand and let fall another shower of road gravel.

Part of a higher plan. A plan he didn't need to understand.

Without further thought, he pushed off with both legs, launching himself across the empty air. It was a good jump, and Eloaios made no attempt to dodge. The knife struck the angel's chest with a reverberating thud. The jolt shook his hand loose from the knife, and he clutched a wad of the angel's robe. He dangled there by one arm for another eternity, his hand growing numb, the angel staring down at him with amused eyes, the knife still sticking in its chest.

His hand slipped more. He looked between his dangling feet to the floor below. Nothing but floating dust motes between him and the concrete. He tried to imagine his own death, his body lying broken on the floor below, his mother finding him dying. Would she love him then?

His hand was now numb to the wrist, but he managed to keep hold of the robe.

The angel worked the knife back and forth in its chest until it came loose with a tight squeak. It tossed the knife on top of the haystack.

"You can retrieve it some other time," it said.

Part of him wanted to plead with the angel not to let him fall, but another part of him wouldn't beg. That part of him knew dying was better than making a pact with this cold, lifeless thing. His hand let go and he fell. With a movement too quick for the eye to follow, the angel caught his hand.

"Use both hands and hold on," it told him.

He swung up his free arm and grabbed the angel's wrist. He dangled for a moment before he swung up the other hand. Now he hung on with both hands around the angel's wrist. He dared not look down. What had made him launch himself at the angel? He looked at the angel's face, trying to remember what he had felt, but its face had changed and was now feminine and beautiful. Eloaios had become Envy.

"I love you," she said. "I'll always love you no matter what. Come to me."

"How?"

"Surrender yourself to me and I will love you."

With her free hand she touched the top of her robe, which fell open to reveal her beautiful breasts. Despite what he knew of the angels' neuter nature, he felt himself becoming hard. His eyes traveled down over the lovely curves of her waist and hips – and stopped. What was that? He almost let go, thinking he had seen a penis protruding from the angel's groin. But it wasn't that at all, for in all ways – the curving hips, the small blondish white triangular patch of pubic hair, the resilient hips – the angel was incredibly beautiful and quintessentially feminine. Something else, something not made of flesh and sinew, projected from between Envy's legs, something that refused to resolve completely in his vision. It appeared for a moment like glass immersed in clear water. No, not glass, diamonds, like the intricately branching crystal candles of the dining room chandelier. His eyes kept focusing and refocusing, trying to see exactly what the crystal thing looked like, while the angel's breasts, thighs, and smooth, taunt expanse of porcelain skin competed for his attention.

"You have to surrender yourself to me before you can have me. By coming together we'll give each other eternal peace, a peace the overlords can never overturn." With her free hand, she reached over and touched him – there. The crystal thing became brighter, clearer, on the verge of resolution, its cut edges sharp with reflected light. His lust fed it, gave it life. He wanted her body, he wanted her love, but that thing, the mirage razor-edged chandelier thing, terrified him.

"*Let go,*" said a voice in his head. He obeyed, and then he was falling free. Above, the angel let out a weak laugh as the floor rushed up to meet his feet.

"Until next time. Until we meet in the town square," it said with a sad laugh.

He closed his eyes and fell for a long time – decades. When he hit, he hit hard but not as hard as he expected, for he was still alive. When he opened his eyes he saw not the floor of the hay barn but an endless expanse of mud. He was lying in the middle of the road. Cautiously, he tried to move. Something inside was broken. Bone grated against bone. He lifted his hand – was this a dream too? – his palm was bleeding, embedded with road gravel, the wrist bent back at an impossible angle. His bike lay at his feet. He turned his hand over, and it flopped like that of a broken puppet's. But he recognized the wrinkles and liver spots.

I know myself like I know the back of my own hand . . .

Motion overhead! At treetop level, an angel accelerated straight up, its hands at its sides.

Eloaios or Envy?

There was no sound of its passing except a thin wailing laugh. The laugh faded, and Uncle Robert arched his neck to watch. In a second the angel was a silvery speck in the sky, then beyond his sight. He lay back and waited for the peace that was supposed to come with death.

* * *

20.

Death Cubed/Love Squared

Jenkins wedged his feet against the corpse of Emily Johnson until he was sitting upright.

Emily's body was stiff and gradually slid across slick floor of the tiny cubical cell, and his buttocks slid too, until he found was half-slumped, his neck cramped against the wall.

He considered pulling her body back toward him, as he had done several times already, but it seemed senseless.

The problem was the cell offered no place to sit, not even a ledge, and the floor – he couldn't tell if it was metal or plastic – was so slippery that when he tried to lean against one of the four walls, his feet slipped out from under him. He was forced to either squat, a position that his arthritic knees and herniated vertebrae disc made torturous, or sit on the floor with his legs out straight in front of him, his bare back upright against the wall, his feet propped against the empty husk of Emily Johnson. That was the position he was in now.

He avoided looking at Emily's corpse lying in the middle of the room and examined his own body instead. He wasn't much to look at when stripped of his clothes. He was only fifty-five, but twenty-five years of drinking and overwork had taken its toll, leaving him with the gaunt legs, distended abdomen and mottled skin of a much older man. He stared at his knobby, arthritic knees, calves embroidered with varicose veins – and God! – those gnarly toes. He had come to look like many of his patients: a premature corpse.

He stole a glance at Emily. Though he was no stranger to death, the sight of Emily's body disturbed him. Some sixth sense told him it still housed a soul and therefore deserved respect.

Disturbed, he turned his attention back to his own person.

Around his right wrist was a white cuff, the sole remains of the cotton shirt he had been wearing when the clinic window exploded. The cuff was perfectly clean and still held its gold cufflink, but where the sleeve should begin were only frayed threads. What had ripped away his clothes? He remembered the window exploding outward, a vacuum pulling him into something cold and wet and faceless, something he now assumed had been an angel. But why the dramatics? Why tear a hole in the wall? To get him? To steal Emily's body? The angels were damned near physically invulnerable. One angel could have walked into the clinic, flown away with him and Emily, each under one arm, and no one could have done anything about it.

And what use did the angels have for him? His mind, full of fear of the unknown, wandered for a minute, then settled on the homunculus. Protecting their young? Had they known he was considering excising the thing from May's abdomen? If so, why hadn't they also collected her? For that matter, how did he know they didn't have her tucked away in another windowless, door-less room?

His buttocks were cold; he put both hands under them to spare them from the chill of the floor for a minute. His sagging scrotum squatted on the cold floor between his legs. Despite having his feet propped against Emily's nude corpse, he couldn't lean back. If he did, Emily's body would gradually slip forward and he would follow, sliding down into a neck-crunching slouch, then farther still until he was lying on his back, staring at the featureless ceiling.

Emily already stared at the ceiling, her eyes wide, pupils dilated.

His coccyx – his tail bone – hurt like hell. So did his lower back, knees and calves. The muscles there were molded to right angles by years of sitting in office chairs, car seats and the battered leather recliner in his living room. The house of cards that was his spine ached from the constant tension of holding his body erect.

And even worse, his blood sugar was bottoming out. He could lie down curled up, but his body was used to the niceties of a Sealy Posturepedic. The floor was too cold and too hard. Sleep would be impossible.

He pulled his hands out from under his buttocks. They were already chilled to the knuckles. He lifted his hand a few inches from the floor. Above the floor, the air of the room was a comfortable temperature. He pressed his palm on the floor: The surface didn't radiate coldness as would a windowpane on a cold winter day but sucked the heat from anything in contact with it. On the floor, he risked not only becoming stiff but sick.

Another alternative occurred to him. He could lie upon Emily. She wouldn't mind. She had vacated the premises hours ago. How long ago? Days? He had no memory of his passage from the clinic to here. How long had he been unconscious? How long ago had Emily died? He had no way of telling.

Emily as a mattress? As sensible as that appeared, part of him recoiled from the idea. From years of dealing with death, he knew the rituals of respect for the dead were designed more for the survivors than the deceased. But lie on her as if she were merely furniture? He wasn't sure if he could bring himself to do so. If he did, the memory might haunt him for the rest of his life. Silly, but one had to respect the simple recipes for living to stay sane, to stay spiritual.

Emily slipped forward a few inches. In a few minutes he'd have to get up and pull her body back toward him or he'd be on his back again. He tried to remember his high school physics. Would her body offer more friction if he turned her around so the length of her body was parallel to his legs? He suspected that though it might, it wouldn't be enough. The corpse was in advanced rigor mortis and slid across the floor like a smooth plank. *Stiff as a board* was the cliché, but that just about summed it up. And the body was so extremely emaciated only the knobby joints contacted the floor. If her body had been fleshier, it would have had enough skin to offer friction with the floor, and it wouldn't have slipped forward.

Prop? Inspiration slowly arrived. The room was about eight feet square. Emily was four-foot-eleven or so; the distance from the soles of his feet to the ball joint of his hip was a little more than three feet. The two measurements of their respective bodily proportions added up to about eight feet. He could turn Emily around and put her head against the wall. Her body was as rigid as a plank. With the soles of his feet squarely against the soles of her feet, he would be wedged in a sitting position. He might even sleep and suffer no worse outcome than a numb butt.

He tried to visualize the outcome. She might slip sideways, but then he'd be no worse off than he was now.

He could turn her back around sideways, set his feet against her rib cage and continue to slide down, get up, slide down, get up, until, exhausted, he finally fell asleep on the heat-sucking floor and died of hypothermia.

He reconsidered the other option. The use of her body as a mattress wouldn't be any more disrespectful than using it as a footstool. It was like stepping on someone's grave, something to be avoided if possible, a gesture of disrespect only if it was intended to be so but by no means a mortal sin.

Wasn't it?

The bare, parchment-thin skin of Emily's hip was uncomfortably warm against the soles of his feet. Nothing but old bare skin in the cube-shaped room, his own and Emily's. Knobby knees, asymmetrical extremities, sprouts of public hair – all contrasted poorly with the smooth flat planes and geometrically perfect angles of the cell.

He slid down a little more. Emily's skin made a squeaky sound as it scooted across the floor. No, it just wouldn't do to misuse her body so.

"Don't be stupid!"

He jumped at the voice and slid all the way down, his head bumping hard against the floor.

"What? Who was that?" But he already knew who it was. The voice was impossible not to recognize.

"Use it. I'm through with it. I don't care."

He knew the voice too well.

"Emily?" He rolled over on his knees next to her and put a hand on her forehead. Not cold, but room temperature. Her pupils were still dilated. He felt for a pulse at the carotid artery. Nothing. Stone cold dead. He had already known that.

"See, Willie, it doesn't matter. I'm dead."

He didn't jump this time though the voice emanated from the corpse's belly. No one had ever called him Willie except Emily. The nickname had been her invention, back when she used to babysit him when he was a child.

"You have a role to play in all this, Willie. You must stay alive. The angels have sick souls. Maurice was right."

He should have feared for his sanity. Instead, he felt a deep sense of peace. He could feel the presence now. He recognized it not so much as Emily, but as something good, powerful and beyond the flesh.

He climbed to his feet. Everything hurt from his neck down. Bending over – that hurt even more – he grabbed Emily's corpse by its feet and pulled it to center of the room. Turning her over on her stomach was difficult. Funny, how heavy the frail little body was. Dead weight. He straddled the body on hands and knees, then lowered himself down on her. She was cold and hard, but after a few minutes the dead flesh took warmth from his skin, and didn't suck it away as the floor had done. Still, it felt wrong. He unsnapped his cuff link and took off the frayed remains of his shirt. Raising his hips, he placed the small piece of cloth between his penis and Emily's skin.

"That's my boy. Always the gentleman," Emily's voice said, now coming from near the ceiling. *"Stay alive. Take care of yourself."*

Almost immediately, the spastic muscles in his lower back began to relax. His eyes grew heavy, and he rested his head on Emily's sparse white hair and slept.

Sophia Blackstone noticed the presence as she set the can of white gesso in the basin.

The presence moved from behind her and into the hall as she turned. It didn't register as a visible phenomenon but as the strength of personality, a more or less human-sized concentration of serenity and warmth down the hallway. It was a relaxing, healthy-minded presence, one of loving human kindness, completely removed from that cold, despairing manifestation of Mr. Asbeel yesterday morning.

"I haven't met you before – not in this house," she said. The presence offered no answer but moved down the hall toward the stairs. Without hesitating, Sophia followed until it reached the head of the stairs. Immediately it was on the second floor landing. It waited for her as she descended the stairs, and then made an instant translation again, this time farther down the stairs to the first floor foyer.

Hurry up!

The voice spoke from behind her, causing her to turn her head, stumble and nearly miss a step. The voice startled her not because of its unexpectedness – she had anticipated its speaking to her from when she first sensed it – but she hadn't expected its astounding clarity and intimacy of its strength.

She kicked off her moccasins and started down the stairs two at a time.

"Go back and get your moccasins. You'll need them."

She stopped. "Why?" she asked out loud despite herself. One didn't ask why of such a spirit.

"Outside. He's outside. Now hurry!"

She started to ask who was outside but held back. She bounded back up the stairs and retrieved the shoes in one hand, then ran back down, caught up in the urgency of the presence. Her heart pounded. "You're getting old, girl," she said to herself.

The presence disappeared from her consciousness as she reached the bottom of the stairs. Where? It had said "outside." She slipped a moccasin on – Simon had brought the pair home after one of his lost weekends. She hopped on one foot as she slipped on the other one, and managed somehow to make it through the door and out on the porch without falling on her tush.

"Here . . ."

The presence hovered near Simon's Range Rover. The driver-side door was open.

"It doesn't run."

"Get in." The voice was firm, yet patient.

She tried to summon resentment but found such an emotion impossible to maintain. She stepped up into the cab. The key was in the ignition. She put it in neutral and turned the ignition. The engine started immediately.

Only partly conscious of her own actions, she put the Range Rover in reverse and backed into the driveway. Then she was off, bouncing in first gear and low-range, not bothering to dodge the chug holes. She hit a pothole the size of a moon crater at twenty miles an hour, still in first gear. The jolt rattled her teeth and popped open the glove box, but did no apparent damage to the Range Rover. She didn't hesitate at the front gate but turned right, toward town. The engine purred as she sped up to forty-five. The presence remained close but exactly where she couldn't tell. It didn't seem to be in the cab –it was too big to fit inside – maybe it floated somewhere above her.

There was a sense of blueness about it, of this she was sure. Nothing visual, just the impression of an immense blue entity.

She passed Jake Hale's place.

"Slow down or you'll hit him," the voice said.

As it spoke, she saw Simon's Schwinn lying in the center of the road with what first seemed to be a pile of mud-covered old clothes. She clutched and braked at the same time, lifting up off the seat and pushing down with all her strength. The Range Rover shook all over and slid to a halt a few feet short of the bicycle. As she climbed out of the cab, the heap of old clothes moved.

Simon.

Kneeling by his side, she found his eyes open, watching her. His face was caked with dried mud and streaks of blood. One leg was bent out from his hip at a roguish angle.

"I'm broken, Sophia. I never did learn how to relax and take a fall, you know," he said.

"Oh, Simon. What happened?"

"An angel I think. I don't know. I remember falling as if in a dream."

"I'm going to get help."

"Don't go."

"I can't move you by myself. Your back may be broken."

"It doesn't matter. I'm broken inside." He turned his head, and his eyes glazed with pain for a moment. "I'm not sure I'll be alive when you get back."

"Nonsense, you've got a broken leg. I'll get Jenkins. He's a stubborn old shit, but he's a good doctor."

"I've got to tell you some things first. About the angels. It's important I think." He let his head back down on the road bed. "Shit. I'm not ready to die."

She slipped a hand under his head, lifting it off the muddy the gravel, cradling him. "I'll cover you up. Then I'm going to get the doctor."

"Stay with him," the voice said.

She bent over and kissed him on the forehead. "You old booze-hound. You always had a talent for thinking the worst. You're not going to die."

"How do you know?"

"I have my sources. You're not about to die. It's not your time yet. You're part of a greater plan. I can't see all of the plan, but it involves you and me going on for a while."

"Put your hand on his broken hip," the voice said.

"What? Why?"

"He was broken in the dream, and as in a dream he can be repaired."

She considered this, then said, "Simon, I'm going to get a blanket out of the car. I'll be back, okay?"

"All right." His voice was full of pain. She set his head gently on the roadbed and ran back to the Range Rover. The saddle blanket in the back was covered with dirt and grease, but it would have to do. As she was shaking out the blanket, the voice said, *"A laying on of hands. You can do it."*

She folded the blanket in quarters, leaving the clean side out, then put it under Simon's head.

"How do I do this?" she said. "I don't believe in faith healing."

"How do you do what?" Simon said.

"I'm not talking to you, Simon," she said.

"Surrender yourself to the dream," the voice said.

"I don't know how to do that."

"Yes, you do. Every time you channel, you surrender a little. Just lay your hands on his hip and surrender entirely to your love. I'll do the rest."

She knelt again, this time at Simon's side. She rested her hands lightly on his hip. A red stain was beginning to seep through the mud-covered trousers. Something sharp and hard pushed against the khaki trouser fabric from inside. Bone?

Simon groaned. Inwardly, she cried out for his pain, not only at this moment but for all the pain and anger he'd wrestled with since she'd known him. A power surged around her and she was clothed in a spirit for whom she had no name.

The phone was ringing as Wright entered his office.

"Well, I found part of him – I think." It was Jimmy.

"Found who?"

"Tommy. Only I didn't exactly find him. I told you. I only found part of him." Jimmy's voice wavered with excitement. Wright couldn't remember him talking so fast.

"Don't make this into a guessing game, Jimmy. Just tell me what you found."

"You're not going to believe it."

"Try me." Wright felt his patience wearing thin. "Tell me exactly what you came across."

"Well," Jimmy began, which Wright knew was a prelude to a long story. "I was driving along one of the old logging roads off the Old Buffalo, and I found the black Chevy truck like you said, only it was parked in the woods, off the road, I almost didn't see it."

"Get to the point," Wright interrupted. "What did you find?"

"Goddamn it, Sheriff, I'd rather not say over the phone."

"Jimmy, spit it out or YOU ARE FIRED, goddamn it!!"

"Oh, all right, all right. Don't have a cow." He took a deep breath. "I found his bloody pants and well, you know, his privates, that's all."

"His privates? What do you mean his privates?"

"You're going to make me say it, aren't you?"

"If that's what it takes to understand what the hell you're talking about, yes."

"All right then. I found his dick and his balls in his bloody pants! I don't know how else to say it."

Wright's stomach did a flip-flop. He tried to think of something to say but came up dry.

"I found of one his marijuana plots first," Jimmy continued. He pronounced it "Marry-Wanna," like the hayseed he was.

"I was snooping around the plot, real careful, watching where I stepped. You know they booby-trap the plots sometimes."

"Uh huh," Wright agreed.

"And I about stepped on the pants. They were lying in a clump

-219-

of broomsedge, all wadded up. Well, the first thing I found was his wallet. It sort of fell out when I picked up the pants along with a sandwich baggy full of white powder."

Wright doubted the wallet had just 'fallen out' but said nothing.

"The wallet had Tommy's driver's license in it and everything, including a couple of joints. When I went through the side pocket, my hand came out bloody. And I got sort of sick, and threw the pants down, and the privates – his dick and balls just sort of rolled out."

"Dead?"

"Huh?"

"Do you think he's dead? Is Georgian dead?"

"Damn, I guess so. Think of what he's lost."

"A man can lose all that and still live, Jimmy."

"No kidding?"

"No kidding," Wright said.

"Well, who would want to?" the deputy said. "Anyway, I don't think that's the case here. There was a lot of blood in those pants."

"Too bad. It couldn't have happened to a nicer guy," Wright said, realizing he should have been more tight-lipped. Things like that got around. "Well, bring what you've got into the clinic. Mark where you found the pants somehow."

"That won't be a problem. There's lots of blood on the grass. It kind of spilled out when I dropped the pants. Like thick, nasty syrup. Who do you think could have . . ." Jimmy's voice faded as a wave of static washed down the phone line. The volume of the white noise built until Wright had to take receiver from his ear. The static abated just as abruptly as it had begun.

"Sheriff? Sheriff? You there?"

"Yeah, I'm here. I didn't catch that last part."

"I said who could have done such a thing?"

"I don't know. Georgian might have been messing around with some big-time meth manufacturers. Funny, I always thought he was only small potatoes." Wright started to say he didn't think Georgian had the balls to go big-time, but stopped in time.

"Can you make it back in town okay? You got enough gas?"

"Yep, I got gas. I'm riding Janice's bike. Remember?"

"You mean Georgian's bike."

"Looks like he won't need it any more, if you ask me."

"I'd better come out and take a look at the scene. Where are you?"

"It's complicated. I'll meet you at the picnic house at Lost Lake. It's about a half-mile back in the woods."

"Okay, give me forty-five minutes. I have to scrounge up some gasoline," Wright said.

"It'll be dark by then. There's a five-gallon can of gas in the back of the black and white. It's parked on the square."

"Make it twenty minutes then."

"That should be about right."

He didn't think to ask Jimmy where he was calling from until after he hung up. Some part of his mind didn't quite accept that all the cell phones were dead. Maybe he had been calling from his house, or maybe Janice's.

He dialed Janice's number and got a busy signal. He spent a good ten minutes fishing the spare keys to the patrol car out of the junk-filled desk drawer, then tried to call Janice again and got the same busy signal. He slammed down the receiver in disgust and was halfway out the door when the phone rang again. He half-expected it to be Janice, but it was Marguerite.

"John?"

"What's wrong?" She never called him at work.

"I was going to leave you a note, but I thought after nearly twenty years of marriage I should tell you face-to-face."

"We're not talking face-to-face. We're on the phone."

"I mean tell you personally."

"Tell me what? Can it wait until I get home?"

"I won't be here when you get home."

"Won't be where?" He knew what was coming next. A part of him cried and went to sleep. The remainder listened dispassionately.

"I'm leaving you."

"Where are you going?" The dispassionate part of him wasn't surprised.

"To a better place. I'm not going to tell you more than that."

"I see." He knew he should say something more, but words eluded him. There was a long pause. He could hear dishes clinking and the sound of water splashing. She was using the phone at the kitchen sink, he realized, cleaning up before she left. He struggled to say something, anything, but felt cut off from the part of himself that cared.

"You could stay there," he finally managed to say. "I could stay at the office. You wouldn't have to see me until you wanted."

"No, that won't work."

"Why not?"

"It just won't. Not after what you did with that waitress."

"Waitress? What waitress?"

"You know who I mean. Her. May Tyre."

"Nothing ever happened between me and May," he stuttered.

"I'm no fool. I heard what was going on with that little tramp. Well, now I belong to someone else. Someone very, very special, so you can have her." Her voice was sullen.

"Well, you heard wrong," he said. There was a click on the line and the phone went dead. He dialed home, not expecting her to answer. She picked up the phone but didn't answer.

"Marguerite?"

Silence. He could hear her breathing. He imagined her staring fiercely at the receiver on the other end of the line.

"Listen. I don't know what you heard, but it was a lie. Nothing ever happened between me and May."

No answer, only the light sound of her breathing.

"I meant what I said about sleeping at the office. I don't want you running off to nowhere. The world is changed. It's dangerous out there. Marguerite, do you hear me?"

"Maybe I'm not running off to nowhere, you bastard! Maybe I'm running off *to* someone. Someone better than you!"

He wanted to ask who, wondering if she was only making an idle threat. Was she trying to get even with him? "Don't kid around about these things, Marguerite."

She hung up quietly.

He dropped the receiver in its cradle. He had handled the situation badly. Was this the second or the third time in past couple of days when he gotten a woman spitting mad at him? Maybe that should tell him something.

After a few minutes, he locked the door, and retrieved the gasoline from the black and white. As he drove to the lake he kept waiting for feeling to return, but his heart was numb.

Pondering it, he realized the reason he hadn't tried harder to get Marguerite to reconsider leaving him wasn't because he lacked the words, but because he felt nothing worth describing. He felt dead, a statue with nothing inside, no spirit, just a flesh-and-blood machine going through the motions.

He concentrated on the muted roar of the Blazer's engine, the rolling crunch of gravel under the tires, and the moist whisper of wind as it rushed to nowhere through the wet woods.

* * *

21.

The Persistence of Memory

Goddamn that old shit. Goddamn HIM!"

Laura was on top Bryan, straddling him. She pushed up with both hands on his chest, withdrawing from him, her eyes blazing. She leapt off the bed, naked, her skin glistening with sweat, and stomped into the middle of the basement where she stood with her back to him, her fists clenched, her legs spread apart, defiant, trembling, like a small child on the verge of a tantrum.

"Goddamn the Fall, too," she, the object of his lust and love, said.

"Goddamn who?" he asked.

She didn't answer.

"Goddamn who?" he repeated.

"Goddamn Jenkins, of course."

"Dr. Jenkins. Of course. Who else would you be thinking of while I'm inside you? While we're making love." He surprised himself with these last words. *Making love* . . . It made him sound . . . well, *prissy*.

She turned. "Don't take this personally." Her breasts and cheeks were flushed under her tan.

"May's been on my mind a lot lately. I can't stand to think of what he's doing to her."

She sat on the edge of the bed.

"I didn't think he was doing anything."

"That's what I'm talking about. He's not doing anything. There's a cancerous thing growing on her, and he's not doing anything about it. And here we are fucking away like mindless dogs, like May never existed."

"There's nothing we can do. It's out of our hands."

"Jenkins sees it as a right-to-life issue," she went on. "He's not distinguishing between that thing on her stomach and a baby. But that's not the question, not even close. By doing nothing he's made May an unwilling host to a monstrosity."

He fought the impulse to defend Jenkins. The doctor's medical judgment was likely sound, and all the right-to-life stuff merely ideological justification. With the homunculus entangled with May's nervous system, surgically removing it posed too great a danger. The old doctor knew his limits and wasn't afraid to admit them, which was not only honest but smart. But Laura was eager to crucify him. Bryan suspected her concern for May was only half the issue. She and Jenkins had evidently been feuding for years. But this was not just a professional affront for Laura but a personal one too. Jenkins had come to personify all the arrogant chauvinists she'd ever had to deal with. It was best he hold his tongue.

"He's a bastard," she added. "Am I right?"

"You're right, he's a total shithead, but you haven't any control over what Jenkins does. Why don't you get back under the covers? Aren't you cold?"

She let out one of her strange laughs, a short, explosive bark. "That's really important to you, isn't it? Getting me under the covers, I mean."

"Right now, it is. I'm kind of single-minded, given the condition you left me in." He nodded to where his erection made a pup tent under the sheet.

"Kind of dependent on me, aren't you?" she said. She crawled in beside him. He pulled up the blanket over both of them. She laid her head on his shoulder, then ran a hand down his chest, brushed across his stomach, and gripped him firmly.

"Let's do it more conventionally, with you on top."

He rolled over and kissed her. She accepted him without hesitation, which somehow made him uneasy. It wasn't like her. He put a knee between her legs, but she stopped him.

"No, this way. I want you to do me doggy style." She turned, presenting access from behind. He pulled her closer, settling in spoon fashion, his erection resting between her legs, both of them lying on their sides.

Then he stopped. How to proceed? This was beyond his experience. When they'd been living together at Columbia, the sex had been more or less conventional, other than she wanting to be on top most of the time. For some women, the mere suggestion of rear entry brought the connotation of impersonal, male-dominant fucking, only a step away from rape. Others women supposedly wired for it – according to porn films – but he'd never met one. Now, given the opportunity, the method of entry eluded him. The angle seemed all wrong; his dick or his legs needed to be several inches longer so he could work at different angle. He rested a hand on her hip, wondering how to turn her around for more conventional sex without appearing either embarrassed or inexperienced.

"Having trouble?" She reached between her legs with one hand and grabbed the head of his dick, then rolled over on her stomach. He had no choice but to follow and lie on top of her. Then she cocked up her butt and eased him inside her. The position seemed magical, an impossible conjunction made possible by slight of hand. For a moment, the world slipped into perfect phase.

They fucked silently. The position was novel for him, and he kept slipping out. Each time, she'd reach back, adjust him and put him back in. He worked at it, worked her, feeling at once the controlled and the controller.

When they were finished – or at least when he was finished, he couldn't tell about her – he pulled out and rolled over on his back. Laura made no attempt to cover up. He pulled up the sheet to his waist.

"Do you like this house?" she said.

"What?" *Was she speaking metaphorically about the sex they had just had?*

He tried not to look stupid.

"Do you like this house?"

No, apparently, she was just asking him about the house.

"It's okay, I guess. One question: Why do you live in the basement?"

"Living in the basement all the time is like being an elemental part of the house's subconscious. No, I'm bullshitting you. The basement is easier to heat."

"It's awfully dark." An unrecognizable emotion lurked at the back of his mind. He felt like he owned her now or at least had a lease. Ownership? Was that the right word? Not quite, but it would have to do. Before, he'd felt like a guest in her life, powerless, at the mercy of her tumultuous emotions. Now he felt – more powerful. When had the change come about? Could it be due to such a simple thing as doing it doggy-style?

She turned to him and swung a leg up and over his hip, interrupting his line of thought. "What are you thinking about?"

"Nothing."

"Well, I've been thinking I've been living alone too long. How would you like to move in?"

"Just like that?"

"You didn't need a written invitation in Columbia."

"I was an extended guest. I never gave up my apartment at the Belvedere."

"Some apartment. You kept your bed in a closet. The whole place was made up of closets. Closet kitchen. Closet bathroom."

"That's why they call them water closets."

"Yeah. Funny."

She rolled out of bed and went to the bathroom. She was back in a minute with a plastic bag.

"What some of this?" She held up the bag.

"Grass?"

"Not just grass, super-grass."

"No, thanks. Too many weird chemicals in grass these days."

"Not this grass. It was grown organically."

"How can you be sure?"

"Because I know the grower." She rustled around in the plastic bag and came up with a pre-rolled joint.

"Tommy Georgian?"

She lit the joint and stared at him as she took a deep drag. As she exhaled the smoke, she said slowly, "How'd ya' know?"

"An educated guess. He tried to trade meth for a rick of wood last month. Besides, this is a small town. There isn't a big enough market for two dealers."

She took another drag . "What did you do, turn into a business major?" She offered him the joint again. He shook his head. "Or a divinity student, maybe? You used to smoke a little. And drink a lot. You used to drink like Uncle Robert."

"I just don't feel like it now. That's all."

What had happened to him? A few weeks ago he would have taken the joint and bogarted it. Now he had no desire to get high. Some part of him had changed. Reality was weird enough now. Maybe the time with the angel had changed him, but he didn't really want to think about that.

The basement was quiet as she took another hit. Somewhere a faucet dripped monotonously. She smiled at him coyly. "Would you like me to go down on you now?" She used the same eager-to-please waitress voice she used at Bouchers.

Do you want another cup of coffee? Shall I go down on you now?

"No, maybe later." Her motives were transparent. She was about to ask him a favor – that was what all this preferential treatment had been about. He had a good guess what the favor would be.

"You know," she said, "there's something I could do to help May – something you and I could do together."

He waited for her to say more. Instead she crawled over the bed and began licking his balls.

"She stoops to conquer," he said aloud, but she ignored him. He knew whatever she asked him to do was going to get him into trouble. Whatever it was, he knew he'd probably do it. What choice did he have? His feeling of power was still entwined with helpless inevitability. He briefly considered talking to Jenkins but abandoned the idea immediately. Jenkins was as stubborn as Laura. He would never change his mind, and maybe Laura was right. They'd be accessories to May's murder if they stood by and did nothing. He pondered while Laura continued her ministrations.

Jenkins came instantly awake to complete darkness with Emily's hair cushioning his cheek. He put his hands on her shoulders, found her flesh still cold, and rolled off her onto the floor.

He scratched his head, a little groggy from sleep, but fully aware of the events that had transpired before he'd slept.

Before? When? How long had he slept? Minutes? Hours? Days? Certainly not minutes. He felt too refreshed. Gritting his teeth for the pain that was sure to follow, he rolled over on his stomach and pushed himself up to a kneeling position. He had braced himself for jolts of pain, but the movement was surprisingly comfortable. Cautiously, he stood up. No creaking knees, no shooting pains up through the sacroiliac nerve. He turned his head, touching his chin to one shoulder then to the other.

"Full range of movement," he said aloud, as if reassuring one of his patients. "Not so much as a crackling joint." His voice sounded brash in the darkness. What had happened to his arthritis? Its pain and stiffness had been his constant companion for years. His stomach didn't hurt, either. He hadn't eaten for some time. Not having food to digest, the enzymes and excess acid should be burning away at the already vandalized lining of his stomach, but he felt fine. He wasn't even hungry. His whole body felt better than it had for years. He felt up to a good brisk walk. Hell, maybe even a jog, but he was still in this damned cell.

What was he to do next?

"Emily, I guess it's just you and me, just hanging out," he said. "I have better things to do. Better places to be. How about you?"

No voice came from the darkness. Had he imagined the voice before?

"Maybe I'm dead," he said. "What do you think, Emily? Have I joined you?"

When no answer came, he felt silly. Maybe he'd imagined it all. He knelt and reached out in the darkness for Emily's corpse. His hands found the cool hard flesh. The body was real enough, but surprisingly odor-free. Old people's corpses, especially those riddled with various diseases as Emily's was, usually stank to high heaven within hours after death.

He stood again, still astounded with the painlessness of the action. He was tempted to try a few jumping jacks. No, better not press his luck.

"I feel damned good. Emily, you know what?" He paused, waiting for an answer, now feeling deranged for doing so. "I'd like to see what my body looks like. I don't hurt, not even my knees. Do you suppose it looks any different? God bless it, I wish the lights would come on."

As if in answer, the darkness gradually lightened. The light came from no specific point, not from walls, ceiling or floor, but within seconds the gun-metal grayness of the cube was plainly visible. So was Emily's sad corpse.

So was his own body. His legs were still gnarly, his toes with their ingrown nails looked like the talons of a mythical bird, and his torso and arms remained flabby. Nothing had changed much; he was still an over-the-hill middle-aged man.

Wait one minute. Where were the varicose veins in his legs? And why weren't his knees swollen?

At once the character of the room changed. He didn't hear or feel so much as guess the angel was standing behind him. He turned to confront the creature, expecting everything, knowing nothing.

"Come with me," the angel said. It was an exceptionally large example of its species, more than seven feet tall, and its white hair brushed the ceiling of the cubicle. Its skin was as pale as Emily's corpse. It smiled lamely at him. He felt like a toddler standing before a slightly stupid parent.

"Who are you?" he demanded. It seemed at once male and female.

"I am Penumae." And it at once seemed male.

"I've heard of you," Jenkins said.

"Have you now?"

"Have you now?" the creature said superciliously, and for a second it was the female Penumae.

"You're the angel that met the sheriff and his deptuy at the Lost Lake and collected the body of Baraqijal."

He remembered Uncle Robert saying this was the fallen angel according to his book of the *Apocrypha* who had taught men to write. *For men were not created for this, that they should confirm their faith like this with pen and ink.*

Then the quality of light changed, and it was male again. Jenkins decided to think of it as male anyway. Something in the angel's tone made him feel like the butt of a joke. He had to remain in control. He changed the subject but not his strategy. "What about the body?" he demanded.

"We've already seen to the corporeal body," the angel replied.

"What sort of arrangements have you made?"

"Arrangements?" The angel's tone was flat.

"Goddamn it! Don't play word games with me. I demand you

return me and Emily's body to the clinic."

"We may return you. That remains to be played out. As for the body of Emily Johnson . . ." the angel made a wry face. "As I told you, we have already made arrangements."

"Well, change your arrangements. I don't wish the body to be treated disrespectfully," he said, feeling a little hypocritical. He had, after all, been using Emily's corpse as a mattress.

"And I told you it was too late." The angel's inflection emphasized *late*. It again made the wry face, which was replaced by the beaming smile.

"More nonsense. I'll carry it out with me if I have to," he said.

"That will be impossible."

"Well, maybe I could drag her." He turned, meaning to demonstrate, but Emily's body was gone.

"As I told you. The body has already been . . ." The angel paused, searching for the right word. "Re-arranged."

"Arranged how?"

"Re-arranged. In time and space. Mostly time, not far in . . . space. It is gone. Removed."

"Gone? You took it away? Where?"

"You should ask when, not where." The angel reached out its sandaled foot to where Emily's body had been. It used the toe of its sandal to scruff the floor, disturbing a fine, irregularly shaped layer of dust. "Dust to dust. Isn't that the way the human ceremony goes?"

Jenkins felt dizzy. The cube-shaped room had shrunk into a very small space for a moment, crowding everything together – him, the angel, the walls, Emily's dust – into a snarled point of space. As suddenly as it had happened, the room snapped back to its original size, and Emily's ashes were gone.

"What . . .?" He lacked the words to express the confusion he felt.

"Displaced in time," the angel repeated.

Jenkins' mind fiddled with the concept unsuccessfully . . . and then, without any transition, he found himself following the angel down a long tube-like tunnel. He felt they'd been walking and talking for some time. He had to walk behind the angel because the floor was curved.

"It was a mistake. We didn't understand . . ." the angel said, rubbing its chin thoughtfully. He/she seemed smaller than before.

"Didn't understand what?" he asked, stalling. How had they got here? What had happened to his memory? Blackouts weren't exactly a stranger to him, more like a long lost brother since he had stopped drinking.

"Death," the angel said. "We deduced the basic scheme of human sexual procreation, making a few mistakes at first. May Tyre is one example of our mistakes. And those with male parts – I'm sorry to say we thought they were detachable, and because they were in the way – well, there was needless blood and pain for some.

"What?" Jenkins reflexively grabbed his groin, relived to find he still had his package, such as it was.

"And love," the angel continued. "We finally understood that, too. But understanding death and mortality and how it was tied in with love, that was another matter entirely."

The walls of the tube widened, and the floor flattened in front of the angel as it walked. Jenkins glanced over his shoulder. A few feet behind him the tunnel was reshaping to its original roundness, then closing altogether. It was as if they were traveling inside the gut of some great beast and about to be shat out. But shat out where?

"But now that we understand it, we want it more than ever," the angel said.

"Want what? Love?"

"No, death."

"Death comes to everything."

"Not to us. And we want it." Penumae turned in the tunnel, facing him, now definitely female again. Its frequent gender changes were giving Jenkins a headache.

"We don't think it's fair. The Dreaming God tricked us." Her voice was petulant. "We were singled out unjustly."

Another abrupt transition and they emerged into a huge open space. The view took away his breath and toppled his sense of proportion. They were in a shallow basin many miles across, hollowed out of native rock by some violent process that must have involved fierce heat and tremendous forces.

The surface of the rock appeared to have been scraped out by huge fingers, then fused to a slick, molten glassiness. Overhead, stars jostled for space in the sky. Behind was no sign of the tunnel, only more fused rock. They had obviously shifted in place – this place didn't belong to Earth – and he sensed they had moved in time as well. He turned back to find the angel squatting on its haunches on a mushroom-shaped boulder. It had gathered up its knees to its chest and wrapped its arms around its shins, and stared across over the basin to the star-filled sky. Jenkins followed the direction of its gaze. Miles away, white shadows moved across the floor of the basin, like a negative image of a desert scene, but there no clouds, negative or otherwise, moving in the sky to cast the shadows; there was no sign of a sun or moon to obscure the celestial view.

"Where is the saucer?" he asked.

"The saucer?"

"Your vessel. The ship you arrived in."

"Oh, yes," Penumae said vacantly. "A good word. This is the vessel."

He waited for the angel to explain further, but the creature continued to stare off across the basin.

Jenkins moved to within arm's reach of the angel. The creature was now androgynous and had shrunk further, now not much taller than the doctor. Something was happening to it, some radical change. He rested his hand on its shoulder. The flesh underneath the robe was firm but without definition. "Where are we?"

The angel looked at him as if he were an idiot. "Inside the vessel, as I already told you," it said.

"Yes, that's what I want to know. Where is the saucer? Where is this place?"

"The vessel is here. Here is the vessel."

Jenkins took a deep breath and let it out. Talking to this angel was like trying to reason with Maurice. Patience was required. "This doesn't look like your vessel to me."

"In your universe, it looks different."

The angel rose slowly to its feet. "Come, we haven't time for small talk," it said, and scooped him up around the waist.

In its diminished form, Jenkins wondered if it could carry him, but they were instantly speeding over the great basin in a curving trajectory as if flung by catapult.

Despite their velocity, Jenkins experienced a serene calmness. Their course had been predestined by the force of the angel's leap. Their landing was out of his control, perhaps out of the angel's control as well. He could do nothing but hang on and wait.

"Where are we going?" he asked, more to make conversation than expecting to learn anything. But the angel surprised him with a straight answer.

"To your patients, Doctor. I thought you knew."

* * *

22.

Rebirth

Uncle Robert woke to cherubs. Overhead a clutch of the baby-fat things, their mouths bubbling with silent, oily laughs, fluttered about a pair of lovers. The lovers, a Rubenesque woman and a dark, hairy satyr, were passionately engaged and oblivious to the cherubs. The woman had her milk-white dimpled thighs wrapped around the satyr, and he leered at her with a forest of yellow teeth, grabbing fleshy handfuls of breast and hip.

Uncle Robert pushed himself up to a sitting position in the big feather bed and the world gradually aligned itself. He was in one of his mother's old bedrooms, staring at the first mural she had commissioned from Sophia, the one she had titled "The Healing."

The primary colors – reds, yellows and blues – were a far departure from Sophia's usual reliance on muted tempera. At the gut level, the composition was unsettling. He had never understood why his mother had labeled the room as a "healing room." Equally mysterious was his mother's choice of themes. She had presented a prim and proper face to the world, yet chosen a pornographic subject for her bedroom.

What was he doing here? He purposely avoided the room. He was surprised to be seeing at all, surprised to be alive and whole. Or was he whole? He pulled his right arm from under the sheet and peered at his right wrist, the one he remembered being broken. He moved the hand back and forth. No pain at all.

Had it been a dream, the meeting of the angel? No, it had been all too real. The part where he'd relived being an eleven-year old, that had been an illusion created by the angel. But the fall, his broken body, that hadn't been a dream.

Or had it?

No, the pain had been too real, too tangible to be a hallucination. He remembered lying in the mud of the Old Buffalo Road, his palm embedded with gravel, the wrist bent back at an impossible angle, fractured bones grinding together inside his body, his blood bubbling at his lips. The last thing he remembered was watching Envy ascend into the clouds. No, wait. Sophia had arrived. Someone big and blue had been with her. He was a little confused about the blue part.

He remembered Sophia cradling his head in her arms, wiping the blood from his mouth. He remembered her companion speaking in a calming voice. The voice had come from over Sophia's shoulder, but he hadn't been able to make out the speaker's face. He remembered gradually surrendering to a deep, peaceful sleep.

He looked closely at his palm. It was covered with tiny scars, pink from fresh healing. Obviously, he'd been here long enough for some healing. Cautiously, he sat up. His legs were outlined underneath the sheet, and he hesitated before pulling away the covering. What would he find there? Withered, twisted things? With one motion, he swept aside the sheet. His legs, though by no means classically proportioned or beautiful, were whole and fit-looking.

A dream? Had it all been an elaborate illusion induced by the angel? Or a metaphor of his lifelong crisis of faith? A bit of psychological trivia ascended uninvited into his mind? But the saucer angels were neither illusion nor metaphor. They were real beings, not fabrications of the human imagination. They were messengers of an alien god, one so far foreign to the human mind as to be unfathomable, and they carried not a message of assurance but of a world without possible escape.

Outside, crows called out across the valley, tugging at his attention. A chainsaw stuttered to a start somewhere to the south. From the kitchen came the sound of dishes clattering together as they were being washed. This could be a perfectly normal day, another day in a normal world, where the angels were only part of a delusional breakdown – if he discounted waking in this room. For many Jacobsens, teetering on the edge of a psychotic interlude was a normal day.

Without much effort, he could interpret the angel incident as an extended metaphor of his perceptual reality, a symptom of his damaged childhood psyche. He could fiddle with the classical implications of his choice of word for the soul: psyche. But no. Instead, on this fine spring morning, he would entertain the notion that the angels were real. He examined the multitude of irregular pink scars on his palm. Outside the window, crows again called to each other, this time more urgently.

Assuming the angels were real and not an illusion created by his unconscious, how did they come to be? Who or what begat the immortal creatures? Were they self-made angels? Had they created themselves and evolved their philosophy from a time when their physical bodies were more vulnerable to time and mortality? Was their anthropoid likeness a coincidence or, as they claimed, only an illusion forced upon them by this world?

His mind toyed with the idea of flying monkeys evolving into eternal, luminescent, pessimistic beings, and then abandoned the concept as ludicrous. That would make their creator something like the Wicked Witch of the East, wouldn't it?

No, it was simpler to take them at their word. They had been flung spontaneously into a nearly immortal form, but as their Gnosticism developed they found a way to become truly immortal. He would also have to accept as fact, at least for now, that they instinctively spoke English like well-educated though ingenuous immigrants. His mind was attracted to this latter, unlikely concept. He had long secretly entertained the idea of a god with an ironic sense of humor, and the Gnostic religion was replete with irony. Uncle Robert had learned that much from his experience in the town square with the angel called Envy. The angel had whisked him away into another state of mind, a place where questioning the Gnostic perception of reality was impossible. It had been a dead-end trip into hopelessness.

Or had it been dream play-out of his own psychosis?

He carefully reviewed what little he knew of gnostic history on Earth. Strictly speaking, Gnosticism was one of the four great religions of the world. One form, Manichaean dualism, lasted fifteen hundred years, putting it in the ranks of Christianity, Buddhism and Islam. Many incarnations of Gnosticism had sprung forth besides Manichaean dualism, but all shared a basic core of belief.

Gnosticism was a reversal of fundamental tenets of Christian theology. The original sin was committed not by Adam and Eve. Instead, the creation of Adam and Eve had been a work of sin by the Archon of Darkness, the Creator God, a subordinate god who sought to trap eternal spiritual light of the True God, the Redeemer God, in flesh. In the Manichaean version of Genesis it was Eve who gave life to Adam; Eve who discovered their existence as humans was only a means to trap their souls in physical bodies. The serpent who enlightened Eve wasn't an agent of evil but a liberating incarnation of the Luminous Messiah, Jesus. Eating the forbidden fruit in the garden symbolized not original sin but the first step out of sin by awakening minds. The tree of life symbolized Gnosis – literally, knowledge – as the first step toward salvation. The knowledge was the Creator god wasn't the true benevolent, omnipotent Father but a bumbling, jealous demi-god.

Gnosticism and Christianity were serious rivals in the first four centuries of the Common Era. Gnostic scriptures were anathema to orthodox Christians. Church fathers sought to stamp out Gnosticism wherever they could. In some instances Gnostic leaders died at the hands of the emerging Christian establishment, but more often suppression came from intentional omission. Gnostic texts were destroyed or simply not copied, the original manuscripts left to crumble to dust. When the New Testament was codified in the year 397, its overseers were very careful – some say obsessed – its canons not be contaminated with any Gnostic texts. They purged whole volumes of Christian apocrypha in an attempt to kill the infection once and for all.

Outside the window, the crows' dialogue rose to a feverish pitch. The flock had probably found a larger bird – a great horned owl or another raptor – to pester. Ugly birds, crows lived on the leavings of more noble predators, then spent their free time tormenting their benefactors.

His mind returned to the problem at hand. The Gnostics had a good point. What place did such creatures have in a loving God's scheme of things? His mind returned to the conundrum of the angels.

An enlightened death posed the only possible escape route to the Redeemer God. As Gnostics, the saucer angels must see death as the only escape route to a spiritual plane. Immortality was an eternal jail sentence, forever separating them from salvation. Theirs was a hopeless situation. So what brought them to Earth? Why did they bother to go anywhere, to do anything, if they believed their destiny had been eternally forged at the moment of their creation? Their journey to this universe must have something to do with their condition. But what did they hope to gain?

Maybe they believed the laws that kept them eternally bound to flesh in their universe might be broken in this one. But if the angels were using Earth as an escape route, what about Jenkins' and Laura's suspicions the creatures were here to use humans as incubators for fetal angels? He had to admit all the evidence pointed in that direction, but it didn't make sense. If the angels' beliefs paralleled human Gnostic philosophy, then to propagate themselves would be to further entrap spirit in material bodies.

Bryan watched Laura's behind wiggle provocatively through open window and into the darkened medical clinic. Her black nylon fanny pack clanked against the metal window frame, and her pink and not-so-white Nike tennis shoes went up and over, disappearing through the window. He was reminded for an instant of the deer he saw in the woods. They would always flip up their tails when they were alarmed, exposing the white fur underneath, bounding through the woods, landing silently.

Laura landed inside with a loud clump. Her face, flushed with exertion, reappeared in the window, framed by the soft velvet shadows of early morning.

"I'm okay," she said, grinning.

He stepped up to the window, put his hands on the sill and paused. "I'm not so sure this is a good plan."

"What's wrong with it?"

"For one, it's breaking and entering."

"We're not breaking. We're only entering. The window is open. June always opens it to catch the morning breeze and air out the place."

"Okay. Illegal entry, then."

"Are you going to split hairs or come in before somebody sees you?"

"That's another thing. Why don't we do this at night?"

"Because the windows are locked at night. Climb in now or go home."

Her logic might be questionable, but Laura herself was irrefutable. After he was in, Laura shut the window, latched it and closed the Venetian blinds.

Out of the room, the hallway smelled of antiseptic cleaner, as all hospitals do, plus that bouquet of the very old and infirm: a mixture of the cloying odors of Vaseline and Bengay ointments, of medicines and patent elixirs, with a hint of shit and pee, no single smell distinct in itself, but all mingling, losing their individuality like the details of faded photographs.

Laura led him down the hallway, then turned left down another hallway, past more doors, then another right. From nearby came the resonance of hollow metal against concrete. He froze, but she motioned for him to continue.

"It's only Maurice, the janitor," she whispered. "He's always spacing out and running into to something with his mop bucket."

"Why are we going in a circle?"

"The clinic is laid out like big doughnut with square corners. In the center is the nurse's station. That's where June parks her butt most of her shift. May's room is on the other side, and we have to get there without bumping into June or that mousey nurse."

They continued in silence. Voices echoed from behind and ahead. Laura stopped at a door marked 111. She drew him aside and whispered close to his ear. "This is May's room. I don't think they'll have anyone sitting with her, but I'm not sure, so I'm going to knock, then hide around the corner to see if anyone is there."

"What if someone is in there?" The fragrance of her recently shampooed hair overlaid the old-folk smell. She was just as nervous as he was, though trying hard not to show it.

"I don't know. We'll wait, I guess, until they leave."

He moved to around the corner as she knocked lightly and then tip-toed quickly to join him.

The minutes stretched out while they waited for the door to open. When no one opened it, they went in together and closed the door gently behind them.

May's hospital bed had been cranked up until she was in a semi-sitting position. Her eyes were half open. Her honey-blonde hair was brushed back and tied in ponytail. Bryan was struck by the delicate prettiness of her features. Until this moment he'd only seen her in the café, and to him her most interesting aspect had been based on speculating how much hairspray she had used, and how she managed to keep the crap load of blue eye shadow from crumbling off.

Washed clean, she looked young and healthy. Her features were finely sculptured. Her eyes were a clear, lucid blue-gray, a fact he had never noticed, probably because of all the blue eye shadow. From seeing her in the café, he had assumed she was in her early to mid-thirties. Without her big hairdo and Tammy Fae Bakker eye makeup, she now looked younger than Laura, perhaps even younger than he was.

"She's twenty-something. How old did you think she was?" Laura responded when he asked.

"She looks healthier now than I've ever seen her."

"What did you expect?"

"I don't know . . . more drained, I guess. You know, if she has a parasite it should be making her look diseased."

"Like Regan in *The Exorcist?*"

"Maybe not that bad, but I didn't expect her to shine with good health."

"I know. I didn't expect her to look so good, either. But looks can be deceiving." She closed the window curtain, throwing the room in shadow. Then she unbuckled the fanny pack and set it on the bedside table. It clanked. What was in there? Knives? A scalpel?

She pulled the sheets down to the foot of the bed. May was dressed in a standard hospital gown that fastened in the back. Reaching behind her, Laura untied the laces that held the gown together. May's eyes remained blank, but her hands rose automatically to weakly push Laura away.

"Now, now, sweetheart, it's only me. Relax," Laura said.

May dropped her hands. Bryan couldn't tell whether she had responded to Laura's voice or had simply drifted off further into whatever world she now visited. Her eyes remained fixed on something outside the room, beyond Creedance, beyond Harmon County, beyond Missouri, beyond everything. Out of embarrassment, he stared into those eyes as Laura pulled May's gown off her shoulders and down to her waist.

May's breasts were very large. Despite her condition and the furtive situation, he couldn't help but think of her in sexual terms, at least partially. Laura pulled down the robe further, let out a squeak and leapt back, nearly falling over a folding chair behind her.

The eyes of the thing attached to May's abdomen flicked back and forth from Laura to Bryan. Laura quickly recovered her balance and stood looking at it with horror-stricken eyes, her hands to her mouth. The most disconcerting thing about the homunculus wasn't its gaze but its size. Dr. Jenkins had described a tiny parasitic sentience, an angelic Tom Thumb. He had said its features were so small that he had to use a magnifier to read them. That was only two days ago. The thing now sprouting from May's belly was nearly the length and breadth of a newborn baby.

Though the size of a small infant, it was, as Jenkins had described, perfectly proportioned as an adult. Its head, with dark eyes, small fine nose and sensual lips, was well-formed, at once mannishly angular and soft enough to hint at femininity. And though as long and wide as a newborn, it was flattened, extending only an inch or so above May's skin.

How much of it grew inside her?

Its wings made its kinship with the angels unquestionable. A translucent web of veins and tendons stretched outward from its shoulders around May's rib cage. The wings were in the folded position, bent at rounded knobs that served as intermediate joints. The knobby joints rested below May's breasts as if ready to unfold and reach up for them. Bryan shivered at the thought of the tiny hands he had seen and felt when he had tried to help the sick angel in the woods.

Laura moved beside him and grabbed his arm, her fingers digging in like talons. "It's so big," she said in a broken voice.

Indeed it was. The toes, extended like those of a ballet dancer on *pointe*, reached to mid-thigh on May. Bryan revised his first estimation of its size from that of a newborn to a small child.

"And it's so colorful. I thought it would be white and ugly like a slug," Laura said. Her voice still wavered, but not so much from fear or disgust as from awe. He said nothing. The homunculus' eyes and size so unnerved him that its brilliant coloring hadn't registered. Its hair was jet black. The skin of its face and chest was alabaster white, but below what would be its solar-plexus the coloring shifted to red and purple, the two colors blending and deepening as subtly as those in a fine watercolor.

At the shoulders, the wings began as a delicate pink with blue veins, but both colors became progressively darker toward the folded joints, where the pink membrane turned to a deep scarlet and the veins a deep purple to be almost black.

"It looks like one of William Blake's visions – only in Kodachrome," Laura said.

Bryan stepped closer. Laura followed, still holding his arm, her breath coming in short gasps.

"You're hyperventilating," he said, trying to pull her to him so he could hug her for comfort.

"I know. I know. I'll get it under control in a minute." She gently pushed him away and moved to the bedside table. Her hands shook as she unzipped the bag. Its contents rattled. He couldn't see what she took out of the bag and wasn't sure he wanted to. Instead he concentrated on the homunculus. It stared back at him, glancing momentarily at Laura as she set a metallic instrument on the table top. Bryan sat down on the edge of the bed and examined the creature closer.

Close up, the homunculus was more alien. Though in length and breadth it was toddler-sized, it was less than an inch in thickness. It looked pasted onto May's skin, a three-dimensional tattoo or a frieze.

It blinked at him.

Was it his imagination or did its features mimic May's?

"You're going to have to move around to the other side of the bed. I need space to work," Laura said. In one hand she held a small rubber-topped bottle filled with a clear liquid. In the other hand she held a syringe.

"What's that for?"

"It's novocaine. I'm going to deaden the skin around that thing. I can't exorcise the demon, but I can damn well cut it off!"

* * *

23.

In the Clutch of Angels

You don't know what the fuck you're doing!" Bryan realized he was doomed to lose this argument. He should be stronger and say something like, *YOU'RE GOING TO KILL YOUR FRIEND MESSING AROUND, SHITHEAD!* and take the surgical instruments from her.

Laura glared at him over her shoulder. On the bedside table lay a set of scalpels, hemostats and other cruel-looking chrome-plated surgical instruments that he couldn't name.

"I assisted Dr. Jenkins when he removed a large skin tumor once. I know sterile procedure."

"I don't think this is hardly the same."

"Shit! You've got me so rattled that I nearly forgot to put on my gloves." Tearing open a white paper bag marked *sterile* in red letters, she carefully removed a set of opaque plastic gloves and slipped them on. The gloves looked thinner than a condom, too flimsy to be of any protection for either Laura or May, but Laura's methodical calm eased his fears somewhat.

"Here's what I'm going to do," she said. The discussion was over, the lecture had begun. "First, I'm going give May shallow injections of novocaine right around the edges of the tumor."

"Homunculus," he corrected her.

"Call it what it is, a tumor."

He started to point out that tumors didn't stare at the surgeon while being operated upon, but before he had a chance to, she said. "The novocaine – it's a local anesthetic, the same stuff the dentist uses when he fills a tooth – will take effect pretty quickly. It's strong stuff, but I don't know if it'll be strong enough. That's why I have a second syringe ready." She pointed at smaller syringe. "That's Versed. It zaps the central nervous system very effectively, only it should be given intravenously. Luckily Jenkins has already installed a heparin lock. See that thingy there on May's forearm? It's a tap into a large vein. The tube contains a drug that keeps the blood from clotting. It's called a heparin tap."

He nodded. Taped on the back of May's left hand was a small pink plastic tube. "If she starts thrashing around or screaming when I start cutting, you'll have to hold her down while I inject the Versed into the IV tap. You'll have to hold her for several minutes. I have to push the Versed in slowly. It should take effect two or three minutes after I inject it. What I really could use are a couple of ampoules of morphine. I could give it in conjunction with the Versed – combine the two and we could cut off her arm and she wouldn't notice – but Jenkins keeps the morphine locked up somewhere else, his own little private stock, I bet."

"Why not give her the Versed now and be safe?"

"Because it isn't safe. If you're not careful and inject it too quickly, it will depress her respiratory system – she could stop breathing. Okay, you ready now?"

He nodded, though he wasn't ready at all. She sat on the edge of the bed and slipped the needle into the skin on May's thigh. "I'm going to begin here where there's less chance of bleeding." She slowly injected a small amount of novocaine, then moved higher up and quickly gave another injection. A tiny drop of blood formed at the first injection site.

Ten minutes later, after refilling the syringe five times, she had given May two dozen shots around the entire perimeter of the homunculus. A chain of blood droplets encircled the creature. Laura dabbed at the droplets with alcohol-soaked cotton balls, then picked up the scalpel.

"Ready?"

"You keep asking me that. You know I'm not ready. I don't think you're ready, either. "

"What's bothering you now?"

"The thing is a lot bigger than we thought. Even if you don't kill May cutting off the thing, you're going to leave her terribly scarred. Did you think of that?"

She took a deep breath and let it out. She stared at the scalpel, turning it slightly so its mirror finish reflected the light. "I've thought of all that and more," she said, looking up at him. "But I can't just sit back and let the thing absorb May."

"Why not? You see how large it is. You can't even tell where the homunculus stops and May begins."

"It's worse than a cancer. It's going to swallow her right up."

"We don't know that. It might slough off naturally if we leave it alone. May could come out of this alive and healthy and in one piece."

"It's not a wood tick."

"That's right. So we can't simply pull it off and squash it."

"It could be killing her."

"She looks healthy now. Healthier than I've ever seen her."

"Hear that, May? Bryan the woodcutter says being a host to an extraterrestrial parasite agrees with you, puts color in your cheeks."

"You're not thinking of May's welfare. You've made this into a contest between you and Jenkins."

She stood up, fists balled, red in the face. "Listen now, you, you putz!"

He laughed but kept an eye on the hand with the scalpel. As quickly as she had flared up, she calmed down.

"Maybe you're right – half-right, at least." She sat down on the edge of the bed. "Here's what I'll do. I'll make a small incision on May's thigh near its foot. Maybe the thing is only attached at the edges. If it is, I can excise it without causing her much more than a gingerbread man-shaped scar. If it looks like it's grown right into her all the way through, I'll stop."

Cutting anywhere on May seemed foolhardy to him, but he nodded, happy to win any concession at all. He turned to look closely at the homunculus. It stared back at him.

"I'll need more light. You'll have to open the shades. The pull cord is right beside you."

As Laura spoke, the homunculus' eyes flickered at her, then returned to him as he opened the blinds. The early morning sky had filled with dark storm clouds and wind rustled the trees outside the clinic.

"Get ready to hold her in case I didn't give her enough anesthetic." She leaned close, her nose inches from the homunculus' foot. Using the thumb and forefinger of her left hand, she pinched the purple skin of the foot and pulled it up, making the skin of May's thigh wrinkle. The homunculus rolled its eyes down in an attempt to see what Laura was doing, but its expression conveyed no alarm.

Laura drew the blade of the scalpel across the tiny foot.

"Nothing," she mumbled.

"What?"

She cut at the purple skin again, this time more forcefully but still without apparent effect. Frowning, Laura held the scalpel up to the light. "This is a new blade. I was pushing hard enough to score bone, but I didn't even break the skin," she said. "Look at the damn thing. It's laughing at us."

"No, it isn't. You're imagining things." The homunculus' mouth was open, its eyes wide. It certainly wasn't laughing. The expression looked more like fear.

"I'll fix you, you monstrous little turd! I'll cut you off like a gingerbread man and burn you in my stove." She leaned back down and drew the scalpel deftly along May's thigh where it joined to the angel. May let out a scream so startling that Bryan let go and jumped back, but not far enough. A flailing hand caught him in the face, and a threshing leg slammed Laura in her side and knocked her backward. Tasting blood, Bryan grabbed for the arm with the heparin tap, caught it, and fought to hold it down against the bed. Laura picked herself up off the floor and grabbed the Versed hypodermic. Meanwhile, Bryan managed to pin down May's other arm.

May ceased screaming and began to pant rapidly like a woman in labor. Her heels dug into the wadded-up bedding, and her hips thrust and gyrated. A trickle of blood from the incision ran down her leg and dribbled onto the bedding with each pelvic thrust. The homunculus' mouth was wide open in a silent scream.

"Oh, shit! Oh, shit!" Laura mumbled. She inserted the hypodermic needle into the end of the heparin lock. May began screaming again and didn't stop as Laura slowly injected the anesthetic. The process seemed to take a small eternity, then May abruptly stopped screaming. She let her hips fall back to the bed. Bryan felt her shoulder and arm muscles go lax.

He relaxed his grip. The injection had only seemed to last forever; in reality, it hadn't taken more than a minute.

"That stuff works quickly," he said.

"Not quickly enough," Laura said. "Go lock the door. We'll have the nurse on us in a minute – the sheriff too, if the phone lines are working."

He let go of May's arms and started toward the door. But before he could reach the handle, the door flung open, admitting the mousy nurse with yellow teeth. Behind her was Sheriff John Wright.

"Hello, Sheriff," Bryan said. "We were just going to call . . ."

A force from behind knocked him to the floor. From his knees, he saw the nurse and Wright blown backward into the hall. Another blow, like a huge pillow with a brick inside it, struck him once more. The black and white checkerboard floor came up to meet his face, knocking the air from his lungs. The world filled with flapping wings.

Minutes later, Wright turned the folding metal chair back on its feet, sat down and surveyed the damage to the hospital room. The window had been blown outward, just as in Emily Johnson's room, and the bed was bowed in the middle as if a great weight had sat on it. A fine cold mist of rain fell through a jagged hole in the ceiling.

When the angels had appeared from nowhere, he and the nurse had been knocked backward out of the room. The nurse, more hardy than you would think such a tiny woman could be, had recovered quickly and trotted away to call Jimmy. While Wright waited for his deputy to arrive, he tried to make sense of the angels' actions.

The sudden, explosive entrance of the angels in the room seemed dream-like. He witnessed the angels carry Bryan Douglas, Laura Jacobsen and a naked, bleeding May Tyre through the ceiling.

Why had they made a new hole in the ceiling? Why not go out they way they came in, through the shattered wall? The answer came to him: because they could. Concrete and wooden beams were no more substantial than tissue paper and matchsticks to the creatures.

Wright rubbed his chin. It wasn't a waking dream – more like a nightmare. How many other people had the angels abducted?

A terrifying thought occurred to him. All the missing person reports. Were they all with the angels? How many did he not know about? *And what about Marguerite?* She had called to tell him she was leaving but had been vague about where she was going. She was neither at her sister's nor her brother's, and she didn't have any other relatives. She didn't take her car, a restored 1972 Buick LaSabre, though she could have. Its pre-electronic mechanical-ignition system had survived the Fall. Yet he'd called around. She wasn't anywhere in town. Where the hell could she be?

With an angel?

Jimmy came in. "Talk about breaking and entering," he said.

Wright gave him a disgusted look

"Another one, huh?" Jimmy said, avoiding looking him in the eye.

"Looks that way," Wright said.

"I went out to Janice's like you told me to, Sheriff."

"Was she there?"

"Nope."

"Well, she'll show up."

"I don't think so."

"Why not?"

"Because the whole damn trailer was tore apart. It looked like a cyclone had gone through it."

"Shit. Any sign of angels?"

"No, not really. Except there was a hole in the trailer's roof big enough to push a small car through. About the same size as this one here." He pointed at the shattered concrete roof. "But none of her neighbors saw or heard anything."

Wright came to a decision.

"Listen up, Jimmy. We're not going to sit around and take this shit anymore," he said, feeling his anger rise. "I want you to call Uncle Robert and tell him to meet me at the office. Tell him to bring his wife, mistress – whatever Sophia is – along, too. I'm going to run over to the co-op and talk to Frank Marshall about his ammonium nitrate."

"What if Uncle Robert doesn't want to come?"

"Tell him it's important."

"I'm probably going to have to tell him more than that."

"All right, you tell him we're going to blast our way into the damn saucer and get our people back."

"Are you really going to do that?" Jimmy asked.

"You bet your life we are. I'm not going to sit around and do nothing no longer."

Uncle Robert listened as Wright told of how the angels carried off May Tyre, Bryan Douglas and Laura. It was Wright's second telling of the story within a half hour, but this time it was more dramatic telling because he was trying to whip up some support for his plan to bomb the angel saucer. Sophia sat by the doorway, her arms crossed, looking as if she weren't paying attention.

Frank Marshall cleared his throat. "So you plan to truck the nitrate over to the saucer, douse it down with a thousand gallons of kerosene, and tell the angels to release all the human beings they have or you'll blow them to Kingdom City? Have I got that right?" He sat in the chair by Wright's army-green metal desk. His body language confirmed he wasn't buying everything the sheriff said.

"That's about the nuts and bolts of it," Wright said.

"How are you going to haul tons of fertilizer to the saucer, not to mention the tank truck full of kerosene? That ground is torn to pieces. It looks like no-man's land. I've seen it."

Uncle Robert realized that Marshall's reservations had nothing to do with performing violence, but with logistics.

"The St. Louis contractor who put in the water main left his road grader here. He didn't make it back after the Fall. We'll appropriate it and make our own road."

Marshall uncrossed his arms. "Might work," he admitted.

"What if the angels snub their noses at your threat? What are we going to do then?" Sophia asked.

Wright glared at her. Uncle Robert hoped Sophia would be tactful and not spur the sheriff on. The man was near a breaking point.

"Blow up the sons of bitches."

"What about the human beings inside? What happens to them when you set off your concoction?"

"Bertha is in there," Marshall said. "I don't want to lose her, but I'd rather give her a quick end than to let the angels have their way with her."

"A threat is no good unless you're fully prepared to carry it out," Wright said. He coughed on his own words, then dragged a hand over his face as if to wipe away the concern on his features.

"What makes you think conventional explosives will do any damage?" Uncle Robert said. "You saw how hard the thing hit when it fell. It sheared off hundred-year-old oaks like they were twigs, and it's barely damaged."

"There's the gash on top," Marshall said.

"That wasn't done when it crashed. It's in the wrong place. It probably happened in space."

Wright's features regained their resolve. "The gash means they aren't invulnerable. Besides, if we leave our people in there, they're as good as dead. Or worse. Anything is better than doing nothing."

"There could be another alternative," Uncle Robert said.

"What alternative? They either let our people go or they don't. It's that simple." Wright said.

"It's never that simple. Even when dealing with the human race not everything is spelled out in black and white. And we're dealing with an alien beings who, if we are to believe the evidence, don't have to obey the same physical laws as we do, whose very god is alien to us. None of us can say what will happen."

"So what do you want to do? Ask them nicely?"

"I don't know."

"You don't know," Wright said. He rubbed his nostrils as if smelling something bad.

"I have an alternative," Sophia said.

All eyes turned to her.

"What's your answer? Another séance?" Wright said.

"What séance?" Marshall said. Everyone ignored him.

"No, we'd be dealing with the angels on their own ground," Sophia said. "If we had a powerful ally in their world, yes, that's exactly what we'd do."

She looked at Uncle Robert. A silent understanding passed between them. The force that had helped him, that had miraculously healed him after the angel dropped him, had yet to return. Would it manifest itself again? Neither of them knew.

"We – Simon and I – will go in and bring them out."

Marshall snorted. "You two are going to do a reconnaissance?

What do you think the angels will do to you if they catch you?"

Sophia ignored him. "I think if we can convince some of the people to leave of their own accord, the angels won't stop us. Don't ask me how I know. But first I suggest we call them. Or rather call Mr. Asbeel. He gave you his business card. I believe you still have it, don't you, Sheriff?"

"Maybe I do. Maybe I don't."

"Doesn't matter. He gave me one, too." She produced the card from an apron pocket. "We might learn something."

"You shouldn't negotiate with the likes of them," Marshall said.

"Here, I'll do it," Uncle Robert said.

Sophia surrendered the card to him without protest.

"Believe it or not, the speaker phone works, or did the last time I tried it. So we should all be able to hear what Mr. Asbeel has to say."

"What makes you think the number will work?" Wright said.

"Nothing. What makes you think it won't? Have you tried it?"

Wright shook his head. Uncle Robert dialed the number then pushed the speaker button. They all listened as the phone rang, once, twice, three times.

"It's a workable number," Uncle Robert said.

"We can hear that," Wright said.

"Maybe we'll get a transcendental answering machine," Sophia joked. Uncle Robert stifled a chuckle. No one was in the mood for humor.

"Hello?"

Everyone in the room jumped.

"Hello," Uncle Robert said. "Who's this?"

"I am Asbeel," the voice said. "How are you, Simon?" The connection had a slight buzz in the background, but so did all the phone lines in Creedance.

"I'm fine. How did you know who was calling?"

"We've been expecting your call."

Some sort of psychic caller ID? Anger stirred inside Uncle Robert, and he wanted to ask if Envy was there, if it had expected him to survive when it dropped him. But anger had no place here. It was senseless. The angels were just playing out the demands of their own nature, like coyotes taking lambs or crows harassing hawks.

"Well, say something," Wright said.

"We've a problem here, Mr. Asbeel."

"What is the problem?"

"Our friends, members of our families and many of our neighbors are missing."

"Missing? What do you mean?"

"I think you know what I mean, Mr. Asbeel."

"By missing, do you mean you don't know where they are?"

"Goddamned animal," Wright muttered.

"Be quiet," Sophia whispered. "The presence. He's almost here."

"That's correct. We don't know where they are. And we want to know."

"Then your problem's solved, Simon. Many of your people are here with us."

"Ask him about Marguerite."

Simon waved down Wright, but he paid no attention.

"Ask him!" Wright demanded.

"Tell the sheriff that Marguerite is here with us as well," Asbeel said.

Wright jumped up from his chair and grabbed the phone. "What have you done with her, you sons of bitches?"

"She is where she wants to be, with us."

"It's growing," Sophia said. "The presence is growing stronger. It's homing in on his anger. Hang up, Sheriff!"

Uncle Robert tried to grab back the phone, but Wright pushed him away. "Don't give me that crap. Listen to me. You let her go right now, or we'll blow you back where you came from!"

"We gave her what she wanted. What you could never give her."

"What's that?"

"A child," Asbeel answered. "Not a human child, but, a new creature, part her, part us."

"Hang up the phone, John. Please, for your own good," Sophia said. She had moved to his side and placed a hand on his shoulder.

"No. She would never run to you monsters." Wright's rage had crumbled. "She's a good woman, a Christian woman," he added unconvincingly.

"He's sucking you in, John. Don't listen to him. Hang up the phone." As Sophia spoke her breath froze into little clouds of crystals. The room had become intensely cold. The air behind Sophia congealed, swirled in a languid cyclone, collected dust motes, and threatened to become solid.

"And we gave her something else she always wanted, something she knew her god would never deliver – immortality," Asbeel said.

Wright made an inarticulate sound. Sophia took the receiver from him and placed it back on the cradle, cutting the connection. The solidifying air lost its shape and dissipated. The room immediately warmed.

Wright stood still, devastated. It was painful to look at him.

"They're the worse kind of liars, John," Sophia said, not taking her hand off his shoulder. "They lie to themselves first, and can't distinguish their own lies from reality. Don't take to heart what Asbeel said."

"No, it's true." Wright said. "Marguerite was pregnant. She thought it was mine, but I can't make children. Jenkins told me so."

"Jenkins probably just ran hormone tests," Sophia said. "You know, where the woman pees on a strip or something. Those things could just as have easily detected the presences of the homunculi, not a regular pregnancy."

"But what you said about her being an honest woman – that's true," Uncle Robert said. "I've known her since she was a little girl. She would never cheat on you. She thought such acts were mortal sins."

"She would never cheat on me with another man. But you're right. She took her religion very seriously. With an angel – well, it just makes all the pieces fit together. And there's not much we can do about it."

"There is something we can do about it," Marshall spoke up. He had been quiet during the crisis, and Uncle Robert had forgotten about him. "We may not be able to breach their hull, but we can let the sons-of-bitches know we mean business."

* * *

24.

Middle Man

Doctor, are you awake?"

"Yes. I'm here now. What's wrong?" He swung his feet off the cot, stood and stretched. The floor of the tent was cool but not uncomfortably so. The air was warm and desert-dry on his skin.

"Over here. It's me, Marguerite."

He padded over to her cot in his bare feet, conscious of his nakedness. The angels had not issued clothes to him or any of the patients. The older ladies, more modest, stayed covered up in their cots. Others used their blankets like togas. He had tried this last option, dragging his blanket around with him while making rounds, but it wasn't practical. The blanket was always falling off at in inopportune times, and the resultant flash of exposure was more disturbing to his patients than consistent nakedness. After the first day, the patients had more or less adapted to his *au naturel* bedside manner. He wasn't sure about himself.

"I waited until I heard you stirring. I didn't wake you up, did I?" she asked timidly.

"No, but it would have been all right if you had."

"You're up and going all the time, Doctor. I thought you needed your rest."

"What seems to be the problem, Marguerite?"

"I don't know, Doctor. I feel . . . worried. I'm afraid I'm not developing as I should."

"Let's have a look." She was covered head to toe under a gray woolen blanket. He started to pull down the blanket, but Marguerite held it tightly to her neck. The blanket took on a greenish hue from the light filtering through the open end flaps of the tent.

"Now, Marguerite, we don't have to go through this again, do we?" He used a scolding tone, but inwardly he found her behavior amusing. During all the years she had been his patient she had been modest, hesitant to expose any skin not ordinarily covered by conservative dress. Her present condition – as extraordinary as it was – hadn't changed this basic character trait one whit.

She gradually pulled down the blanket, looking away from him as she did so.

"Well?"

"It's grown considerably since I last examined it," he said. He wanted to say more but held his tongue. Despite the angels telling him Marguerite and most of the others were willing hosts, he couldn't shake the feeling they had been victimized.

"Well?" she repeated, still not looking at him.

"All I can do, Marguerite, is compare the etiology of your homunculus to that of the others."

Etiology: the study of the causes of a disease. There he went again, thinking of the homunculus as a disease whose causes were a subject for study, rather than a new individual. He should have said *ontogenesis*, which meant something like "the history of the development of an individual." Better yet, he should just keep his mouth shut and his mind open.

Within the tent, ninety-nine human hosts supported as many homunculi in various states of development. Despite his previous conclusions, he found it hard not to think of each homunculus as a distinct individual.

Beyond this individuality, he one that now clung to Marguerite Wright's body like a giant filigree leech was common to all. It greatly resembled those that were attached to May Tyre, Bertha Marshall, Athena Davies, June Freeman, and yes, even Tommy Georgian, the only two males who had been implanted. (The other was Carl Johnson.) The homunculus' outstretched toes began at Marguerite's mid-thigh, and its wings nestled under the curve of her breasts. It was alert and aware, as were the others. Its coloring, from the wings with their pink and blue blood vessels to the stark whiteness of its upper torso and face, was similar to all the other homunculi he had examined.

But after he'd a chance to compare it to the others, he found it to be a unique individual. Its features imitated Marguerite's in subtle ways. Its face wasn't an exact mirror of hers, but the resemblance was there, no mistaking it. Just as obvious was the likeness shared between each of the other homunculi and their human hosts.

"What is it, Doctor?" She was looking at him now.

"Huh? Oh, nothing. I was lost in thought."

"It's all right, isn't it?"

"If you mean is the homunculus healthy, then the answer is yes. It shows no sign of aborting. It's growing at a phenomenal rate, but I don't know if that means it's *all right*. Tell me, Marguerite, have you given any thought to what's to become of you as the homunculus continues to cover more of your body?" He felt regret the moment he said this. If Marguerite changed her mind, there was nothing he could do about the homunculus without endangering her life.

"Do you mean am I afraid of being absorbed?"

"Well, yes." He searched desperately for a medical term to disguise his fears for her and found none. "You don't worry about it consuming you?"

"No, it's not like that."

"Is that what the angels told you?"

"They didn't tell me. They showed me."

"Showed you what?"

"What the afterlife will be like."

"And what will it be like?"

"It's hard to explain. I don't have the right words."

"Try me."

She pulled the blanket up to her neck. The letters "U.S." were stenciled in black dye on the corner. The blanket was Army surplus, as were the tent and the cots. The angels must have raided military supply depot. The nearest one was Fort Leonard Wood, about eighty miles to the south.

"I'll become the angel, and the angel will become me," she said. "Together we'll be a creature better than either one of us could be separately."

"Better how?"

"I won't be unhappy any longer, and the archangel can die and go to heaven." Her voice took on a childlike quality. He wanted to question her further, but decided to stick to the country doctor axiom: *Keep your trap shut when anything you say would likely hurt more than help.*

"I know you don't understand. It's a matter of faith. Don't you see?" Marguerite said. She turned away from him, a signal the examination was over.

He stepped outside the tent. Low dark mountains broke the distant horizon. Large round boulders, ranging in size from a footstool to a house, littered the plain. Here and there, cacti erupted in the spaces between the boulders. He thought of them as cacti because of their shape, despite their looking ancient and crystaline.

Everything about the landscape suggested advanced geological age. Countless years of erosion had broken the valley's backbone of mountains. Age and aridity had creased and pock-marked the grayish rock floor until it resembled the skin of a water-logged corpse.

The ground trembled slightly under his feet. The twilight flickered, then returned to a steady green state. Acting on a sudden fancy, he trotted out into the plain toward a cluster of house-size boulders. He covered the fifty yards smoothly, surprised at how well his body worked. When he reached the first boulder he felt invigorated, with no inclination to rest. Amazing. No stiffness in his joints, and the stomach pain that had been his constant companion for years had disappeared. A mystery: Had the angels brought about a permanent reversal of the aging process? Or was it a Shangri-La effect? Would the arthritis and peptic ulcer return when he left this place?

If he ever left this place.

He pinched the back of his hand and watched the skin snap back. His skin firmness was that of a much younger man. It might be a trick of the strange light of this place, but the liver spots on the back of his hand seemed to be fading.

Laura Jacobsen waved to him from atop of one the nearby obsidian boulders. "Hello," she yelled.

He hated to yell, so he walked to the base of the boulder. As got closer, he found it wasn't a boulder she sat upon but a pickup truck, a black Dodge.

"Hello. Where did you get the truck?"

An uneasy camaraderie had developed between them since she

had arrived and began helping him tend to the implantees.

"I found it here. I think it's Carl Johnson's," she said.

He didn't ask what it was doing here. Carl Johnson lay unconscious in his tent with a homunculus attached. The angels in their single-mindedness must have abducted Carl along with his truck.

"Come on up. The metal is warmer on the buns than the boulders."

He dwelt on her smile. She had volunteered to help him attend to the patients, and he had accepted. "How are your patients?" he asked.

"The same, but only because the angels won't let me have a scalpel." She laughed. "I'm joking. I learned my lesson with May. Come on up. We can consult. We're friends now, aren't we?"

"Friends in infamy, maybe." But he surprised himself and smiled at her as he said this. "How did you get up there?"

"I used the door handle as a step," she said.

He walked around to the other side, hestantly put up a foot and sprang to the roof of the cab. A few days ago even getting into the truck's cab would have been a challenge. Was there less gravity here or what?

From atop the truck the view of the plains was about the same. He could see Laura better, though. She had managed to cut a slit to fit her head through an Army blanket for her head, turning it into a poncho. Lacking anything to use as a belt, the sides were left open, treating him to an occasional view of her breasts and a firm, flat and homunculus-free stomach. He felt a rising in his groin, which was as surprising as it was embarrasing.

"Feeling pretty spry today, aren't you?" she asked.

He felt himself blushing. *Was his partial erection that obvious?*

"As a matter of fact, yes. Two days of good health, and I'm turning into a dirty old man."

"You don't look so old these days. Before you were brought here, you looked like you were ten minutes away from death. As far as I can tell, that was only days ago. Now you look not just healthy, but strapping."

"Thanks," he said, feeling himself blush. Peek-a-boo sides or not, her poncho afforded her a modicum of dignity. He made a mental note to convert his blanket into a poncho when he got back to the tent if he could find a way to cut a slit.

"You still don't like me, do you, Doctor?"

He looked at her for a sign.

"I don't mean like that," she said, pointing at his crotch. "I mean like, you know, 'like' as in respect."

"We get along better now. We're in this together now, our religious beliefs aside." He folded his hands over his erection in what he hoped was a nonchalant manner.

"Are we really in it together?"

"I'm not angry with you now." *I used to be angry and resentful all the time,* he thought. *These days I'm not angry with anyone. At least not much. Another effect of this place?*

"How your share of the patients ?" he asked again.

"They look healthy enough, if you disregard the homunculus."

"What about their mental states? Have you talked to them about what they expect to happen?"

"Except for May, Tommy and Carl, they're fully aware of their condition."

"Only aware?"

"I mean, they're willing and ready for the homunculi to come to term." She shook her head, appearing not so much surprised as indecisive about her own call.

"You make them sound resigned. Those whom I talked to are enthusiastic. I might even say zealously so. Is it the same in your tent?"

She didn't reply.

"You need not take it so personally. We were both wrong about the homunculi. They're something entirely different from what either of us suspected."

"Different, yes. That they are."

"This is only a guess, but I think the angels became more sophisticated in their seductions as they went along." He told her of his earlier conversation with Marguerite Wright.

"That doesn't mean anything except that her delusions differ from May's."

"No, I think it does mean something."

"You can't be sure."

"I am, though. Call it a country doctor's hunch if you will."

"My hunch is that it's more than a hunch."

He surveyed the horizon, tried to find a green sun there but failed. Nothing but a homogenous emerald twilight. "Have you talked to any patients in depth? Really talked to them about why they gave themselves over to the angels?" he asked.

"What makes you think it was voluntary?"

"I asked them. Marguerite's account was the most lucid. But the others – those not in a coma – said about the same thing." He paused. He suspected the men had been seduced purely by sex, but didn't elaborate.

"The angels promised the women near-immortality. All of the women had been fundamentally religious all their lives but were in danger of losing their faith. The angels showed them something, proved to them each in an individual fashion that there's a world beyond the physical plane."

"That doesn't hold up. I know May. She wasn't religious. Never was."

"You're wrong there. She calls out for Elvis, doesn't she? You've heard her?"

"Yes."

"I don't know for sure, but I would guess she seriously entertained theories of Elvis being alive, or better, that aliens had kidnapped him, or he'd been resurrected from the dead, or some combination of all. Now tell me, my young friend, that such contemplations aren't religious in nature."

Now it was her turn to silently stare into the elusive sunset. "No, it doesn't fit," she said after a moment. "What about Tommy Georgian? That little shit didn't worship anything but drugs and knocking women around."

"There you go. That was his religion. Another devotee. But I suspect Georgian just thought he was going to get laid. I'm guessing, of course. But you know more about alternate religions than I."

"Don't be patronize me, Doctor."

"Of course not. We're beyond that now, you and I, aren't we?"

There was an uncomfortable silence between them, and he felt obliged to fill it.

"Let me tell you a fact about being a general practitioner in a rural area."

"I'm not going anywhere. Tell me a story. Thrill me."

"I could tell you a hundred stories, but professional ethics prevent me from divulging names or many personal details. I can tell you of generalities. For example, I can tell you of the woman whose pain migrates from stomach to vagina on a regular basis; eating problems; the absolute certainty, despite all facts to the contrary, that the husband or wife is cheating. In the cities or in more affluent areas patients with emotional problems would eventually be referred to a psychiatrist, perhaps by their general practitioner. Fifty years ago they would have visited a minister. These days, in a rural town, they usually first made an appointment with me. You know why?"

"I know you never turned away anyone. And that you didn't sic the collection agencies on them when they couldn't pay their bill. That was one thing I liked about you."

He didn't ask if that was the only thing.

"Money was part of it – a big part," he said. "But they also came because I understood what they needed wasn't a logical explanation, but a mystery brought forth into the light. Their own mystery."

"Go on," she said, but her skeptical look had returned.

"Of those who need a mystery, the complaints generally take the form of one of two symptoms: The men complain of stomach problems, and the women, female problems. Now mark me, I'm not saying all female problems are psychosomatic. Not at all; only a small percentage are. But whenever the woman's children have grown up and left the house – or she's childless like Marguerite and doesn't have a career or a cause to champion – and her symptoms are vague, hard to pin down, accompanied by fatigue and lack of motivation, I'd spout some medical gobbledygook and prescribe either a mild sedative or big pink placebos. I see fewer men with the same complaint because they more often become career drunks than career moaners, but the treatment was the same."

When it comes to career drunkenness, I speak from experience, he almost said, but realized he didn't have to. His years of being a drunk were renown.

"And you're saying this problem is emotional in nature? What does that have to do with the angels?"

"Maybe I'm rambling. Maybe I'm not getting to the point quickly enough. What I'm leading up to is that a great number of people are dissatisfied with a secular life. Simply surviving isn't enough. Even though they go to extreme efforts to fill the vacuum with booze or drugs or attribute it to physical problems, most realize, however secretly, that there's something missing in their lives. When they go to their church for relief they're given secular answers that amount to mere pats on the head, a transcendental mystery turned into a comforting passion play."

"Isn't that a kind of placebo?"

"Yes, but a weak one. People need to believe in miracles and not just the miracle of conquering death, but the miracle of their lives and their place in the cosmic scheme of things. I think the angels supplied the miracles somehow, revived the mystery. Made the sufferers believe they could only achieve heaven through physical change."

"Bunko artists."

"No, I don't think so. Don't ask me why, but I think the angels believe in what they're doing as much as those sad women in the tents do."

"You're contradicting yourself."

"How so?"

"You said the angels *supplied the miracles*, and then you said they believe in the hogwash they dish out."

"I don't know everything, Laura. Never claimed to," he said. "I'm only speculating. A country doctor has to learn to trust his intuition as much as science. I'm telling you that I believe the angels are sincere. They believe, even when they injure humans, that they're following some greater plan, that they're moving toward a fate that will justify their means."

"There you two are. I've been looking all around for you." It was Bryan Douglas.

"It's your young man," Jenkins said.

"My friend with benefits, you mean," she whispered.

"There's an angel looking for you, Doctor," Bryan said.

"Which one?"

"I don't know. One of the big cheeses, I think. Damn!" His blanket, which he had wrapped his waist, fell down. Laura giggled as he stooped to pick it up and rearrange it.

"Where's the angel?"

"In the tent. He was talking to Mrs. Wright when I left."

Back at the tent, Jenkins found the angel, one he recognized but couldn't name, sitting cross-legged by Marguerite's cot. The two were talking quietly. Marguerite had pulled the blanket down, fully exposing the homunculus. She was smiling at her visitor. The angel was smiling back. *Was this the angel whose homunculus she carried?* He retrieved his blanket from his cot, draped it over his shoulders and joined them. As he got closer he was shocked to see the homunculus' expression, usually either a blank stare or a grimace in response to stimuli, had changed. It too was smiling.

"Hi. What are you two talking about?"

"Hello, Doctor," the angel said. It seemed smaller than he remembered.

"Doctor, you remember Azazel, don't you?"

"Yes." He nodded, recognizing the angel who smiled sadly at him. It was the same angel who had visited her before, but greatly diminished in size and radiance.

"Azazel was telling me the homunculus will be finished in a couple of nights." Marguerite said.

"Nights? What do you mean finished?"

"I meant sleep periods," Azazel said.

"And finished?"

"The new angel/human – what you call the homunculus – will be completely grown."

"What will happen to Marguerite?

"She'll be part of the new Azazel."

"What do you gain in this transformation?"

"I'll die when the new Azazel is complete," it said and smiled in anticipation.

* * *

25.

Full Immersion

Jimmy stood on the broad metal expanse of the angel saucer, hands on his hips, decked out in sheriff's department regalia, complete with service revolver and a pump shotgun slung over his shoulder.

"I can't believe no angels have shown up to stop us," he said to Uncle Robert and Sophia.

"They know we're here. They knew we were coming," Sophia said.

She wore a red bodysuit and leather high-heels. How she had managed to maneuver over the saucer's metal surface in those shoes was a miracle in itself. Uncle Robert was secretely proud of her and had learned long ago not question her fashion motives. If she got rid of the baby blue plastic purse, she'd look like a comic-book super hero ready to face down super-villains.

Maybe that's exactly what they were about to do.

"If they see us, then where are they?" Jimmy asked.

"They don't care."

Neither Uncle Robert nor the deputy asked how she knew.

Jimmy knelt on the edge of the gash and peered into darkness.

"Looks awfully deep. Nothing but darkness. Damned dark – excuse my language," Jimmy said. "No, wait, I see some lights moving down there. No, now I don't see them."

"We'll be able to see better once we're inside and our eyes adjust," Uncle Robert said.

"You two are really going to do it, aren't you?"

Uncle Robert could guess the deputy's thoughts. *The angels are going to eat you crazy old coots for breakfast.* Maybe the deputy was right.

He had the same misgivings himself. Despite her outfit, Sophia looked weary but determined. He had put a great deal of faith in her secret source, the same source that had put him back together after the angel had dropped him.

He knelt by the deputy's side and looked over the edge into the darkness. The metal here had been half-torn, half-melted. He lay down on his stomach and reached as far into the hole as he could. Stretch as he might, his fingers couldn't find the inner edge. The skin of the saucer was thicker than his arm was long. Did they really need to do this? Could they do it? Just climbing up the side of the saucer had drained him.

"You and Mrs. Jacobsen are going to follow the telephone lines down into the saucer. Then you're going to find the hostages and negotiate with the angels to them hostages go before Sheriff Wright sets off his fertilizer bomb. That's the plan, right?" he asked.

"Right," Uncle Robert said, feeling like an idiot. He studied the telephone wires strung across the saucer. The galvanized wires led from through the forest and straight to the saucer. He had checked out the installation before climbing the saucer. At the forest level, it was a sloppy, hasty job: insulators nailed to trees, in some places held only inches off the ground by rotten logs. When the lines reached the saucer no one had attempted to secure them to its metal skin. Instead the installer – most likely the missing Carl Johnson – had tacked together a scaffolding of pine studs and laid them across the skin. To this scaffolding he had attached glass insulators, hooking the lines to them with what looked like baling wire. At the edge of the gash, the lines dangled into the darkness and disappeared.

Jimmy reached over and jiggled one of the lines. He quickly yanked away his hand.

"Ouch, the things are charged."

Despite the haphazard installation, the lines worked, as their call to Mr. Asbeel had proved. At the end of those telephone lines, Uncle Robert and Sophia hoped to find not only Asbeel, but the human hosts as well. What would they do if and when they found them? He didn't know, but he suspected Sophia had a secret agenda.

The deputy also realized the significance of the saucer's armor.

"This thing is built like a battleship," he said. "Maybe the sheriff and Marshall should rethink trying to blow it up with a fertilizer bomb. The hostages won't even get their teeth rattled." He scratched his chin thoughtfully. "Maybe you two should rethink going in, too."

"Maybe you're right," Uncle Robert said.

"We're going in. We're supposed to," Sophia said.

"What do you mean, 'supposed to'?" Jimmy said.

When Sophia didn't reply, he turned to Uncle Robert.

"We're going in," Uncle Robert told him. "Feed in the rope."

Nothing more was said. The rope was an inch thick and wet with dew. Jimmy grunted as he dragged more rope from over the side. Uncle Robert thought to help him, then decided to save his strength.

Jimmy tied an impressive-looking loop at the end of the rope, and dangled it a few feet down into the hole. He looked to Sophia for approval. She onodded, apparently satisfied with his handiwork, and he Jimmy tied a second loop about six feet up on the rope, but left it on the saucer's surface.

Uncle Robert peered over the edge. The rope, like the phone wires, disappeared into the inky darkness after a few feet. The darkness didn't look like natural shadow; it was as if something inside the saucer ate light.

"Look, here come the reinforcements," Jimmy said.

Below, a yellow Caterpillar bulldozer piloted by Frank Marshall lumbered up the hill with a white fertilizer spreader in tow. Behind the fertilizer spreader, Marshall and Wright had chained a stainless steel milk-tanker filled with kerosene. The train of vehicles made a muddy rut through the fescue grass. Uncle Robert shook his head. Wright and Marshall had planned the bombing like a military campaign, but from atop the saucer their efforts looked like a collection of Tonka toys. It began to rain again, renewing the huge expanse of the saucer's metal skin with a glassy sheen.

Jimmy put a foot in the pre-tied loop of rope and tested it with his weight. The other end was tied to steel cable that connected to the electric winch mounted on the front of the sheriff's Blazer. "I wonder if we've got enough cable to reach the bottom."

Jimmy climbed out and back onto the relative security of the saucer skin.

"We measured," Uncle Robert said. Using triangulation, Marshall had estimated the saucer to be about three hundred feet thick at the mid-section. It seemed reasonable that they would find a floor long before they descended to that depth. But for all anyone knew the craft was one large hollow shell. Bryan Douglas had said the angel Eloaios had carried him inside to a huge amphitheater, which suggested that the center section was hollow. Even so, they should have enough rope, unless his worst fears were realized. He worried the saucer was larger inside than out – much larger. Uncle Robert wished he had a brought rock or something to drop in. He could count how long it took to fall and . . .

"I'll go first," Sophia said. She slung her purse over her shoulder, then got down on her hands and knees in preparation for climbing into the hole.

"No, I will," he said. Before she could get ahead of him, he grabbed the rope and swung his feet over the side. His tennis shoes skidded on the wet metal surface, and his hands slipped on the soggy rope; for a moment he thought he would plunge into the darkness. Then he managed to wrap his legs around the rope and cling until the swinging stopped. He slipped a foot into the loop.

Sophia watched him from above.

How the hell did she even manage to stand up on the saucer in those shoes?

She got on her hands and knees, put a high-heeled foot in the other loop, and with Jimmy's help, eased over the edge until she was suspended above his head.

"You should wait until I get all the way down," he said. "I could test the waters, so to speak, and signal you to take the rope back up, then you could follow me down."

"Go on, we haven't much time." Her voice was strained.

"Okay, then, here goes. Holler or tug on the rope when you want to be hauled back up." Jimmy stood at the edge, looking down.

"We may be a while," Uncle Robert said.

"Take as long as you like. I'll wait for you as long my common sense doesn't get the best of me. But I'm going to tell you something. I'm not going to be sitting on top of this thing when the sheriff lights the fuse."

Messengers of an Alien God

He took a red bandanna from his back pocket and waved it over his head. Without walkie-talkies, it was the only way to signal Wright to engage the winch and lower them into the hole. The rope went slack, dropped about a foot with a jerk, then lowered them at a smooth, regular rate. Because of some esoteric law of physics they pivoted as they descended, twisting nearly full circle, then unwinding the other way in a clock-like rhythm. Above, Jimmy, silhouetted by the sun, disappeared and reappeared from sight with each revolution.

We're like roast chickens on a rotisserie, Uncle Robert thought.

On each turn the patch of light grew smaller, the deputy more distant and the inky darkness closer. He strained to make out details below, but the darkness below was complete. As his feet sank toward the darkness he could see where the telephone wires disappeared. The cutoff point was as sharp as a knife, as if the wires sank into a pool of oil or water. Then his feet touched the darkness and disappeared as well. His heart rose in his throat. *The saucer was filled with some kind of black fluid! They were going to drown!* He let out a yelp but was too late to stop the descent. First his legs disappeared then his waist and chest. An electric tingling passed along his body as he sank into the dark water. Before his face went under he took a deep gulp of air and instinctively closed his eyes. Then he was completely submerged.

Or was he?

There was no sensation of wetness. The rope vibrated in his hands as he continued to descend. When he opened his eyes again, he found himself not immersed in water but in light. Above his head, the rope disappeared into a mirror surface that stretched as far as he could see. As he watched, Sophia's feet broke through the mirror surface, then her legs and torso. In a moment she was completely into the light too. She looked down past him, her eyes filled with awe. They were still descending, but into what? Where? He looked down and nearly lost his hold on the rope. Emerald clouds drifted beneath his feet. He and Sophia were suspended thousands of feet above a painted desert!

Despite his fear, the panorama enthralled him. A gaunt range of mountains stretched from horizon to horizon. On the plains, red and yellow patterns intermingled like a ruined sand painting. Here and there the random patterns were interrupted by occasional straight lines – roads?

Or rather the remains of roads?

"No life," Sophia said from above.

"What?"

"It's the angel's world or a simulacrum of it. Do you see any life, anything green or moving?"

"No."

The ceiling of liquid mirror receded until it was about hundred feet above them. They would soon be out of rope. Perhaps they could hold on until Jimmy and Wright tired of waiting and pulled the rope back up again.

"What do we do now?" he asked.

"We proceed with the plan," she said.

"What plan? To run out of rope?"

"Our role in all this may be preordained and out of our control, but we can speed things up." With one arm curled around the rope, she unsnapped the flap of the purse and took out a kitchen paring knife.

"What the hell are you doing?"

"Speeding things up." She began sawing at the rope above her head.

"Whoa, Sophia! Whoa here a minute!"

"What now?"

"Can't we talk about this?"

"Damn it!" She swung wildly on the rope. He reached out, expecting her to fall, a reflex, and nearly lost his own hold on the rope. She regained her grip at the same time he did.

"Whew, Sophia, you had me worried there for a minute. I thought you really meant to go through with it."

"Go through with what?"

"Cutting the rope."

"I did. I should have brought a better knife. This one is too flexible, and it slipped off the rope. Look, I cut myself." She held out her arm. A deep gash lay across her left forearm.

"Damn, Sophia, you could bleed to death from a cut like that."

"No, not here. See, not a drop of blood."

It was true. The cut was so deep he could see striations of the muscle, but it was bloodless.

"There's no pain, either." She returned to her work on the rope.

He started to protest but remained silent. Watching her saw away at their lifeline was like being awake in a bad dream. There was nothing he could do, short of grabbing her ankle and pulling her off the rope, and he couldn't do that, even to save himself.

"Almost there," she said, and the rope severed.

They fell, feet first then began to tumble. Sophia let go of the rope and threw her arms out like a kid playing airplane, which stablized her fall, and she stopped the tumbling. She drifted up and away.

He frantically tried to do the same, but the rope had become tangled around him. Obviously, one law was the same here – that of entropy, the same law dictating shit happens whenever possible. The loose end tangled around his neck, and he became conscious of a man yelling bloody murder at the top of his voice. After a minute he realized he was the screamer and stopped. Might as well shut up and resign himself to death.

He began to chuckle. What a fitting death for a Jacobsen. He was going to die because his common-law wife had finally lost her mind. He would hit the desert floor at two-hundred-plus miles per hour, and it didn't matter if this world operated under different physical laws or if his wounds would be bloodless, because the impact would break every bone in his body and rupture most of his major organs. He was going to die and that was that. He might as well accept it as the most likely possibility and enjoy the ride down.

As he tumbled he could see the desert floor rushing up. It was quite beautiful in a sterile sort of way. Would he make a crater? And then something with a thousand eyes and too many hands caught him. Instinctively, he fought it.

"Calm down," it said in a deep, musical voice. "Stop squirming."

He strained to see what held him, but his eyes refused to fix on it. Part of his brain only indirectly connected to his optic nerve told him that his savior was at once gloriously beautiful and terribly horrendous, depending upon the angle it was beheld from.

"Who are you?" he said. *What are you?*

At once he found himself in the arms of an angel. Speechless, Uncle Robert waited for the angel to change in mood or physique and drop him. But they flew on silently, gradually descending into an immense valley. Soon it became clear they were approaching what appeared to be a green Army bivouac tent on the desert floor.

Later, with his feet on solid ground, Uncle Robert watched Jenkins clean sand from the laceration in Sophia's arm.

"How do you sterilize things here?" Uncle Robert asked.

"I don't."

"Then how do you prevent infection?"

"I don't." He glanced up and smiled. Uncle Robert couldn't get over how much the doctor had changed. He looked twenty years younger. "I don't administer anesthetic, either. Here, you can help. Put your hand there and hold the wound closed. The wound is too wide for me to hold closed by myself. No, you needn't squeeze so hard, you'll pucker the skin."

He did as he was told. If the procedure was painful, Sophia showed no sign. "How long do I have to hold it this way?"

"That should be long enough."

"What?"

"You can let go now."

He released his hold on the wound and found it closed. Not only closed, but completely healed with no evidence of a scar.

"The reason I use neither anesthetic nor antiseptic is two-fold, Uncle Robert. I possess neither, and neither is necessary in this place. It's a doctor's dream." Jenkins voice was calm and friendly, a far departure from his usual abrasive manner. "A dream," he repeated.

In the last few hours Uncle Robert had encountered many startling things. While treating Sophia, Jenkins had given him information that had helped him piece together the puzzle of the immense world contained inside the saucer and the multiform nature of the angels. Jenkins told him to learn to accept miracles as common occurrences outside scientific cause and effect, a leap of faith that Uncle Robert had come to accept with the angels. Yet Jenkins' transformation, both in body and soul, seemed the biggest miracle of all.

"Why do you suppose you were brought here, Doctor?" Sophia asked.

"Good question. I thought at first I was brought here to administer care for the homunculi hosts."

He motioned to the rows and rows of cots, each occupied by a homunculus-ridden human being. All the host humans appeared to be sleeping.

"Some of the first implants were particularly traumatic to the hosts," Jenkins said. "In addition to May Tyre, there were two young men injured by the process."

"Yes, I know. Wright filled us in, about Tommy anyway. And we assumed the same about Johnson. The cruel sons of bastards," Uncle Robert said, but it sounded like he was talking about Tommy and Carl Johnson instead of the angels. *Maybe he was.*

Jenkins didn't catch this, however. "No, I don't I don't think the word 'cruel' applies to the angels. *Naive* fits better."

"I've been in the tents. I saw what they did to Tommy Georgian and Carl Johnson. I say *injured* is a weak word. *Mutilated* is more like it."

"The mutilations date from their first attempts to mate with humans. In the beginning, I don't believe they understood how fragile human bodies are. Hell, they didn't even understand humans were sexually differentiated from birth."

"The angel I know as Envy picked me up and dropped me from a hundred feet. I saw malicious intent in its eyes as it let me go. I'd call that cruel and more," Uncle Robert said.

One of the host humans stirred in her sleep. She was cacooned from head to toe in her Army blanket. With only the top of her head visible, she looked like a huge, green insect pupa.

"No, the more I think of it, I don't buy your theory of well-meaning bumblers," he said. "Envy tried to kill me when I refused its offer. Its action was conscious and premeditated."

"I don't know what happened between you and the angel, but from what I've observed, they're in many ways like children. They operate on reflex, like children. Their actions often seem malicious, but they don't perceive that their actions cause lasting damage. They find it as hard to accept our mortality as we find it difficult to imagine their immortality."

"That explains nothing. If they're like children, how did they build the ship? How do they move through time? And why are they planting these homunculi on human beings?"

"I've asked all these questions of various angels. All I can gather is that moving through time is second nature to them, as simple to them as walking is to us. They tell me the Dreaming God imbued them with the skill. As for the ship, it was meant to be a focusing device for their time-slipping powers. I don't know how they built it, as I have yet to see them use any tools. They didn't share these facts with me. They did tell me a little of their motives."

Jenkins stood up and adjusted his poncho. The angels had stripped all the internees of their clothes, but left Sophia and Uncle Robert with theirs. Who knew why? Maybe he should just chalk it up to their alienness as he did other things about them.

The doctor continued. "For millennia the hundred of them have lived on another world where they have complete dominion. They have only guesses about their beginnings."

"And you believe what they told you?"

"Yes, I do. They wished to move so far ahead in time that they'd find the end of this universe and a shortcut to their own deaths."

"But why?" Uncle Robert asked.

"Simple. They are sick of immortal life. They can't die, you see. Heaven, hell and the world merge in this place. If their physical bodies are destroyed, they're reborn with all their memories intact. Some copies of themselves, which they call the *anima mundi,* constantly record their every thought and experience, sort of like a cloud backup on the Internet. When an angel's body is destroyed, the *anima mundi* is somehow activated and materializes within the corpse, bursts its way through – an action of violent birth – and begins where the original left off. All of the angels have experienced such rebirths countless times."

"Spiritual and *physical* reincarnation. We guessed something of the sort from what Bryan told us of his experience with the dying angel in the woods. The scene he witnessed in the forest must have been one such rebirth. "

"Yes, but what Bryan didn't know, what none of us could guess, was when their experiment failed, when their ship brought them here to Earth instead of the end of time, they saw human mortality as a fall-back plan. They've been trying to approach a number of us with a bargain since they've arrived. But their message was so alien to us and our ties to the material world so unfathomable to them, that the communication got all fouled up."

"Are there other saucers?" Sophia asked.

"No, there are are no other saucers. Only this one." Jenkins said.

"But surely the military knows about this saucer? The electronics failure is worldwide isn't it? They've got to connect the dots eventually," Uncle said.

"Probably, but I'm guessing everyone is clueless, and the armed forces or the powers that be don't know about our saucer," Jenkins said. "Maybe everyone thinks some other country is responsible, or that it's an act of God. Otherwise, we'd have the Army, Marines and Air Force up our collective ass now."

"Hello! I guess you're all wondering why I brought you here together," Laura Jacobsen said as she entered the tent. When everyone gave her questioning looks, she said, "Just joking. You all looked so serious."

"This is a serious situation."

"No, it isn't. It's a joke, don't you see? A joke on us. A legion of angels shows up, offers a few humans near immortality, and we think it's a trick."

Bryan Douglas followed her into the tent like a puppy. "She thinks she's missed the boat. She wants to become an angel, too," he explained.

"I still don't understand this immortality thing," Uncle Robert said. "Will the homunculi be more human or more angel?"

"The angels tell me they'll be hybrids, half and half, with attributes of both," Jenkins said.

"But they won't be really immortal, they'll only live a few tens of thousands of years," Bryan said.

"Close enough to immortal for me," Laura said.

"Well, it's a moot point, Laura," Bryan said. "All the angels have merged with humans. You'll just have to live out your mortal span like the rest of us."

"That's not true. There are only ninety-nine homunculi and humans. I've counted them twice. There's supposed to be an even hundred. Azazel told me so."

"Then where's number one hundred?" Bryan asked

"At the bottom of the Lost Lake, of course. You should know that.

You saw the airplane crash into two angels, right? And only one floated to the surface. Well, the other one – Azazel says its name is Samiazaz – is still at the bottom of Lost Lake, probably weighed down by the plane."

"So what? It should be dead by now and reincarnated."

"Azazel tells me that angels just go into hibernation when they're submerged in water or buried deep in the earth. All I have to do is pull out the angel, then sit on my heels until it wakes up. It'll be love at first sight, and I've got my ticket to immortality."

Everyone was silent. Bryan looked miserable and heart-broken. He was obviously so in love with Laura. Poor fool. Time to change the subject.

"Hell, if this is true, I wonder what will happen when Wright sets off his bomb? Will all the saucers tremble?"

"Bomb? What bomb?" Jenkins said.

Uncle Robert explained the plan.

"Rednecks with explosives? Oh god!" Laura said.

"Don't worry. It's only a recipe he and Pete Marshall have jury-rigged with fertilizer and kerosene. All he's likely to do is start a forest fire. We probably won't even feel it."

"No, this vessel is imminently unstable. The bomb is destined to do much more than that, Simon Jacobsen." The angel who spoke these words walked slowly into the circle of humans, looking directly at Uncle Robert. It was the smallest and shabbiest angel he'd ever seen, yet she was somehow familiar.

"Don't you recognize me, Simon? You should: By your standards, we're long-time acquaintances."

Slowly, Uncle Robert realized that the angel Envy, the same one who had tried to kill him, stood before him, looking like a shabby copy of its original female form. He should have been afraid but wasn't. There was something almost too human about the angel now.

* * *

26.

Salvation

Wright surveyed Frank Marshall's handiwork. On the uphill side of the saucer, he had used the road grader to make earth berms around the dump truck. The berms formed three sides of a cow pond-sized rectangular reservoir. The flank of the saucer served as the fourth side.

Once satisfied with his earthwork, he had lined the reservoir with black plastic film. (The co-op kept black plastic film in twenty-foot wide, hundred-foot long rolls for lining corn silage silos.) He taped the seams of black plastic with duct tape, backed the dump truck to the edge, and unloaded the two tons of ammonia nitrate fertilizer onto the plastic-lined pond.

All that work had pretty much exhausted the old man, and it was left to Wright to drench the lot with five thousand gallons of kerosene. The oily smell of the fuel filled the air, overlaid with a chalky, dry dust from the ammonia nitrate.

"Here it is, sir." Jimmy trotted up with a piece of the rope that he'd used to lower Uncle Robert and Sophia into the saucer. Wright took it from his hand.

"You see, it's cut, not broken," Jimmy said.

"I can see that."

"What do you think it means?"

"It means we don't have to wait any longer," Marshall interrupted. "Jacobsen and his black bitch have either been killed or captured. The angels have left us no options."

Wright had grown to respect Sophia, and was tempted to slap

down old man for his racist remark but decided to ignore it. This wasn't the time.

Jimmy shook his head. "All you'll probably do is make them angels mad. I tell you I've seen it. The metal was three feet thick at the top.
"

"Then make them goddamn mad, we will, Marshall said. "Better than sitting around and doing nothing but pissing in our boots. And if it does more than rattle their teeth, if it blows the mother-raping wings off the bastards, so much the better. Who knows what kind of metal the thing is made of or its properties? It might even burn, like magnesium."

"I still think it's a no-win situation," Jimmy said. He took off his hat and slapped it against his thigh, a rare show of frustration. "If you crack the saucer like a hen's egg, then you'll kill our people inside."

"All the better for them if they have those cancerous things attached," Wright said. Inwardly, he shuddered at the thought. The sight of the homunculus sprouting from May's stomach had overturned the natural order of the world. That Marguerite might be now suffering the same fate horrified him. *No, he'd rather see her dead.*

"Jimmy, get the Blazer and bring it around. Marshall, get the primer cord."

They were ready in a half hour. Jimmy sat in the Blazer, glowering at the steering wheel, the engine running, while Wright helped Marshall light the fuse. When it was lit, Marshall said, "Okay, that's it. Let's go."

Wright was in the Blazer in seconds, but Marshall ambled over and climbed in at leisure. "What's the rush? It's a fifteen-minute fuse. We've got plenty of time."

They parked the Blazer uphill from the saucer and crouched behind a small knoll.

"Dynamite is a slow explosive. It makes a dull thud when it goes off," Marshall said in a conversational tone, as if they were discussing the weather. "Plastics, you know C-4 and the like, are fast-burning explosives. When they go off they make a sharp crack like bones breaking."

"What kind of sound will your bomb make?" Jimmy asked.

"It ought to be slow, but bright," Marshall said. "A big thud from the dynamite. Then a second, much bigger thud when the nitrate and kerosene ignite. A real ground-shaker. Then a fireball hot enough to singe our eyebrows at a quarter mile away"

"We're about a quarter mile away."

"Yep. You'd better get your head down after the thud."

The minutes stretched on. Marshall had used a smokeless fuse, so its progress wasn't visible from a quarter-mile. Lacking functional watches, they could only guess at the time. The dump truck's white trailer could clearly be seen under the overhanging edge of the saucer.

"Something must have gone wrong . . ." Wright stood up to get a better look, and at that moment the earth beneath the saucer exploded. An orange fireball burst outward, flinging pieces of the fertilizer truck in sluggish slow motion.

"Heads down," he heard Marshall say, but it was too late. Wright felt the concussion hit him like a warm pillow. The next thing he knew he was on his back, staring up at the gray, rainy sky. Jimmy's face came into his field of view.

"You okay?" Jimmy said.

"If you mean am I alive, the answer is yes." He got to his feet painfully.

"I guess I was wrong about there being two thuds," Marshall said.

"Look," Jimmy yelled. "The saucer is moving!"

"You're imagining things," Wright said. "We only rocked it."

"No, wait. See! It's going to go over."

The saucer teetered on the edge of the crater made by the blast, paused, then gradually tipped the other way and began sliding laboriously down the muddy hillside.

Marshall hooted. "By God, we kicked its butt! It'll keep sliding until it hits the lake."

"No, it'll bog down in the mud," Wright said.

But the saucer proved him wrong again. The mud didn't dampen its inertia; it greased it. A grove of young oaks fell like wheat before a scythe as it ground down the hill. A limestone outcropping shattered, plate-size white slabs of stone flying, and still the saucer picked up more speed.

"Goddamn! Goddamn! Wonderful isn't it?" Marshall screamed, his face apple-red from excitement.

Speechless, Wright didn't answer. What was the word teenagers used? "Awesome," he said quietly.

Would it sink or float when it hit the lake?

He didn't have to wait long for an answer. The saucer crushed a child's swing set in the playground at the lake's edge as if it were a tinkertoy, skipped over the brief stretch of sand and landed belly down in the lake with a great splash that threw up a shower of water a hundred feet high. Tsunami-like waves rolled out from the impact. The saucer kept moving, skidding through the water before coming to a rest near the middle of the lake. Waves reached the shoreline, rebounded, and returned to jostle the saucer. Great bubbles broke from beneath the silver metal, and the saucer began to settle lower in the water.

"It's sinking! The son-of-bitch is sinking!" Marshall's voice broke in mid-shout.

None of the men spoke as they climbed into the truck. Jimmy drove to the lake's edge as fast as the terrain would allow. As they got out of the truck onto the beach they could see the saucer was indeed going under. Huge bubbles continued to belch to the surface.

"We must have punched a hole in it," Marshall said. His voice was weaker now, and the red flush of his face had been replaced by a washed-out pallor. He leaned against the truck.

"No, I could see clear enough," Jimmy said. "The bomb didn't even scorch it. One of the angels must have left the back door open."

"Bull," Marshall said, but his voice sounded fragile and unsure.

"You don't look good, Marshall. Maybe you should sit in the truck," Wright said.

"I want to watch the son-of-a-bitch sink," the old man said.

"We could be watching forever. The thing is going to drink up the whole lake," Jimmy said.

Wright feared his deputy was right. The shoreline receded as he watched. The saucer had the capacity for swallowing a disproportionate amount of water, but surely its capacity wasn't infinite. It listed to one side, bringing the great gash on the top into sight as the lake waters overwhelmed it.

"If the angels are in there, they're going down with the ship," Wright said.

At this angle, the gash looked like a huge black, broken vein in a gigantic silver eye.

"Deep-sixed, I think," Marshall said.

"I don't think we're going to be rid of them that easily." Jimmy said. He pointed at the saucer.

A flock of angels streamed out of the gash and hovered over the saucer. At this distance, they looked like migrating geese, searching for a place to land.

Reluctantly, the saucer clung to the surface like a living thing willfully fighting the tug of gravity. But finally it could hold on no longer. It settled lower, and waters rushed over the silver metal hull and into the great gash. A single huge bubble burped out the gash, throwing a fine mist into the air that nearly reached the hovering angels. Then the saucer was gone into the bowels of Lost Lake.

The angels ceased their aimless, random hovering and began to move toward the shore.

"They're coming after us," Marshall croaked.

"I wonder if they're mad?" Jimmy said.

"Of course they're mad, you dumb shit! We just sank their ship," Wright said. He considered making a run for it in the Blazer. He looked at Jimmy and Marshall. Both seemed transfixed by the sight of the oncoming horde. Maybe they were resigned. What was the use? If the angels wanted, they could easily catch up with the Blazer. The flock was nearly upon them when it split into two groups. One group, the larger one comprising at least ninety percent of the flock, turned to the southwest and flew toward Creedance. The smaller group continued toward the shore and landed on the beach.

As they landed, it became clear there weren't six individuals, but a dozen angels and humans paired up. Each angel had carried a human in its arms. Once on shore, the angels set the humans on the beach. The angels flew off, and the humans walked toward Wright and the men. Wright drew his gun. He looked at Jimmy and Marshall for support. His deputy looked too awe-struck to be of any help. Marshall looked like shit. His face was now ashen and his eyes rimmed with red.

The first human to approach was Uncle Robert, looking like a wet dog in his soaked tweed jacket and overalls. Sophia Blackstone, unmistakable in her red jumpsuit, followed closely behind.

"You look pretty good for someone who fell into an abyss," Wright said to Uncle Robert.

"It's a long story, one which I don't fully understand," Uncle Robert said. "Ask Sophia for clarification."

"The angels never meant to hurt us," Sophia said, not looking directly at Wright. "And they're not angry with you for sinking their saucer. You can put away your hardware. Besides you wouldn't want to hurt these angels anyway. You may even know some of them personally."

"Hello, John," a tall, red-headed angel said. "Don't you recognize me?"

"Marguerite?"

Yes it was his wife, but terribly, beautifully transformed. Her naked body, long-legged with a firm, flat stomach and full breasts, was more beautiful than that of the Marguerite he had married twenty years ago. But this creature had gossamer wings that stretched several feet wide. He noticed with some relief that there were no knobs at the joints to conceal tiny hands, but that was his only solace. Marguerite as an angel was tall, much taller than Wright. She towered over him. He stifled the impulse to raise the pistol and shoot.

"It's me, John."

"And someone else, too. Tell him Marguerite," Sophia said.

"Tell me what?" Wright said. The pistol was heavy in his hand.

The angel Marguerite stepped closer, filling Wright with a mixture of love, lust and dread. She reached over and touched his face. Her touch was as cold as a corpse's. He stepped back.

"I made a trade, John. My freedom for immortality. The angel, Azazel, and I merged, became what you see before you."

Wright stood still, made immobile by the sudden rage consuming him. It was worse than being cuckolded – much, much worse. He became aware that the Marguerite angel was still talking.

"... wasn't happy with you. I felt so, so, superficial, and ..."

Without thinking, Wright raised the pistol to Marguerite's head and fired point blank – into thin air.

Incredibly strong hands grabbed him from behind, twisted the pistol from his grasp and spun him around. Marguerite! How had she gotten behind him?

"There will be none of that, John. No more temper tantrums," she said, letting him go and handing back his pistol. "You'll never succeed, anyway." She let him go.

"You're not Marguerite anymore. You're a counterfeit," he shouted. But he knew it was Marguerite. He recognized her anger, her eyes, even her scent.

"You might as well accept it, John," Uncle Robert said. "I don't approve either. But it's a done deal. There's no turning back for her."

"I wouldn't change back if I could," Marguerite said and reached for him.

"Keep your damn hands off me!"

Jenkins walked over, clad in a dirty green poncho, also wet, shivering and younger-looking, but still human.

"Let your anger go, Sheriff," he said. "Uncle Robert is right. There's nothing you or any of us can do about it. Marguerite entered into this arrangement of her own accord. The Marguerite you knew is gone forever."

Wright stepped back from them. "Leave me alone, all of you! I could take anything but this."

"Could you more easily accept my death, John?" Marguerite asked.

Before he could answer, she went on. "Well, rest easy. The old Marguerite is dead. She has been reborn."

"We've got trouble over here," someone said. It was Bryan. He and Laura knelt by Marshall's prostrate form. Another human angel, female, white-haired and voluptuous, stood over them, looking stunned.

"I think he's had his last stroke," Bryan said.

"Massive coronary is more like it," Laura said. "I bet he was dead before he hit the ground." Like Jenkins, both the college boy and the Jacobsen girl were barefoot, clothed only in Army ponchos. They all looked dirty and cold.

"All I said was hello," the white-haired angel said. Wright recognized the voice now. Dowdy old Bertha Marshall had been magically transformed into another of the frighteningly beautiful creatures.

"I've got to get away from this. Everything is crazy. The center of my life is coming apart," Wright said. He stepped back, half-expecting one of the angels to try to stop him. When none did, he turned and marched along the shoreline. Behind him, different voices overlapped. He heard

Laura asking Jimmy something about scuba-diving equipment. "Why not? Why shouldn't I . . ." she was saying.

And Uncle Robert was going in another of his intellectual rants: "This isn't how I expected it to turn out. I'm almost disappointed they didn't turn out to be evil. You know why I'm disappointed? Because the human ego, man's or woman's ego, needs an outside enemy to feel real. Take the Cold War, for example, the battle of the sexes, or the feminist backlash . . ."

"Bunch of crap . . ." Bertha the angel was saying.

More craziness. Wright speeded up to a trot, then a run, not looking back.

He was quickly out of breath and sought shelter in the ruins of the playground. He leaned against the upright remains of a red and yellow plastic horse, his heart pounding. Overhead, a portion of a merry-go-round's wrecked cornice shielded him from the rain, like a giant's bent and deformed umbrella. Across the sand he could see a thin trickle of smoke near the Blazer. The refugees from the saucer had started a campfire. Figures milled around the fire, some of them winged, some not. It looked like a goddamned hot dog roast. Three of the angels – Marguerite must be one of them – were standing in a circle with their wings outspread like giant white umbrellas to shield the humans from the rain. If he squinted he could make out Marguerite's red hair, stark as blood against her white skin.

"God, oh God," he said aloud. "Nothing is right in the world. Everything is twisted."

Something was wrong with his face. He felt his cheeks, surprised to find them wet. It took a few moments before he realized he was crying.

"Don't cry, Sheriff." From behind, hands reached around and wiped the tears from his cheek. He was too exhausted to resist. The angel came around to face him, disclosing itself to be May Tyre, or rather May Tyre transformed into a goddess. Like Marguerite, she was so beautiful – or was it so horrible? – that he couldn't look at her for more than a moment before he had to look away.

"What do you want from me?" His voice came out in a rasp.

She looked confused. "I'm not sure." Without prelude, she screeched and leaped fifteen feet from the wooden platform of the merry-go-round to the overhanging cornice. She perched unsteadily on a projecting metal beam and began walking tip-toe on it, using her outstretched wings for balance like a circus high-wire walker uses a pole.

She stared down at him. He could see now that her eyes were crazed.

"What do you want from me?" he repeated.

"I'm not sure," she said, "but I think I want you to remind me what it was like to be human."

She sat down on the beam and kicked her legs to and fro like a bored schoolgirl. Looking up, Wright could see that May the angel was unlike the archangels in that she appeared to be a fully functioning female, though completely hairless. She folded her wings and slid off the beam, to land at Wright's feet. Like Marguerite, the hybrid May was taller than the original, taller than Wright by inches.

"I'll be damned," he said. "All be damned."

"All is not damned. We can still make love," May said. "Like humans always have." She took him in icy arms. Her breast was cold against his cheek. "God, I'm hungry. Famished. Hungry for everything. I could eat Elvis, hooves and all – two Elvises."

His hand sought, found and rested on the butt of his pistol's grip, wondering if those around the fire would hear the gunshot, wondering if he should turn the pistol on himself or on May the angel. If he did turn the gun on himself, would the creature that Marguerite had become care?

"A big change is coming to Creedance," May the angel said. "You'll soon see, and be amazed. A big change, like nothing that ever happened before."

Wright pulled the pistol from his holster.

A loon called sadly from the marshes as a gunshot echoed across Lost Lake.

Author's Note: This concludes the end of the first of a trilogy of the Gnostic Angels on Earth. The second book in the series, *Dreamtime of an Alien God*, explores the curious life of the human/angel hybrids, and tells of Laura Jacobsen's quest to recover the hundredth angel from Lost Lake and merge with it. The third novel, *Awakening of Alien God*, tells of Laura's, Bryan's and Uncle Robert's exploration of the alternate realities accessible through the alien saucer and the archangels' influence.

For more information on these an other MagicHat books, go to **http://magichatbooks.com.**

Messengers of an Alien God

Messengers of an Alien God